THE SUNSET HOUR

EAGLE BROTHERHOOD SERIES

KAT LE VEQUE

OLIVERHEBERBOOKS

AUTHOR'S NOTE

They call themselves the Eagle Brotherhood.

We've all got 'that' group of friends. People we've bonded with that just 'get' you and you get them. Whether you bond over common interests, or a job, of even just mutual friends, we've all found that connection at one time or another.

Same with the Eagle Brotherhood.

It started with five Americans. They were young, brilliant, idealistic, and met during a semester abroad. When I first wrote this series, many years ago, it was originally called the American Heroes series. It was supposed to be about guys who knew each other as young men, but who went on to live their own lives and have their own adventures. Ordinary guys in extraordinary circumstances was how I described it. There were only five in the beginning, but somewhere along the line, we added two Brits as 'honorary' members. There are actually more books slated to be written, but I just haven't gotten around to it yet. One of the Eagle Brotherhood — Nash Aury — even has a sequel mostly written to his book, so this is really a series that has a lot of growth potential. And why not? It centers around men who are honorable, chivalric, and end up facing some really stressful and, in a few cases, dangerous situations. Some explainable, some not. That's the fun of it.

But it all had to start somewhere.

Each Eagle Brotherhood book starts out with the same "*How it began*" preface so you, as the reader, knows where these guys connect because they don't appear in each other's stories. It's a rather interesting connection, but one that opens up the hero of each tale — and eventually the heroine — to one heck of a story. These guys are connected to me as much as to each other.

They really are a true brotherhood.

I hope you enjoy the stories in this series because they were a labor of love to write. You don't have to read them in any particular order:

The Burning Hour
The Sunset Hour
The Secret Hour
The Unholy Hour
The Devil's Hour
The Killing Hour
The Ancient Hour

Happy reading,

AQUILA FRATRUM

Seven men.
Each with a story to tell.
Welcome to the world of the Eagle Brotherhood.

Years ago, five Americans on a semester abroad met at the home of their sponsor in Yorkshire, England. They were taking the same course at the University of York, including the son of their host. But it wasn't the course in International Law that bonded them. It was an incident from that time, something that happened on a dark and stormy night in an alley behind a bar in York called *The Calcaria.*

It is something that changed their perspectives forever.

These days, the men who once called themselves the *Aquila Fratrum* or the Eagle Brotherhood — a name based on the Americans who were military-based at that time — have gone forth in their lives. They are men in normal, everyday professions who succeed in extraordinary things. Their paths aren't smooth, and they aren't perfect, but they understand more than most that life is never about the smooth or the perfect. It is about the imperfect and the difficult. It's even about the unexplainable.

And, above all else, light overcomes the darkness.
Aquila Fratrum.
Ordinary men who have lived extraordinary circumstances.
And the women who love them.

HOW IT BEGAN
MORE THEN TWENTY YEARS AGO, THE CALCARIA, YORK

MICK MCCONNELL, PROPRIETOR

"Beck." A big man with a crown of auburn hair spoke with a drunken slur to his words. "Beck. *Seavington!*"

The blond Californian on the other side of the table, who had been half-lidded as he watched a group of women across the darkened room of the pub, jerked at the sound of his name as if he'd just been slapped.

"What?" he said, looking at the man with the auburn hair. "Christ, Phipps. Can't you just leave me alone for a minute?"

Archer Phipps struggled not to laugh. "Why?"

"Because you're breaking my powers of concentration, you ass."

That broke the table out in snorts of laughter. The man seated next to Beck, big and blond and with a mega-watt smile, put a hand on Beck's shoulder.

"What in the hell are you concentrating on?" he said, leaning over to see what Beck might be seeing. When he spied it, he gestured. "Over there?"

Beck full-on pointed to the women across the pub. "There."

"Those?"

"*Those.*"

"Well... what are you trying to do by staring at them? Just go talk to them."

Beck scowled at the man. "Because I'm trying to lure them with the power of suggestion, Trevor," he said. Then, he looked around the table and pointed. "It works. Colt over there has a laser stare. He doesn't even have to say anything — women know what he's thinking just by the expression on his face. Isn't that right, Sheridan?"

Colt Sheridan, clean-cut and square-jawed, waved an annoyed hand at the man he'd spent nearly every day with for the past six months. "Some of us don't have to be obvious," he said. "Look at Nash. All he has to do is give them one of those sexy, down-home expressions and they're falling all over themselves. I don't have anything on him."

Across the table, Nash Aury, the quiet and diplomatic sort with a Louisiana drawl, laughed softly. "It's all in the face," he said, gesturing to the big dimples in each cheek. "I don't have anything y'all don't have, but we don't have anything that Serreaux has, so maybe we should just give it up and let him take the lead."

The group looked over at Ethan Serreaux, a man with a French parents even though he was born in America. Dark-eyed and dark-haired, he looked like he'd just come off the pages of a men's magazine. When he saw that the entire table of semi-drunks was looking at him, he smiled lasciviously.

"*Belle fille,*" he said in his best Maurice Chevalier impression. "*Asseyez-vous sur mes genoux et dites-moi à quel point vous me voulez.*"

Everyone burst out laughing except for Beck, who slowly banged his forehead on the table. "You sound like Pepe Le Pew," he said. "Shut *up!*"

More laughter, most especially from Archer and the last man of their group, a giant of a figure who wasn't part of their academic group. Fox Henredon was in the process of obtaining his Ph.D. in Archaeology with an emphasis in Egyptology from Oxford. In fact, he'd come back a few months ago from a dig near Aswan and when he visited his best friend from grade school, Archer, he'd come across the Americans temporarily housed in Archer's pad. He'd gotten on so well with them that they'd made him an honorary member of their group. But not just the group — of their secret society, as well.

Aquila Fratrum.

The Eagle Brotherhood.

The whole secret group was really meant as a joke, but the basis of it — the honor, the patriotism — they took seriously. Three out of the five Americans had come from Annapolis and all five of them were majoring in International Law, hence the purpose of the semester abroad course. Archer was taking the same course, and he'd been the host house, and given that they were all within a few years of each other age-wise, they'd all bonded over common likes, common dislikes, and a passion for adventure.

It was a guy gang like no other.

But tonight, they were drinking to the group that would soon be separating. The course at the University of York was finished and the Americans would soon be heading back to their native lands, but promises of reciprocal visits had abound all evening. Nash, in particular, had invited everyone to New Orleans for the holidays because his family, having made their money in sugar, had a massive house that could accommodate everyone. Beck, Cord, and Colt had already committed to it, but Ethan had family obligations he needed to get out of. Archer was trying to figure out how to break the news to his parents, who were possessive of his time, while Fox was on the verge of committing. He'd never been to New Orleans and a street named after liquor intrigued him. As the Brotherhood planned their next gathering, Beck stood up from the table.

"I need to find the loo," he said, looking around. "Where is it? Back behind the bar?"

The problem was that he was drunker than the rest of them

and probably not in great shape to find anything, so Cord stood up next to him.

"Back in the corner," he said. "Come on, little brother."

He had Beck by the neck, pulling him back behind the bar where there was a dark corridor that led to bathrooms and the kitchen. The term 'little brother' was essentially referring to Beck's age because he happened to be the youngest out of their group. But he was also the toughest. Beck Seavington could out-fight anybody, Fox included, and Fox had participated in underground fight clubs during his earlier college days. He'd won money at it, too.

But Beck's fists were quite lethal.

The Navy wanted him that way.

Cord went with Beck so he wouldn't get into any trouble. Cord was an enormous man, having played football, and the rumor was that he was being scouted by the NFL. He wasn't a fighter by nature, but no one was going to test of man of that size. He'd just push the scrapper, Beck, in front of him, anyway, and let the career Navy man do the damage.

Every group had a scrapper.

It smelled like stale booze and bleach back here and the door to the men's room was locked. Beck rattled it but it remained fixed. With a heavy sigh, he looked at Cord.

"I can't wait," he muttered.

Cord tipped his head in the direction of the door to the alley out back, which was next to the kitchen door.

"Outside?" he said.

Beck nodded, which nearly threw him off balance, and charged through the back door. Cord followed him and they ended up in the dirty, damp alley behind the bar. It smelled worse out here, like garbage and animals. There were crates against the wall, broken down cardboard boxes, and little else. There were two ends to the alley, but they were standing closer to the end that dumped out onto the street where *The Calcaria* was located. Beck was looking for a discreet place to relieve himself when the back door smacked back on its hinges again, spilling forth the rest of their group.

"I think we're done with this place," Archer said, rubbing his eyes because the alcohol was messing with his vision. "There's another pub down the way called Valhalla. Let's go there."

Beck had found a spot behind some crates. "Are the women more proactive there?" he asked. "I mean, will they actually come up and talk to you? I don't think my mind control is working."

Archer grinned. "Do you seriously want a woman that approaches you?" he said. "The wooing of a woman is an art, Beck. You don't want some nervy woman up in your grill, do you?"

The others snorted in agreement. Ethan and Nash were by the back door, leaning back against the wall, as Colt went to stand next to Beck. Fox went to stand with Cord, maybe as a lookout since they really shouldn't be pissing in an alley, when three men suddenly appeared from what was a small walkway between buildings. It was dark, so no one really noticed, until one of the men walked up behind Colt and put a knife to the man's back.

Then, everything changed.

The drunken, happy mood was gone.

"Easy, big man," the man said. He was short, with a dirty jacket, but the knife he'd produced was quite large. "If you want to keep your kidney, you'll relax, mate."

Everyone froze — Ethan, Nash, Archer, Fox, Cord, Beck, and most of all, Colt. But his features never changed expression, even as he felt the prick of cold steel against his right kidney.

"If you're looking for money, you're too late," he said steadily. "We're coming out of the bar, not going into it. We've spent our money."

The man in the dirty jacket grunted as his friends also produced big knives. "Somehow, I doubt it," he said. "We were watching you inside. I think you're from money, so you've got more where that came from, Yank. I think all of you have more."

With that, his friends began to move. One of them was heading for Ethan while the other one was heading for Archer. The group, as a whole, instinctively started to back away from the men approaching, but Fox refused to budge. At seven inches over six feet, he had that luxury of being stubborn.

"You blokes really think you're going to rob guys who are twice your size?" he said incredulously. "You're either incredibly stupid or way too overconfident."

"I'll go with stupid," Cord muttered.

Fox quickly agreed with him. "Stupid, for sure," he said. "There are seven of us and three of you. You may be able to take out a couple of us, but there are five of us left who will break your fucking necks. Are you ready for that?"

That brought some pause to the man's companions, but the man in the dirty jacket poked Colt enough to draw blood.

"Give me your fucking money!" he hissed. "Another word and I'll cut a hole in this man big enough to stick my hand through!"

Colt didn't even flinch when the man jabbed him. He kept his right hand up while his left once reached into his pocket for his wallet. But as he was doing that, and the other two men with knives were advancing on Ethan and Archer, no one happened to be watching Cord.

And that would be their fatal mistake.

"*Quaere ferro scopum tuum*," Cord suddenly mumbled. "*Oboedite mihi!*"

Inexplicably, the man holding the knife to Colt's back jerked. He jolted. His hand flew up and the big blade he'd been forcing on Colt flew up and into his own throat, straight back through so that the tip came out of the back of his neck. It went through him like a bullet. As he staggered back and fell to the ground, his friends were momentarily startled and that gave Cord the opportunity to turn against them.

"*In molles venter it ferrum*," he growled, lifting a big fist as if to punch the men straight in the face. "*Utrumque vestrum!*"

The men screamed as the hands holding the knives came up and plunged the blades into their bellies as if they had a mind of their own. They went down as Ethan, Nash, Archer, Fox, Beck and Colt made haste to back up, away from what was evidently going on. No one knew what was happening and it was best to get clear considering knives were slashing all over the place.

At least, everyone but Cord backed up. He pointed a finger at the men who had just stabbed themselves in the belly.

"*Ferro ad carnem, ferrum ad os,*" he said in a low tone. "*Collum secari debet.*"

The men with knives in their bellies suddenly withdrew those knives and stabbed themselves in the neck, three or four times, until they could stab no more. They simply lay there and bled as Cord turned to his stunned group of friends.

"We need to get out of here," he said quietly. "Before the cops come. *Quickly.*"

No one moved. They stood there, eyes wide at what they'd just seen. Colt, who was the closest to Cord, grabbed him by the arm.

"What in the hell just happened?" he asked in awe. "What did you do?"

Cord looked back at the men bleeding out on the alley floor. "I protected us," he said simply. "We really need to go."

"Protected us *how*?" Fox was at Cord's side, his handsome face seriously. "What did we just see, Cord? Hypnosis of some kind?"

Cord scratched his head. "No," he said reluctantly, looking at the curious group. "Can we just get out of here, please?"

"Not until you explain," Fox said.

He was serious. No one was moving, not really. Exasperated, Cord sighed heavily. "Fine," he said. "I did it to save Colt's life. That guy was going to kill him."

Colt, who had blood running down the right side of his torso, stepped forward. "He probably was," he said. "Nobody is disputing that. But *what* did you do?"

Cord looked at his friend. "It's not something I really talk about," he said hesitantly. "I haven't... I haven't done that stuff since I was younger, but you all know I'm descended from Abigail Williams. When we all talked about our families and stuff, I told you guys that I was descended from one of the chief accusers of the Salem Witch Trails."

"You did," Colt said as his gaze moved to the men on the ground. "But what does that have to do with it? And done *what* stuff?"

Cord was clearly reluctant. "My dad likes to call us Casters," he said. "Abigail Williams was an accomplished witch and that trait is passed down in my family, like red hair or freckles. Only it's some kind of power we can summon. What you saw was a spell. I turned their knives against them."

"You're a witch?" Colt repeated in shock. "Seriously, Cord? Like — magic?"

Cord didn't answer. He just started walking, very quickly, and the others instinctively followed. They came to a walkway that led out onto the street and, nearly running, they headed up towards the main road.

"Yeah, like magic," Cord finally said as they came to the main avenue. "You saw it. I can't explain it more than that, but I wouldn't have done it if I thought we could have gotten out of that without Sheridan missing a kidney. Just... do yourself a favor. Forget you ever saw it."

"Wait," Ethan said as they began to walk, very quickly, towards the area with the car park. "We can't just leave. No matter what happened, or how it happened, we have to call the police."

"And tell them what?" Cord said. "That we got attacked and that I used a spell to turn the weapons against the guys who attacked us? They would think we were nuts."

As Ethan shook his head in disagreement, Archer grabbed him by the arm and pulled him along. "They would want to know who stabbed those guys," he said. "They'd take our fingerprints and find out that none of our fingerprints were on the weapons. How in the hell are we going to explain that?"

Ethan wasn't sure, but he didn't like running from a crime scene. "Guys, we can't leave," he said, trying to drag his feet. "We were witnesses to what happened. We have to..."

Cord suddenly came to a halt and grabbed Ethan by the shirt. "What do you think is going to happen?" he hissed. "Ethan, I don't want to run any more than you do, but I'm the one who killed those guys. That's the bottom line. And I'm not doing time for it and I'm not going to show the York Police how I turned those weapons against them, so forget it. We're not calling anyone. We're getting out of here and you are giving me your word that you'll never repeat what you saw. I need you to swear that to me."

Ethan could see how upset Cord was and he put up his hands in a gesture of surrender. "I swear that I'll never repeat it," he said. "Don't worry about that. But if anyone else saw us…"

"Who is going to see us?" Cord said, letting go of his shirt. "No one saw us. We're going to fly home tomorrow, anyway, and we'll be out of here. Done."

Ethan nodded, but he wasn't happy about it. Even if he wasn't happy, at least he understood. The entire group began walking again, very quickly, with the car park in sight. Beyond that, freedom.

Freedom from something they hoped wouldn't come back to haunt them.

Cord most of all.

"You… you really *did* that?" Beck finally said. He was still astonished by what he'd witnessed. "How in the hell did you learn how to cast spells?"

Cord school his head. "I told you," he said. "It's in my blood. But I don't like talking about it, so let's just drop it… okay?"

"But we saw it."

They had reached the car park by now and Cord came to an abrupt halt, facing the group. He was normally a congenial guy, but the event had him spooked.

"I know you guys saw it," he said. "But you need to swear that you will never repeat it. You will never tell anyone. Because if you do, I'm going to be in a shitload of trouble. How in the hell am I going to explain to anyone that I used witchcraft to kill some criminals?"

"But it was in self-defense," Ethan stressed. "No one is going to convict you, or any of us for that matter."

Cord's frustration bled through. "But we would have to explain *how* it happened," he said. "Don't you get it? One question would lead to another, questions you don't want to answer. Trust me."

Nash, who had been silent for the most part, put a hand on Cord's shoulder. "Cord, where I'm from, voodoo and witchcraft are part of the culture," he said quietly. "I've seen things I can't explain, so I believe what you're saying. I know what I saw. You have a gift, but it's a gift people don't understand. We've all witnessed something tonight that was... well, pretty damn amazing."

Cord registered some relief as he realized he had the support of Nash. The guy wasn't going to hound him. After a moment, he looked at the rest of the group. "You know, we've joked about calling ourselves the Eagle Brotherhood, but I think we really *are* a brotherhood now," he said. "We've experienced something that could have cost us our lives. It was small, but it happened. You saw something you shouldn't have seen because I did something I shouldn't have done. But to protect you guys... I'd do it again. I hope you know that."

"I feel like I owe my life to you," Colt said, reaching out to shake Cord's hand. "You were brave to do what you did, Cord, knowing... well, knowing that it wasn't something for all to see. But you did it and I'm grateful. I'll take an oath of silence on the Eagle Brotherhood if that's what it'll take. To protect you because you saved my life, I'll do anything. And if you ever need me, no matter where I am, I'll come. That's a promise."

More hands began shooting out, covering Colt and Cord's hands. It was a vow, a promise, not to discuss the event that bonded them more than a school or allied nations could. It was a bond that went deeper now because they harbored a secret. More than that, they had crossed into the realm of a brotherhood that would protect or kill for one another.

The true test of a brotherhood.

It was an oath that would take to their graves.

Wherever life would take them.

ONE

"MOMMY!"

It was a hazy day at the beach. The pearlescent sands on the shore of the stretch of beach along the Hotel del Coronado in San Diego, California, was alive with tourists and beachgoers. There was even a collection of men in wetsuits, rubber dinghies and equipment about fifty yards to the south of the hotel, which wasn't an abnormal sight since Coronado Island also housed a naval base.

Waves crashed and gulls screamed on the lazy, hazy day, adding to the sense of terrestrial paradise that California was so often accused of being. But the cry from one of her young daughters had Blakesley Thorne running for the water's edge.

"Mommy!"

Her middle daughter, five-year-old Crosby, was pointing frantically to the rolling surf while three-year-old Charlotte jumped up and down beside her sister. Blakesley's heart was in her throat as she looked to the area where Crosby was pointing.

"Cadee got pulled in!" Crosby hollered.

Blakesley yelped with terror, seeing her eight-year-old daughter's blond head bobbing a few yards off the sandy shore. The water was rough but not too terribly; still, Cadee must have gotten too close after being repeatedly warned. Tearing off her jacket, Blakesley threw it onto the sand as she ran towards the water.

"Crosby, stay up on the sand!" she yelled. "Watch Charlotte!"

People began to notice what had happened as the panicked young mother dove into the surf. Some began yelling for lifeguards, others began yelling for general help. People began running towards the water as the cry for help spread like wildfire, down the beach and up onto the hotel grounds.

Men in jeans began pulling off their shoes, preparing to follow the woman into the water, but the call for help had soon reached the men in wetsuits down the beach. As the tourists and beach-goers removed shoes and sweatshirts in preparation to help, the men in wetsuits swung into action. There was no delay.

The black rubber assault crafts were moving, engines gunning, with several men in each black, little boat. The other men in wetsuits raced up the beach, diving into the water and swimming furiously towards the child in distress as a couple of men in the dinghies dove into the water once the boats drew close.

The surf was pounding, the water churning, as Blakesley reached her struggling daughter. She had no idea that two dozen men in wetsuits were upon them. As she tried to grasp her child to pull her back to shore, a black rubber dinghy rolled up beside her and arms reached down to pull her up into the boat.

Startled, she could see other arms reaching down to collect Cadee as men in rubber suits lifted her up. So many arms were around her daughter, lifting her to safety as the water churned and crashed around them. The boat's engine engaged and Blakesley fell sideways, onto the floor of the watercraft, as the dinghy grounded itself onto the white sand beach.

"Are you okay?"

Someone was reaching down to pull her up off the bottom of the wet and sandy boat. Blakesley pushed the hair from her eyes, gazing up into the face of a big, bald man with pale green eyes. She nodded, a bit disoriented, straining for a look at her daughter.

"I'm fine," she said, twisting her neck around. "Cadee? Honey, are you all right?"

Someone was lifting her out of the boat. Blakesley suddenly realized she was standing on the beach as a host of men in wetsuits surrounded her. Another man in a wetsuit had Cadee in his arms, climbing out of the boat and handing the girl over to her mother. Blakesley threw her arms around her daughter, struggling not to cry.

"Cadee, are you all right?" she asked again. "What happened?"

Cadee Masterson gripped her mother's neck, sobbing and coughing. "I don't know," the girl wept. "We were playing by the water and then a wave came. It washed me away."

Blakesley held her daughter tightly, feeling a vast amount of relief wash over her as she realized her daughter was safe and sound. "Oh, my God," she gasped. "I was standing there the whole time. I just turned my back to put the camera on the towel and...."

She felt stupid even as she said it. She could have kicked herself a thousand times over for being foolish enough to turn her back on her frolicking daughters, but it wouldn't do any good. She couldn't possibly feel any worse than she already did. But Cadee was safe and that's all that really mattered.

Relief brought on tears and Blakesley closed her eyes, water dampening her sun-kissed cheeks. Crosby and Charlotte found her, little Charlotte sitting on both her shaken older sister and her mother in an attempt to get close. She didn't like to be left out of hugs, of any kind. As Blakesley opened her arms to her other two daughters, she noticed the host of rubber-clad men surrounding her.

Gazing up, she could see several concerned faces gazing down at her. One man in particular was crouched next to her and Blakesley looked at him, startled to see an extraordinarily handsome man looking back at her. His blond hair was cut short, his chiseled features embracing full lips, intense green eyes, and a big cleft in his chin. He looked like he just stepped off a movie set.

When their eyes met, he smiled and she felt a distinct sense of giddy shock at the sexy smile and big dimples in his cheeks.

"Thank you so much," she said gratefully. "All of you – thank you so much for saving my daughter. I don't know what I would have done if... if she...."

The man beside her cut her off, but not unkindly. "We're glad to help," he said, his voice deep and smooth. "Are you sure she's okay? I can have a medic take a look at her if you want."

It began to occur to Blakesley who the men were. Coronado Island had a naval base and it was obvious that these men were part of a detachment from the base. She tried to pull her daughter out of the crook of her neck so she could see for herself how the little girl was, but Cadee wouldn't let go. She clung like a leech. Blakesley smiled weakly at the blond man.

"She's okay," she said softly. "She wouldn't be holding me with a death grip if she wasn't."

The man returned her smile before turning to the men around him and issuing a disbursement command. Immediately, the group disbanded, jumping back into the dinghies or running back down the beach. The tourists and beachgoers who had been gathered around started to disburse also, especially when the men in wetsuits began waving them away. Nothing was worse than a looky-loo crowd.

Shortly, it was just Blakesley, her daughters, and the blond man in the wetsuit. He stayed right next to her, watching the little girl in her arms, listening to her coughing.

"Really, I think we're okay," Blakesley assured him when the crowd wandered away. "I can't tell you how much I appreciate your help. That really scared the crap out of me."

The blond man's grin returned. "It doesn't sound like she swallowed any water," he commented. "Her coughing seems clear."

Blakesley nodded, feeling her daughter's frantic breathing calming. "Are you guys doing some training or something?"

The man nodded vaguely. "Or something," he replied, snickering at her when she grinned. "Are you sure she's okay?"

Blakesley nodded. "She's fine," she said, firmly pulling her daughter off of her. "Cadee, can you say thank you?"

Cadee turned to the blond man, pushing her wet blond hair out of her cherubic face. "T-thank you," she hiccupped.

He smiled at her. "You're welcome, honey," he replied. "Are you sure you feel okay?"

Cadee nodded wearily. "Yes."

Suddenly, the youngest girl was standing in front of him, studying him with the naked curiosity that most three-year-olds have. She had curly blond hair and enormous blue eyes, very angelic in appearance.

"What's your name?" she asked.

The man extended his hand. "My name is Beck," he said. "What's your name?"

"Charlotte Claire Masterson."

She said it very fast, with an adorable little lisp. "It's nice to meet you, Charlotte Claire Masterson," he shook the little hand she placed in his big palm. "What are your sisters' names?"

Charlotte pointed to her oldest sister. "That's Cadee," she said, then pointed to the middle sister. "She's Crosby."

Beck's gaze moved across the two older girls, skimming over Blakesley, before returning to Charlotte. "What's your mom's name?"

"Mommy."

He laughed softly as Blakesley grinned. "I'm Blakesley," she said softly, extending a sandy hand. "There's no way I can repay you for saving my child, but you have my eternal thanks. You really do."

Beck took her sandy hand in his big mitt, shaking it with tender strength. "Like I said, I'm glad we could help," his gaze lingered on her. "Are you here on vacation?"

She shook her head. "No," she said softly. "We live here. Well, we just moved here, this weekend in fact."

His smile grew, revealing straight white teeth. He had a drop-dead, gorgeous smile. "Welcome to San Diego," he said. "But next time, watch out for the surf here. It can be strong."

"I figured that out the hard way."

He snickered softly, drawing chuckles from Blakesley. The man had a very soothing manner about him, something that helped calm her down tremendously. Just as he opened his mouth to say something more to her, Charlotte suddenly put herself between Beck and Blakesley. She didn't want to be left out of the conversation.

"I'm three years old," she announced.

Beck pretended to be impressed. "Three years old," he repeated. "You're practically an old lady."

Charlotte grinned brightly. "No, I'm not!"

Blakesley watched her youngest daughter engage in conversation with the man in the wetsuit and, inevitably, her gaze fixed on him. She couldn't help but watch him closely, for he was a truly handsome male specimen. He had enormous shoulders and hands, and his eyes had a very cute way of crinkling when he grinned. She couldn't tell how tall he was because he remained crouched down next to her, but he had a truly easy manner with her daughter and she appreciated that immensely. But bold, little Charlotte would talk to anyone, however, so Blakesley thought she'd better put a stop to it so the man could get on with his day.

"Charlotte, honey, can you and Crosby please go and get our stuff?" she interrupted when there was a break in the chatter. "I think we should go now and I'm sure Mr. Beck has to get going also. He has things to do."

Charlotte bolted off with Crosby scampering after her. Cadee even climbed off her mother and wandered after her sisters, leaving Blakesley and Beck alone. When Blakesley realized she was alone with the handsome stranger, her heart began to beat a little faster, perhaps with excitement. She really wasn't sure. It had been so long since she'd experienced that kind of giddiness that she couldn't be sure of anything. She was sure any ability to feel something like that had died long ago. Casting him a somewhat shy grin, she brushed off her hands of sand and rose to her knees.

"You've been our guardian angel today, Mr. Beck," she said, holding out her hand again. "I really appreciate all you've done."

Beck smiled and took her hand, shaking it again but holding it when he probably should have let it go. He let his gaze move over her exquisite face, so beautiful and sweet. She had long hair, honey blond in color, and gorgeous bluish-green eyes that had a catlike tilt to them. With a big dimple in her left cheek and brilliant smile, he could have stared at the woman all day. It was a surprising reaction from a man who didn't pay a lot of attention to women since his ex-wife left him for someone who didn't serve in the Navy or deploy for months on end. Women just meant trouble for him and he mostly avoided them. But this woman, for some reason, had his full attention.

"You're welcome," he said, standing up and gently pulling her to her feet. He was still holding her hand, greedily, soaking up the last few moments of her soft flesh before she would inevitably pull her hand away. "Are you ladies heading home for the day now? You shouldn't let a little mishap spoil your fun, you know. Once the haze burns off, it'll be a beautiful day."

Blakesley smiled and, as he had known, pulled her hand from his grip and began to brush off her pants. "We've been here since early morning," she told him. "We're staying here at the hotel so I'm sure this won't be our last trip to the beach today."

Beck glanced up at the towering white Victorian hotel with its terra cotta-colored roof and tall, cupola-shaped spire that was a landmark in San Diego. It was big, beautiful and historic.

"You just moved to San Diego but you're staying in a hotel?" he cocked his head curiously.

Blakesley nodded, turning to watch Crosby and Charlotte run circles in the sand. "I've always wanted to stay here," she admitted. "It's just for this weekend. Our house is still being cleared out and... well, anyway, I'm sure you don't care about that, so we're just at the hotel for the weekend."

His face was creased in a permanent smile as he gazed down at her. She was a couple of inches over five feet, deliciously curvy, with tantalizing cleavage that he could see encased in a pink bikini top beneath a flowing white shirt. In fact, it was a struggle not to look at that amazing cleavage as he looked her in the eye. When he opened his mouth to say something, Charlotte abruptly crashed into his legs as she and her giggling sister chased each other. He instinctively reached down to keep the little girl from tumbling.

"Whoa there," he cautioned gently. "Careful."

Crosby was grabbing at Charlotte, who screamed and clung to Beck as if the man could save her. Beck began to laugh but Blakesley reached out and grasped her daughter, pulling her away from the big man in the wetsuit.

"Sorry." She cast Beck an apologetic look. "She can be rather, uh, friendly."

He just shook his head. "She's sweet," he told her. "No worries."

Blakesley smiled broadly, flashing him that big dimple in her left cheek, and Beck was growing more enchanted by the moment.

"Well... thank you again," she said sincerely. "It's been very nice meeting you, Mr. Beck."

He realized she was preparing to leave him. He didn't want her to leave, not in the least. He was feeling a great amount of disappointment at the thought. He started thinking furiously of a way not to end the conversation.

"Actually, Beck is my first name," he told her. "It's Beckham, but everybody calls me Beck."

Blakesley nodded in understanding. "Nice," she said, coming to realize that she, too, was glad the conversation was continuing and she, too, realized she wanted to keep it going. "This is an obvious statement, but you evidently have something to do with the naval base on Coronado. I hope saving my daughter didn't interrupt anything."

He shook his head, his blond hair glistening under the hazy sun. "We just finished up," he told her. "We were heading back."

"What were you doing?"

"Secret stuff. James Bond stuff."

"Seriously?"

"Seriously."

Blakesley laughed softly. Along with his soothing demeanor and stunning, blond good looks, he was also very charming. There was no reason on earth she should give the man a second glance, but she did. She couldn't help it. He really did look like a movie star with his attractive face and muscular build. Now that he was on his feet, she could see that he was maybe a foot taller than her five foot two inches, not inordinately tall, but his frame was just plain big. He was a very big man all tucked up into that skin-tight rubber suit, something that didn't go unnoticed by her and probably every other woman on the beach. She couldn't imagine he had any shortage of female companionship, or was perhaps even married, so she allowed herself to feel giddy in his glorious presence and nothing more. There wasn't any point.

"Well," she began to glance around to where Cadee and Crosby were now picking up their towels. "I guess we'd better get going. It was really good to meet you, Beck."

His brilliant smile grew. "Beckham Raymond Seavington the Third," he told her. "If you ever want to name your next kid after me, now you know."

She laughed. "That's not likely to happen, but thanks for the information."

His face fell dramatically. "You don't want to name your next kid after me?"

She couldn't stop laughing, backing away from him partially because Charlotte was pulling at her and partially because he was making her feel hot and giggly.

"I didn't mean it that way," she told him. "No more kids for me. Three girls are enough."

He was back to grinning, shrugging. "Your husband doesn't want a boy? Beck's a good name, you know. It'll go with Masterson really well."

It was an exceptionally leading question but Blakesley didn't get defensive about it like she usually would. She could see that he was trying to probe her and, against her usual reaction, she let him. She had nothing to lose.

"No husband," she told him, still backing away as Charlotte pulled. "Nobody at all. You'll have to get someone else to name a kid after you."

Beck just stood there and grinned, waving at her when she waved at him and turned back to her daughters. He stood there watching her pick up towels and bags, watching her deliciously round buttocks in her wet Capri pants as she herded the girls up towards the hotel. There was something so sweet and fluid about the way she moved, the way her shiny hair blew softly in the breeze. Enchanted was a very appropriate word for what he felt when he looked at her.

When Blakesley turned around and saw that he was still standing there watching her, she waved at him again and he waved back. She was feeling giddy and self-conscious, knowing that he was standing there watching her, but she couldn't help the grin on her lips as she pulled her girls back towards the hotel. It was nice to feel like that again, even if it was only fleeting. She could feel his gaze on her as they made their way to the hotel doors, daring to turn around to see if he was still there and rather surprised to find that he wasn't.

A glance down the beach, both north and south, didn't show the man. There were all sorts of people on the sand, but no man in a wetsuit. He had literally vanished. As she held the door open for her girls, she noticed something out in the water, paralleling the shore and swimming north in the direction of the naval base. It took her a moment to realize it was him, evidently unconcerned with the two-mile swim to the base grounds. It *was* rather James Bond.

With a grin, she followed her girls into the hotel's posh and cool depths.

TWO

"HEY, THANKS FOR WAITING FOR ME," Beck said sarcastically as he entered the big barracks at the Naval Amphibious Base Coronado where his team was stationed. "You're lucky I made it back."

There were about twenty men spread out over the barracks, which were more like a small air hanger than an actual building. There were offices, a conference room, lockers, a shower area, and a big, wide-open area used for staging. Most of the men were checking their weapons but some were beginning to change out of their gear. They looked up at Beck as the man walked wearily into the barracks, dripping wet.

"Sorry, sir," a young seaman was sitting on the floor going through his equipment. "Commander Aguirre ordered us back to base."

Beck's gaze moved off towards the locker area where the officers kept their equipment. "He did, did he?" he muttered, running his hand over his drying hair and thinking that his operations officer would soon be getting a foot shoved up his ass. "I'm going to have to have a talk with Mr. Aguirre."

The seamen spread out over the floor pretended to be busy, but grins and glances passed between them as Commander Seavington made his way over to the officer's area. Things could get lively between the unit commander and his second, Lt. Commander Aguirre, at times.

Beck walked up to the bank of lockers where two men were in various stages of undress. Operations and Tactics Officer Robert "Butch" Aguirre caught sight of Beck as he approached, a big grin crossing his face. Butch was a big man with a heavy combat background, bald as a cue ball and looking a lot like Mr. Clean. He was a little rough around the edges but there was no one better qualified on a mission. He also happened to be one of Beck's closest friends.

"Thanks for taking off," Beck scolded. "I had to swim back."

Butch grinned and turned back to the pack he was reloading. "Quit your crying," he said. "I wasn't about to interrupt you."

"What do you mean?"

Butch looked at the other officer, Chief Petty Officer Anthony Solis. He was young but extremely smart, with jet black hair, black eyes, and an efficient manner about him. The kid was first generation Italian American and Navy to the core. Solis grinned at Aguirre but quickly looked away so Seavington wouldn't see him.

"That sweet young mother you were talking to," Aguirre fought off a grin as he pretended to focus on his equipment. "There was no way I was getting in the middle of that."

Beck scowled. "There wasn't anything to get in the middle of," he said, grumpy, and yanked his locker open. "I was just making sure she and her daughter were okay."

Butch shook his head. "Beck, I've known you for ten years. Never, in that time, have you departed from your command-and-control mode to talk to a civilian. I don't blame you, though, She was pretty sweet."

Beck didn't say anything as he began to peel himself out of the wetsuit. Any snappy reply he could think of had him sounding defensive or, worse yet, guilty of what they were suggesting. But the truth was that they were right. He started feeling a little unbalanced at the thought.

"Whatever," he growled. It was all he could think to say. "Where's Davis?"

He was referring to their commanding officer, a hawk-like man who was always integrally involved in any operation they performed, even exercises. He had been out on a small cruiser watching his men conduct exercises in a Combat Rubber Raiding Craft. Many of the S.E.A.L. teams had specialties, like counter-terrorism or demolitions, but Beck's team specialized in land ops, assault craft boarding and rescue, and they had been at it for two days straight. Butch shrugged to Beck's question.

"Not sure," he said. "He was here a minute ago, looking for you."

Beck rolled his eyes. "Great," he muttered. "The CO comes looking for me and I'm AWOL."

"Was it worth it?" Butch wanted to know.

Beck looked down at him. "Was what worth it?"

"Talking to her."

Beck dug into his locker, debating on what, or how much, he should say. He pulled out a dry tee shirt.

"Yeah," he muttered. "It was worth it."

Butch and Anthony perked up, all ears now that Seavington was talking. "Really?" Butch said. "That's great. Are you going to see her again?"

Beck lifted his big shoulders. "Maybe," he said. "I don't know. We really didn't talk about it."

"Did you get her number?"

"No."

"Name?"

"Blakesley Thorne."

Butch looked at Anthony and winked. "Blakesley Thorne," he repeated, rather dreamily. "Very nice. So do something about it. Ask her out."

Beck shrugged again. "Maybe."

Butch threw up his hands, turning to Anthony. "Do you hear this guy?" he jabbed a finger at Beck. "If it were me, I sure wouldn't wait. He meets a woman he actually says more than two words to, which means he's seriously attracted to her, but he's not sure if he's going to ask her out? What a loser."

Anthony grinned, looking at Beck, who was pulling out a dry pair of pants. "Maybe he just doesn't want to rush anything," Anthony said. "Maybe she's not really his type."

Beck looked at the pair. "Oh, don't get me wrong; she's my type," he said. "But... oh, hell, I don't know. I just don't need this kind of trouble."

Butch laughed softly and slapped him on the back. "You need to get laid."

As Butch and Anthony snorted, Beck just shook his head at them. "That's the last thing I need," he said. "But maybe... well, maybe I could take her to dinner. If she'll go. She may not even like me, you know."

Butch's smile faded. "You let that bitch ex-wife convince you that no woman would want you because of your job." He stood up from the bench he had been seated on. "You've let her do that to you for four years, Beck. Enough is enough. If you like this Blakesley, then ask her to dinner. The worst thing that can happen is you have a good time."

"Or she turns me down."

"There's only one way to find out."

Butch was right. There was only one way to find out.

———

The Sun Deck Restaurant at the Hotel del Coronado offered California dining al fresco with the Pacific Ocean as the backdrop. Dusk was gentle on this night, a soft breeze blowing off the water as the patio fire pit offered a bit of warmth in the cool wind. There was a beautiful moon above and everything would have been quite romantic had Blakesley had a special partner to share the evening with.

But she didn't. She hadn't in well over a year, not since Ed had been sentenced and packed away in Folsom Prison. Blakesley sat facing the water, her second glass of wine in hand as Charlotte slept on her lap, thinking back to the days when her ex-husband hadn't been a murdering cheat. As she had done so many times over the months since Ed's crime spree, she wondered when in the hell the man she had fallen in love with had gone so wrong. It just didn't make any sense to her, not after all this time, and Ed couldn't seem to explain it. So she shut him out of her life, out of her children's lives, and made every effort to move on as if he had never existed. It was a past she couldn't get away from but one she desperately wanted to shake.

It was important to move on for her children. Cadee, having recovered from her near-death experience, was enjoying a chocolate brownie with vanilla ice cream while Crosby indulged in a hot fudge sundae. Charlotte had been too exhausted to stay awake for the treats after dinner and slept soundly on her mother. As the girls ate, Blakesley sat and watched the waves pound, glancing at the happy families dining around them and trying not to feel too depressed that she was single with her girls. It wasn't so much that being single bothered her, because it didn't. She just felt bad for her girls being without a father.

"Mommy!" Crosby had a mouth full of ice cream. "Can we do movie night?"

Blakesley looked to her daughter, thoughts shifting from her depression to the posters they had seen in the hotel lobby for a kids' movie night hosted by the hotel. It was some Disney movie that the girls had seen five hundred times, but they still wanted to go. During the summer months, the hotel hosted the movie night for kids so their parents could have a few hours of kid-free time. There was face-painting and games. She looked at her watch.

"Do you really want to go?" she asked, noting the time.

Crosby and Cadee nodded vigorously. "Please, Mama?" Cadee begged.

Blakesley sighed, nodding her head. It would be something fun for the girls to do and Lord knew they needed it. So much of their young lives, as of late, had been serious and depressing. So she woke Charlotte up, who very much wanted to see the Princess movie again and told the waiter she would return. Blakesley walked the girls through the sumptuous hotel lobby and over to the KidTopia recreation center where other kids were gathering, signing them in for the movie night.

Leaving the girls hadn't been particularly easy. She stood there and watched them integrate with the other children that were running around, feeling some separation anxiety but fighting it. The girls were already having a good time so she wandered back out to the patio restaurant and sat by the fireplace, feeling the heat from the golden flames lick at her as she gazed up at the darkening sky.

She'd never felt more alone in her life.

"At the risk of using an overused line, is this seat taken?"

The voice came from behind her. Blakesley wasn't even sure the question was meant for her until she realized there was no one else within ten feet of her. Startled, she looked over her left shoulder to see who had asked the question.

Beck stood about five feet away, smiling at her, and Blakesley's jaw dropped with surprise. He was in street clothes, jeans and a white collared shirt with rolled-up sleeves, and looking completely different from when they had met earlier in the day. The truth was that she probably wouldn't have recognized him on the street, except he had a smile that lit up the room. It was all teeth and brilliance – she definitely recognized the smile. Closing her agape mouth, she looked around just to make sure there wasn't someone else he was speaking to.

"Are you talking to me?" she asked, grinning.

His smile grew. "I am." He made his way towards her, looking somewhat timid. "I was driving by the hotel and thought I'd stop to see how your daughter was doing after her brush with death."

Blakesley realized she was feeling giddy again at the sight of him. She was so shocked and pleased that she almost didn't know what to say.

"She's fine," she assured him, looking at him with a mixture of curiosity, suspicion and pleasure. "How in the world did you find me?"

He threw a thumb back in the direction of the hotel entry. "I was at the front desk about to ask them if they could call your room for me when I saw you walk through the lobby. I followed you out here."

"Oh," she accepted his explanation. "I just dropped the girls off at a movie night gig. The hotel has activities and face painting for the kids."

"Sounds like fun."

"Want to get your face painted? You'd look great with a big butterfly on your nose."

He laughed. "I'll have to pass, but thanks."

She laughed because he was, her gaze lingering on him. "It's really sweet of you to check on Cadee. You didn't have to."

He shrugged. "No problem," he said. "No ill effects?"

"None that I can see," Blakesley shook her head. "She was eating like a pig earlier. Do you want to see her for yourself?"

He shook his head, waving her off. "No, that's not necessary," he said. "If you say she's fine, I believe you. Let her watch her movie."

Blakesley nodded, smiling as they slipped into awkward silence now that the surprise of his appearance had faded.

"Uh... well, it was really sweet of you to check in on her," she said again. "She'll be sorry she missed you."

His green eyes glimmered at her, reflecting the light from the patio fire pit. "I'm just glad she's okay," he said, feeling the same awkwardness that she was but he had no intention of leaving. "So... how's Mom doing after the wave fiasco?"

Blakesley laughed softly. "Fine," she said. "Although I will admit, it freaks me out every time I think about what would have happened if you guys hadn't come to our rescue. I'll admit I'm not a very good swimmer."

His easy smile broadened. "Now that you're living in California, you'll have to learn."

She waved him off. "I was born and raised in California, so that has nothing to do with it," she told him. "I'm from Los Angeles. I just never liked swimming very much. I was always one of those girls who would rather look cute on the beach than get my hair wet; hence, I never really learned how to swim very well."

He was warming to the conversation, thrilled that the initial awkwardness had passed. Maybe if she warmed enough, too, she would ask him to sit next to her. "I get it," he pretended to be wise to her. "You were the girl that all the boys wanted to pick up on."

She feigned outrage for a few seconds before breaking down in giggles. "That sums it up pretty well," she said, sighing heavily. "Oh, let's face it; I was a vain little witch. Now I try and raise my daughters to be the opposite. Girls like me always seemed to attract the worst kind of men."

By the time she finished, her smile was gone and, embarrassed, she turned back for her chair if only to give herself something to do. She'd said too much and was feeling humiliated for it. She pointed to the chair next to her.

"Can you sit for a minute?" she asked, purely to change the subject. "Are you in a hurry?"

"No."

"I'd love to buy a drink for the man who saved my child's life."

He'd been waiting for that invitation since the moment he arrived and gladly took the seat next to her, although he didn't want to seem too eager so he tried to be casual about it. He was so casual that he ended up stumbling into the chair and trying not to look like an idiot in the process.

"Thanks," he said, hoping she didn't notice that he tripped over his feet. "Are you sure I'm not interrupting anything?"

"Not at all," she assured him, waving over the waiter. "Like I said, they're at movie night. I have at least two hours to kill until I have to pick them up."

"Are you sure you want company? I mean, I really didn't come here to interrupt you. You said you were on vacation so maybe you just want to chill without chatting it up with a stranger."

It seemed to her that he was a bit nervous. She could tell just by the way he was rambling. The big, beefy Navy man was actually nervous and she suppressed a smile. She was thrilled, of course, but she also decided to have a little fun with him.

"So...," she leaned forward on the table, folding her hands and looking at him seriously. "You were just driving by the hotel and decided to come in and see how Cadee was?"

He was sucked in by her big, bluish-green eyes. "Yes, ma'am."

He answered as if he were facing an inquisitor and the smile she had been trying to hide was threatening to burst forth. "Where were you going?"

"How's that?"

"I asked you where you were going when you were driving by the hotel. You said you were driving by. Surely you were going somewhere unless you were just driving aimlessly."

"I wasn't driving aimlessly, ma'am."

"Where were you going?"

"It'll cost you a drink to find out, ma'am."

She did grin, then. The waiter was standing next to the table and Beck ordered a domestic beer. When the waiter went off to fetch it, Beck returned his attention to Blakesley.

"Until my drink arrives and you get the answer to your question," he lifted an eyebrow at her, "I get to ask some of my own."

Her eyebrows rose in mock outrage. "What?"

"You heard me. I'm invoking my right to ask questions, too."

She sat back in her chair and collected her wine, biting a grinning lip. "All right," she agreed. "Go for it."

"You said you're from Los Angeles?"

"Born and raised in Pasadena. I was on the Tournament of Roses Rose Court in nineties. If you don't believe me, look it up. I was Princess Blakesley Amelia Thorne." She presented a much practiced Rose Parade wave complete with the stiff cup-shaped hand and swiveling wrist.

A faint grin played on his lips. "I would believe that implicitly," he agreed. "You definitely look like a princess."

She smiled, flattered. "Thanks."

"You're welcome." He sat forward, folding his enormous hands on the tabletop. "But I'm not finished yet. Pasadena isn't a bad town. Why'd you move down to San Diego?"

Her smiled began to fade and she took a sip of her wine. Beck watched her, thinking that maybe that hadn't been the right question. He'd been so excited about sitting at the same table with her that maybe he had been too overbearing. Maybe he had asked a question with too personal an answer.

"Sorry," he said softly. "You don't have to answer that if you don't want to."

She looked at him, forcing a smile. "It's not that," she said, somewhat subdued. "It's just a complicated answer."

His smile returned. "Like I said, you don't have to answer it if you don't want to," he said, rather eager to change the subject. "So... what do you do for a living, Mrs. Masterson? Is that a safe question?"

Her smile turned genuine and she laughed softly. "It's Blakesley Thorne. I took back my maiden name after my divorce," she said. "And you wouldn't believe me if I told you."

His eyebrows lifted. "Should I guess?"

She laughed again. "You can try."

He pretended to think. "A super model?" He watched her giggle and shake her head. "A pediatrician? A spy?"

"No, not even close," she shut him up. "When I was in college, I started cleaning offices at night for money. It worked with my schedule and paid well. I started getting more and more clients just by word of mouth, so much so that I started employing my friends to take the jobs I just didn't have time to do. Eventually, I grew the business into one of the most successful industrial janitorial companies in the state. I sold it last year so I could pursue my dream."

He was listening intently. "What's your dream?"

She smiled bashfully. "My college degree wasn't in business," she admitted. "It was in Art. I paint. I want to open my own art gallery."

He was staring at her. After a moment, he simply shook his head. "That's a pretty amazing story," he said. "You're telling me that you built a big janitorial business and you weren't even a business major?"

She nodded. "Weird, huh?" she sipped at her wine again. "I sold it to a national chain for a lot of money, at least enough to keep me comfortable the rest of my life. I was lucky."

He wriggled his eyebrows in agreement, in surprise, as the waiter brought his beer. "So you moved down here to open your art gallery?"

"I'd really like to. I'm going out with a real estate agent next week to look at some storefronts."

His intense green eyes were warm on her, inspecting her, digesting her life and dreams as she explained them. He held up his glass of beer to her. "I think it's great that you can live your dream," he said sincerely. "Good luck on your art gallery."

She lifted her wine glass, smiling as she clinked it against his. "Thank you," she said sincerely. "I really hope it works out."

He took a big gulp of beer, savoring it. "If you have as much talent for art as you do for business, then you shouldn't have a problem."

She shrugged modestly, glancing at him and realizing he was studying her intently. From the moment he had appeared, his eyes had never left her, but his manner wasn't threatening or lecherous. It was kind, curious, and very interested. His expression was enough to make her cheeks grow warm and her heart started doing that weird fluttering thing again.

"So...," she sipped at her wine, looking away and hoping he didn't see that her cheeks were flushing. "Now that I've bought and paid for you for the price of a beer, you're going to answer my questions."

His easy grin returned as he regarded her. "Ask away."

"Were you really just driving by the hotel tonight?"

"What do you mean?"

"Did you have someplace else to go and just happened to stop by?"

He sighed heavily, but not without a huge grin on his face. Suddenly, he couldn't seem to look her in the eye as he fidgeted with his glass.

"What's the penalty for perjury?" he wanted to know.

She bit her lip to keep from laughing. "I'll take my fork and stick it in your eyeball."

He burst out laughing. "Ouch," he moved the silverware out of her reach. "In that case, I'll tell you the truth. But swear you won't laugh."

"I won't."

He took another deep breath and fixed her in the eye. "No, I didn't have anywhere else to go," he told her. "I came here tonight because I wanted to see how your daughter was. That was a scary experience for a little kid. But I also… oh, hell, I can't believe I'm telling you this, but I guess I have nothing to lose now so I might as well. What I really wanted was to see you again and hopefully get the chance to ask you to dinner."

Blakesley waited for more of an explanation, but it was apparent he was finished. His rationalization was all packaged up neat and tidy. She lifted her eyebrows at him.

"Seriously?"

"Seriously."

"You came to ask me out?"

"I was hoping to."

"But you don't know the first thing about me."

He shrugged. "I know you're about five feet and a couple of inches, you have beautiful hair and the most beautiful face I've ever seen." He threw caution to the wind. "You said you didn't have a husband, so I thought… oh, God, now I'm starting to feel stupid, but I thought maybe you'd let me take you out. If you're not interested, I totally understand. No harm in asking, I guess."

She just looked at him, a smile playing on her lush lips. "Let me get this straight," she was deeply flattered but couldn't resist teasing him. "You're telling me that based on the five-minute conversation we had on the beach today, a conversation that wasn't under the best of circumstances, that you want to take me out?"

He was starting to feel really foolish. "That's about it, ma'am."

"If you call me 'ma'am' again, I'm going to put that fork in your eyeball."

He grinned, toying with his beer glass. "Sorry. Habit."

She forgave him with a smile. "So tell me about yourself, Mr. Navy."

He lifted his eyebrows thoughtfully. "My name is Beck Seavington, I'm a commander in the United States Navy, and I'm assigned to a detachment out Naval Amphibious Base Coronado. I was born and raised in San Diego, California, attended the United States Naval Academy, and graduated in 1990 in the top two percent of my class with dual degrees in International Law and Mechanical Engineering. Is there anything else you'd like to know?"

Her eyes were glimmering warmly at him. "Are you married?"

He gave her a curious expression. "Do you really think I'd be here if I was?"

Her smile faded. "Sorry," she said softly. "I wasn't trying to insult your integrity."

He shook his head. "You didn't." He watched her, noticing she wouldn't look at him as she finished the last of her red wine. "But I'm guessing you asked for a reason."

She did look at him, then. "What reason?"

"You tell me."

She looked back to her wine. "Maybe...," she whispered. "Maybe someday I will."

He let it go. She was very protective, he could tell. But he was a patient man. He intended to find out why this lovely, sweet and funny woman was so guarded. He drained the last of his beer.

"You didn't answer me," he said as he set the glass down.

She looked at him. "What's that?"

"Whether or not you'll let me take you out to dinner."

"We're having dinner now, aren't we?"

He shook his head. "We're having drinks."

"Then let's order dinner."

"You haven't eaten yet?"

She shook her head. "I fed the girls earlier but I wasn't hungry."

His smile returned. "Then let's get the waiter over here."

The evening flew past as they conversed over dinner and more drinks. Beck hadn't been out on a date in so long that he felt like a giddy teenager through most of the meal, engaging in further conversation about the art gallery she wanted to open but steering away from her reasons for moving to San Diego. It seemed to be one of a few subjects she wouldn't talk about but despite that, she was very easy to talk to and he talked more than he probably had in his entire life in just a couple of short hours.

Beck discovered that she loved horses and dogs, but hated anything to do with the water, ironic considering he was in the Navy. She also loved horse racing, football and NASCAR, something he loved as well, so they bonded over talk of Talladega, the San Diego Chargers and the Kentucky Derby. He came to discover she was a smart cookie who knew her stats on horses, race car drivers and football players. He was impressed to the bone.

But along with his growing respect and interest, he was also increasingly aware that she was very guarded with her private life or personal information. He knew where she was born and raised, but little more than that. He was becoming increasingly curious but he refrained from asking any more personal questions, afraid he would scare her off. He was enjoying her company so much that he sincerely didn't want to spook her. He wanted to have many more nights just like tonight, getting to know a very sweet and beautiful woman that he was extremely attracted to.

It was close to ten in the evening when Blakesley's cell phone went off. Thinking it was the KidTopia center calling to let her know to pick up the girls, she answered. As Beck sat back and finished off his third beer, Blakesley's expression went from relaxed to tense all in a short few seconds. Beck listened to a few short exchanges, nothing he could really make heads or tails out of, until she signed off and abruptly shut off the phone.

The mood, which had been light and fun only a few moments earlier, was now uncertain and tense. Beck watched her put the phone back in her purse, her expression dark and somber.

"Everything okay?" he asked softly.

She looked up at him as if startled by the question. "What?" she said before she could really think about it, then shook her head and regained her train of thought. "Oh... it's nothing. Hey, I think it's about time for me to pick up the girls. Do you want to come with me and see Cadee for yourself?"

He smiled faintly, toying with the empty beer glass. "Sure," he said, his intense eyes riveted to her. "Can I ask you something?"

She forced a smile at him, the gentle and funny man she had shared two wonderful hours with. Truth be told, she was coming to like him a great deal.

"Ask away," she said, forcing the jovial mood.

He sat back, watching her carefully. "I realize that I just met you," he began, "but I have to tell you, I've never had a date like this in my life."

She cocked her head curiously. "What do you mean?"

He lifted those big shoulders, searching for the correct words to describe what he was feeling. "Well," he laughed softly, embarrassed. "I don't get out much. My work keeps me pretty busy, so there's very little free time. I can't even remember when I was last out on a date, so this... this is like something out of a fantasy for me. Here I am, at the Del, sitting with a beautiful woman I seem to have a lot in common with. It never even occurred to me when I woke up this morning that this would be the end of my day and I want to thank you for that."

Blakesley smiled, a genuine gesture. "That's a really sweet

thing to say," she said sincerely. "Thank you. I've really enjoyed this evening, too."

He met her smile, still looking somewhat embarrassed as he continued. "I guess what I'm trying to say is that even though I just met you, already, I feel like I know you and I feel a lot of concern for you. Hell, I kind of feel responsible for you and your girls after what happened this afternoon. I know you just moved here and all, and you've got three beautiful, little girls and are undoubtedly really busy, but I was kind of hoping we could be friends."

Her smile grew. "I'd like that."

He looked surprised. "Really?"

She nodded. "You're really easy to talk to and, to tell you the truth, I don't get out much either."

"It seems like you have a lot to keep you busy."

She half-nodded, half-shrugged. She began to fidget with her empty wine glass again. "Life had been really busy the past few years," she admitted.

He was watching her closely, the way her lashes fanned out over her cheeks when she blinked, the way her elegant hands gripped the wine glass. She seemed pensive again, distant.

"So we're friends, right?" he asked quietly.

She forced a smile, eyeing him. "Yes."

He leaned forward on the table. "Then from one friend to another, from a guy who really doesn't have any ulterior motive other than he just wants to help if he can, why are you so guarded?"

She looked at him as if shocked by the question. An expression crossed her face, like one of sorrow and longing, that was quickly replaced by that same forced smile he had seen all night when they danced around a subject she didn't want to talk about. She let go of the wine glass and reached across the table, gripping one of his enormous hands.

"I appreciate the concern, I really do," she said sincerely. "But you can't even imagine... I came to San Diego because I need to start fresh with my girls, away from... well, away from the madness that has been my life over the past couple of years. If I told you about it, you'd run screaming from this table and never look back. I just made a friend and I don't want to lose him, so even though I appreciate your concern, I'd rather just let it all lie. It doesn't matter, anyway."

He held her soft fingers tightly as he gazed into her blue-green eyes. "Probably not," he said quietly, his voice soft and deep, "but I thought I'd ask anyway. I wasn't trying to be nosey."

"I know."

"Whatever is troubling you, it's pretty evident."

She just smiled at him, feeling his big fingers caress her hand. "I'm sure it is," she whispered. "But it's my problem. I'll deal with it."

He simply nodded, slowly, as his other hand came up to hold on to her. Her hand looked tiny wrapped up in his big mitts.

"If you need help, you'll let me know?"

She smiled gratefully. "I will."

"Can you tell me what that phone call was about?"

"Why?"

"Because you went from happy to sad all in a split second." He cocked his head slightly, eyeing her in the moonlight. "Is it an ex? Is he harassing you?"

She laughed softly and squeezed his hand. "No, nothing like that," she assured him. "Although it... oh, hell, it doesn't matter. Look; I'm just a nice, normal girl without any weirdness or vices that just got caught up in a bad situation. I'm trying to put distance between that bad situation and my family so my girls won't have to deal with it."

He just looked at her. "You're not making any sense at all. You realize that, right?"

She pulled her hand from his grip and started laughing, running her hands through her hair in a frustrated, oddly nervous gesture. She gazed up at the stars as if they would help her navigate her way through this delicate subject. After a moment, she simply shook her head.

"All right," she said with resignation. "You want to know all about me? Okay. Here goes. I was married to a man for almost ten years and we owned a few businesses together, including three successful restaurants in Hollywood, Pasadena and Irvine. We had a great life, or so I thought, until about two years ago. That's when things went crazy."

He was hanging on every word. "What happened?"

She looked at him, matter-of-factly. "We had a big house, private schools, and had everything we could possibly want. I thought we were happy, but I was wrong. In August almost two years ago, at around midnight, there was a knock on my front door. I was still awake, waiting for my husband to get home because he had a business meeting that ran late, which was nothing unusual. Because of the restaurants and the odd hours, he was always coming home late. Anyway, I open the door and the police were there. So were several media vans. Apparently, my husband wasn't so much at a business meeting as he was at our restaurant in Hollywood with a woman he'd been seeing for about a year. I guess she wanted more than to just be a mistress and threatened to tell me about the affair so my husband, seeing that he had everything to lose if this happened, strangled her. He tried to cover up the crime by getting rid of the body but one of the kitchen staff saw what happened and called the cops."

Beck stared at her, horror in his expression. "Oh, my God," he muttered. "That's terrible."

She nodded, shrugged, as if she really didn't care anymore when the truth was that she did. The shame, the horror, followed her around on a daily basis and she cared very much. She couldn't believe she was actually telling him all of it but the more she talked, the more it came spilling out.

"Didn't you hear about the Hollyhock Murder?" she asked him. "It was all over the news for, like, six months. Hollyhock was the restaurant in Hollywood where it happened. Ed Masterson was convicted on second degree murder and sentenced to life without possibility of parole at Folsom State Prison. He's been in there for almost a year and I have all but wiped him from my life and the lives of my children."

Beck wriggled his eyebrows sympathetically. "I don't blame you. I would have done the same thing."

She grew subdued as she thought on the past year of her life that she really didn't like to think about. "The trial drained any mutual assets we had to pay his legal bills," she said softly. "Everything we had together was gone. Fortunately, I'd kept the janitorial service as my personal asset, so at least the girls and I weren't destitute. I'm still able to provide for my children. That call you heard was about our house."

"What house?"

She looked up from her fidgeting fingers. "The house here in San Diego," she told him. "It belonged to my mother, who passed away about the same time Ed went to prison. The house has been in our family since it was built, but since my mom and dad retired to Palm Springs years ago, my mother rented it out to my cousin and his family. Now the house belongs to me and I evicted them because I want to live in it, only my cousin wouldn't go peacefully. Remember I told you this morning that I was staying at the hotel until my house was cleared? The eviction warrant was served today. That call was from the Sheriff's Department telling me that they finally got my cousin out of the house."

Beck sat back in his chair, understanding now why this beautiful, sweet woman seemed so protected. She had a lot going on, a horrible situation that she didn't deserve. When he had asked her why she had seemed so guarded, he never imagined a story like this. It was, in truth, a little shocking. Before he could say a word, Blakesley suddenly stood up and collected her purse.

"So," she seemed abrupt and businesslike, "now you know the truth and I'm sure this will be the last I'll see of you, so I want you to know that you will always have my gratitude for saving my daughter's life today. I owe you everything. You seem like a really sweet and grounded guy, and I thank you very much for a lovely evening. It's been a long time since I've had such a nice evening out."

He stuck out a big hand and grabbed her by the wrist before she could get away. "Wait a minute," he said firmly. "Where are you running off to?"

Blakesley wasn't as strong as she was pretending. Tears were right on the surface, tears she didn't fully understand but she knew had something to do with embarrassment and disappointment.

"I'm going to get my girls," she said tightly. "Then I'm going to go see if my cousin trashed my house."

He stood up next to her, still holding her wrist. He was a good foot taller than she was, towering over her.

"You're not going anywhere," he said softly, firmly. "Sit down. Please."

She shook her head, struggling not to look like an idiot and burst into tears. "I can't," she whispered, refusing to look at him. "I really have to get the girls. The movie has been over for ten minutes."

"The girls are fine," he said steadily. "I want you to sit down a minute. I need to talk to you."

She looked at him, anguish on her face. "No, please," she begged softly, trying to pull from his grip. "Look, Beck, I appreciate your concern and interest in me. It's really very flattering and very sweet. But... I really have to go."

He could see that she wasn't going to sit back down again. He didn't let go of her as he pushed his chair in.

"Okay," he said steadily. "I'll go with you to get the girls. You promised I could see Cadee."

Blakesley struggled to compose herself, not knowing what more to say to him. She let him lead her back into the hotel, the quiet corridors that would lead to the main lobby. She couldn't help but notice the vise-like grip on her wrist had eased up and now he gently held her hand.

His palm was big and warm, safe, and she liked the feel of it. But she was also feeling vastly uncertain, her thoughts moving in so many different directions as they traversed the quiet corridor with its elaborate red and gold carpet. She found herself looking at his left hand as it held hers.

"Have you ever been married, Beck?" she asked softly.

"Yes," he replied. "For fourteen years."

"Kids?"

"One. A girl."

"How old is she?"

"Fourteen years old."

"What happened?"

They emerged into a corridor that would take them into the main lobby. "My ex got tired of having a husband deployed for months and years at a time."

She looked up him. "Years?"

He nodded. "I was in Iraq for two separate tours, about two years each, and I've also done two tours in Afghanistan." He looked down at her. "I get deployed all over the world, sometimes with only a twelve hour notice depending on the mission. She didn't like that. It's hard to live with that kind of instability and it was tough on my daughter, too."

They emerged into the lush lobby. It was an enormous place with wood paneling and expensive furnishings, emulating the Victorian-era portion of the original hotel. There were more people around them now, families with children or couples enjoying the posh and intimate setting.

"What do you do for the Navy that they would deploy you like that?" she wanted to know.

He came to a stop and faced her. "Well," he grinned slightly, "since you told me your dark secrets, I guess I can tell you mine. I command a team."

She looked confused. "A team?"

"S.E.A.L. team," he clarified. "We're based out of Coronado. We deploy worldwide at a moment's notice and in the end, she just couldn't handle that. Not that I blame her."

She gazed up into his strong, handsome face. "That's pretty dangerous stuff from what I've heard."

His grin broadened. "Sometimes."

He resumed their walk, still holding on to her hand. Blakesley found herself taking a second look at the man, his muscular body and stunning blond looks. He looked like a god and moved with the stealth of a cat. He had power and grace, an unusual combination. The more she watched him, the more enamored she became, which would spell disaster for her fragile heart when she never saw him again. She was coming to think that maybe it would be better if they just separated now and be done with it.

"Are you deploying again soon?" she asked. "Is that why you guys were training on the beach?"

He shook his head. "That's normal routine," he told her. "As far as I know, I'm here for a while. At least long enough to take you out to dinner again."

She pulled her hand from his and came to a halt, watching him come to a stop and casually turn to her. Her expression was serious.

"Look," she said quietly. "I appreciate how kind you've been to me all evening and even when I told you my story, you were kind enough not to run, at least not right away. You don't have to feed me lines about future dates just so I won't feel bad about chasing you off. In fact, it would probably be best if we just said our good-nights right now and leave it at that. I don't blame you in the least for what you must be thinking, so you don't need to stroke me. You can leave right now with no hard feelings."

He cocked an eyebrow at her, putting his hands on his hips. "How do you know what I'm thinking?"

"I don't, but I can guess."

His brow furrowed. "You've known me for a total of six hours and already you know what I'm thinking?"

She puckered her lips irritably, perhaps apologetically. "I didn't mean it like that, but I'm sure you...."

He waved a big hand at her, interrupting her. "You don't have any idea what I'm thinking. All I'm thinking is that I've met a very beautiful woman who's trying to get rid of me. If you're not interested in seeing me again, then just say so. Stop trying to turn it around like I'm the one with the problem."

She calmed somewhat, looking rather distressed. "Is that what you think? That I'm trying to get rid of you?"

"Well, you *are*."

She sighed, putting a hand on his big arm. "It's not for the reasons you think," she said. "Seriously, I would give anything to get to know you better. I've had the best evening I've ever had in my life tonight and I can see what a wonderful guy you are. But I've got this cloud following me around and I can't let anyone else be subjected to it, not even a new friend. It wouldn't be fair to you."

He just looked at her. "I'm a big boy. I can handle myself."

She met his gaze, longing and hope in her expression. "You really don't know what you're saying."

"So not only do you think you know what's on my mind, but you also don't think I know what I'm saying?"

She started to giggle. "You're a tough nut, you know that?"

The corner of his mouth twitched with a smile. "You have no idea."

"So you're saying that I couldn't get rid of you even if I wanted to?"

"Do you want to?"

She cocked her head coyly. "I let you hold my hand. Obviously, I don't want to get rid of you too badly if I let you do that."

"What happens if you let me kiss you?"

She laughed. "That's like sleeping together. We're automatically engaged."

He chuckled. "Wow," he stroked his chin thoughtfully. "I need to pace myself, then."

She looked at him pointedly. "Still want to hang around?"

"If I can kiss you without having to marry you."

She laughed and resumed walking towards the KidTopia area. Beck followed on her heels, enchanted.

"No promises, Commander," she eyed him flirtatiously. "But you don't make a lot of sense, you know."

"Why?"

"Because my sob story didn't chase you off, but the threat of engagement does?"

His grin was returning. "Maybe," he shrugged casually, shoving his hands in his pockets as he watched his feet move over the red and gold carpet. "I won't marry again. I can't do that to someone I love."

"Never say never. You may meet a girl in the future that changes your mind, you know."

He cast her a long glance, grinning, wondering against his better judgment if he already had.

THREE

BLAKESLEY AWOKE the next morning to brilliant sunlight streaming in through a crack in the hotel's blackout curtains. The beam was hitting her right in the eye and she groaned as she rolled over, away from the violent white light. It was a sweet and quiet Sunday morning, lazy and beautiful on the shores of the Pacific.

In the adjoining room, she could hear the girls stirring. A glance at the clock showed it to be a little after nine in the morning. As she lay there and listened to her children in the next room, her thoughts drifted to the night before and Beck Seavington.

For a moment, she wondered if she might have dreamed it. Of all of the unexpected occurrences in her life, and there had been a load of them, she could have never imagined a group of S.E.A.L.s saving her daughter from sure death and the additional surprise of their commanding officer showing up to ask her out on a date. Happy things like that just didn't happen in her world. At least, she'd forgotten if such things ever did. Thinking on the handsome, blond naval officer, a smile creased her lips. He really was a doll.

Rising from bed, she stuck her head into the bedroom where all three girls were sitting on one bed watching cartoons. Telling Cadee to watch her sisters for a few minutes, Blakesley quickly took a shower, shaved and washed her hair. All the while, she kept reliving the evening, up to and including the part where she and Beck picked their girls up from their movie night.

Charlotte was thrilled to see Beck again, while Cadee was her usual sweet but shy self. Crosby couldn't have cared less because she wanted ice cream. Mom told her no but Beck somehow managed to buy her an ice cream bar in the hotel's gift shop. Crosby was thrilled while Blakesley just shook her head reproachfully. Beck grinned his sly and sexy grin and Mom was putty. Score one for Beck and Crosby.

But it didn't end there. Somehow, he talked her into not heading out to the house that night but, instead, just taking the girls back to their room and putting them to bed. While Cadee stayed close to her mother on the elevator ride up and the long walk down the hallway, Crosby and Charlotte had attached themselves to Beck. Crosby had one of his big hands while Charlotte had the other, and they escorted him down the hall chattering about sharks and seagulls and Barbie dolls. It had made for a comical conversation and more than once, Blakesley had glanced back at Beck to find him grinning at her. She smiled back.

He'd left them at the door to their hotel room without anything more than a word of goodnight. He was very respectful and made no move to enter the room. Blakesley had watched him move back down the corridor towards the elevator banks, wondering if that would be the last she ever saw of him. In spite of his assurances, she wouldn't have been surprised and she tried not to let that bother her. But the truth was that she was deeply disappointed.

Turning off the shower, she dried off and dressed quickly, knowing that it would be little time before the girls were demanding breakfast. After doing her makeup and hair, she got the girls into the shower and cleaned them up, getting them dressed and ready for the day. She had promised them Sea World and, like a pack of elephants, they wouldn't forget even though she hadn't been specific about when they would go. They had already done the San Diego Zoo two days ago so she figured she might as well get Sea World over, too. She had a feeling once they moved into the old family homestead, all of her attention would be on fixing the place up and not on amusement parks. Might as well enjoy Sea World while they could.

So she got the girls ready in their cute shorts and tee shirts, hats and white tennis shoes. Dressed in Capri cut jeans and a tank top that showed off her full, natural C cup breasts, Blakesley packed a bag for the trip to the park with sunscreen, granola bars and other goodies. She even had a folding stroller for Charlotte, who tended to ride more than she walked because she got tired easily. With her long, silky hair pulled back into a casual ponytail, she herded the girls out the door so they could eat breakfast and head to Sea World.

The lobby was fairly busy mid-morning with people checking out and checking in. There was a bakery on the lower level and when they stepped off the elevator, she directed the girls towards the stairs that led down to that level. Lugging the stroller and the big bag that carried all of their junk was a burden, but one she was used to. Still, it was difficult when Charlotte was already having a meltdown because she wasn't wearing the right hat and she kept trying to pull the bag away from her mother. Blakesley calmly soothed her daughter as they made their way through the lobby and towards the stairs.

"Good morning," a voice brought them to a stop before they could hit the stairs. "I was hoping I'd catch everybody before you went on with your day."

Blakesley turned, startled, to see Beck walking up with a steaming cup of coffee in his hand. She couldn't help the extreme joy that sprang to her heart at the sight, thrilled that all of that talk last night hadn't been a load of crap. So far, Beck Seavington was proving himself to be a man of his word, a faith that she didn't have much of these days. This morning, for the moment, he had restored that faith.

"Good morning," she greeted, looking both surprised and pleased. "What in the world are you doing here?"

His green-eyed gazed locked on her even as grumpy Charlotte

ran to him and took his hand. "Having coffee," he lifted his cup obviously.

She cocked an eyebrow, noting he was dressed in a tight gray tee shirt that showed off his beautifully muscular physique, black combat pants and big, black combat boots. It looked to her like he was in some kind of casual military uniform and it looked rather spectacular on him. It was enough to flutter her heart, as he seemed to be so capable of effortlessly doing.

"Do you always come to the hotel just for coffee?" she asked, suggesting with her tone that she already didn't believe him.

He had eyes only for her. "Okay, I lied," he admitted. "I was hoping to take you ladies out to breakfast."

She grinned. "Are you serious?"

He returned her smile. "Absolutely," he nodded. "I've been here since seven thirty this morning, watching everyone who stepped off the elevators and knowing, eventually, you girls would show up."

"You could have just said something last night."

"I didn't think about it until after I left." He looked at the stroller and bag in her arms as if just noticing them. "Going somewhere?"

She nodded. "Sea World," she replied. "But we need to eat first. We'd love to have you join us."

His grin broadened. "It's been years since I've been to Sea World."

Blakesley had only meant that he was welcome to join them for breakfast but she didn't have the heart to correct him. Besides, the thought of spending the day with him was a giddy one. She didn't see any harm in it.

"Uh... well, okay, then," she shrugged her shoulders, smiling. The she pointed to his pants, his standard issue boots. "You look like you're going to work, though."

He shook his head. "That was earlier this morning. I don't need to be back on base until tonight."

She lifted her eyebrows. "You were working this morning? But it's only ten o'clock."

He winked at her as Charlotte tugged on his hand. "The Navy isn't a nine-to-five job, trust me."

She simply smiled, watching Charlotte tug on him until he looked at her. As Beck and Charlotte engaged in a conversation about donuts, Blakesley's gaze lingered on the big blond, inspecting his enormous shoulders and muscular biceps. The tee shirt did nothing to conceal his amazing physique and she found herself a little warm over the sight. Tearing her eyes away, she collected the bag and stroller and headed for the stairs.

"Here, let me get that." Beck took the stroller from her as they headed down the stairs. He had Charlotte in one hand as they moved. "Can I take the bag?"

Blakesley shook her head. "I've got it, thanks," she replied as they reached the lower level, glancing over her shoulder at him. "So... no training today?"

"No," he replied. "This morning was just mundane stuff. Believe it or not, part of my job is paperwork, so I did that this morning."

"Oh," she said as he walked up beside her. She alternately watched him and her daughters as they walked up ahead. "Look, you really don't have to go to Sea World with us. I'm sure there are a million other things you could be doing."

He looked at her. "There you go, trying to discourage me again. If you don't want me to go, just say so. No hard feelings."

She lifted her eyebrows. "Why do you always think I'm trying to discourage you? I just don't want you to feel pressured or obligated, that's all. It's hard to turn down three little girls who are excited that their new friend is going to Sea World with them."

They had reached the little bakery and the girls ran on ahead to see what was in the bakery case. Beck came to a halt at the entry to the shop, causing Blakesley to pause because he was partially blocking her way. He faced her.

"It wasn't the girls who asked me to go, it was you," he said quietly, without force. "Look, we could just sit in the coffee shop all day as far as I'm concerned. I was just looking forward to spending more time with you and getting to know you a little better, that's all. I told you last night that if you weren't really interested in me to just let me know. Now I'm starting to think that maybe you're the one feeling obligated to include me in things because I keep showing up on your doorstep like a little, lost puppy."

She gazed up at his handsome face, cocking her head with thought. "You know," she said slowly, "we've run into this type conversation a couple of times and it's underscoring something pretty obvious."

"What's that?"

"That we're two emotional people who are concerned for each other's feelings. I'm afraid of offending you and you're afraid of imposing on me."

He smiled weakly, nodding his head after a moment. "You know what's funny?" he snorted softly. "I always steer clear of women because I'm just not very good with them. When my marriage was over, I drowned myself in work like there wasn't anything else in the world. I can't even honestly tell you if I've been on a date since Sharon divorced me. I've just kept myself bottled up and focused. But yesterday was the first time in four years that I felt myself come out of that bottle, the moment I laid eyes on you. Now I can't think of anything else but you. If I get emotional, it's because I haven't had to deal with feelings of any kind since Sharon left and took Lizzie with her. Maybe I just don't know how to control myself around you. You make me feel every-thing I'm afraid of."

Blakesley was stunned. Beck Seavington was so different from the men she had been exposed to in her life, something so fresh and honorable, that he was everything she could have ever hoped for. But the majority of her was terrified to open herself up and accept what he was telling her because she knew, without a doubt, that she could feel the same way about him.

All giddiness aside, she just wasn't sure she was ready to and it scared the hell out of her. What had started out as sweet flirting and conversation yesterday had moved too quickly to something else. Overwhelmed, she could feel the tears in her eyes. Impulsively, she put her hands on his broad chest and kissed him on the cheek.

"And I'm everything you need to stay away from," she whispered. "Beck, I think you're sweet and amazing, and your kindness has touched me like I haven't been touched in years. But... but I want you to go back to the base and forget you ever met me."

His face was taut with emotion. "I can't."

"Yes, you can. Please. I want you to."

"Please don't ask me to. Don't do this...."

She touched his face, a gentle touch with a warm, gentle hand; something Beck hadn't felt in years. It was enough to melt him completely. But she quickly removed the hand and turned away from him.

"It's been such an honor to meet you," she murmured, tearing up. "Please go. I'm asking you to."

"I can't."

"I want you to."

"Please... don't."

She just shook her head and turned away from him, going to her girls. She asked them what they wanted to eat, wiping at the few errant tears that had escaped onto her cheeks. She couldn't even bear to look back to see if Beck was still standing there. The thought of it was ripping her insides out. But she focused on her girls, those little beacons of salvation that had kept her sane throughout her darkest days and bought them rolls and donuts for breakfast.

By the time she was brave enough to turn around, Beck was gone and the collapsible stroller was propped up against the wall where he had been standing. Fighting back the tears, she went to collect the stroller when a piece of paper fell out and drifted to the floor. Picking it up, she saw that it was his business card.

When Cadee and Crosby wanted to know why she was crying, she couldn't tell them.

———

The bar was called Nicky Rottens, which was appropriate considering that's how Beck felt – rotten. He sat in the midst of the bustling sports bar on an early Sunday evening, nursing his fourth beer between what had so far been nine intermittent shots of tequila, while life and happiness went on around him. He didn't even care.

They were blasting a Padres' game over his head but he wasn't watching it. He was just sitting, staring out the window onto the busy street, feeling truly disappointed for the first time in many years. Normally, he never let a situation involving a woman get this far, avoiding disappointment by cutting things off before they really got started. It made for a fairly celibate life, but that was safer than the alternative. Half of him was pissed off that he had let himself feel something for Blakesley, while the other half of him was simply grossly depressed that she had sent him away.

"Hey," a familiar voice wafted in behind him and Beck turned to see Butch pulling up a bar stool next to him. Butch grinned when their eyes met. "I've been calling you for hours. Why aren't you picking up your phone?"

Beck sighed heavily and tuned back to his beer. "If I wanted company, I would have picked up the phone."

"I know," Butch flagged down the bartender at the end of the bar. "Here I am anyway."

The bartender came over and Butch ordered a beer. Beck downed the rest of his and ordered another.

"How'd you find me?" Beck asked.

"The same way you always seem to find me," Butch replied. "Your phone has location navigation, remember? You insisted the entire team get it when we got new phones last year."

Beck turned to look at the man, irritated. "Why are you here? Why aren't you home with Gina?"

"Because," Butch met his gaze. "Anytime Beck Seavington won't pick up a call, something's wrong. What's wrong that you're getting yourself drunk on a Sunday night?"

Beck just sat there looking at him. Then he rolled his eyes and leaned heavily on the bar. "I blew it," he muttered. "Oh, God, I totally blew it."

"Blew what?"

Beck ran a hand over his face, wearily. "Blakesley," he said. "I blew it."

The beers arrived and Butch collected his glass. "Blew what?" he repeated, his brow furrowed. "What happened?"

Beck took a big drink of his beer. "I went back last night to the hotel to ask her out to dinner," he said. "We had a great time. She's sweet, beautiful, smart, successful... she's everything. She's perfect and she's way too good for me. But she's also carrying around some serious emotional baggage thanks to an ex-husband who murdered his mistress because the woman was going to tell Blakesley about the affair. She said it was called the Hollyhock Murder. Did you ever hear of it? I haven't. Anyway, the ex is in jail and Blakesley is trying to start a new life for her daughters. I gotta tell you - her story was really crazy. You'd think she'd be a basket case because of it, but she's got a good head on her shoulders and she's really trying to move forward. I admire that."

Butch was waiting for the punch line, where Beck blew it, but nothing was forthcoming. "And?" he pressed.

Beck's jaw ticked glumly. "And I went back over to the hotel this morning to take her and her little girls out to breakfast," he said. "I was so glad to see her, you know? The moment I laid eyes on her, she just lit up my life. She invited me to go with her and her girls to Sea World and I was so excited at the prospect of spending the day with her that I said things I shouldn't have."

Butch took a drink of his beer. "Like what?"

Beck put his hands over his face. "I told her that I felt alive for the first time in years because of her and that she makes me feel things I've been afraid to feel," he pulled his hands away from his face, grossly depressed. "Oh, man, I just let it all come out. I said so much that I shouldn't have. I came across like an emotional cripple and scared her off."

Butch was looking at him with some sympathy. He and Beck were old and good friends, and he knew how guarded the man usually was about his feelings. He was always in control, one of the characteristics that made him such an excellent military commander. They didn't come any cooler or steadier than Beck Seavington. It was surprising to hear that he had gone on an emotional binge that had evidently backfired on him.

"How do you know you scared her off?" Butch asked. "What did she say?"

Beck sighed heavily and took another drink of beer. "She asked me to leave," he said. "She was really sweet about it, but she told me to go. So I did. And I've been here ever since."

Butch drew in a long, thoughtful breath, wondering how he could advise his friend out of this one. He felt kind of guilty, like he had somehow contributed to this by egging Beck on to ask the woman out in the first place.

"Well," he said slowly, trying to think of something of comfort to say. "It's not like you were married to her or with her for years. You just met her. So it ended; so what? It never really got started. You had a nice dinner with a beautiful woman that made you feel good. It was a good night. It just wasn't mean to last."

Beck was fairly well drunk, but not so drunk that Butch's words didn't have impact. He looked at his friend. "But that's not what I want," he insisted. "I want it to last. She's the one I've been waiting for my entire life, Butch. You just don't get it."

Butch wasn't going to get into it with him. Beck was drunk, a rare occurrence, but he could become very emotional and combative when drunk. Butch was a fairly big man but Beck had a right cross that could take down a charging bull. Butch didn't want to lose teeth.

"Look," Butch put his hand on Beck's shoulder. "Let's get out of here, okay? Let me take you home."

Beck just shook his head. "I don't want to go home," he told him. "I want to sit right here and drink myself to death."

Butch sighed. "Beck, you're going to hate me for saying this, but you need to stop drinking. If we get a call, Davis is going to have your head if you're plastered. You need to sober up, son."

"What I *need* is Blakesley."

"I'm not sure that's going to happen. You need to forget about her."

Beck didn't want to hear that, draining the rest of his beer before Butch could stop him. Butch helped him stagger out to the parking lot, where Butch put him into the passenger side of his truck.

Butch drove him back to his own house so he could keep an eye on him, but not before Beck threw up the contents of his stomach in the gutter once the truck came to a halt in his driveway. Butch's wife helped her husband drag Beck inside and put him on the couch before returning outside to hose down the puke. She was pretty cool about it, mostly because she was as concerned for Beck as her husband was.

Beck didn't wake up until his cell phone rang almost eleven hours later.

————

Monday morning dawned bright and clear. Blakesley knew this because she had been awake in the pre-dawn hours, drinking coffee and sitting on her patio watching the sunrise. Her room faced the ocean and she could see a section of the naval base to the north. Her chair was positioned so she had a clear view of it.

Sea World had been fun for the girls, a depressing disaster for her. All she could think of was Beck and how she had essentially chased him away. It had been her fear talking and she'd spent a sleepless night wondering if she had done the right thing. As the sun climbed over the Pacific, she was coming to think that she'd made a big mistake.

Beck hadn't been pushy. He had been honest. She'd held his business card in her hand all night, glancing at the numbers, the email address, the name, wondering if she should just throw caution to the wind and call him. By the time the sun rose, she'd made a decision. For better or worse, she would stick with it.

Turning on her cell phone, she stared at the numbers on his business card for about ten minutes before summoning enough courage to call. Closing the patio doors so she wouldn't wake the girls, she waited nervously as the phone rang six times, waiting for him to answer but disappointed when it went to voice mail. At the sound of the beep, she tried not to come across like an idiot.

"Hi, Beck," she said softly. "This is Blakesley. I just wanted to call and tell you... well, I wanted to tell you how sorry I am about yesterday. You were honest with me and I guess it just freaked me out. I'm so sorry I told you to go away. I was just overwhelmed with what you had said and... and I didn't have the guts to tell you that I've been thinking the same thing. So I suppose I can tell you now and hope you don't hate me or think I'm some crazy witch. I'm really sorry if I hurt your feelings and I hope you can forgive me. If... if you want to call me back, my number is 310-322-9222. If you don't want to call me back, I totally understand. Take care of yourself."

She hung up the phone, fighting off tears, and went back inside. As the girls slept into the morning, Blakesley showered and dressed, focusing on what she needed to accomplish that day. She had already arranged for a babysitter through the hotel because she planned to go to the house that morning to inspect it before her one o'clock appointment with the real estate agent to start looking at gallery spaces. It was a busy day and not one she wanted to drag the girls along.

At around nine in the morning, the babysitter arrived. She was one of the young women who worked at KidTopia, so the girls were already acquainted with her. Blakesley ordered room service and had cereal and fruit waiting for her children when they finally woke up. Blakesley wanted to make sure she was there with the babysitter when the girls woke up so they wouldn't be freaked out, but they were fine with Ashley the babysitter, who had brought coloring books and a couple of games with her to keep them entertained. Charlotte was already sitting in Ashley's lap within the first few minutes, so Blakesley collected her purse and keys and told Ashley to call her with any little problem or question. Ashley, coloring a clown along with Charlotte, waved her off.

Dressed in tight jeans, a red, wrap-around blouse with a deep "v" neck, gold platform sandals and her usual jewelry, she looked sleek, sexy and stylish as she took the elevator down to the lobby. Blakesley was admittedly a clothes hound and she liked fashionable clothing, so she knew how to project a sexy yet professional image. It was something she had worked hard at as a businesswoman and, fortunately, she had made enough money in the past to support the habit.

Her long hair was loosely curled, tumbling down her back as she stepped off the elevator and out into the lobby area, slipping on her designer sunglasses before she even left the hotel. When she reached the door, the doorman held the big panel open for her and she stepped out into the Victorian-style *porte cochere* where the valet stand was. The entire area was lush with plants, cobblestones and carved benches, and a soft sea breeze blew in from the west.

Digging in her purse for her valet receipt, she didn't see Beck until he stood up from one of the benches and blocked her path. Startled, she almost tripped as she came to a halt and he smiled weakly at her.

"Sorry," he said softly. "I seem to have a habit of surprising you every time I show up."

Blakesley yanked off the sunglasses, her sea-colored eyes wide on him. "Beck," she gasped. "I... I called you this morning. I left a message..."

"I know." He cut her off gently. "I got it. That's why I came."

Blakesley threw caution to the wind. Now was not the time to show reluctance or uncertainty. She reached out and touched his arm.

"I'm sorry," she whispered fervently. "I'm so sorry I told you to go away. I didn't mean it. I couldn't sleep all night because I knew it had been a mistake to tell you that."

He was shaking his head even as she spit out the words. He put his hands on her shoulders, gently yet with unmistakable power, and pulled her towards him.

"I shouldn't have said what I did," he countered, interrupting her. "I don't know why I did, but you had every right to be freaked out. You must have thought I was some kind of incredibly needy person, telling you all of that when I had only just met you. If anyone is sorry, it's me. I'm so sorry I said those things to you. I shouldn't have."

Her hands were on his chest, her warm palms against his tee shirt. She realized his arms were going around her but she didn't particularly care.

"You were just being honest," she insisted, her guard completely down. "I can't fault you for being honest. But you have to understand... after what happened to me over the past couple of years, I'm still kind of messed up a little. Now *I'm* being honest. I see in you someone that I would love to get to know and it really scares the hell out of me on so many levels. That's why I told you to go away. I was just scared. But I'm so sorry I did."

He was caressing her arms gently, listening to her halting speech. After a moment, he smiled at her. "I think you and I are both pretty afraid of getting involved with someone, but I have to tell you, when I look at you, I'm just not afraid anymore. I'm willing to be open about it and see where it takes us."

She looked at him in disbelief. "Really?"

"Really."

"Even after everything I've told you?"

"Even after that. If you've even got half the strength and character I think you have, then you won't be damaged forever. Neither will I. Maybe... maybe we'll fix each other in some ways, better than we were before. I'd sure like to explore the possibility."

She thought on that, thinking it was an offer she couldn't refuse. She bit her lip thoughtfully. "So where do we start?" she wanted to know.

He grinned at her. "Are you saying that you're willing?"

She nodded, then shrugged, giggling. "I'm willing if you are," she said. "Besides, I don't like the alternative. I don't like the thought of never seeing you again."

His smile faded, the green eyes riveted to her. "Me, either," he admitted. "So... can I kiss you now?"

"I thought you were going to pace yourself."

"I lied."

She snickered. "Sure you can kiss me, but you know what the consequences are."

"A fork to the eye?"

She laughed. "You need to get your consequences straight before we can continue. I told you a kiss was like sleeping together. We'll have to have a shotgun wedding."

He moved lower, pulling her against him gently. Blakesley's breathing quickened, her heart doing that wild fluttery thing, as his lips came close to hers.

"No, it's not like sleeping together," he whispered. "That will be much, much different."

She barely had time to draw in a breath as his mouth closed over hers, a sweet and gentle kiss that quickly turned heated. He was a wonderful kisser, not sloppy, but rather soft and sensual, and Blakesley quickly succumbed to him. Her hands moved to his face, holding his dimpled cheeks as he kissed her deeply. But just as things started to heat up, he pulled away.

"Oh, God," he groaned. "You're right. It's like sleeping together. That's the sexiest kiss I've ever had. Where's the shotgun? I'll go peacefully."

She grinned at him, reaching up to wipe her red lipstick off his lips. "You're pretty good at that."

"Thanks. So are you."

She laughed, realizing they were in a fairly heated clutch in a public place and reluctantly pulling away purely for decency's sake. She wiped at her lips to catch any smeared lipstick as she faced him.

"I was just heading out to check out the house and then meet with the real estate agent," she said. "I hate to cut this short, but I'm sure you have other things to do today."

He shrugged. "I don't have anywhere to go until later this afternoon."

She lifted her eyebrows. "Do you want to come with me? We could get to know each other a little better, you know, just hanging out and all. I'd like the company."

A sexy smile took over is whole face. "I was waiting for you to ask me that." He held out his elbow to her. "As long as you're okay hanging out with a guy in fatigues. I'm not really supposed to be wearing these out in public, but I left the base rather quickly after I got your message. Actually, I sort of flew over here."

She'd only been focused on his face and hadn't really noticed he was in his NWU Type II working fatigues until that moment. It made him look big and tough. His rank insignia was pinned to his collar along with what she would later learn to be the S.E.A.L. insignia with the eagle holding a trident, and the name "SEAV-INGTON" was emblazoned over his right breast. She shrugged.

"You look like G.I. Joe," she teased.

He snorted. "He's Army."

"Okay, so you look like Navy Joe."

"There *is* no Navy Joe."

She just grinned and took his elbow as they made their way towards the valet stand. "I think I have a lot to learn about the military."

He patted her hand. "Don't worry about it," he said. "I'm a good teacher."

She had no doubt that he would be.

FOUR

AFTER COLLECTING Blakesley's BMW from the valet, they took off in the direction of the Coronado Bridge. A massive expanse of green steel, it linked Coronado Island to the mainland, spitting out traffic into the southern end of the city of San Diego. Blakesley wasn't entirely sure where she was going but she had navigation in the car, so the soft female voice told her where to turn and where to go. Beck sat in the passenger seat, grinning at her when she accidentally ran a red light.

"You should have let me drive," he told her.

She made a face at him, looking at the street signs. "This isn't a boat," she told him. "Leave the driving to us landlubbers."

He laughed at her. "Next time, I drive."

"Are you always so bossy?"

He lifted his eyebrows. "Yes, pretty much. I'm a take-charge kind of guy. Sorry. I'll try not to do that anymore with you. I don't think you'd appreciate it."

She just grinned, glancing over at him and watching him wink at her. "So, bossy guy, tell me what prompted you to join the Navy," she asked.

He shrugged, looking out of the window to watch the scenery

pass by. "My dad was Navy," he said. "I was always surrounded by it so there really wasn't much doubt that I would."

"Do you like it?"

"Love it."

"Even when you're deployed for years?"

He cocked his head thoughtfully. "That's just part of the gig," he told her. "I've been to parts of the world and seen things that, with a normal job, I would have never done or seen. Even when I was in college, I studied in England and it gave me a group of friends that I still consider brothers to this day. They were the first real 'team' I ever had. But the point is that the Navy has provided me with a lot of opportunities."

"Have you always been on a S.E.A.L. team?"

"No," he shook his head. "When I first got out of the academy, I was stationed on an aircraft carrier. After a couple years of that, I volunteered for sub duty and spent a few years on a fast attack sub. But I got bored of that. I wanted to get out and do something."

"Like the S.E.A.L.s?"

"Yes," he turned to look at her. "I've been on the teams for almost fifteen years. It's been my calling."

"At least you're doing something that you love," she said, making a left hand turn when the navigation told her to. "I don't know much about them other than a movie I saw once, but I know enough that you can't really talk about what you do."

He grinned coyly, looking out of the window again as they drove through downtown San Diego. "I can tell you but then I'd have to kill you."

She giggled. "That's an old, overused line."

"In my case, it happens to be true."

She gave him a scaredy-cat face and pretended to button her lips. "Then I won't ask you anything."

He snorted, lifting a big hand to affectionately touch her shoulder. "You can ask all you want," he told her. "But whether I answer you is another matter."

They were heading out of the city and into more residential areas now. "Can you tell me what the coolest thing you ever did?"

He thought on that a moment, looking from the window and watching the houses go by. "Well," he said contemplatively. "Since you're an artist, you might appreciate this. When I was on a tour in Iraq, the museums in Baghdad had moved all of their artwork and antiques to various areas all over the country to protect them from the bombings going on. I can tell you that I saw stashes of relics and art that would make your head spin. Things that were thousands and thousands of years old. It was really amazing."

She glanced at him, smiling. "Does stuff like that interest you? Ancient relics and art?"

He nodded. "It does, because it's so precisely done. Maybe it's the engineer in me, but it has always fascinated me how ancient man had the skill set to do things thousands of years ago that, even now, takes modern equipment and computers to accomplish."

"Aliens helped them."

He chuckled. "That would not surprise me." He noticed they were heading into the gently rolling hills near the Presidio, the oldest section of San Diego east of the Old Town center. "Hey, do you really know where you're going?"

"Quiet up over there or you can walk."

He smirked. "Would you really make me walk?"

She cast him sidelong glance. "Yes."

"I'm feeling insecure and threatened right now."

She started laughing, giggling because he was. It was a sweet, funny moment between them, building a relationship that seemed to be growing with a great ease. As the car wound its way deeper into the residential area, the conversation died but it wasn't uncomfortable. Beck put his hand on the back of her chair, his fingers brushing her shoulder now and again. Blakesley could feel his touch, electrifying her. She fought to keep her focus on the road and not on his fingers.

They were in a very old section of the residential area and also a very exclusive one. Beck began to look at the houses with more and more curiosity, big Spanish-style structures with big lots. They were old and expensive. When he turned to ask her if she was sure she was in the right neighborhood, she suddenly took a right into a big driveway shrouded by dozens of mature Eucalyptus trees.

"This is it," she said, pulling slowly into the driveway. "I have to tell you, I'm a little scared about what I'm going to find. This house is so old that it's really going to break my heart if it's terribly damaged."

Beck wasn't sure what to say to that so he just put a hand on her shoulder to comfort her as she pulled up the driveway, which wasn't so much a driveway as it was a small road. The grounds were pretty extensive and Eucalyptus trees were mingled with gigantic, mature oaks and carob trees, very typically Californian.

It was a fairly lush property but overgrown and unkempt. The entire lot sat on a section of a big hill with a deep canyon running alongside it, all overgrown and dense. By the time the house finally came into view, Beck was in for a surprise.

The house seemed to be in two wings, mirror images of each other. The first thing he noticed is how thick and fortress-like the walls were, great expanses of plaster that were whitewashed on an imperfect surface. There was a balcony on the second floor of both wings, the heavy, dark wood in stark contrast to the brilliant, white walls. There were wrought iron railings on the iron exterior staircases that led from the balconies to the ground floor, all very intricate and element-worn.

As they pulled to a stop in front of the house, he could see that the attic vents on the pitched roofline were shaped like a cross. He climbed out of the car, rather fascinated with what he was witnessing. The house looked like an old California mission that had been converted into living quarters. Without even knowing anything about the house, he could see that it was very old and very early California authentic.

"So this is the house?" he asked with some amazement, turning to look at her as she rounded the front of the car. "How old is this place?"

Blakesley came to stand next to him, peering up at the house just as he was. She seemed to have a look of great satisfaction and affection on her face.

"Really, really old," she told him. "There's quite a story attached to it."

He wriggled is eyebrows. "No doubt," he said. "What's the story?"

Initial inspection finished and pleased to note that at least the exterior looked intact, Blakesley pulled out a key and began walking towards the wing nearest the driveway. There was an enormous Spanish-style door with great wrought iron detailing staring them down.

"Well," Blakesley said as she fumbled with the key. "My great-great-great grandfather came to San Diego back when California was still part of Mexico. He fought in the Mexican-American War at the battle of San Pasqual, which isn't far from here. He was rewarded for valor in the battle, married a Mexican woman, and settled down in San Diego as one of the first town marshals after California joined the United States."

Beck watched her fiddle with the very old lock on the door. "Wow," he exclaimed softly. "That's very cool. So you didn't move to San Diego as much as you were just coming back home again?"

She smiled, having difficulty turning the old tumblers. "Something like that," she agreed. "Anyway, he built this house in 1847. It's one of the oldest homes in San Diego and somewhere around here, there used to be a sign declaring the Benjamin and Dulcinea Earp Home a State of California Historical Landmark."

He gently pushed her aside to see if he would have better luck with the old lock. "Earp?" he repeated. "Like Wyatt Earp?"

She nodded as he managed to move the tumblers. "Benjamin Outsen Earp was a younger brother of Nicholas Earp, Wyatt's father," she told him. "My mother's father was an Earp, but he had two girls, so my mother inherited the house when he died. Her name was Mollie Earp Thorne. This is the first time in one hundred and sixty years that an Earp hasn't owned the house."

He managed to get the door open but he didn't go in. He handed her back the key and stared at her. "You're related to Wyatt Earp?"

"He's my cousin several generations back."

He lifted his eyebrows with amazement. "That's pretty darn cool. I've never met anyone famous."

She grinned. "You still haven't," she said as she pushed the door open. "Shall we go in?"

He stepped back, gesturing in gentlemanly fashion for her to enter first. The first thing that greeted them was a spectacular wrought iron staircase inlaid with exquisite Spanish tile, twisting up to the gallery on the second floor. But even though the staircase was intact, they immediately could see that someone had marked up the walls with black and green spray paint and two of the big stained glass windows that overlooked the staircase were broken. Blakesley gasped in horror at the sight.

"Oh, no," she breathed, eyes on the glass windows. "Those windows are well over one hundred years old. I can't believe they damaged them."

Beck followed her into the house, glancing around at a structure rarely seen. The walls were enormously thick and old adobe tile lined the entry floor. There seemed to be several levels as well – two steps led into a room to their right while directly in front of them, a small flight of stairs led down into a room beyond. He couldn't see much of it, but there were certainly stairs everywhere, all inlaid with gorgeous Mexican tile. The distinctive ambiance of Old California was everywhere.

Blakesley went into the room on their right and he followed. This room was enormous, at least forty feet in length, with a big vaulted ceiling and great oak beams stretching across the length of it. Two enormous wrought iron chandeliers hung from the ceiling with only one light bulb between them, and an enormous second floor gallery ran the length of the room on the east side of the chamber. He could see three doors up off of the gallery, leading into darkened second floor rooms. The floor of the room was very uneven, and very old, tile, and it seemed as if the entire place was old and dusty and run down. Even so, the grandeur was not lost. Beck stood in the doorway, looking at the room with surprise.

"Holy Smokes." He ran a hand through his cropped blond hair. "This is a hell of a room."

Standing in the middle of the room, Blakesley turned to him and smiled. "Back when the house was first built, this was the public section of the house. Did you notice there are two wings?" When he nodded, she continued. "My great-great-great grand-daddy used this as kind of a marshal's office and courtroom and public gathering place all rolled into one. Although the Whaley House in old town San Diego was used as the main courthouse, this was kind of an annex for the marshal. Come here and take a look at this."

She waved him to follow and he came up on her heels as she went into a smaller room just off the main room, one that sat under-neath the galleried second floor. It was very dark inside, the old tile floor uneven and worn. Stuck against one wall of the small room were two very small cells with ancient iron bars.

Grinning, Beck took a look at the old cells, the doors having long since been removed. The iron was extremely old, with big, fat rivets holding pieces in place. When Blakesley opened up the blinds over the windows, letting bright, white light into the room, he squinted at the brightness but never lost sight of inspecting the cells.

"This is one of the most amazing things I've ever seen," he told her. "Who knew something like this still existed around here?"

She smiled, watching him run his big hands over the iron bars. "The whole house is like this," she told him. "It was built for public use and since it's been in the family since it was built, nothing has really been changed. The other wing was the family living quarters and it's laid out pretty much like this wing. I was thinking about restoring all of this and opening this wing to the public for tours. There's a lot of history here that people would pay to see and the income would help pay for the upkeep."

He nodded at her plans, her logic, his green-eyed gaze moving over the low-ceilinged, rather run-down, room.

"I think that's a great idea," he said sincerely. "I'd pay to come see it. I know a lot of people who would."

She grinned. "I hope so."

He took his eyes off the old iron, fixing on her, seeing such a bright and lovely woman. He was becoming more enamored with her by the second. He reached out, taking her soft hand in his big, calloused fingers. The touch was pure magic.

"Show me more," he asked softly.

She did. Blakesley took him through the entire wing, the upstairs rooms that once had been used for traveling judges and lawmen, the one and only bathroom in the wing that had the oldest fixtures Beck had ever seen, and even a small room in the southeast corner of the house with exterior access that used to house horses. Then she took him to the second wing, which was attached to the other wing by a tiled and overgrown courtyard complete with fountain.

This had been the wing where her cousin and his family had lived for several years and this, they quickly discovered, was where the true vandalism had happened. Every room had damaged walls, windows or fixtures, which sent Blakesley into a mournful depression. Most of the fixtures were original and priceless, and the great adobe walls were going to be difficult to repair. They had even torn a couple of the interior doors off their old hinges, leaving twisted messes in their wake.

Beck inspected the wing along with her, remaining silent as she lamented the damage. He felt sorry for her, of course, but he also felt a good deal of disgust for the person that created the damage. They had even stuffed paper, wood and other debris into the chimney of the enormous fireplace in the big living room. As Beck stuck his head into the fireplace to get a better look at the blockage, Blakesley went into the kitchen to see if she could find something with which to dislodge the mess. Maybe there was a broom or something they could use.

Finding a small utility room off the kitchen that had an exterior door leading to the yard, she was rummaging around in a small closet when the back door suddenly jerked open and a body entered.

Startled, Blakesley screamed when she came face to face with a dirty, unfamiliar man. He seemed equally startled. She screamed again when he seemed to grab her purely as a reflex action, but her fear was short-lived when Beck came flying through the kitchen, dropping the man with a crushing blow to the jaw. He fell like a stone as Beck grabbed Blakesley and pulled her out of the utility room and back into the kitchen.

"Are you all right?" he asked, his arms still around her. "Did he hurt you?"

She was trembling, pressed against him tightly. "No," she gasped, shaking her head. "He just scared me. The back door flew open and there he was, and it just scared me."

Beck still held her close, his gaze on the body in the next room. The man was old and bearded, dressed in a green jumpsuit or something like it, all ratty and dirty, that made him look like some kind of maintenance worker. They could smell him from where he stood; he smelled like old, moldy leaves. Giving Blakesley a comforting squeeze, he gently cupped her face, kissed her cheek, and went back out to the utility room.

Beck stood over the man, now beginning to stir, and jabbed him with a steel-toed boot.

"Hey," he said, his voice low and controlled. "Get up."

The man groaned and began to roll around. Blakesley crept back into the utility room, huddling behind Beck's big presence as Beck shoved the man again with his boot.

"Get up," Beck commanded again.

The man rolled onto his belly, lifted his head and shook it. "Hey!" he groaned, peering up at Beck and Blakesley. "Why'd you do that?"

"Who the hell are you?" Blakesley demanded, still wedged in behind Beck. "What are you doing in my house?"

The man pushed himself up onto his hands and knees, looking up at Blakesley. "Who are you?"

"I own this house. Who are you?"

The man sat back on his heels, still shaking off the bells from Beck's blow. "Name's Mike," he said. "I work for Jimmy."

"Jimmy?" Beck repeated.

Blakesley stepped out from around Beck, now looking more curious than scared. "Jimmy?" she said. "Jimmy Armstrong?"

"Yep," Mike nodded his head, looking up at the pair and rubbing his jaw where Beck clobbered him. "Where is he?"

Beck looked at Blakesley, confused. "Who's Jimmy?"

Blakesley put her hand on his arm although she was still looking at the man on the floor. "My cousin," she said softy, her voice growing louder as she addressed Mike. "He doesn't live here anymore. He left yesterday. What did you do for him?"

Mike shrugged. "Tried to keep the place from overrunning itself," he said. "Cuttin' trees, vines, fixing the plumbing, that kind of thing. This place is a lot of work. He moved out yesterday, you say?"

"Yes," Blakesley answered. "I live here now."

Mike stood up, weaving unsteadily. His gaze was on Beck, the enormous, blond man with the pan-sized fists. He pointed a finger at him. "Did you bring your own army with you?"

Blakesley looked at Beck. "Kind of," she said, biting off her smile when Beck winked at her. "Look, Mike, I don't mean to be rude, but I don't need anyone working for me."

Mike looked at her, looking rather surprised. "You don't?"

"No."

"Then who's going to keep the place up?"

Beck cocked an eyebrow at him. "Not you, that's for sure," he said pointedly. "This place looks like hell. And who trashed it? Can you seriously say you didn't know Jimmy moved out? Where in the hell were you when he was knocking holes in the walls and breaking windows?"

Mike blinked at the big man as if startled by the words, rubbing his jaw again. "I... I was down in the canyon," he said, looking uncomfortable and averting his gaze. "I live down there. I didn't hear nothing."

"How's that possible?"

Mike shrugged, inching away from Beck and moving towards the door. "I sleep down there," he told him. "There's an old shaft that's been around since the old days. I live in it."

Blakesley's curiosity had her. No longer fearful or confused, his words had her interest. "A shaft?" she repeated. "What kind of a shaft?"

Mike looked at her. "It's dug into the side of the canyon," he told her. "It used to be a place they'd hide from the Indians and Mexicans back in the old days. You know there was a lot of trouble around here back when this house was built. My dad's granddad told me so. He was just a young kid, but he remembered the trouble."

"Show me," Blakesley commanded.

Unfortunately, Blakesley wasn't dressed to make it down the narrow trail leading down into the canyon. In her five inch heels, she could barely make it through the rocky backyard. By the time they reached the path that led into the canyon, she was thinking that she would have to do this another time when she had better shoes on.

Beck agreed because she had been holding on to him since they'd walked out of the house. Every little rock or dip had her teetering, so by the time they reached the canyon edge, she was forced to admit she could make it no further. Mike kept going down the canyon, ignoring Blakesley's and Beck's calls to return, finally disappearing in the bramble. The two of them stood at the edge of the overgrown canyon, peering down into the heavy foliage.

"Well?" Beck turned to her, hands on his hips. "Do you want me to go down and get him out of there?"

Blakesley shrugged. "If it doesn't involve covert operations, C-4 explosives and big knives, then I'd don't suppose it's worth it to you, huh?"

He laughed. "I can get him out of there in less than two minutes using my wits and bare hands. Want to see?"

She laughed in return, shaking her head. "He's just some old man," she waved him off. "You'd scare him to death and probably give him a heart attack."

Smiling, Beck scratched his head, turning to look at the gully again. "I'm not sure I'm comfortable with a homeless guy living down there while you and your girls are living in this big, old house all by yourselves." He looked at her, his smile fading. "Let me go down there and get him out."

She lifted her eyebrows at him. "And do what with him?" she wanted to know. Then she waved him off. "We'll worry about him later. Right now, I want to finish looking at the family wing and then I've got an appointment with the real estate agent. Still want to tag along? I can take you back to the base if you're getting bored."

He just looked at her, refraining from commenting that she was trying to get rid of him again. He was coming to see that the repeated comment was making him look insecure and he didn't like it. So he took a few steps towards her, bent over, and scooped her up into his muscular arms.

"Come along, Princess." He began to head back towards the house. "I don't want you to twist an ankle on those sky-high shoes."

Blakesley wrapped her arms around his neck, smiling at him, her face very close to his. "I kind of like this," she murmured. "I could get used to getting carried around."

He looked at her, grinning. "If you keep wearing shoes like that, I'm going to have to."

She giggled. "My closet is full of shoes like this."

"It's a miracle you haven't broken your ankle before now."

"Maybe. But they look really good, don't they?"

They went through the back porch and into the kitchen, where he set her carefully on her feet. "They look amazing," he agreed.

"But you're a gorgeous woman, with or without the shoes. You could wear a potato sack and you'd still be the most beautiful woman I've ever seen."

She smiled bashfully. "Thank you, that's really sweet," she replied, her eyes glimmering at him. "But I want you to do something for me."

"Anything. What?"

"Say my name."

He cocked his head curiously. "Come again?"

"I said I want you to say my name."

"Why?"

"Because I've never heard you say it."

He scowled at her, but there was a smile on his face. "Sure I have."

She shook her head. "No, you haven't, not since we met yesterday. I want to hear you say it."

He just looked at her. Then, he put his arms around her, pulling her feminine softness firmly against him. He gazed down into her lovely face, studying the fine lines, acquainting himself with the curve of her pert, little nose. The more time he spent with her, the more he felt himself falling for her, and falling hard. He couldn't even throw out a rope to stop himself. He didn't want to.

"Blakesley," he whispered.

She gazed up at him, watching his lips as he spoke her name. "You don't like my name," she accused him.

He lifted his eyebrows. "Why do you say that?"

"I can just tell. I know it's a weird name, but it's a family name on my dad's side. It was his mother's name."

"Do you like it?"

"It's grown on me," she responded, her arms winding up around his neck. "In school, I really hated it so the kids just called me Blake."

He absolutely melted as her arms went around his neck. An embrace from her was like nothing he had ever experienced before and he pushed his face into the side of her head, nuzzling her, inhaling deeply the sweet smell of her.

"I think your name is sweet," he whispered, kissing her ear, her cheek, "but I'll call you whatever you want me to."

His mouth found hers, engaging in a heated kiss as tongues plunged deep, tasting, teasing. Beck was so wrapped up in it that he ended up backing her into a wall, trapping her, his big arms around her, his hands drifting over her arms and back. Blakesley had her arms around his neck, his head, like she was trapping his head against her, and when she sucked on his tongue, Beck nearly lost his mind. With a growl, he picked her up and set her on the kitchen counter.

Blakesley wrapped her legs around his waist, holding him tightly as they furiously kissed one another. Beck's hands were beginning to roam, gaining confidence, as he went from stroking her back and arms to gently cupping her bottom. When she didn't stop him, he grew bolder and squeezed, pulling her body up against him, her legs parted and his body wedged in between them even though they were fully clothed. He sincerely wished, at that moment, that they were not. He'd never been more attracted to a woman in his life.

His mouth went to her neck, gently but passionately suckling her skin, and a hand began to gently pull back the neckline of her red blouse. He pulled it off her right shoulder, baring her skin, and his lips suckled and kissed the sweet-smelling flesh. It was heavenly. He could hear her grunting with pleasure, her hands on his head, her face in his hair. He made no move to touch her breasts or grab at them, but he continued to slowly and steadily pull her blouse off her shoulder, exposing the swell of her right breast. Still, she didn't stop him. Beck got bolder.

He hadn't been with a woman in over four years. Now, he had the woman of his dreams in his hands and he was overwhelmed with desire. If she wasn't going to stop him, he wasn't going to stop, and the blouse was pulled further and further down, exposing her bra. His mouth was on her cleavage now, that delightful cleavage he had noticed the day he had met her, encased within a sexy, pink bikini. Half of her blouse was pulled down to her waist, her black bra exposed, and very gently, he pulled the bra down her right breast, kissing the flesh as it became exposed bit by bit, until he finally uncovered her breast completely.

Blakesley cried out softly as his hot mouth clamped over a tender nipple. She began to pull at his uniform, unbuttoning it, and Beck went right along with her. He wanted her as badly as she wanted him, not stopping to think about the consequences or implications. All he knew was that he wanted her so much that he couldn't stop himself from pulling her shirt down around her waist, unhooking the bra and pulling it off her body. It landed in the old sink.

His uniform was coming off in pieces, the utility jacket followed by the tee shirt underneath. Naked from the waist up, he threw the jacket on the old adobe floor, lifted Blakesley up by the waist, and deposited her onto her back on the laid-out jacket. Mouth on her luscious breasts, he unfastened her jeans without any resistance whatsoever. In fact, she was working on his pants and he pulled her jeans off just about the time she unfastened his belt. Panting, he pulled off her teetering shoes and yanked her jeans off in one clean move.

He was back on her in a flash, her sweet, curvy body drawing his lust like he'd never experienced in his life. His mouth was on her waist, suckling the flesh, moving the blouse around so he could get to it, while his hands unfastened his pants and lowered them to his knees. Blakesley was pulling off her underwear, pulling him down to her so hard that he heard her grunt when he fell on top of her. Trembling, his lips came down on hers, so full of force and passion that he cut her lip on his teeth. He could taste her blood.

He was between her legs, their bodies naked from the waist down, and his big arousal pushed at her. Blakesley was panting, crying softly for want of him, her hands moving to his thick erection as she guided him into her. When he felt her slick, wet heat, he thrust firmly into her, listening to her gasp with wild pleasure. She was exquisitely tight and hot, and he thrust again, feeling her legs wrap around him and draw him in deeper. He put a big hand behind her head to protect it from the hard floor while the other slipped under her buttocks, holding her tightly against him as he began to move.

His mouth was on hers, kissing her deeply, as he made love to her on the old adobe floor. He couldn't even think that he had just met her. All he knew was that he felt things for her that he had never felt in his life, passion and interest and feelings of attraction that he couldn't control. It was more than sex; it was a demonstration of feelings that had completely overwhelmed him. There was emotion involved, something that started with his tender kisses and ended every time he thrust his big erection into her eager body.

Blakesley was nearly incoherent with arousal, feeling every move and every touch with the greatest of pleasure. He was burying himself so deeply in her body that she swore she could feel him touching her womb, the pleasure-pain sensitivity of it quickly driving her towards her release. She'd never made love like this in her life; nothing had even come close. Beck was sexy as hell, a spectacular form of a man that she had never seen equaled. But he was also sweet and sensitive and intelligent, and she found the combination wildly attractive. She was feeling something for him, something fast and deep, and the fact that they were having sex without having even known each other a full day didn't mean anything to her. It was right and she knew it. She wanted all of him.

Beck's thrust grew harder, firmer, and he ground his pelvis against her every time he plunged deep. He suckled her nipples as he thrust, listening to her gasp with pleasure. It was moving and beautiful and powerful, and after one particularly deep thrust, he felt her orgasm around him, a faint cry of ecstasy peeling from her lips. He continued to make love to her, feeling another orgasm a few moments later. Their lovemaking was reaching frenzied proportions and he could feel his body climaxing.

He tried to pull out of her but her legs were locked around him, holding him deep, and as he reached around to unwind her legs, he released himself hard. He grunted, pulling out of her sweet body, letting the last of his orgasm die on her belly. Still gasping and squirming, Blakesley reached down and gently grasped his erection, stroking it, milking it, feeling him twitch and listening to him groan as she prolonged his pleasure.

Breathing heavily, Beck finally opened his eyes to look down at her. The sight of her naked body, open to receive him, was enough to cause him to heat up again. He could feel it. He'd never seen anything so spectacular or arousing. He just wanted to hold her. But as he lowered his lips to gently kiss her, she suddenly lifted her hands, with his body fluid on her palms, and laid the back of her hands against her face. As he watched, she burst into tears.

"Oh, my God," he hissed, gathering her up, trying to look her in the eye. "Blakesley, I'm so sorry. I'm so, so sorry. I shouldn't have... but I thought we were... oh, my God, I'm so sorry. Please don't cry."

She wouldn't look at him no matter how hard he tried. She wept deeply. But then she took her hands off her face and wrapped her arms around his neck, pulling him down against her and hugging him tightly.

"It's... it's okay," she struggled to compose herself. "You didn't do anything wrong. Don't apologize."

He held her snuggly. "Then why are you crying?"

She wiped at her face, her nose, pulling back to look him in the eye. "I don't know," she said honestly. "I guess... I guess it's because we shouldn't have done that but I couldn't help it. I wanted to so badly. Not because I was horny but because... I'm just so attracted to you, Beck. Everything about you is so wonderful and strong and grounded and... oh, hell, I'm the one who should apologize. I should have stopped you but I didn't. I was overwhelmed with you."

He watched her, seeing joy and sorrow and fear. He kissed her cheeks gently.

"I'm never going to get over this," he whispered. "If I never touch another woman again as long as I live, I'll be okay with that because that was pretty much the most amazing experience of my life. I can live on that forever."

She closed her eyes as his mouth moved over her forehead. It was pure heaven. "I hope you don't have to," she cooed. "I hope I don't have to."

He stopped kissing her, taking the time to study her amazing face. "I don't even know what to say." He brushed a lock of hair from her face. "The last time I tried to say what I felt, I freaked you out. I'd never get over it if I freaked you out again."

She smiled, putting her hands on his face and watching him kiss the backs of her hands. "Then maybe we shouldn't say anything right now," she whispered. "Maybe we should just get dressed and get on with the day, and figure this all out later."

"You don't think we should talk about it?"

"Not now," she said. "I don't know about you, but I think... I think I just need to sit on it for a while."

He nodded after a moment, not wanting to force her. "Fair enough," he kissed her again, sensuously, feeling the power of attraction between them rock him down to his toes. It was difficult to pull away. "You've got some art galleries to see."

She smiled, touching his face one last time, as he pushed himself off of her and pulled her into a sitting position. Silently, he handed over her underwear and jeans, standing up and turning his back discreetly as he fastened his pants to allow her some privacy. He could hear her moving around behind him as he picked up his tee shirt and utility jacket, pulling them on as she shuffled around behind him. He was fastening his jacket when he glanced over his shoulder to see if she was dressed, noting that she was fully clothed and leaning against the counter as she pulled on her shoes. He smiled when their eyes met.

"Ready?" he asked.

She nodded, wiping at her mouth, which was now lipstick free. "Yes," she said. "Are you?"

He nodded. "Affirmative."

She grinned at the very military-sounding reply, gesturing to the back door. "Can you make sure that's locked? I left my purse out in the living room."

He nodded, heading back to the door to bolt it, wondering if it would do any good with old Mike running around. He probably knew all the secret ways to get in. Finished securing the door, he left the kitchen and headed back into the living room with its thirty foot ceiling and gigantic, plugged fireplace.

When he got there, Blakesley was fixing her lipstick and touching up her face. He stood there a moment, watching her, appreciating the allure of a beautiful woman. He also realized that he felt incredibly attached to her now that he knew her on an intimate level, far more than he could have imagined. The act of passion in the kitchen had brought his feelings for her to an entirely new level and he still wasn't over it. It lingered in his mind. It scared him a little.

Blakesley put her compact back in her purse and caught him looking at her. She softened when their eyes met, a smile on her face.

"What are you thinking?" she asked. Before he could answer, she put her hand up to silence him. "Forget I asked that. Come on. Let's get going. Do you want to drive this time?"

He opened his mouth but she turned around and tossed him the keys before he could get a word out. He caught the keys. "Sure, baby. Whatever you say."

"Don't wreck my car," she teased.

"I wouldn't dream of it."

He followed her out of the house, pausing to watch her wrestle with locking the front door. He took the keys from her again and locked it himself. They went back over to the other wing to make sure it was locked, too, and he handed her back the house keys. She took the keys, put them in her purse, and smiled at him.

"Are you hungry?"

"A little."

"Then let's go get some lunch before we meet the real estate agent."

"Sure," he paused as she took a step towards the car. "Can... can I hold your hand? I mean, are you okay with that?"

She smiled and reached out her hand, clutching his big fingers. "Completely."

He held her hand tightly as they headed towards the car. "How about putting my arm around you in public?"

"Okay."

"Kissing you in public?"

She lifted an eyebrow at him as he unlocked the car and opened the door for her. "That depends," she said. "If it's anything like back in the kitchen, then...."

He grinned, somewhat devilishly, which she found extremely sexy. "I'd never do that in public," he assured her. "Only in private with no audience, I promise. I wouldn't disrespect you that way."

She softened. "I know you wouldn't," she assured him. "Kissing in public is fine, so long as it's appropriate."

"Good," he held the door as she climbed in. "I can do that. I'm sure if I don't, you'll let me know."

"You bet I will."

"I never had any doubt."

He could hear her giggling even after he shut the door.

FIVE

BECK TOOK Blakesley to a restaurant down in the Gaslamp Quarter of San Diego, one of the most popular tourist spots in town that had street after street of restaurants and shops. It was set in the older part of town, with gas lamp streetlights, hence the name, and it was always overflowing with people because of its location to the major hotels, convention center, and docks.

Beck drove the BMW perhaps a bit more carefully than he did his own truck, thinking the car cost more than he made in a year. It had every amenity known to man, from the inboard navigation to the heated and cooled seats to the chilled glove box for drinks. He was actually a little nervous driving down to the Gaslamp Quarter as it started to dawn on him that Blakesley was fairly well off and probably used to the finer things in life. She'd never made any secret of it but it had never really occurred to him until now what might be financially expected of him.

The incident in the kitchen seemed to change everything and he was taking everything more seriously now, including his ability to treat her the way she was accustomed. By the time they entered Brian's 24 Restaurant, Bar and Grille, he was beginning to feel distinctly nervous about it. But Blakesley was oblivious to his mental dilemma as they were seated, smiling at the décor of the place.

"This is really cute," she said, looking around as the hostess handed her a menu. "Have you been here before?"

He nodded, picking up his own menu. "A couple of times to watch football."

"You and your friends?"

He flipped the page of the menu. "We come here to drink, watch the game and pick up women," he looked up at her, grinning, when she laughed. "I'm just kidding about the last part. I've never picked up a woman in a bar in my life."

"Me, either," she teased. "Seriously, I'd like to meet your friends. Well, that is, if you want me to. You may not want me to."

He looked at her as if she were insane. "Are you kidding?" he snorted. "I'll be lucky if they don't try to steal you away from me. In fact, you met a couple of them yesterday but you didn't know it. Some of the guys that helped pull you and Cadee out of the water."

She looked at him, the smile fading from her face. She closed the menu and grew serious. "You guys were lifesavers, literally," she said. "But I was wondering something."

"What?"

She shrugged, fingering her water glass. "I know you've been a S.E.A.L. for a lot of years, but I was wondering if you've ever been injured."

He suspected these questions would come at some point, but he didn't think they'd come so soon. He closed his menu.

"That depends on what you mean by injured," he said evenly. "What I do... well, it's not safe sometimes. There's always the risk of injury or death."

She nodded. "I realize that," she said. "I've already admitted I really don't know a lot about S.E.A.L.s other than what I saw in a movie once, but even if that movie exaggerated, it looked like it was really dangerous stuff."

He nodded faintly. "I told you that it can be."

"How dangerous?"

He sighed and reached across the table, grasping her hand. "Do you really want to talk about that right now?" he asked. "Baby, it's dangerous. I carry weapons. I've been shot at. I've been shot. It's pretty hairy sometimes. But it hasn't killed me yet and I don't expect it to. I expect to retire in a few years and grow old with a beautiful woman by my side."

The waitress interrupted to take their order. Blakesley ordered a Cobb salad and Beck ordered a Monte Cristo sandwich. When the waitress walked away, Beck picked up Blakesley's hand and kissed her fingers.

"It's too soon for you to start worrying about this," he told her. "Let's just enjoy getting to know each other, okay? We'll worry about the rest of it as it comes."

She looked at him pointedly. "It wasn't too soon for us to sleep together," she said. "Why is it too soon to worry about what you do for a living? You've already roped me in hook, line and sinker and if I'm going to fall for a guy, I want to know what I'm getting in to."

He held her hand, toying with her fingers, gazing at her steadily from across the table. After a moment, he let go of her hand and stood up, coming over to her side of the booth and sitting down next to her. He put his arm around her shoulders and she laid her head on his big shoulder, feeling him kiss her forehead.

"What do you want me to tell you?" he whispered.

"I want to know if you've ever been seriously injured."

"Yes."

"How seriously?"

He sighed again, his arm tightening around her. "I took a bullet to the groin and another to the abdomen," he said softly. "Because of the situation, it was six hours before they could airlift me to a carrier for medical attention. They weren't sure if I was going to make it, but I did."

She was quiet a moment. "When did this happen?"

"Four years ago. Sharon divorced me while I was recovering. It was the last nail in the coffin as far as she was concerned."

She leaned against him, her arm going across his chest to hold him just as he was holding her.

"Have there been any other times?" she asked quietly.

"I was wounded twice before, but nothing critical. I survived."

She sighed faintly, hearing his heart beating strong and steady in her right ear. "Well," she said after a moment. "Thanks for being honest with me."

"Does it change your mind about me?"

She shook her head and lifted it, looking at him. "No," she said honestly. "But it does worry me. I guess I'm just going to have to learn to deal with it."

He smiled at her, kissing the tip of her nose. "I want you to listen to me and listen closely, because it's important." His green eyes were intense. "I really love what I do. I make a difference and that means a lot to me. Most people can't say that. But with you... you've been such an unexpected piece of heaven that for the first time in my life, I find myself thinking of something other than my career and myself. Does that make any sense?"

She nodded seriously. "It does," she said. "But you've only known me a day, Beck. You can't make a big life-changing declaration. It's too soon."

"Is it?" he fired back. "Someone just told me she's been roped in hook, line and sinker."

Her eyes narrowed at him, but it was good-natured. "Ah ha," she muttered. "I can see he is using my own words against me, clever boy."

He laughed at her sense of humor. "So have I," he admitted. "By you. I feel like you're what I've been waiting for my entire life, Blakesley. I'm sorry if that freaks you out, but it's the truth. I want you to hear it."

She hugged him, not staying a word, but the waitress came with the food and she was forced to let him go. They ate in relative silence, although he was on her right side and, being right handed, she jabbed him with her elbow a couple of times as she ate, playfully, knocking the fork out of his hand at one point.

Beck sighed heavily, fighting off a smirk, and picked up his sandwich with his hands. She dropped a piece of avocado on it and he responded by throwing a French fry in the middle of her salad. She ate the French fry and made sure to put a piece of lettuce in his maple syrup cup. On and on it went, with giggles and soft laughter, until the meal was over. When all was said and done, Beck had eaten about a quarter of her salad and she'd had about half his French fries. But lunchtime had never been so fun.

Blakesley was drinking the rest of his Coke when the bill came and she snatched it from the waitress before he could get his hands on it. His brow furrowed.

"Hey," he snapped his fingers, gently demanding she turn the check over to him. "Give me that."

She shook her head and pulled out her wallet. "No way," she said. "I'm buying."

He lifted an eyebrow, making his displeasure obvious. "I can afford to pay for lunch, you know."

She pulled out her credit card. "I know," she said. "But I'd like to pay if that's okay with you."

He couldn't help but notice all of the credit cards she had in her wallet and it reminded him of the paranoid delusions he had on the way to the restaurant. He scratched his head, watching her hand the check and the credit card over to the waitress. When the woman left to run the card, he looked at Blakesley.

"Uh... can I say something?" he asked.

She nodded. "Of course."

He shifted uncomfortably. "Well," he began. "For a Naval officer, my pay isn't too bad. Hazard pay is like double overtime, so I don't do too poorly. I mean, I own my own home and I live comfortably. But I noticed... well, to be honest, I noticed that you seem to have expensive tastes. You drive an expensive car."

She lifted her eyebrows. "What's wrong with a woman being able to support herself like that?"

"Nothing," he said quickly. "Nothing at all. But I just want you to know that I don't live like that. I live, well, averagely."

"So what are you saying?"

He was losing control of the conversation. "I don't know," he shook his head. "I guess I'm saying that although I would like to spend all the money in the world on you, the truth is that I can't. I'd love to buy you cars and expensive clothes and expensive trips, but I don't have the funds for that. I'll do whatever I can, but I hope it doesn't become an issue that I can't spend like a king."

She frowned. "Am I coming across like super high-maintenance?"

"Not at all," he assured her. "But it's obvious that you have money and I really don't."

She cocked her head, not quite sure how to take him. "So... if I pay for lunch, or take us on a trip to Vegas, do you feel like that's emasculating you?"

He sighed, his hand on her shoulder. "No, honey, that's not what I'm saying," he shrugged his shoulders. "I don't know what I'm saying. I guess I was just trying to make it clear that I'm not rich."

She took pity on him, snuggling up against him because he looked depressed. "Neither am I, by a lot of standards," she assured him. "But I do have a little money and I'm not ashamed of that. I sold my cleaning company for several million dollars, but some of that was sucked up in taxes, I invested a big chunk of it, and the rest of it is mine to do with as I please. If I pay for lunch, or take us on a trip to Las Vegas, I'm really happy to do it, okay? I'm not trying to show you up, I promise."

He smiled at her and kissed her cheek. "And if I want to pay for a trip to Vegas?"

"Then I go first class and stay in a suite at the Venetian."

His face fell. "Seriously?"

She laughed at him. "No, of course not," she said. "If you want to pay for a trip to Vegas, I'm thrilled to go, even if we go on Greyhound."

He rubbed her back affectionately and kissed her cheek again as the waitress brought the credit card and receipt back to the table.

"I wouldn't do that to you," he said. "But I do like to drive."

She threw up her hands like she was at a rock concert. "Woo hoo!" she exclaimed happily. "Road trip!"

He smirked at her as she signed the slip and put the credit card back in her wallet. Lunch had been an enlightening and joyful experience. In fact, the entire day had been hugely eventful, something he wasn't sorry about in the least. He was quite happy to be swept along with it.

Climbing out of the booth, he pulled her out after him, holding her hand as they left the restaurant. Heading down the street in the bright California sunshine, he couldn't ever recall feeling so happy. He was falling for a beautiful woman who seemed to feel the same way about him and he was thrilled. As they neared her car, his cell phone rang. He paused to answer it as Blakesley hit the remote and unlocked the car.

Blakesley climbed into the driver's seat and turned on the car, rolling down the windows and opening up the sun roof as Beck stood on the sidewalk and talked on his cell phone. She was thinking about the real estate agent she had to meet in fifteen minutes, looking on her inboard navigation to find the best route to the real estate office, when Beck opened up the door and climbed into the car. She looked up at him to ask him if he knew the neighborhood they were heading to but he cut her off.

"Can you take me back to the hotel, please?" he asked. "I need to get back to the base."

He seemed rushed so she immediately put the car in gear and headed out. "Sure," she said. "Do you want me to just take you straight to the base?"

He shook his head. "No," he replied. "I need to get my truck and it's at the hotel."

She pulled into traffic and sped up. "Is everything okay?" she asked.

He just picked up her hand and kissed it without answering. Feeling increasingly concerned, she tried not to let it show but was unsuccessful.

"Will I see you tonight?" she asked quietly.

"I don't know yet," he replied vaguely. "I'll give you a call when I can."

She fell silent as they took a couple of turns and ended up on the road heading for the Coronado Bridge. Blakesley gunned it and flew over the bridge, passing over the great, blue body of San Diego Bay without noticing the clear water or bright sky. She was focused on making it back to the hotel, which she could see from the bridge.

The bridge dumped out onto Fourth Street and she took a left on Orange, which took her straight to the hotel. There was a massive parking lot on the east side of the hotel and she pulled in as Beck directed her to his truck. They found the dark blue Chevy half-ton parked under a tree and she pulled in behind it. When she put the car in park, he turned to her.

"I can't even tell you what this day has meant to me," he confessed. "I just want to thank you. It's been amazing."

She stared at him, the big, bluish-green eyes beginning to tear up. "You make it sound like I'm never going to see you again."

He cupped her face with his big hands, kissing her cheeks sweetly. "No, baby girl, not at all," he whispered. "But I've got to go and I really don't know how long it will be until I see you again. Something is going on and they need me to be a part of it."

She sniffled, trying not to cry. "Is that all you can tell me?"

"Yes."

She accepted it. "Okay," she said, her hands moving to his face, his shoulders. "Just... just so you know, I'm only going to be at the hotel another couple of days and then the girls and I are moving into the house. That's where I'll be."

He grunted with some displeasure. "I really wish you wouldn't move into the house just yet," he said. "I'm not comfortable with that old guy living back in the canyon."

"I have nowhere else to go."

He frowned. "You can use my house. It's about a half mile from here."

She shook her head. "That's such a sweet offer, but I wouldn't feel comfortable doing that. My girls are messy and I'd hate to wreck something."

"You won't wreck anything."

"You're sweet, but I'm going to decline again. Thank you so much."

He didn't look happy but he didn't push. "If you won't use my house, then can you go to a cheaper hotel for a while until you get that house under repair? I just don't get a good feeling from that place and it worries me."

She shrugged. "I guess," she said. "I need to think about it."

He kissed her cheek, her lips. "Please do," he whispered, pulling back to look at her. "I'll call you as soon as I can and give you some idea of when I'll be back, okay?"

"Okay," she nodded. "Please... please take care of yourself. I don't want anything to happen to you."

He smiled and kissed her deeply, tasting her sweetness, inhaling her scent. He would tuck it away in his memory to sustain him for the time they would spend apart.

"I really...," he caught himself. "I adore you. Remember that, okay? And I swear I will be back."

She nodded, her eyes big on him. "I adore you, too," she whispered. "Take care of yourself."

He smiled and kissed her one last time before bailing out of the car and moving swiftly to his truck. Blakesley put her car in reverse and backed away so he could pull out. She sat there, watching him drive from the parking lot. She prayed it wouldn't be the last time she ever saw him.

Calling the real estate agent, she rescheduled their appointment for another time and spent the rest of the day on the beach with her girls. She just didn't feel like checking out storefronts. She felt like staying close to home, close to the base where Beck was.

When he finally called her, sometime around ten that night, it was to tell her that he wouldn't be able to call her for the next few days. She understood but she was unhappy. He was unhappy, too, but he had a job to do, as he soothingly explained to her. She was calmed by his soft manner and sweet words, hanging up the phone after only a few minutes because he had to go.

Blakesley didn't get any sleep that night, either.

SIX
SEVEN DAYS LATER

HE COULDN'T STOP THINKING about her and nearly got himself killed.

It had been a quick jaunt to Mexico to deal with a cartel that had ambushed an American diplomat, so it hadn't been a truly dangerous or critical mission, but it had been dangerous enough. The Mexican cartels were as well supplied with munitions as some armies, so the team had gone in with their usual caution. What they hadn't counted on was the entire small, sleepy village in the province of Sinaloa to be part of the cartel. Beck had been parlaying with a local official when the guy's son had clocked him, right in the face.

That had started a firefight that wiped out the entire village along with the cartel.

And now, they were back.

It was well before dawn as the transport landed in Coronado. As usual, Beck was the last man off the plane, lugging his gear down the stairs and onto the tarmac. He was heading for debriefing, which would take a couple of hours before Davis would let them rest and then they'd return to go through it again.

But all he could think about was getting to Blakesley.

That's what got him clocked by the son of the official. He'd been talking to the man, who happened to own the only jewelry store in town. Beck took his attention off his surroundings to look at a silver necklace the man had in a case and that's when it had happened. It had been annoying more than anything because other than a big bruise, he wasn't hurt. But it could have easily been a bullet and not a fist that had come flying at him.

He considered himself lucky.

Therefore, his thoughts were of Blakesley as he sat through debriefing with a diagram of the town on the table in front of them. He got through his portion of it, sitting through the other guys and their recollections, before Davis finally let everyone go home to clean up and rest a bit. And with that, Beck went back to his locker to collect his wallet and keys only to be ambushed by Butch and Anthony, who wanted to know where he was going in such a hurry. They already knew, so it took very little needling for Beck to confess. Anthony suggested that Beck swing by wholesale flower market that his friend owned to buy Blakesley some flowers just to show her how much he'd missed her.

Beck thought it was a damn fine idea.

Back in his truck and heading for the flower market as dawn began to break, he found himself thinking of his first marriage. He never tried bringing flowers home to Sharon when he'd come back from a mission or deployment because it wouldn't have worked, anyway. That made him a little uncertain. He started thinking that he needed to talk to someone who wouldn't tease him about the situation or tell him what he wanted to hear. When he came to a red light, he went to his contacts in his cell phone, found a number, and hit dial.

A familiar voice answered through the car speakers.

"Are you even out of bed yet?"

Beck snorted. "Of course I'm out of bed," he said. "I didn't even sleep last night. I've been on a plane and you know I can't sleep on a plane."

The man on the other end chuckled. "I remember coming

home from Cancun with you a very long time ago and you slept the entire way."

"I'd been drunk for a week, Cord. Of course I'm going to sleep. But that's not usual with me."

Cord Trevor laughed. "I know," he said. "I'm just giving you crap. So what has you calling me at the break of dawn in California?"

"You on duty?"

"Not anymore," Cord said. "We had a hell of a storm last night and I'm heading home, but I've got a few minutes. What's up, Beck?"

Cord was a firefighter in Salem, Massachusetts and had been for several years. Now that Beck had his attention, he wasn't sure where to begin.

"I need some advice, I think," he said. "I met somebody."

There was a pause. "Met somebody?" Cord repeated. "Who?"

"A woman."

"Oh," Cord said as he realized what Beck meant. "Hey, good for you. I'm happy for you. How long has this been going on?"

"Not long," Beck said. "I met her a few days before I was deployed for about a week. That's what I'm coming back from and I need some advice."

"About what?"

Beck was feeling increasingly uncomfortable. "Okay, here it is," he said. "We hadn't even known each other twenty-four hours when we slept together. It was totally spontaneous, but we did. I swear, Cord, I've never been so attracted to a woman in my life. Her name is Blakesley and she's just... she's just everything. She's beautiful and sexy and smart. She's way too good for me. Since I went away right after we slept together, I need to know... how should I handle seeing her again? Should I assume we'll pick up where we left off? What if she's had time to think about it and doesn't want to see me again? What if she thinks the whole thing was a big mistake?"

"Hold it right there," Cord said. "Beck, you need to stop. Don't you say those things to her or she'll think you're emotionally unstable."

"Christ, I know," Beck said, running a hand over his face. "I'd like to say it's my exhaustion talking, but it's not."

"No, it's not, because your bitchy ex-wife did everything she could to damage your confidence."

"Yeah," Beck said quietly. "I already had a failure with Blakesley once and she was willing to overlook it. But I don't think she would a second time."

"Then don't," Cord said firmly. "Look, little bro – ask her straight up if she still feels the same way she did a week ago. If she says yes, you're fine. If she says no, then at least you know. That's better than not knowing. But face it with the same bravery you would face a thousand Afghan rebels with. Would you get all needy and uncertain in a combat situation?"

"No."

"Then don't do it with her. She doesn't deserve that and neither do you. Okay?"

Beck felt better. "Okay," he said. "Thanks, Cord. I knew I could count on you."

On the other end of the line, Cord snorted. "Always," he said. "I'll always be here to keep you from making an ass out of yourself."

"God knows, you've done that enough."

"You owe me."

"I do," Beck said. "I'll name a grandkid after you or something."

"Ha!" Cord said. "Why not your firstborn with Blakesley?"

"I'll think about it," Beck said, grinning. "Hey, speaking of kids, how are the boys doing?"

"Great," Cord said. "Chris and Kyle have football practice these days and Cole is getting along. And I've got a new neighbor who might turn out to be my Blakesley."

"Really?" Beck was interested. "Tell me about her."

"Not much to tell right now," Cord said. "I just met her. She's a physician with the emergency department over at North Shore. She just moved in with her two kids."

"Divorced?"

"Divorced and gorgeous."

Beck grinned. "Then I wish you all the luck," he said. "If I can ever give you some advice, call me."

Cord snorted again. "Relationship advice from you?" he said. "Don't make me laugh. But I appreciate the offer."

Beck couldn't resist. "I know how you are," he said. "You charge in and take control, even in a relationship."

Cord couldn't deny it. "I've been known to, yes."

"Just take this one slow and easy. You've got your kids and they don't need women coming in and out of their lives."

"Don't I know it," Cord said. "They've never reacted well to anyone I'm dating, at least Cole hasn't, but we'll see. At some point, they have to realize their Dad needs to be happy, too.

"Don't we all."

"Sounds like you're about to be."

"Sounds like you are, too."

"Let's hope so."

With that, Beck thanked his friend again and hung up the phone because he was coming to the offramp that would lead to the flower market. His thoughts were quickly turning away from Cord and to Blakesley. He was glad he'd called his old friend, glad to get advice from his perspective. He couldn't depend on Butch for that kind of thing because Butch, more than Cord, was a charge in and take control kind of guy. Somehow, Beck didn't think that would work well with Blakesley.

It was just a hunch he had.

With the flower market dead ahead, he had his day mapped out for him.

SEVEN

IT HAD BEEN seven days since Blakesley had last seen Beck. Seven long, lonely and depressing days.

Never mind that she just met the guy and never mind that she'd known him less than a week. She felt his absence like a heavy weight, remembering his handsome face and wondering, on the seventh day of their separation, if she had really just dreamed him. Maybe he wasn't real at all. She was starting to think he was just a ghost, a wisp of a dream she once held close to her heart. She just wasn't sure anymore.

After checking out of the Hotel del Coronado on Tuesday night, she had moved to an Extended Stay Hotel that was literally over the hill from the house. It was so close that she could visit the house daily and frequently, meeting with contractors and beginning the slow process of restoring the place.

Although the structure had been lived in since it had been built, so much of it needed to be updated that she had taken Beck's advice and checked into an Extended Stay. It just wasn't worth it to stay in a house under construction and she felt much better with the girls being in a safe and controlled environment, with clean toilets, clean linens, and all the comforts. Fortunately, the girls were easy-going enough that staying in a hotel didn't bother them in the least. As long as they could watch cartoons, they were content.

The better news mid-week was that their former live-in nanny, who had chosen to stay in Los Angeles when they had moved to San Diego, called Blakesley on Thursday to see how the girls were but also to see if she could have her old job back. It seemed that she missed the girls very badly and was willing to relocate to be with them. Blakesley gladly flew Nikki King to San Diego from Los Angeles the next day and picked her up at the airport, much to the delight of the girls. They had missed Nikki very much, a young woman without a social life who had been taking care of the girls since Cadee was born, and they were one big, happy family again.

With Nikki tending the girls, it freed up Blakesley to focus on the house. She had found a contractor with experience in restoring historical homes and by Saturday, he was busy at work getting rid of the spray paint on the walls and repairing the holes. He was also remodeling the kitchen, and the hammering and tearing out of old fixtures was in full swing. They had to be very careful since the floors were the original adobe and so were the walls, so the restoration was slow-going for the most part. Also, because the house was a State Historical Landmark, Blakesley had gotten the State of California involved and they had sent an art historian to ensure that nothing out of the ordinary was damaged, touched or rearranged.

In all, it had been a very busy week. On this mild Monday morning, she had arrived at the house after dropping Nikki and the girls off at the San Diego Zoo. She planned to go get them later in the day, after she had seen the house and met with the real estate agent she still hadn't seen since her arrival in San Diego.

The contractor was already at the house and as Blakesley entered the family wing, she could see that the green spray-painted wall had been completely repaired. They were whitewashed again on the imperfect adobe surface, the look of which she loved. Wrought iron contractors were taking down the big chandeliers in the main room to restore and rewire them, while a chimney repair guy was unplugging the massive fireplace.

It was busy already and Blakesley met briefly with the contractor to find out what he was attempting to accomplish for the day. Satisfied with his punch list, Blakesley left the man alone to do his job as she wandered through the kitchen to see what the landscaper was doing with the property.

She stood by the edge of the canyon, watching the landscaper and his army of men cut back the overgrowth off to the south. It was a huge area and she was thinking it might be a good spot for a pool. She could envision a big play area for the girls. Shielding her eyes from the bright morning sun, she was watching the landscapers when she heard movement over to her left.

Climbing up through the bramble was old Mike. He was looking curiously at the activity going on, startled when he spied Blakesley several feet away. She was looking right at him. He fled, ducking back into the overgrowth, and she ran to the edge of the canyon.

"Hey!" she called. "Mike? Where are you going?"

Only the sounds of rustling bushes and birds answered. Blakesley tried to see down the canyon, straining to catch a glimpse of the elusive former maintenance man.

"Mike!" she called again. "Don't run away! Please?"

He didn't respond. She could hear a lot of movement below, but she couldn't see anything. With a heavy sigh, she turned away from the canyon and back towards the house but was caught off guard by a body in the kitchen doorway.

Beck was standing in the portal. He wore a snug gray tee shirt, black utility pants, and big, black combat boots. His hair was dirty and his face unshaved; she could see it from where she stood, and he also had a big red welt on his left cheekbone. But all of that was overshadowed by the enormous bouquet of red roses he held and the uncertain expression on his face.

Blakesley gasped at the sight of him, her hands flying to her mouth as if to hold back her surprise. Her eyes were wide on him as he smiled timidly.

"Hi," he said in that gentle, deep voice.

Blakesley realized there was a lump in her throat. She was so glad to see him that she could hardly breathe.

"Hi," she replied, swallowing hard.

He took a timid step out of the house, onto the porch, just looking at her. "I just want to know," he said, "if you still feel the same way you did seven days ago."

The lump in her throat grew. "You've been counting the days?"

He nodded. "It's been nine thousand, nine hundred and sixty-four minutes since I last saw you," he whispered. "I've missed you for every one of those minutes. I got back to base less than an hour ago and picked these flowers up on the way over here, hoping you still remembered my name."

She smiled and tears filled her eyes. Quietly, she made her way over to him, her eyes alight with everything she was feeling. It was glorious and warm and spiritual. She stopped just short of him, letting out a weepy chuckle as she lifted up her right foot.

"Look," she told him. "I'm not wearing high heels. I'm actually wearing shoes I won't fall down in when I walk in the yard."

He laughed softly, looking at the little white tennis shoes on her feet. "I'm proud of you," he said, his eyes moving back to her face. "But you could have worn the heels. I would have carried you around."

She started laughing and the tears rolled down her cheeks. She was at a loss for words, so glad to see him that she couldn't verbalize it. But he wasn't rushing at her with his arms open, and she was feeling timid and uncertain, too. She pointed at the flowers.

"They're gorgeous."

He extended them to her. "They're for you."

She reached out and took them, holding them against her chest. "Thank you," she murmured sincerely. "They're the most beautiful flowers I've ever gotten."

His smile faded, his expression growing intense. "I don't want to freak you out, Blakesley," he said, "but I just wanted to tell you how much I missed you. All the way over here I was thinking about what I would say to you, but the best I could come up with was that I missed you. That pretty well sums it up."

The tears were overtaking her and she moved closer to him, gazing up into his handsome face with the flowers clutched to her chest.

"Yes, I still feel the same way I did when you left me a week ago," she whispered. "And yes, I missed you as badly as you missed me. I'm so glad you're back."

"Really?"

"Really."

His smile returned, only now, it wasn't timid. It was bright and sexy. "Can I kiss you?"

She nodded, lifting her mouth up to him even as he swooped down on her. The flowers got smashed as he pulled her into a crushing embrace, but he couldn't have cared less. He had her in his arms again and that was all that mattered. He swore that he was never, ever going to let her go, not ever. He could feel her sobbing against him and he tasted her salty tears as she threw her arms around his neck. The flowers ended up on the ground.

Beck had her up in his arms, kissing her so furiously that she could hardly draw a breath. Arms around his neck, Blakesley jumped on him so that her legs were wrapped around his waist and he just held her there, hands supporting her thighs, kissing her happily and passionately.

"I wrote you some letters while I was away," he said between heated kisses. "I brought them with me."

"Letters?" she repeated as he suckled her lips.

"Love letters," he told her, hoping it wouldn't send her out of his arms. He hadn't told Cord about them, fearful of what the man would say about him being needy, but the cat was out of the bag now. He was going to be honest about it. "I'm not very good at it, but I tried. I wanted to tell you what I was feeling."

She pulled back to look at him, her lips red from his forceful kisses and her expression serious.

"It's too soon to say that kind of stuff, isn't it?" she murmured.

His heart fell a little. "Maybe," he gently kissed her jaw, her cheek. "Maybe not. I don't know if falling in love really has a timeline."

He could feel her breathing quicken. "You're... you're falling in love?" she asked.

He sighed. "I guess," he whispered, meeting her gaze. "That's what I meant about not freaking you out again. I couldn't take it if...."

"I love you, too."

He froze mid-sentence, his eyes widening with shock. "You do?"

Blakesley nodded and started crying. Her head fell forward, onto his shoulder.

"Yes," she sobbed, holding his neck tightly. "I do. I really do. But I'm so scared... Beck, being separated from you was hell. I know that's why your wife left you and I'm sorry if I don't like it, either, but I'll try to get used to it. I promise I'll try."

He held her tightly, so tightly that he was squeezing the air out of her lungs. "Baby, it's all right," he assured her, absolutely giddy with what she was saying. "Don't worry about it. We'll work something out, I promise. I don't want to be away from you, either. Please don't cry about it."

"I'm not crying about it."

"You could have fooled me." He rubbed her back when she sobbed rather dramatically, kissing the side of her head. He couldn't help the smile on his lips. "I love you, too, baby. I love you so much."

Blakesley clung to him, all wrapped up around him, as he hugged her and soothed her. It was as sweet a reunion as it could possibly be, something he had hoped for but didn't really believe would happen. He'd spent seven days wondering if she would have realized, upon reflection and separation, that she really wasn't as attracted to him as she thought. He had been terrified about it. Now, he couldn't believe things were better than when he had left.

Blakesley slowed her tears, pulling her face from the crook of his neck and wiping at her eyes. She still had one arm firmly around his neck, looking at him with a sad, wet face. He gazed back at her, thinking he'd never seen anything more beautiful in his life. He was a man in total, utter love.

"What happened?" she sniffled, touching the red lump on his cheekbone.

He grunted. "I was fighting three hundred pissed-off Mexicans and one of them clocked me."

She grinned in spite of herself, knowing he was teasing her and suspecting she could ask the question twenty different ways and he would never give her a straight answer. She was coming to figure that out about him.

"You went to Mexico?" her eyes narrowed. "Did you bring me anything?"

He grinned. "Like what?"

"Tequila," she said. "Jewelry, perfume or designer handbags."

He laughed softly. "I wasn't shopping."

"You can't go to Mexico and not shop."

He cocked his head at her, studying her sweet face. "I brought you two dozen red roses."

She gasped as if just remembering, releasing her hold on him and gasping again when she saw what happened to her flowers.

"Oh, no," she knelt down, picking up the smashed flowers. "I'm so sorry. I didn't mean to take such bad care of them."

He knelt down beside her and helped her collect them. "All things considered," he winked at her as they stood up, flowers in her arms. "The flowers were a small sacrifice for such a spectacular hug."

She smiled and went back into the kitchen with Beck on her heels. A couple of laborers were stripping years of soot off the ceiling as she propped the roses up in the old sink, put in the stopper, and began to fill it up with water. Beck crossed his big arms and leaned back against the counter, watching her try to fix the broken flowers. He tore his eyes off her long enough to look around the old, torn-up kitchen.

"Please don't tell me you're staying here with the girls," he said quietly.

She looked at him. "No," she said. "I took your advice and moved to another hotel. We're at the Extended Stay over in Mission Valley."

"Good," he said firmly. "I'm glad you listened to me."

She shrugged. "It made sense," she said. "This is no place for three little girls. They'd just be in the way. The contractor tells me that the house won't be ready for at least six weeks, so I guess we're going to call the hotel 'home' until then. I'm not real thrilled about that because Cadee and Crosby will be starting summer school in a couple of weeks, but I guess there's nothing I can do about it."

"Have you enrolled them yet?"

She shook her head. "Not yet."

"How are they doing?"

She smiled. "Fine," she said. "My nanny from Los Angeles joined us a few days ago, so they're very happy and taken care of. They're at the zoo right now."

"And you're here overseeing the house."

"That about sums up my life for the past week."

She turned off the faucet, finished fussing with the roses, and turned to him. She reached up and ran a hand over his forehead, his cropped blond hair. He closed his eyes, savoring her gentle touch.

"What about you?" she asked with concern. "You look so tired. What are you going to do now that you're back?"

He kept his eyes closed as she ran her fingers across his scalp, gently moving down his face to his dimpled chin. He was enjoying every second of it, having dreamed of moments like this in the days they spent apart.

"I haven't slept much," he admitted, his eyes rolling open. "I don't have to report in until tomorrow. I was hoping to spend the time with you."

She smiled faintly and leaned against him, her face upturned to him. Beck unfolded his arms and wrapped her up in them.

"The girls are going to be at the zoo most of the day," she said. "So I'm thinking that you and I should go someplace with a bed so you can rest."

He lifted his eyebrows at her. "If you and I are someplace with a bed, resting is going to be the last thing I want to do."

She giggled. "I have something else in mind."

"What?"

"Please," she caressed his cheek again. "Just... let me do something for you."

He couldn't refuse. He'd been waiting for this moment his entire life and he only just now realized it.

Blakesley took Beck back to the hotel where she and the girls had a suite. The first thing she did was have him sit down and take off his shoes, and while he was unlacing his boots, she went into her bathroom with the big, deep-soak tub and began running him a bath. He could hear her moving around in the bathroom as he pulled his shoes off, feeling more exhausted by the moment.

He pulled of his tee shirt and wearily rose, heading into the bathroom that now smelled like something flowery and lemony. There were bubbles in the bathtub and he wasn't too sure about that until she turned around and demanded he remove his pants. He did without hesitation. He was all set to pull her against his naked body when she side-stepped him and made him get into the tub.

Disappointed, he did as he was told. As Beck settled back against the tub, Blakesley busied herself over at the bathroom counter. He sighed with contentment, feeling drowsy with the heat and thinking maybe a bubble bath wasn't such a bad thing, all the while watching her curiously as she made her way back over to him. She had something on her hands and she sat on the back of the tub and began rubbing his shoulders.

He audibly groaned as she began to massage him with some kind of oil that didn't smell too girly. In fact, he rather liked it. The more she rubbed, the more relaxed and content he began to feel, an outcome of seven days of brutal conditions that he could have never imagined. Blakesley had magic fingers as she rubbed his tense shoulders and neck, moving down his arms and then back to his neck again. He soaked it up, savored it, falling half-asleep as she rubbed until she made him sit forward so she could get to his back.

Blakesley massaged his back, using techniques she had learned from a girlfriend who was a masseuse, rubbing out the knots and taking the time to become acquainted with his body. Their passionate rendezvous in the kitchen seven days before hadn't afforded her a real opportunity to study him, but as she rubbed his tense flesh, she studied every inch of tanned skin.

As she had noticed from the onset, the man was just plain big, with big muscles and big hands. He had a very broad chest, something she took the time to explore as she had rubbed his shoulders and arms. But as she ran her hands over him, she could also see that he was scarred and bruised. He had a particularly large bruise on his right kidney, a big, greenish blob. He had another bruise on his right arm, a big one, and both of his hands were scraped up pretty good. All of his knuckles had scabs and scrapes on them. The more she massaged him, the more injuries she seemed to notice. The man looked beat to hell.

After taking about ten minutes on his back, she had him sit back in the tub and she brought out the body wash and shampoo. Beck opened his eyes long enough to suspiciously eye the products, hoping nothing was particularly girly-smelling but willing to go along with her anyway, but fortunately, she happened to have a sample of the Hermes unisex-scent body wash. She let him smell it, and approve it, before lathering up one of her sponges and going to work on him.

As Beck lay back against the tub, he seriously thought he had died and gone to heaven. Never in his life had he known such attention or pleasure, from anyone, and as Blakesley silently washed his shoulders and back and chest, he just sat there and enjoyed every single minute. She had him lift one big leg out of the tub, which she washed, and then the other. She even washed his hair with it. All soaped up, she put the sponge aside and used the little hand-held shower fixture to rinse him off. By the time she was finished, Beck was putty. He was exhausted, warm, massaged and limp, so she popped the tub drain and had him get out.

He did, staggering because he was so exhausted and relaxed, and she wrapped a towel around him as she pulled him out to the bedroom. He fell on the bed, still damp, as Blakesley did her best to dry him. She could only get to the back of him because of the way he had fallen on the bed and before she reached his head, he was snoring heavily on the sheets.

With a smile, she stopped drying and pulled the covers up over him. He had said that if they went someplace with a bed, resting would be the last thing on his mind, but that was not the case. She couldn't imagine what the man had done over the past seven days but she was pretty sure she really didn't want to know. All she knew was that he was here now, he was safe, and she was happy.

She sat down next to him on the bed, hand on his damp head, and watched him while he slept.

———

"Beck?"

He heard his name, whispered in his ear in a deliciously sensual female voice and he smiled. It was sweet and heavenly. In the haze between sleep and consciousness, he heard his name a couple of times, murmured by an angel.

"Beck?" Blakesley rubbed his back gently. "Beck, are you awake?"

Beck became lucid, instantly awake when he realized someone

was trying to wake him. He rolled onto his back to find himself gazing up into Blakesley's lovely face. It was the best thing in the world he could wake up to as far as he was concerned and he smiled sleepily at her.

"Hi, baby," he mumbled, putting a big hand up to gently cup her head. Then he pulled the arm back to look at his watch. "What time is it? I feel like I've been asleep for years."

"It's around three," she said even though he was looking at his watch. "I hate to wake you, but I need to go get the girls and I didn't want you to wake up and find out I was gone. Do you want to go with me or do you want to stay here and sleep?"

He was already sitting up. "I'll go with you," he said, groggy, running his hands over his face as if to rub the sleep from his mind. "I'll get dressed and we can go."

She grasped him as he staggered up. "Slow down," she told him. "We've got some time."

He just winked at her and teetered his way into the bathroom as the towel Blakesley had put around his waist when he first got out of the bath fell off onto the floor. Blakesley watched his naked buttocks as he entered the bathroom and shut the door, disappointed when her peep show was cut short. The man had an amazing ass. In fact, she'd spent the past four hours watching him sleep and had come to the conclusion that pretty much everything about him was amazing. That was becoming increasingly evident.

Beck was dressed and wide awake in little time, taking the time to wash his face and at least make an attempt to clean up. He bought a caffeinated energy drink from the hotel's vending machine as they left the lobby and passed their way out to the parking lot. The day was moderately hazy with fairly mild temperatures, not entirely out of character for the bay area of San Diego, with the air smelling heavily of pungent carob trees.

Blakesley drove, letting him relax in the passenger seat and down his drink. He commented on the traffic, the weather, and mentioned that he felt the need to go to Sea World because he had missed out on the other day. He liked the whales. Blakesley grinned at him, feeling his big hand affectionately on her shoulder as they made their way from Hotel Circle Drive along the 8 Freeway to the San Diego Zoo, about four miles away. By the time they reached the zoo, he was wide awake and making dinner plans. Blakesley just went along, thrilled to be listening to him, whatever the subject.

They pulled up to the zoo's entrance with its big zoo sign and lush landscape where Cadee, Crosby, Charlotte and Nikki were waiting. A sea breeze was bending the eucalyptus trees, scattering leaves. When Blakesley put the car in park to load the girls up, Beck climbed out of the car and the two younger girls went crazy.

Beck found himself surrounded by two very happy little ladies. Charlotte held one of his hands and Crosby held the other as they told him about the zoo. They liked the monkeys in particular because the monkeys would smell their own butts. They laughed hysterically about that. Blakesley and Nikki loaded up the car with the stroller and diaper bag as Charlotte showed Beck her scraped knee, which got his immediate sympathy. Crosby wanted to know if he was sympathetic enough to buy them ice cream, but according to Blakesley he wasn't.

Disappointed, Crosby climbed into the car after Cadee as Blakesley secured Charlotte in her car seat. Homely and over-weight Nikki was very quiet and shy when introduced to Beck, and she climbed into the back 3rd row seat with the stroller and diaper bag for company as Blakesley started up the car and off they went.

Beck was very definitive where he wanted to go for dinner but since it was only three in the afternoon, the girls simply weren't hungry yet. More than that, Charlotte had missed her nap and she was growing very grumpy. Blakesley made the call to go to the house so the girls could see it, and also so she could see how successful the contractor had been in clearing out the fireplace in the family wing. It would kill some time and give the girls a chance to see their new home.

The contractors were just starting to pack up when they pulled into the long, tree-shrouded driveway. There were squirrels running around on the overrun grounds, and Cadee and Crosby were excited as they spied the rodents. Charlotte had fallen asleep in her car seat and when Blakesley pulled the car to a stop in front of the mirror-image wings, Nikki volunteered to stay with Charlotte. Cadee and Crosby gladly bailed out of the car along with Blakesley and Beck. Crosby ran towards the public wing while Cadee walked up calmly beside her mother and held her hand.

"Crosby!" Blakesley called after her daughter. "Stop when you get to the front door!"

Crosby, curly blond hair waving behind her like a banner, streaked across the driveway, the rocky yard area surrounding the public wing, and came to a halt on the very old porch. She hung all over the old, rusty wrought iron banisters that hugged the exterior staircase.

"Mommy!" she yelled. "Where does this go?"

She was pointing up the stairs. "Up to some rooms," Blakesley told her. "Get off the banisters, please. They're very dirty."

Crosby climbed off but not right away. She lingered just to reinforce to her mother that the woman couldn't tell her what to do. Beck watched the spunky little girl, trying not to grin at her, as he followed Blakesley and Cadee to the front door. Just as Blakesley opened the front door, the contractor was heading out.

They nearly ran into each other and Blakesley jumped out of the way, startled. The contractor, a great big man in his late fifties with a big mustache and belly, laughed.

"Sorry, Ms. Masterson," he said. "I didn't hear you."

Blakesley waved him off. "No harm," she said. "Did you get the fireplace unplugged in the other wing?"

The big man nodded. "Unplugged and partially repaired," he said. "We rewired the chandeliers in the big hall today. All in all, we got a lot done today. Go see for yourself."

Blakesley smiled happily. "I will."

"See you tomorrow."

"Okay, thanks," Blakesley waved at him as he continued on to his truck.

The open door screamed "come in" to Crosby, who darted into the public wing and disappeared. Blakesley let go of Cadee's hand and darted in after her.

"Crosby Anne!" she called. "Come back here now."

They could hear giggling somewhere back in the maze of rooms. Beck, following Cadee into the house, wriggled his eyebrows when Blakesley turned around and gave him an exasperated expression. He grinned.

"I'll see if I can find her," he said, pushing past her and Cadee.

Blakesley watched him go, taking Cadee's hand again, her one obedient child, and went into the giant hall to see to the newly repaired chandeliers. She could hear Beck's soft, firm voice calling for Crosby and the little girl's high-pitched giggles. Blakesley took a moment to pause and listen, thinking that Ed Masterson had never shown such interest in his girls. The man had provided well and had shown up appropriately at school plays or parent nights, but he'd never truly shown the makings of a caring or considerate father.

They were qualities that Beck most definitely had. It endeared him to her all the more and the man took on another dimension in her eyes. With a smile reflective of her thoughts, she trusted Beck to corral Crosby and went to inspect the repaired chandeliers.

Corral was an appropriate term. In fact, Beck was thinking he needed a lasso as Crosby darted in and out of rooms, hiding beneath old desks and then emerging on the other side and running away. In truth, it was very cute and very funny, and Beck figured she couldn't really get into any trouble if he had her within his sights. Crosby was a handful, no doubt, with her mother's porcelain features and lively personality. The little girl ran into a smaller room that had an outlet into a larger room that flanked the main hall, so Beck casually doubled back into the larger room and waited for her to emerge. She did and ran straight into him.

Beck hauled her up, gigging and squirming, and carried her upside-down into the main hall where Blakesley and Cadee were. Blakesley was peering up at the old antique chandeliers when she heard them coming, smiling when she saw how Beck was holding her daughter. He righted her as he came to a halt next to Blakesley, setting the little girl gently to her feet.

"Thank you," Blakesley said to him, then looked at her squirrely daughter. "No more running away, okay?"

Crosby just grinned, an impish gesture with her two missing front teeth. She was holding Beck's hand, twisting around impatiently. "Okay."

"Promise?"

"Uh uh!"

Crosby suddenly fell to her hands and knees and crawled in between Beck's legs, rabbiting towards the back of the house. Giving Blakesley a wink, Beck calmly but swiftly took off after her. He pursued her into the room off the big hall, hearing her over in the room on the southeast corner of the house, the one that they used to keep horses in with great double doors that had long been nailed shut to prevent exterior access.

Quickly, he ran around to lock the second door that led off into the room with the two old iron cells. It was the only other way out of the room. Then he came back around to the open door leading into the horse room and as he stood there, he could hear her giggling. She was evidently hiding from him so he just stood there, getting a fix on her position based on her giggles. It was like radar, a talent that had served him well in his chosen profession. Beck had the hearing of a bat.

"What are you doing?" Blakesley was suddenly standing beside him. She alternately looked up at Beck and into the darkened room. "Where is she?"

Beck put a finger to his lips in a silencing gesture. He pointed to a corner that had what looked like an old tack closet built into it, with ragged doors hanging slightly ajar. There was movement inside.

"I don't know what happened to Crosby," he said loudly. "I can't find her."

Blakesley grinned; she was on to his game. "Poor Crosby," she said dramatically. "I guess she's lost in this big house. We'll never find her now."

"Too bad," Beck lamented. "Who am I going to eat ice cream with?"

Blakesley fought off the giggles. "Well, I hope she likes it here," she said loudly. "I'm going to miss her. But she really needs to watch out for the toe-eating bunnies."

Beck looked at her, a smile on his lips. "Toe-eating bunnies?" he repeated. "That sounds scary."

"It is scary," Blakesley agreed. "There are bunnies that live in the cupboards and closets in the house and they like to nibble on the toes of naughty little girls. I forgot to tell her that."

Beck was grinning by now. "I don't think I like that," he said, looking to see if the tack cabinet was still moving. "Do you think they'll nibble on her?"

Blakesley nodded firmly. "Absolutely," she announced. "The only way they won't is if she's a very good girl and doesn't run from her mother."

Beck was close to laughing and he pressed his lips together, struggling not to chuckle, as the tack closet suddenly burst open and Crosby jumped out.

"You're kidding, Mommy," she announced, a big grin on her face. "There are no bunnies in the closet."

Blakesley leaned confidently against the doorjamb. "How do you know?"

Crosby was very sure of herself as she danced around over by the tack closets. "Because the bunnies won't bite me!"

"Why not?" Blakesley wanted to know.

"Because!" Crosby insisted. "They...!"

Her daughter was there and in the next second, she was gone. The old floor gave way and Crosby fell through, down into the dark oblivion.

EIGHT

STARTLED, Beck rushed forward with Blakesley on his heels, dropping to his belly as he came near the hole in the floor. He held out a hand to the terrified mother.

"Stop," he told her. "Stay there in case this floor gives way some more."

Blakesley did as she was told but she was in a panic. "Crosby!" she cried. "Baby, can you hear me? Are you all right?"

Beck very quickly inspected the floor around the hole before he inched forward, just to make sure he wouldn't fall through as well. He could hear Crosby whimpering down in the hole as he stuck his head in.

"Crosby?" he couldn't see a thing; it was pitch black. "Honey, are you okay?"

Crosby suddenly let up a big wail. "It's dark!"

"Are you okay?"

"I wanna get out!"

Beck began looking around for a way to lowering himself into the hole when he noticed what looked like old wooden slats built into the side of the hole, like ladder rungs. It began to occur to him that, perhaps, this wasn't just a freakish hole beneath the house but something more structured. It was odd and startling.

"I'm coming," he told her, sliding his big body over to the side of the hole where the rungs were. "Hold on. I'm coming down to get you."

Blakesley moved from her spot several feet away, rushing to Beck as he moved for the edge of the hole.

"What are you doing?" she asked.

He could hear the fear in her voice. "I'm going down to get Crosby," he told her, his manner professional and no-nonsense, but he realized how that must be coming across to her so he softened. He had a tendency to sound harsh. "It's okay, baby. She's conscious and talking, and she doesn't sound like she's too far down, so I'm just going to go down and get her, okay?"

Blakesley nodded, total fear yet total trust in her eyes. "Okay."

Beck winked at her but simultaneously pointed a finger at her. "You and Cadee stay back," he told her. "Are there any flashlights around here?"

Blakesley shrugged anxiously. "I don't know," she said, her tone bordering on tears. "I think I have one in my car."

"Can you please go get it?"

Blakesley nodded again, taking Cadee fearfully by the hand and racing from the room. Beck heard their footsteps fade away as he very carefully began to lower himself into the hole.

"Crosby?" he called down to the child. "Did you hurt yourself?"

He could hear her crying softly. "I bumped my knee," she wept.

Beck very carefully lowered himself onto the old ladder, old slats of dusty wood that had to be a hundred years old. They also appeared well-used, piquing his curiosity as he began to carefully test his weight on them. They seemed sturdy enough so he was willing to take the chance because he had to get down to Crosby. Even if he had to jump, he was going to get to her.

The wood creaked dangerously under his weight as he made his way down. Dust and the smell of cold, damp earth surrounded him. But he was also very curious. He could see that the walls had been carved out and the hole itself was about four feet or more in diameter, definitely not a natural phenomenon. Someone had taken the time to carve this out, so along with the uncertainty, he was feeling some fascination.

"Crosby?" he called again because he wanted her to know he was with her. "Talk to me, baby. Did you hurt anything else when you fell?"

He could hear her sniffling. "No," she wasn't sobbing anymore but she was very unhappy. "Is this where the bunnies live?"

Beck grunted softly, thinking that his and Blakesley's stories to scare Crosby into obeying were about to backfire.

"No, baby," he said softly. "The bunnies don't live down here."

"Are they going to bite my toes?"

"I promise, they're not down here," he told her. "Nobody is going to bite your toes."

Surprisingly, he hit the ground after only about ten or so feet. It was very dark except for light from the hole above and he looked around, spying the blond little girl just a few feet away. He went to her, kneeling down beside her. Before he could check her for any injury, she jumped up and threw her arms around his neck. Beck picked her up and held her.

"It's okay," he comforted, rubbing her little back. "I'll get you out of here."

"I don't like the dark." She squeezed his neck fearfully.

"I know," he soothed her. "I'm going to take you out right now."

"Beck?" Blakesley was calling from above.

He turned in the direction of the open hole. "Down here."

"Is Crosby okay?"

"She seems to be."

"Can I come near the hole?" she asked.

"Carefully."

After a couple of moments, he could see Blakesley's face peering down at him. "I found a flashlight," she said.

"Toss it down," he told her. "Try not to nail me in the head with it."

He heard her giggle as an object came flying down, missing him by inches and thumping against the ground. With Crosby in one big arm, he bent down to pick up the flashlight and turned it on.

A whole new world opened up in the white beam of the LCD flashlight. A tunnel branched off from the bottom of the hole, disappearing in darkness. There were old boxes and tools and other unidentifiable objects lining the walls of the tunnel, covered in dirt and cobwebs, and decades of oldness.

Surprised and curious, Beck shined the flashlight on the walls of the mouth of the tunnel, seeing all sorts of words and engravings, like people had lived down in the depths and scrawled out their thoughts and feelings. He got an overall impression of eeriness as he inspected a few of the passages, words such as "diablo" and "muerte" being recognizable. Almost everything he could see was written in Spanish.

In all, he only took a few seconds inspecting his surroundings because he had a five-year-old clinging to him, but his brief inspection was enough to feed his curiosity. It was also enough to feed his sense of caution and foreboding. He wasn't sure he was comfortable with any of it.

Backing up towards the old ladder, he looked upward to see Blakesley looking down at him.

"I'm going to bring Crosby up," he told her.

Beck began to deftly climb the old ladder with only one free hand. He held Crosby tightly against him with the other. Blakesley positioned herself at the top of the ladder, listening to the floorboard groan and praying they wouldn't give way as she held her arms out for Crosby. Beck lifted the little girl up to her mother as he drew within range and Blakesley scooped the child up, holding her fast as she scurried away from the hole. She was gone from the room when Beck pulled himself from the hole.

He found Blakesley sitting on the staircase by the entry, holding Crosby and rocking her gently. Crosby was crying again, cuddled up against her mother, as Beck stood over them both for a moment before crouching down and putting a big hand on Blakesley's shoulder.

"Is she okay?" he asked. "I didn't get a good look at her. It was pretty dark down there."

Blakesley's nose and mouth were buried in the top of Crosby's blond head. She looked up at Beck, the bluish-green eyes watery with emotion.

"She seems to be," she confirmed. "No broken bones or big bleeding wounds. I'll get her back to the hotel and into the bath and get a better idea."

He smiled, squeezing her shoulder before putting the same hand on Crosby's blond head.

"You sure you're okay, honey?" His smile broadened when their eyes met. "You took quite a fall."

Crosby wiped at her wet eyes, smearing dirt on her face. "Y-yes," she sniffed. "Are you sure you didn't see any bunnies?"

Blakesley looked confused as Beck shook his head and squeezed her little hand. "No bunnies, I promise." He stood up, looking at Blakesley. "Maybe we should take the girls back to the hotel for now. I think Miss Crosby has had a big day."

Blakesley nodded, standing wearily until Beck reached out and took Crosby from her. He cradled the little girl as Blakesley followed him out into the late afternoon sunshine. As they neared the BMW, they could hear Charlotte's high-pitched voice. Beck opened up the door and Charlotte practically threw herself out.

He had a good grip on Charlotte as her mother came to the rescue, putting the little girl back in her car seat. As Charlotte fussed, Beck put Crosby into the car and snapped on her seat belt.

"You take the girls back," he told Blakesley. "I'll follow in my truck."

Blakesley finished with Charlotte and turned to Beck. "I'm going to have Nikki take them back," she said quietly. "I want to see what that hole is all about."

He shook his head at her. "I'm not sure that's a good idea," he replied. "You should probably call the City or the Fire Department

and have them check it out. That hole was purposely built underneath that floor and more than that, it had a tunnel that branched
off from it. I'm not exactly sure, but it seemed to me that it ran off
in the direction of the canyon behind the house."

Blakesley's eyebrows lifted. "Seriously?" she gasped. "Could
you see anything? I mean, what did it look like?"

"Like an old tunnel with loads of old stuff cluttering it up," he
replied. "You may even want to call a museum. It looked like a treasure trove down there."

He could tell, just by the look on her face, that she wasn't going
to leave the house before she saw it and he knew that, very shortly,
he'd be back down in that hole. It was just a hunch he had.

"I really want to see it," she half-demanded, half-pleaded. "I'll
send the girls back with Nikki and we can take a quick look.
Please? If this is under my house, where my girls are going to live,
then I really want to see what it's all about."

He knew better than to argue. He was coming to see that
Blakesley Thorne was very determined in most aspects of her life
and not one to take no for an answer. It was a rather diva quality
but, truth be told, he didn't really care. He liked her that way. After
a moment, he puffed out his cheeks and sighed heavily.

"All right," he agreed. "Send the girls back and we'll take a
look."

She lit up with a bright smile. "Awesome."

He pointed a finger at her. "But just a quick look," he insisted.
"And I want you to stay with me, okay? It could be very dangerous
down there and I don't want either of us getting hurt. Agreed?"

"Agreed."

He wasn't sure he believed her but he did the gentlemanly
thing and didn't dispute her. Blakesley handed her car keys over to
Nikki and told the young woman to take the girls back to the hotel
and get them into the bathtub. Nikki pulled out of the driveway,
very carefully, driving like a grandma as Blakesley and Beck
watched the SUV slowly pull out onto the road and disappear.
When the car vanished, Blakesley turned to Beck.

"Can we take a look now?" she asked.

He nodded, going back over to his big Chevy half-ton pickup and unlocking it. He dug around in the utility box behind the front seat until he came up with a flashlight of his own. By the time he turned around, Blakesley was gone and he ran back into the public wing, nearly running her over when he found her just inside the front door messing around with her flashlight. As it was, he bumped into her and she staggered from the force of his momentum.

"Hey." She pretended to frown at him as she adjusted the flashlight. "Slow down, slick."

He grinned, his hand on her arm to both steady her and keep her from getting away. "Sorry to say that I don't trust you, but I don't."

Her frown was real. "What do you mean?"

"I mean that you'll pretty much do as you damn well please and end up in that hole no matter how much I tell you to be careful." When she opened her mouth to argue, he simply pulled her against him and kissed her soundly to shut her up. "You're a bossy, stubborn and determined woman, but I kind of like that."

She grinned up at him, all wrapped up in his big arms. "It takes one to know one."

He met her grin. "I've got forty men under my command who jump when I say jump." He rubbed his nose against her, gently. "I have a feeling I know four women who won't jump when I give the word."

She laughed softly, her arms going around his neck. "That's not true," she insisted. "Maybe we will sometimes. Once in a while. Or not."

It was his turn to laugh and he kissed her again, a couple of times, softly and sensually. "I don't care if you do or you don't," he whispered. "You just tell me how high you want me to jump and I'll do it without question."

She made a noise that sounded a lot like a purr and slanted her lips over his, kissing him with power and passion. Beck picked her up and she wrapped her legs around his waist, holding fast to him as tongues tasted and lips suckled. They were losing control again, as they had in the kitchen, but this time, Blakesley put on the brakes. As Beck began to fondle her breasts, she pulled her mouth away from his.

"Not now," she breathed, although his hands on her breasts were heating her up. "It's not that I don't want to, but there are bigger priorities right now."

He was unbuttoning her white blouse, his mouth on the swell of her cleavage. "Bigger than this?"

His words were muffled against her flesh. "Yes," she insisted, although weakly. He was moving on her nipples and she knew that once he did that, all would be lost. "I'd really like to see the hole and then get back to the hotel to make sure Crosby is all right."

He sighed heavily and came to a halt. He had just managed to pull her bra away from her left breast and the rosy nipple was inches from his mouth. He could see it and nearly taste it. But her words had some impact on him.

"Sorry," he murmured. "I got carried away."

She smiled at him as he still held her breast, his mouth very close to her nipple. "That's okay," she insisted. "I don't mind. But we'll find time for this later and give it the attention and respect it deserves. Crazy, passionate sex in the kitchen is excusable once, but twice, it's just opportunistic and cheap. Like that's all we care about."

He looked rather pained by her words and let go of her breast, the green eyes full of distress. "Oh, my God, you're right," he hissed. "You're absolutely right. The first time... it just all happened so fast. I just wanted you so badly but to do it where we did it... in a kitchen like that, on the floor... I'm so sorry, baby. That wasn't respectful at all, was it?"

She kissed him, pulling her bra and blouse back over her exposed breast. "It was an amazing experience and one I don't regret," she told him quietly. "But you and I aren't in this just for spontaneous sex wherever or whenever we feel like it, are we?"

"Hell, no."

"So we need to show some self-control and give that kind of intimate display the seriousness it deserves. It means something deep to me and I hope it means something deep to you."

"Of course it does," he kissed her and lowered her to the ground. "I'm really sorry. It's just that when I taste you, I just can't help myself. Something about you just makes me lose control."

She grinned. "There's no reason to be sorry," she said. "I feel the same way you do."

He smiled, somewhat reluctantly, and kissed her again as she took his hand and led him back towards the room with the big hole in the floor. He held her hand tightly, still feeling guilty that he had been so willing to make another cheap display of sex but thankful she had righted his senses. He struggled to focus on the task ahead of them and not on his lack of self-control with a woman who clearly overwhelmed him.

Blakesley let go of his hand when they entered the room with the big hole over near the tack closets. She stood back, eyeing the unsteady scene, as Beck took several steps into the room and crouched down to better inspected the floor. It seemed to him that it was leaning somewhat, like the hole in the floor had created a big sinking point that dragged down the rest of the flooring, so he wasn't too sure that more of the floor wasn't about to give way. He sighed heavily.

"Baby," he turned to look at her. "I'm just not comfortable with this. Everything in this room looks unstable to me and I just don't think it's safe."

She stood by the door, taking his words seriously because it looked to her, too, like everything in the room was tilting towards the hole.

"I don't disagree with you," she said, "but I'm afraid that once I call the City about this, they'll block off this entire wing while they study this and I may never get to see what's underneath. They'll have it all sectioned off for study for God knows how long. You know this house is a historical landmark, so the State of California is going to get involved, too. Everything in that hole belongs to my family. I'd really like to see what's down there before I'm kicked out and never get to see it again."

He sighed again, looking back to the hole before rising to his feet. "Okay," he said reluctantly. "But you stay with me, and you hold on to me, and you do exactly what I tell you. Okay?"

She nodded and walked up behind him, holding his hand tightly. He gave her a wink and squeezed her hand and, very carefully, led her towards the gaping hole.

It was still daylight outside but the sun was beginning to set. Since the electricity wasn't live in this room, there were no lights to turn on so they fired up their flashlights. Beck went to the side of the hole with the ladder on it, taking a good look at the edges of the hole before putting his foot on the first rung of the ladder.

"It looks like this room wasn't built on a raised foundation," he said, shining the flashlight around the hole. "If you look at the edges of this hole, you'll see packed earth beneath the floor with the exception of this pit."

She was holding on to him as he began to descend. "So this entire room isn't about to collapse?"

He shook his head. "Now that I can see what's under the floor, I don't think so."

"But it looks like it's leaning."

"I know it does, but I don't think it's going anywhere."

Beck took four or five rungs before holding his hand up and helping Blakesley find her footing on the ladder above him. Another five rungs and he was on the floor of the pit. He took Blakesley by the waist when she was halfway down, lifted her up, and set her on the floor beside him.

Blakesley shined her flashlight around the surrounding pit, noting the crude dirt walls that still looked like they had pick marks on them. Awed, she timidly put her hand against the side of the pit.

"Wow," she breathed softly. "Somebody dug this out."

Beck was already shining his flashlight down the tunnel. "They sure did," he said softly. "With picks and shovels and who knows what else. The question is why?"

The smell, the dankness, was starting to creep over Blakesley as if only now noticing it. They were deep in the earth, like a grave, and although she wasn't claustrophobic, she really didn't like the sense that they were buried alive. She pondered Beck's statement on her family's history, searching for a logical answer when a thought suddenly occurred to her.

"Remember what Old Mike said?" she said, her hand on the dirt wall. "He said that there was a room dug into the side of the canyon, where people back in the old days would hide from Indians. Maybe this tunnel is part of that safety system."

Beck stood at the mouth of the tunnel, shining his bright, white light into the murky darkness.

"Maybe," he said quietly, then held out a hand to her. "You wanted to look so let's go look."

Blakesley took his hand and followed him to the tunnel entry. She was spooked and curious, excited and wary. As the beam of her flashlight fell on the wall, she could see the Spanish writing etched into the earth. She was instantly fascinated.

"Oh, my God," she gasped. "What is this?"

He looked at what she was indicating and took a closer peek. "I saw this when I pulled Crosby out of here earlier."

"It looks like Spanish," she said, trying not to get her fingers all over the writing but understandably curious. "I don't really know Spanish. Do you?"

He nodded. "Part of my job is to be multi-lingual because we deploy in so many different countries. Every man on my team knows at least one other language. My languages are Spanish and Tagalog."

Blakesley was looking at the scratching on the wall. "What does it say?"

He shined his flashlight on the faded writing, scratches in the hard-packed earth wall, blowing away the years of dirt that had settled. After a moment or two of studying the words, he looked unsettled.

"Oh, brother," he sighed. "You're not going to like this."

She looked concerned. "Why not?"

"Because from what I can see, it says 'camino del pinche'."

"What does that mean?"

He looked at her. "Road of the Damned."

Her eyes widened. "Seriously?"

"Seriously."

She looked uncomfortable as she began to look around, as if expecting devils to come jumping out of the walls. "Why would they call it that?" she wondered.

He shook his head. "I have no idea," he said. "Do you still want to have a look down the tunnel?"

She nodded, although with less enthusiasm than she had shown earlier. "Just a quick look," she said uneasily.

He squeezed her hand. "Quick enough," he said, shining the flashlight down the pitch black passage. "Watch your footing as you walk. There are things all over the ground."

Blakesley fell in behind him, shining her light at the floor and seeing all sorts of implements tucked up against the walls. They were rusted and dusty, like a thousand years old, and she received an overall impression of being caught in a time capsule. It was like people had just dumped stuff and left, ghosts from times past when the West was truly wild. There were old crates, shovels, bits and pieces of what looked like forks or knives, old lanterns, and then she suddenly came to a halt. Her eyes widened.

"Look," she pointed to the wall. "Is that an old rifle?"

Beck saw it, kneeling down to take a better look but not touching it. He inspected it closely, the shape of the barrel and the firing pin. He blew on it, blowing off decades of dust, and took an even closer look.

"I'll be damned," he finally shook his head. "It's a Winchester Model 1885 single-shot rifle."

Blakesley peered at it. "Really?" she said, surprised. "Do you know much about them?"

He shrugged. "Maybe a little more than most," he said. "Weapons are kind of my thing. This rifle was manufactured between 1885 and 1920, but this one looks like one of the first models ever made because of the full barrel and the high walls on either side of the hammer. Can you see it?"

Blakesley had no idea what he was talking about but she nodded as he pointed, smiling at him when he looked at her with a happy grin. It was a neat little treasure.

"That's really cool," she said, looking around. "It makes me wonder what else we'll find down here."

Beck stood up, clutched Blakesley's hand, and continued very slowly down the tunnel. The ceiling was fairly low, so he kept hunched down to avoid hitting his head. The beam from the flashlight danced along the walls, the white LCD stream hitting the old and dank walls. There was more writing on the walls as they moved further back and Beck paused to read what he could of it. Most of it was scratches, bits of words he couldn't make out and nothing particularly organized, but there was one passage that he could make out down near the floor. He could see the deeply carved words and he bent over, shining his light on it.

El hombre malvado,
yo maldigo el día que conocí usted y le puedo y su familia
nunca sabe un momento de la paz sobre esta tierra.
Pueda todos sus almas son maldecidas.

Blakesley had initially been watching him read but was distracted by something on the dirt floor reflecting the weak light. She let go of his hand and crouched down beside it.

"Oh, my," she gasped. "Look at this."

Beck turned from the words on the wall to see that she had a pair of eyeglasses in her hand, old-fashioned, with the lenses remarkably still intact. He crouched down beside her.

"That's pretty amazing," he said, looking at them as she put them in the palm of her hand. "The lenses are still intact."

She was looking at the wire frames closely, the faded silver color. "How old do you think they are?"

He shook his head. "I have no idea," he replied. "Pretty darn old, I'd say."

Blakesley was still looking at them. "What does that passage say on the wall?"

Beck was kind of hoping she wouldn't ask that. His green-eyed gaze moved to the carefully etched words buried deep in the earth. He debated how much to tell her but opted for all of it because, at some point, someone might translate the entire passage and he didn't want her to become upset with him for not being entirely truthful. He sighed heavily.

"This is another one of those doom and gloom passages," he told her.

She looked up from the glasses. "Why? What does it say?"

Beck looked at the writing. "Well," he grunted, standing up. "Loosely translated, it says, 'Wicked man, I curse the day I knew you and may you and your family never know a moment of peace upon this earth. May all your souls be damned'."

Blakesley's jaw dropped and she stood up next to him, the glasses still in her hand. "Are you kidding me?" she exclaimed softly.

He looked at her. "It would be easier if I was. My first inclination was to lie to you just so it wouldn't scare you."

She put her hand on his arm sincerely. "I'm glad you didn't lie," she said. "I didn't mean it the way it sounded. I didn't mean to question your honor."

He bent over and kissed her on the forehead. "I know you didn't," he looked back at the words. "But, I have to tell you, this whole tunnel is getting creepier and creepier."

She nodded fervently. "No joke," she looked around. "Where do you think this tunnel ends up?"

He shrugged. "Like I told you earlier, it leads off to the east towards the canyon but I have no idea what's at the other end. It could be caved in for all we know."

Blakesley shined her flashlight back the way they had come, seeing the faint light from the floor hole in the distance. "Maybe it was an escape tunnel that led to the canyon," she said. "Why else would it be here?"

Beck's flashlight was shining in the opposite direction, looking into a dark hole with debris cluttering the way. "Any number of reasons," he said. "It could be a smuggler's cave, or built for storage, or maybe an escape route like you said. I'm sure there are experts who can tell us for sure."

She nodded. "I'll call the City in the morning and let them know about this."

Beck nodded in agreement, but it was absently. His vision was locked on to something against the wall of the tunnel about twenty feet away, something that looked like a pile of clothing or bags. It was a big, dirty lump crumpled against the wall. It took him a moment to realize that there were a pair of pants and a coat dressed on something he initially thought was a mannequin. Gradually, he realized it wasn't a mannequin; it was a body. He could see a skeletal hand protruding from one of the coat sleeves.

Startled, Beck positioned himself so he was blocking Blakesley's view; he didn't want her to see it, whatever it was. His heart began to race and his palms started sweating.

"Seen enough?" he asked her as casually as he could. "We should start heading back."

She didn't sense his change in demeanor, completely oblivious to his edgy expression. "Okay," she sighed, holding up the hand that still held the old spectacles. "What should I do with these?"

He wanted to get the hell out of the tunnel. "Just take them with you," he told her, turning her around for the pit. "You can show the girls and tell them about your adventure."

Blakesley let him turn her around and gently guide her back

the way they had come. She was still looking at the glasses, fascinated by them, as they passed the rifle propped against the wall. She pointed at it.

"Do you want to take that?" she asked. "Do you think it's valuable?"

He looked at the dusty old weapon. "I'm sure it's valuable from a historic standpoint," he said, trying to get her moving without shoving her. "We should probably just leave it there and let the experts handle it."

Blakesley nodded and continued on, seemingly in no hurry to leave while Beck was doing all he could to keep her moving and prevent her from backtracking. Just as he opened his mouth to bring up the subject of dinner, a huge booming sound came from back behind them coupled by a great and unearthly howling.

The noise shook Blakesley right out of her skin. Terrified, she screamed and bolted for the pit, flying so fast that Beck lost his grip on her. Last he saw she was already in the pit and heading for the crude ladder. As a trained military man, and Special Ops at that, Beck didn't run. He turned to face whatever it was, balling his fists and preparing for a fight. He held the flashlight steady as he inspected the depths of the tunnel for the source of the sound but didn't see anything. In fact, it all looked suspiciously still and he cautiously made his way back into the tunnel.

The booming sound came again, followed by more howling and banging. Flotsam from the ceiling floated down in the beam of the flashlight but Beck didn't waver as he moved further back into the tunnel, passing the skeletal corpse without even looking at it. There was debris scattered around him but he didn't take his eyes off the flashlight beam to look around. He was more concerned about who was making the tremendous noise. More than that, he wasn't going to back down. It wasn't in his nature.

The mystery monster was now starting to make a ruckus. Dirt was flying in great clouds and there was a lot of banging going on. Beck just kept walking, his flashlight beam fixed on the area back in the tunnel where the sounds were emanating from. There was more debris back here, an old dresser and a very old Grandfather clock covered in dust and cobwebs.

Everything smelled of damp and oldness. It was like an antique trove, but Beck wasn't distracted. He was on a mission. The noise grew closer and he eventually walked right into the source.

NINE

OLD MIKE WAS BANGING up a storm in the darkness. He had been so busy slamming things around that he didn't see Beck until it was too late. Even though it was nearly pitch-dark in the beam of the flashlight, Beck swooped in on the old man and grabbed him, pinning him up so he couldn't move. Mike tried to kick and swing his fists, but he was no match against Beck's strength and experience. The old man grunted angrily.

"Hey!" he yelled. "What are you doing? Let me go!"

Beck had the old man's back against his chest, arms pinned to subdue him. "I've got a better question," Beck fired back. "What are you doing?"

"I live here!" Mike spat. "I told you I lived in the canyon!"

"This isn't the canyon," Beck said. "This is a tunnel that leads under the house. Is that something you made use of, maybe to spray-paint walls or break stained glass windows?"

Mike was squirming. "I didn't do that," he insisted. "I don't go back in that tunnel!"

Beck didn't like the answer and began lugging the old man back the way he had come. "Sure you don't," he said sarcastically. "You just about scared the crap out of Miss Thorne, so I'm going to let you explain to her what you were doing down here."

Mike grunted and twisted but he was no match for Beck. Beck hauled the old man back down the tunnel, hitting his broad shoulders a couple of times on the narrow tunnel walls. Mike howled as he was pulled further back into the tunnel.

"Don't come back here!" he yelled. "Don't you know it's cursed?"

Beck just lifted his eyebrows at the ramblings of the old man. He continued back into the tunnel, finally emerging into the pit. The setting sun provided enough light into the room, and into the pit, that Beck was able to see his way up the old ladder with a combative captive in hand. He literally had old Mike by the scruff of the neck, pulling the old man up with him as he emerged into the darkened and abandoned room.

Blakesley was nowhere to be seen. With the old man now in a choke hold, Beck called for her.

"Blakesley?" he called out. "Where are you?"

He heard a faint response so he emerged from the pit room into the big hall, dragging Mike with him and seeing Blakesley standing far down the building by the front entry. In the dim light, he could barely see her. As he came near her with his unwilling prisoner, she ran to him.

"Oh, my God!" she exclaimed as she saw Mike. "So it wasn't a monster down there after all?"

Beck shook his head, letting the old man go as he reached Blakesley. Actually, he sort of threw the man down and Mike ended up in a heap at Blakesley's feet. Furious, rubbing his neck, Mike looked up at the two of them.

"You didn't have to do that," he scolded Beck. "What's wrong with you, hurting an old man like that?"

Beck was in professional mode and in no mood for a mouthy old man. "Shut it," he pointed a finger at him. "Now, I want you to apologize to Miss Thorne for scaring her to death. Do it or you'll be very sorry."

Mike believed him. Lord howdy, he did. He looked up at Blakesley, his expression between defiance and submission.

"I... I didn't know it was you," he said. "I thought... maybe it was someone come to rob me."

Blakesley opened her mouth but Beck cut her off. "That's not an apology," he growled.

Mike didn't like his tone and he looked fearfully at Blakesley. "Sorry I scared you."

Beck bent over to apparently intimidate the old man even more, but Blakesley put her hand on his shoulder, pulling him away from Mike. She put herself between Beck and the old man.

"What were you doing down there?" she asked.

Mike felt better with her doing the talking. "That's where I live."

"In a tunnel?"

He shrugged. "I don't live in the tunnel," he said frankly. "That's a cursed place. I live in the room by the canyon."

Blakesley still wasn't clear on what he meant, but one thing he said caught her interest. "Cursed?" she repeated. "What's cursed?"

"The tunnel," Mike repeated. "Don't you know it?"

Blakesley shook her head. "No," she said, half-fearfully. "Why do you say it's cursed?"

Mike's dark eyes took on a strange glitter. "Because of him," he said. "He used to keep people down there that he wanted to disappear, or worse. He used to do his business down there."

He wasn't making any sense and Blakesley put up her hands to slow him down. "Wait a minute," she said. "Who are you talking about? Tell me the story from the beginning because you're not making any sense."

Mike sighed heavily, calming now that Blakesley had called off the big, blond man. He shifted on the floor, moving to the bottom stair of the ceramic-tiled staircase and planted himself. He seemed to be pondering her question.

"Don't you know anything about this house?" he asked. "You bought it – somebody should have told you."

Blakesley was trying to follow him but not liking what she was hearing. "This house has been in my family since it was built," she said. "The builder was my great-grandfather several times over. I know he was the marshal in the early days of San Diego and...."

Mike waved her off. "Ben Earp was an outlaw. Don't let no one tell you different."

"Why?"

"Because he was a mean man who bootlegged whisky, robbed stages, ran a saloon full of prostitutes, and then would murder people who tried to stop him." He pointed at Blakesley in a matter-of-fact sort of way. "Ben Earp came out here back when the Mexicans still had California. He married a local Mexican woman and he was like a big bandito in this area. He was the law but he only enforced it if there was something in it for him. Otherwise, he'd shoot you just as soon as look at you."

Shocked, Blakesley looked at Beck. He met her gaze, not sure what to say to her. He could see how uneasy she was as she turned back to Mike.

"Who told you that?" she demanded.

Mike shrugged. "Everybody knows that," he said. "Read your history. You'll see. Ben Earp was a bad man."

"I know my ancestor and from what I know, he was just the town marshal. I never heard or read anything about him being an outlaw."

Mike cocked an eyebrow. "Do you think your family would have told you he was bad? That makes them all look bad, including you. You need to read the history of San Diego and find out what Ben Earp was really like."

Blakesley didn't have a swift answer for that so, lacking the ability to do verbal battle on the subject, switched the focus. "Why do you say the tunnel is cursed?"

Mike settled in for a good, long story. " 'Cuz," he went on. "My grampa told me this story and he got it from his grampa, who knew Ben Earp personally. It's not just the tunnel that's cursed, but the whole house. The whole family, too. Seems that Ben Earp stole from the wrong person and his family has been cursed ever since."

"Who did he steal from?"

"Bouchard started it," Mike said frankly. "He was a pirate who used to sail around California back in the old days. Have you ever heard of him?"

Blakesley shook her head but Beck piped up. "I have," he said quietly, looking at Blakesley. "He was a big pirate back in the days of the missions."

As Blakesley nodded in understanding, Mike continued. "Back in the old, old days when Bouchard sailed around, he got a hold of some cursed gold down in Mexico somewhere. Some say it was Aztec gold stolen by the Spanish, and the Aztecs put a curse on it. So ol' Bouchard goes through a big string of bad luck and someone tells him it's the gold that's causing it. Well, sailors are a superstitious bunch, so Bouchard dumps the gold off at the San Diego mission. The padres were glad to get it until they started suffering their own bad luck – restless Indians, drought, famine. You can look in your history books and it'll tell you how badly the mission suffered during that time. Anyway, the padres start figuring out that Bouchard's gold is the cause of all their misery, 'cuz it all started when the pirate gave them the gold, but being good men they didn't want to just give it to someone and put the curse on them. Still, they had to get rid of it."

Blakesley was hanging on every word. "So what did they do?"

Mike scratched his nose casually. "They all knew that Ben Earp was corrupt and a thief. Nobody in town liked him but they were all afraid of him, including the padres. According to my grampa, the padres made it easy for Ben to steal the gold. They let him know they had it, where it was, and ol' Ben slipped in one night and took it. That way, the padres are rid of it, Ben's got the stolen gold, and the curse continues with him."

Blakesley looked a little stunned by the story. "But that doesn't explain why you said the tunnel is cursed."

Mike threw a thumb back in the direction of the pit. "Because that's where ol' Ben kept his ill-gotten gains, including that cursed gold," he said. "Ben would keep people he didn't like down there, chained up like in a dungeon. Once, he kept a wealthy Mexican down there and ransomed him to his family, but the man didn't live to see daylight again. He died down there. You see his writings all over the walls."

Blakesley was seized with uneasiness, with some sorrow. "Is he the one that wrote about the road of the damned?"

Mike nodded. "That's what it is. That tunnel was the road to hell for some." As Blakesley struggled to absorb what he was telling her, Mike continued on. "Now, I'm curious. What's your relationship to Ben Earp?"

Blakesley was clearly distracted and uneasy. "He's my great-great-great grandfather," she said. "My mother was an Earp."

"Mollie or Kelly?"

She was instantly suspicious. "How do you know that?"

Mike shrugged. "Because I knew the Earp girls," he said. "My family has been in San Diego as long as yours. Mollie and Kelly were real dolls back in the day."

Blakesley's suspicious stance eased. "My mother was Mollie," she said. "She passed away last year. That's why the house is mine now. I bought it from her."

"Hmpf," Mike grunted thoughtfully. "Sorry to hear that. But she never told you about the Earp Curse?"

Blakesley shook her head. "No," she said. "She never talked much about her family, really. I just know the lineage and our relationship to Wyatt, but not much else. I just got the impression that there wasn't a whole lot to tell."

Mike's dark eyes were fixed on her. "So you didn't know?"

"No."

He took a thoughtful breath, looking around the structure as if the walls could confirm his story. "Has your family had a run of bad luck?"

She thought on his question, fear creeping into her veins as she pondered the deeper implications. "Well," she started off slowly. "My mother was killed by a drunk driver. We've had our share of illnesses, financial ruin, and things like that. My aunt's home in

San Diego burned down twice before they decided not to rebuild and moved to Las Vegas. And then there's me...."

She stopped, not wanting to go any further. She was starting to feel very uneasy and incredibly depressed. Beck, increasingly resistant to Mike's wild stories, stepped in before things got out of hand.

"Your stories are entertaining, I'll give you that," he said. "But curses are a bunch of bullshit, so don't waste any more of her time with that kind of crap. What we need to focus on is figuring out where you're going to live. You can't live in that hole anymore, so I suggest you start figuring out where you can go."

Mike looked stricken. "I don't have nowhere else to go," he told Beck. "I've lived in the canyon for twenty years."

"Not anymore," Beck said firmly. "There's some homeless shelters downtown. I'll call and see if the Salvation Army has room for you."

Mike jumped to his feet. "I don't want to go!" he said. "You can't make me!"

He suddenly bolted from the room, racing back towards the room with the pit. They could hear him banging around in the increasing darkness. Beck started to follow but Blakesley stopped him.

"No," she had him by the arm. "Leave him alone. I don't care if he stays here tonight. I'll call social services tomorrow and see if we can't get someone out here tomorrow to take him and his belongings out of here. But for tonight... just let him be. I don't want a big battle on my hands tonight."

Beck immediately backed down, taking one of her hands into his big, warm palm. He didn't agree with her but respected her decision. "Okay," he conceded reluctantly. "So what do you want to do now? Are you ready to get out of here?"

She nodded, somewhat subdued. "I am," she sighed. "I guess I just need to go back to the hotel and digest all of this."

Beck had her hand as he led her towards the front door. "You're not taking all of that curse crap seriously, are you?"

She shrugged weakly. "It would explain a lot."

"Including me?"

She looked at him, his impish smile, and broke into soft laughter. "No, baby, not you," she pinched his cheek affectionately. "You're the best thing out of all of this."

He was glad he had been able to lighten her mood. He didn't want tales of curses and outlaws clouding her up. Moreover, he was looking forward to spending the evening with her because he honestly didn't know what would happen tomorrow when he reported to work. There were some things heating up, things he couldn't talk about, and he suspected he might be deployed again fairly soon. He didn't want anything to wreck this night.

The sun was nearly down by the time he led her from the structure and secured the old, big lock. He wasn't even sure why he was locking the place considering old Mike could come and go as he pleased through the jagged pit in the floor. Still, he locked it up and took Blakesley's hand as he walked her over to his truck. He opened the door for her, like a gentleman, and then climbed in the driver's seat and took off.

Although he didn't look at her, he could see Blakesley turn and watch the house fade in the distance as they drove off. He knew her mind was still working on curses and Wild West stories.

The truth was that his mind was kind of working on them, too.

TEN

CROSBY HAD a big bruise on her left butt cheek that Blakesley wouldn't let her show to Beck, for obvious reasons. She also had scraped palms and a scrape on her knee, which she eagerly showed Beck and received the hoped-for sympathy. It even earned her a spot on his lap and she sat happily, demanding his attention and mostly getting it.

Arriving at the two-room hotel suite around dinner time, the girls were already bathed and in their pajamas. Blakesley knew that Beck wanted to take them out to dinner, a notion he quickly quelled when he saw that the three little girls were already ready for bed. He suggested they order pizza but the hotel suite had a kitchenette with a two-eye stovetop and oven, and Blakesley offered to cook. Beck didn't argue with her. He was just glad to be spending the time with her, no matter what they were doing. In fact, he was rather looking forward to a home-cooked meal. He couldn't remember when he last had one.

The evening quickly morphed into an oddly domestic situation, something Beck hadn't experienced in over four years. He went with Blakesley to the market, following her around while she purchased chicken and asparagus, and other goodies for the girls. He would casually walk behind her as she pushed the cart up the aisles, bending over to kiss her neck or pat her butt when no one was around. She giggled, swept away with his flirting, feeling extremely lucky to be with him. She hadn't enjoyed such flirting in years and wasn't hard pressed to admit she had missed it. Beck seemed to bring it out in her and she responded to him without reserve.

So they flirted and charmed their way through the market and after they put the groceries back in the car and climbed in to return to the hotel, he pulled her into his arms and kissed her ferociously. Blakesley turned herself over to him completely, not giving any thought to the fact that they were making out in the supermarket parking lot. Eventually, Beck forced himself to pull away, groaning reluctantly when she turned the car on and backed out of the lot. His eyes drifted over her great figure, her full breasts, and he had to look away because he could feel himself growing aroused. The woman had an overwhelming effect on him and he was loving every minute of it.

He helped her with dinner as much as he was able, but the truth was that she was very efficient in the kitchen and he eventually sat back with Crosby and Charlotte on his lap and watched her cook. Nikki bustled around setting the coffee-table with place settings and helping with little tasks, freeing Beck up to just watch Blakesley as she worked.

It was a hugely settling and comforting feeling to be with her, watching her prepare dinner, holding two little girls on his lap who poked at his nose and then screamed with delight when he pretended to bite their fingers. He couldn't have hoped for anything more divine. He also realized, with increasing fear and excitement that he would give everything he owned to be able to come home to Blakesley and the girls every night. He had told her once he would never marry again because he couldn't do that to someone he loved. Now he wasn't so sure.

When the chicken, rice and asparagus dish were done, he carried Crosby and Charlotte out to the living room where Nikki had set up their dinner table. Crosby didn't want to be put down, however, and neither did Charlotte, so he ended up sitting on the floor with a little girl on each knee, trying to eat around them. Blakesley had tried several times to remove the girls but they had put up such a fuss that Beck told her to leave them alone. Blakesley sat down next to him while Cadee and Nikki sat across the table.

Blakesley hardly ate any of her meal. She was too busy watching Beck with her daughters, little girls whose own father had been so absent in their young lives. Charlotte fed Beck pieces of asparagus, dropping more on the carpet than she was actually getting into his mouth, while Crosby stuffed her face with chicken and bounced up and down on Beck's big knee. It warmed Blakesley's heart hugely to watch Beck with her girls, finding herself more and more enamored with the man. He was so gentle and sweet with them, and that touched her deeply.

"You obviously have a way with little girls," she complimented, smiling when he looked up from his food. "How often do you see your daughter?"

He opened his mouth to speak but Charlotte pushed a piece of asparagus in it. He laughed and thanked her before refocusing on Blakesley.

"Not often enough," he said quietly. "Her mom took her to San Francisco when we divorced, so I don't see her often at all. We email back and forth all of the time, but it's just not the same."

Blakesley shook her head sympathetically. "You said she's fourteen?" she cocked her head. "Is she in high school yet?"

He nodded, shoveling rice into his mouth. "She's a freshman," he told her. "She's a member of the French Club, a math genius, and has a boyfriend, which I'm not too happy about."

Blakesley fought off a grin. "She's got to grow up sometime, Dad."

He was focused back on his food, which Charlotte was trying to commandeer as her own. "I haven't seen her much in the past four years," he said, somewhat glumly. "I guess I still see her as that ten-year-old who cried herself sick when her mom and I divorced. It's hard to see her as a young lady."

Blakesley stroked his arm comfortingly, removing Charlotte's spoon from his rice in the same movement.

"Are you planning on seeing her this summer?" she asked. "Maybe you can fly her down here and take her to Sea World. You've been wanting to go."

He shrugged. "My schedule is so dicey that it's difficult," he said. "I could fly her down tomorrow but if I'm suddenly called away, I can't just leave her on her own. My best chance of seeing her is if I take a couple of days and just go up to San Francisco."

Blakesley was stroking his arm. "You can bring her down here to visit and if something happens and you get called away, I'll watch out for her and make sure she gets on a plane home."

He looked at her, surprised. "You would?"

She smiled. "Of course."

He was seriously considering it. "That's a really generous offer," he said. "Are you sure you wouldn't mind?"

She shook her head. "Of course not," she insisted. "You can just introduce me as a friend of the family. I'd be happy to look out for her if you can't."

He just stared at her. Then, he lifted Charlotte and Crosby off his knees in succession, setting the girls down in front of their plates. He stood up as they started to whine and looked at Blakesley.

"I need to talk to you outside," he said in a low voice. "Right now."

Curious, not to mention slightly concerned at his tone, Blakesley left the girls with Nikki and followed him out into the hall. It was still and quiet in the corridor as he faced her.

"Look," he held out his hand as if grasping at his thoughts. "I'm going to say this here and now since you brought it up. I don't want you to be a friend of the family."

Blakesley's brow furrowed. The way he said it and the tone in which he said it had her totally misunderstanding him.

"Sorry," she said defensively. "I'm not sure what you thought I meant, but I wasn't trying to... oh, forget I even said anything.

I'm sorry I did. I was just offering to help you see your daughter."

He realized she had misinterpreted him and he grasped her by the wrist. "Blakesley, baby, that's not what I meant at all," he could see he had offended her and he was trying to pull her to him as she struggled to pull away. "I just meant that you're more than a friend. I don't want you to be just a friend. I want you to be much more than that."

She stopped struggling although her expression was still guarded. "What do you mean?"

He lifted her hand and kissed her fingers. They tasted like asparagus. "Baby, I love you," he murmured. "You know I love you. I don't want to be with another woman as long as I live. I only want to be with you."

She was cooling down, coming to understand what he meant. "Okay," she replied slowly, although still unsure what he was driving at. "I love you, too. That's why I was offering to help you see your child."

His jaw ticked and he took her other hand, pulling her against his big torso. It was clear that there was much on his mind.

"I guess I should make myself clear," he said gently, looking her in the eye. "When people ask me if I'm seeing someone, I want to tell them that I am. If they ask me if I have a girlfriend, I want to say that I do. I guess I'm asking your permission to say that."

A smile spread across her lips. "You have it."

He grinned in response, genuinely happy and relieved. "Thank you," he said sincerely. "I don't want to see anyone else, not ever."

"Good."

"I don't want you to see anyone else, either. We're together, just you and me. Is that clear enough?"

She laughed in understanding. "You had that commitment when you asked if I would be your girlfriend," she said. "No worries, Beck. I don't want to see anyone else, either. I just want to see you."

His grin grew and he kissed her, wrapping her up in his big

arms. He hugged her tightly, feeling happier than he had in years. He felt like he was walking on clouds.

"I was thinking something else," he said. "Your house isn't going to be ready for weeks, even months, especially now that we've discovered that tunnel. I'm not comfortable with you and the girls living there. That house is so old and God only knows what else is running underneath that house. I want to make sure it's completely safe and repaired before you and the girls move in."

He was being very cautious, very protective, and she appreciated that but she wasn't sure where he was going with it.

"Okay," she said as if she were waiting for him to say more. "So what do you want me to do?"

He was holding her tightly against him, gazing down into her big, bluish-green eyes. "I was thinking that I could rent a bigger house for all of us," he said quietly, almost hesitantly. "Someplace that was safe for the girls and some place where I could come home to you... you know, a place for all of us to live. Together. We could live there together and I can watch over all of you, at least until your house is finished."

He was starting to ramble, as if fearful of the words even as they came out of his mouth. She was very touched by his suggestion but she was also very torn.

"That's so sweet of you to think of us," she said sincerely. "But don't you think it's a little soon for us to be talking about moving in together?"

He sighed faintly. "Yes," he agreed, "but the truth is that I can't stand the thought of being away from you, or going home tonight and sleeping alone. I... I'm just so happy, Blakesley. I've never felt like this in my life. I want to come home every night to those little girls who cling to me and want to know if sharks can smile or why I wear a watch with a whole bunch of different numbers on it. I deal with so much death and sorrow, and you and your girls make me see the beauty in life. It's the greatest thing I've ever experienced."

She was watching him with tears in her eyes by the time he was finished. "That's so sweet," she murmured, blinking away the tears. "But... I really need to think about things, Beck. I have my children to think of and I need to make their lives as stable as possible right now. You have no idea what they've been through. If it were just me, there would be no question, but I have my girls to think about. I hope you can understand that."

He nodded, although it was clear that he wasn't happy. "I wouldn't do anything to disrupt or hurt them, I hope you know that," he said. "I... I guess I fell in love with them, too, the first time Crosby coerced ice cream from me, the moment I pulled Cadee out of the water, and the moment Charlotte asked me if I'd play Barbies with her. I fell in love with all of you, Blakesley. I've spent so much time training myself not to feel emotion that when I do feel it, it overwhelms me."

She wrapped her arms around his neck, leaning her forehead against his chin. He kissed her forehead, her temple.

"I do understand," she whispered. "Believe me, I do. The girls and I have spent years dealing with murder trials and conflict like you can't even imagine. Charlotte has never really known her father. She was only a year old when he was arrested. She really doesn't remember him, and when I see how she's bonding with you, it touches me more than you know and I feel like there's hope for all of us. Please... just give me time to think about all of this. It's all happening so fast and I just don't want to make a bad decision."

"I understand. I'm not happy about it, but I understand."

She smiled up at him, kissing him sweetly a couple of times but pulling away before things got heated. They grinned at each other in the dark hall as she put her hand on the door. Things were moving fast and hot, and they were both struggling to keep a clear mind about it. Still, neither one of them could deny the joy of the situation as two lonely people found love again.

Beck followed her back into the suite where Charlotte and Crosby had finished everything on his plate. Beck went to his empty plate, gave the girls an exaggeratedly shocked look, and pretended to cry. That brought on loud laughter from the little girls who proceeded to jump back onto his lap when he sat down again. Grinning, Blakesley went back into the kitchen and put more food on his plate, pulling the girls off of him so the man could eat in peace.

Tired from a day at the zoo, Charlotte and Crosby turned into cranky monsters as their mother pulled them into one of the bedrooms and then emerged a few moments later with blankets and teddy bears. Then she sat on the couch with both girls in her arms, all wrapped up in their blankets and toys, and began to hum to them.

Beck watched her as he ate, her sweet manner with the children, the gentle rocking motion and soft singing. It was so sweet to watch. Although Cadee was too old for that kind of comfort, she climbed on the couch and sat next to her mother as a brightly colored cartoon danced across the television screen. Beck finished his dinner watching Blakesley and the girls settled down for the night.

Nikki cleared up the table and washed the dishes. Beck offered to help her but she was so shy and terrified of him, he ended up giving her a wide berth because she was so skittish. He went to sit on the couch on the other side of Cadee, sitting back and watching the animated cartoon also.

Cadee, the most reserved out of the three girls, gave him a wide-open curious look now that her sisters weren't jumping on him and demanding his attention. Her big, bluish-green eyes drifted over him, inspecting his shirt, his pants, his boots. She took the time to digest everything about him because she was very deliberate like that.

"Why are you in the Navy?" she finally asked.

He looked down his right shoulder at her. "Because I wanted to serve my country and help people."

She thought on that a moment. "Have you saved other girls from the water like me?"

He smiled. "No, not like you," he told her. "You're special."

"Why?"

He shrugged. "Because you're just about the prettiest little girl I've ever seen. I couldn't let anything happen to you."

Cadee pondered his statement. She seemed much more introspective and somber than her two younger sisters. "Do you go away a lot when you're in the Navy?" she asked.

He nodded, shifting so he was more turned towards her. "I do," he said. "I go all over the world and help people."

"But you come back."

"I always come back."

Cadee's expression grew serious. "My dad went away but he's not coming back," she said frankly. "I don't want you to be our friend if you're going away and not coming back."

On Cadee's other side, Blakesley frowned and opened her mouth to scold her daughter but Beck silently waved her off. This was between him and Cadee. He could tell that, from the beginning of their association, she had been stand-offish from him. Even though he had essentially saved her life, she wasn't going to make it easy for him like her sisters had. Now her feelings were starting to come out. He made sure he was looking her in the eye when he spoke.

"I understand that your dad went away," he said quietly. "But he went away for different reasons. I go away for my work but I always come home again."

Cadee didn't back away from him. She continued to stare up at him, studying him. "My dad said he'd be back, too, but he won't," she said. "He went to prison because he did something very bad. He made my mom cry. She cried all the time, like when the people came to take the house and when the police came a lot. I told my dad not to come back because he just made my mom cry. You better not make her cry, either."

It was a fairly bold threat from an eight-year-old but Beck took it seriously. "I swear I would never intentionally do that, baby girl," he said sincerely. "Your mom is very special to me just like she's special to you. I would never hurt her and I would never make her cry, I swear. I think you're a pretty special girl to be so concerned for your mom like that."

Cadee thought about what he said, turning to look at her mother and seeing that there were tears on her face. Blakesley had both arms wrapped around her other daughters and couldn't spare a hand to wipe them away. Cadee was very deep and very protective of her mother, a big burden for an eight-year-old girl. It was hard for Blakesley to hear Cadee express her fears to Beck.

"Well...," Cadee's gaze lingered on her mother before she turned back to Beck. "As long as you don't make her cry, I guess it's okay if you're our friend."

Beck smiled faintly. "Thanks," he said sincerely. "I'd really like to hang around with you girls. I miss my own daughter so it helps me not be so sad all the time."

"What's your daughter's name?"

"Elizabeth," he told her. "Elizabeth Beatrice Seavington, but we call her Lizzie."

"I heard you say that she lives in San Francisco."

He nodded. "She does."

"And she has a boyfriend?"

Beck made a very comical, very unhappy face. "Yes," he muttered.

"Does her mom have a boyfriend?"

Beck was a little taken back at the blunt question. "She has a husband. She married him last year."

Cadee turned to look at her mother. "Are you going to marry my mom, too?"

Beck took a deep breath and grinned nervously. "I just met her," he said. "It's a little early to ask that question, I think."

Cadee turned those big, bluish-green eyes on him. "But you like her, don't you?"

"I like her a lot."

"So don't people get married when they like each other a lot?"

"Cadee," Blakesley had all she could stand. She had to stop her nosey daughter before Beck was backed into a corner. "Stop with the questions. It's time to get ready for bed."

Cadee shrugged and climbed off the couch. Smiling, Beck watched her disappear into the bedroom, turning back to Blakesley and wiping his hand across his forehead in mock relief.

"Sheesh," he muttered. "I feel like I've just been given the third degree."

"I'm sorry," Blakesley whispered because the girls in her arms were now asleep. "She doesn't say much but when she does, everything comes spilling out."

Beck thought back on what Cadee had said, especially the part about people coming to take the house away and cops coming to the house a lot. He was starting to understand just how bad things had been for Blakesley and the girls over the past couple of years and his heart ached for them.

"Don't be sorry," he said, his green eyes lingering on her. "So you lost your house?"

Blakesley nodded after a brief hesitation. "Ed's legal bills drained everything," she explained. "I had separate assets and on the advice of my lawyer, kept everything separate even when the house went into foreclosure. Everybody asked me why I let the house go and the best I could do was explain to them that the house only had bad memories for me. I wanted to let it go. I wanted to get my girls the hell out of there and away from everything that house represented."

He nodded his head faintly. "There's nothing wrong with that."

Blakesley wriggled her eyebrows, almost ironically. "My parents thought so," she said. "They couldn't understand it, especially when I offered to buy the house down here from my mother's family. I just felt like I needed to get back to my family roots and start fresh."

"Did the house cost you a lot?"

She hugged Charlotte to still her when the little girl stirred in her sleep. "It sits on two acres of prime San Diego land," she told him what he could already figure out. "My mom's sister really wanted a lot of money for it. It was her son living in it, renting it, and she wanted the money for him. The home was appraised for almost three million and that's what I paid for it. Ironic considering my cousin trashed the place even though the money I paid for it was going to him to buy him a new place to live. What an ass."

Beck's eyebrows lifted. "Three million?" he repeated. "I've never known anyone who paid three million for anything."

She smiled faintly. "Don't tell your friends that your girlfriend is a cash cow, okay? I don't want to find the entire base of Coronado Island at the house sponging off of me."

He laughed. "Nobody is sponging off of you, especially me," he said firmly. "In fact, I'll buy dinner tomorrow for everyone, okay?"

She smiled over the top of Charlotte's sleeping head. "Don't you like my cooking?"

He stood up, his gaze warm on her. "I love it," he said, "but you really need to let me pay for some things, okay? You're going to give me a complex."

She just smiled up at him as he stood over her, looking at the little girls in her arms. "Want to help me with these two?" she asked.

He nodded, reaching down to scoop up Crosby. "Be happy to," he grunted softly as he held the little girl against his chest. He nodded his head in the direction of the bedroom where Cadee had disappeared. "In there?"

Blakesley stood up next to him, cradling Charlotte. "In there."

Beck hadn't tucked a child into bed in years and he wasn't hard pressed to admit he had missed it. There was one big king bed in the room and a fold-away couch, which Nikki slept on, so all three little girls were put into the big bed and covered up. Cadee was still awake when her mother tucked her in, her big eyes gazing up at her mom.

"What are we doing tomorrow?" she asked.

Blakesley kissed her daughter on the forehead. "I'm not sure," she whispered. "Maybe we'll go back over to the new house for a while."

"I want to go to the beach."

Blakesley lifted her eyebrows. "You do?" she shrugged. "Well, I suppose we could."

Cadee looked over at Beck, who was standing at the end of the bed. "Will he go, too?"

Blakesley glanced back at Beck. "If you want him to."

Cadee was still looking at Beck. "I guess so."

Beck could sense her hesitation, still, and he put his hand up. "I've got to work tomorrow, so don't worry about me. You ladies have fun at the beach."

Cadee didn't say anything as Blakesley kissed her again and stood up, turning off the light. Bidding Nikki a good night, she and Beck went out of the room and shut the door. They wandered into the living room area with its nondescript couches and still-running television. Beck sat first and pulled Blakesley down onto his lap.

"Alone at last," he whispered with a smile, pulling her close.

Blakesley returned his smile, wrapping her arms around his neck and hugging him tightly. Beck held her close, nuzzling her neck, allowing himself the freedom of no reserve, no doubt, in what he was feeling for her. His day had started out with concern and fear for what might or might not be happening between them, so the ending to the day was more than he could have hoped for.

Just as he pulled away from her neck to kiss her on the lips, he caught sight of a little body standing next to them. Startled, he found himself looking into Cadee's big eyes.

The little girl was staring at him. She hadn't even looked at her mother, all curled up in Beck's lap. She was looking right at Beck.

"You can come to the beach with us if you want to," she said. "Will you teach me to swim like you do so you won't have to save me anymore?"

He smiled at her. "I really do have to go to work tomorrow, but if I get off in time, I'll come to the beach and teach you to swim like I do. Okay?"

Cadee nodded, looked at her mother, and then turned away. But suddenly, she turned back around again and put her arms around Beck's neck, hugging him. It was as if all of the fight suddenly drained out of her and she needed and wanted that comfort.

Beck pulled her up onto his lap, too, holding both Blakesley and Cadee in his big arms. Blakesley, one arm around Beck and the other around her daughter, smiled at him over the top of Cadee's blond head. He winked at her.

They put Cadee back into bed and closed the door again, returning to their couch. The first thing Beck did was turn off the television and pull Blakesley down onto his lap again as he sat. She curled up on him, her arms around his neck, pausing to breathe in the quiet stillness of the room with just the two of them. He leaned against the back of the couch, cuddling her, relaxing and feeling the peace. It was the first day in a week that he'd been able to experience it.

Blakesley didn't say anything as she lay against him, hearing his heartbeat loud and steady in her right ear. He seemed very content just to lay there and hold her, and she was content to let him. But soon enough, he began to snore and she lifted her head, seeing that he had fallen dead asleep. She knew how exhausted the man was so she very carefully began to climb off his lap. He stirred immediately.

"Where are you going?" he demanded groggily.

She leaned over and kissed him. "You're exhausted," she whispered. "You have two choices; either you sleep on the couch or you drive home and go to bed. What's it going to be?"

He rubbed at his eyes, trying to wake up. "Neither," he told her. "I want to sit here with you. I haven't seen you in a week."

She smiled. "You'll see me tomorrow," she said softly. "You need to sleep, Beck. I don't know what crazy stuff you've been doing this past week, but it's very clear that you've got some kind of sleep deprivation. You need to go to sleep."

He sighed heavily. "I really want to just hang out with you tonight."

She kissed him again and he pulled her down against him, kissing her hungrily. "We'll see each other tomorrow." She was trying to pull away from him but she wasn't doing a very good job. "Are you going to go home?"

He shook his head, his mouth devouring her lips. "No," he said, his lips against hers. "I'm going to stay here until you kick me out."

She laughed, her arms going around his neck as his hands began to roam. This time, Blakesley didn't stop him. In little time, they were in her bedroom with the door closed and Beck took his time with her. Every stroke, every kiss, every touch meant something. Emotion he hadn't let himself feel in years was spilling out all over the place and he couldn't stop it. Her flesh was sweet and her body incredibly responsive, and he took her twice before midnight. It was the best night of his life.

They fell asleep together, cuddled up, but he woke up before dawn and dragged himself into the living area and fell back asleep on the couch. He didn't want three little girls getting up and finding Mom in bed with her new friend.

He woke up three hours later to a three-year-old trying to put Cheerios in his mouth.

ELEVEN

"SO... did the two dozen roses work?"

It was about nine in the morning. Beck looked up from the dispatch he was reading on his iPad to see Butch standing next to his desk, grinning. Anthony was standing slightly behind Butch, a smirk on his face. The question had come from Anthony and Beck took his focus away from the iPad screen.

"They did," he replied. "Thank your florist guy again the next time you see him. They worked like a charm."

Anthony's grin grew. "Good," he said. "So what happened?"

Beck couldn't help the smile creeping onto his lips as he set the iPad down and leaned back in his chair.

"She's a very special lady," he said discreetly. "That's all I'm going to tell you."

Butch looked at Anthony. "Look at his face," he said confidently. "He got laid."

Anthony chuckled as Beck gave Butch an intolerant look. "I spent yesterday with her and her girls, she cooked dinner, and here I am." He pointed a finger at Butch. "And if you go around telling everyone I got laid, I'm going to lay *you* out, maybe permanently. Keep your mouth shut because this isn't a cheap one-night stand."

Butch's face lit up. "You *did* get laid!" he exclaimed. "Congratulations, Beck. When's the wedding?"

Beck looked disgusted as he turned back to his iPad. "I've only known her a week," he said flatly. "She's sweet and wonderful and, like I mentioned before, way too good for me, but she seems to like me anyway. I feel like the luckiest man on earth and I won't let you make fun of me for it."

Butch was still smiling as he sat on the edge of the big, metal desk. "I'm not making fun of you." His joviality eased considerably. "I'm serious. I'm really happy for you, you know that. Also, I was curious about your lady-friend so I looked up the Hollyhock Murder like you mentioned. She really went through all that?"

Beck looked up at him. "I don't know anything about it. I've purposely not done any research on it. If she wants me to know, she'll tell me. I feel like I'm prying into her business if I look it up."

Butch could see his point, sort of. "I think it would be better if you knew what you were getting in to," he said quietly. "You know you're my best friend, Beck, but I have to tell you, the Hollyhock Murder was pretty crazy. Your lady-friend's ex-husband is a pretty bad dude."

In spite of his declaration of not wanting to pry into Blakesley's business, Beck found himself interested. "What do you mean?"

Butch shrugged. "He was some big shot restaurant owner and the celebrities went to all of his restaurants," he replied. "The article I read said he hooked up with one of his waitresses and had an affair. The girl had a cocaine habit according to what I read, and he got hooked into that also, you know, paying millions of dollars for drugs and all that. Turns out that his mistress had ties to the Colombians, so the guy got roped into doing drug deals out of his restaurants and using the businesses as a money laundering front. Anyway, when the woman wanted to make the affair public, he killed her and got caught. What I read said that the Colombians made a couple of unsubstantiated attempts on your lady-friend's life so she couldn't testify against her ex even though the cops said she didn't know anything about his drug dealings. She didn't tell you any of this?"

Beck was staring at him, shocked. "Not a word," he said. "Like I said, she will when she's ready to."

"Does it give you second thoughts about hooking up with her?"

Beck shook his head definitively. "It makes me want to go to Colombia and kill every goddamn bastard associated with the drug cartel. Did you read anything about continued threats against her?"

Butch shook his head. "No," he said. "It was really just a sentence about it and not much more. You'd have to ask her if there's been anything else."

"I'm not going to ask her anything. When she's ready to talk, she will."

Butch watched him turn back to his iPad again. He could sense the man's angst about it so he let it go and changed the subject somewhat. "So when do we get to officially meet her?" he wanted to know.

Beck wouldn't look at him. "I don't know," he said. "I'm trying not to rush this. If I bring her around here and introduce her to you, I feel like I'm pushing way too fast. I don't want to scare her off."

Butch wouldn't be put off. "Can I at least invite you and her over to dinner?" he asked. "Gina is dying to meet her."

Beck glanced up at him. "Maybe," he said. "Just give me a week or two and let us get to know each other a little more. Coming to your house for dinner is a big step. We're hanging out at the beach over by the Del this afternoon, so just give me some room to work, okay?"

Butch slapped him on the shoulder and stood up from the desk. "Whatever you say," he said, noticing that Beck was fairly interested in the dispatch he was reading. He pointed to the iPad. "What's going on?"

Beck sighed faintly, reading the confidential report, debating how much to tell them before they were fully briefed by the entire team's commanding officer, Captain Davis. Each S.E.A.L. team was divided into three troops, consisting of anywhere from forty to sixty men each. Each individual troop consisted of a Troop Commander, which happened to be Beck for his particular group, a Troop Senior Enlisted Officer, which was Butch, a Targeting/Operations Officer, and a Chief Petty Officer, which was Anthony Solis.

There were all sorts of different officers, enlisted and other specialized personnel that could make up the teams, including Combat Service Support, Administrative Support, Operations, Intelligence, Communications and so on, but Beck's particular team was tightly configured and very specialized in their area of expertise – rescue land ops, assault craft boarding and rescue.

Beck's kind of work didn't have a lot of prep time because it was usually, with rare exception, something that had less than a twelve-hour notice. His team was a true first response team to hostage or hostile situations, usually going in hot and heavy, and usually with massive resistance. Some teams had the luxury of weeks or months of planning; Beck's team did not.

Which was why the luxury of the dispatch Beck was reading was something unusual. They had advance notice of an enemy operative on a Navy frigate heading for the Panama Canal who, according to Intelligence, was planning on detonating explosives in the canal. It sounded cheesy and like something out of a bad James Bond movie, but it happened to be extremely serious. Disabling the Panama Canal could be catastrophic for Navy vessels deployed from San Diego en route to the Atlantic and all points east. It was a very big deal. Intel suggested it was an al-Qaeda operative, which made matters worse. Worse still, evidence pointed to a dirty bomb, which would be devastating.

Beck opted to tell Butch and Anthony all of what the dispatch said. The subject of Blakesley was forgotten as they shifted to work-related issues. Captain Davis joined them about a half hour later and the entire team was briefed on the situation with the frigate. An NCIS team would be joining them for the op, basically Navy cops, and it would be Beck's team's responsibility to board the frigate, locate the operative, and disarm any explosives that might be on the ship. They still weren't entirely sure there was anything actually on the ship, but they couldn't take the chance that somehow, someway, al-Qaeda had actually infiltrated the Navy.

Speculation was that this had been in the works for years with a mole and wasn't because some enlisted swabby had been bribed or coerced to participate. It was further speculated that San Diego had been targeted because bases like Norfolk on the east coast were so heavily watched. The terrorists were shifting focus from the east coast to the west.

The frigate had sailed two days before and would be at the Panama Canal in another two. That gave the S.E.A.L. team twenty-four hours to meet the ship and board it before it entered the canal. They would be departing at nine o'clock that night for a flight down to Panama where they would meet the ship at sea. After that, it was anybody's guess as to how dicey this mission would become. It threatened to be a big one.

Beck was all business as they went about making preparations for the trip down to Panama, but the truth was that he was aching inside. He didn't want to leave Blakesley again, not so soon, but he had no choice. They had known about this for a couple of weeks now, whispers on the rumor mill, and now it had become fact. This was what they trained for and what they got paid for.

Still, his heart sank. Come hell or high water, however, he was going to see Blakesley before he left. He had things he wanted to discuss with her. But before he did anything, he had a phone call to make.

———

The day had turned out surprisingly hot, the third day in a heat wave that only seemed to be getting worse. It was a perfect beach day, with hot white sands and pounding blue surf. Blakesley, Nikki and the girls had returned to the beach on Coronado Island near the Hotel del Coronado, mostly because the girls liked the beach and Blakesley liked the fact that it was near the naval base.

Blakesley sat in a beach chair beneath a bright blue and pink umbrella. She was spread out on a big blanket, with colorful towels strewn about, with the sea breeze lifting the tassels on the umbrella. She was reading an Elliot Jentry novel, a great romance set in the bayous of Louisiana, as Nikki and the girls played a few feet away, building a sand castle for the Barbies that Charlotte had brought. Cadee was reluctant to get near the waves, so Crosby and Nikki kept running down to the water's edge, scooping up water and sand and bringing it back for the girls to build with.

At noon, Blakesley took the girls over to the B & S Bar inside the hotel and ordered a couple of club sandwiches to take out. All Charlotte wanted was strawberries and French fries, so she got that, too, plus a smoothie for Nikki and cookies for Cadee. She ended up with quite a feast and took it back out to the beach where the wind blew and the seagulls screamed overhead. The moment she unpacked the sandwiches and the girls began to eat, the gulls landed nearby and kept moving in closer, waiting for the chance to steal some food.

When lunch was over, Charlotte fell asleep on the shaded blanket but Nikki, Cadee and Crosby went back to castle building. Blakesley covered up her sleeping daughter with a towel and sat back on her chair, relaxing as Cadee and Crosby decided that they needed to build a new castle and razed the old one. They kicked it down as Nikki tried to talk them out of it. Just as Blakesley was getting back into the book, a shadow fell over her legs and warm lips gently kissed her cheek.

Startled, she looked up to see Beck smiling at her. He threw his big body onto the blanket beside the chair, stretching out and getting comfortable.

"Hi, baby," he greeted. "I've been up and down this beach looking for you."

Blakesley put the book down, very happy to see him. "Are you finished?"

"For the time being."

"Do we get to have you for the rest of the day?"

His smile faded. "For the rest of the afternoon, at any rate," he replied. "Did you girls eat yet?"

She nodded. "We did." She pointed up to the hotel. "But we can go inside and get you some lunch if you're hungry."

"I hate to be a pain, but I'm starving."

Blakesley smiled at him and called over to Nikki to tell her she would be gone for a few moments. Beck pulled her up off the chair and began to walk with her over to the hotel, her hand tucked tightly in his. Blakesley was in the pink bikini he'd first seen her in, with a sexy flowing sarong around her waist. Beck kept glancing over at her, distracted and aroused by all of the flesh she was showing. In her sunglasses and big hat, she looked divine and he was swept away with the vision. He'd never been so proud in his life to be with someone, which made the prospect of leaving her all that more heartbreaking.

They made it into the same bar where Blakesley had gotten the sandwiches earlier and she talked him into sitting down and eating in peace. They sat on the patio, she with a diet drink and him with a big, fat burger. They sat close to each other as he ate, discussing the call she had placed to the City of San Diego earlier in the day about the mysterious pit and tunnel at the house and also the calls she had made to the renovation contractor telling him to seal off the room until the City got up there to check it out.

Beck heard all about the engineers that were heading up there later in the afternoon to assess the hole and the archaeologists from the State of California that were flying down from Sacramento. Blakesley seemed excited about it. He was sorry he was going to have to miss it. Just as he was finishing his burger, he heard a familiar voice come from behind.

"Hey, Beck." Butch walked up behind him, slapping him on the shoulder. "Funny seeing you here. I swear I can't get away from you."

Beck wiped his mouth and looked up, rolling his eyes when he saw Butch and Gina standing next to their table. Obviously, they couldn't wait to meet Blakesley and Butch and his wife had done some recon of their own. Beck cocked an eyebrow at his friend, thinking he should have never told the man where he would be spending the afternoon.

"Hey," Beck replied, although by his tone it was evident he wasn't happy to see Butch. Beck indicated Blakesley. "Blakesley, this is Butch Aguirre and his wife, Gina. Butch and I work together."

Blakesley smiled happily at the pair, shaking their hands in succession. "It's really nice to meet you," she said. "Have you guys eaten? Do you want to sit down?"

Butch was sitting before she even got the words out of her mouth, pulling out a chair for his petite, round and dark-haired wife. "Thanks," he said. "We just came down here for lunch and I saw Beck sitting out here. Now that I have a close look at you, I can see why he wants you all to himself. She's too gorgeous and young for you, Beck."

Beck wriggled his eyebrows. "I told you she was."

Blakesley looked between them, seeing that she had been the topic of conversation at some point. "I'm not too young," she insisted. "Thirty-five isn't too young."

Butch threw a thumb in Beck's direction. "He's seven years older than you are," he said. "You can do better than this old man."

Blakesley sensed the humor so she wasn't offended. "I kind of like old men."

Butch chuckled, seeing that Beck didn't seem too pleased at his appearance in general so he changed the subject. "So," he said to Blakesley. "I hear your daughter is doing okay after her little adventure last week."

Blakesley nodded. "She's fine," she replied. "Thanks to you guys. I told Beck I don't know what I would have done had you not been there to save us both. I owe you."

Butch waved her off. "No need," he said, slapping Beck on the shoulder as the man took a last bite of his burger. "All in a day's work, eh? Normally, we're beatin' the crap out of people or blowing shit up, so it's a nice change to be able to save a life once in a while instead of take it."

Blakesley's smile faded somewhat. Whereas Beck was much more discreet about his job, Butch apparently didn't have that same tactful mechanism. It was a little disturbing.

"Well, I appreciate it," she said after a moment. "Do you two have any kids?"

Gina nodded, speaking before her big-mouthed husband could. "A boy," she said. "He's three. We just dropped him off at preschool."

Blakesley's smile returned. "Sweet," she said. "I love that age. What's his name?"

"Robert William Aguirre the Second," Gina replied. "But we call him Spike. Dad is Butch and his boy is Spike."

Blakesley laughed softly. "I love it," she said. "I have a three-year-old daughter. Maybe you can recommend a good nursery school for her."

As the women warmed up to each other, Beck swallowed the bite in his mouth and grabbed Butch discreetly by the neck, pulling his ear to Beck's mouth.

"I'm going to kill you," he whispered. "What in the hell are you doing here?"

Butch saw that Blakesley happened to be looking at him at that moment and he smiled broadly, slapping Beck on the chest with the back of his hand.

"I just wanted to spend some time with the wife before we deploy," he said loudly, waving down the waiter. "We've only got the afternoon, so I wanted to make the little woman happy by spending some quality time with her and she wanted to come to the Del."

Blakesley's smile vanished and she looked at Beck. "You're deploying?"

Before Beck could reply, Butch spoke up. "Yes, ma'am," he said, taking a menu being extended to him by the waiter. "I'm sure

Beck has told you that this kind of turnaround isn't unusual with us. We'll be gone weeks at a time, be home for a couple of days, and then ship out again. That's normal. Our schedule doesn't run like anyone else's; we're called out when we're needed at the spur of the moment. We're flying out of here again tonight at zero hundred hours."

Blakesley was sitting back in her chair, all of the warmth and humor gone from her expression. "Oh," she said, sounding rather depressed. "That... that must be tough on the family."

Gina was looking at her own menu. "It is," she admitted. "Butch has been gone so much the past three years that Spike barely recognizes him when he comes home. It's tough on the kids."

Blakesley was focused on her. "It must be hard on you, too."

Gina nodded and closed her menu. "It is," she replied. "But you get used to it. All of the wives of the men on the team hang together and support each other. We're like our own little family when the men are away. You're going to have to get used to it, too, if you're hanging out with Beck. He's always the first man out and the last man to return. His bitchy ex-wife gave him hell for it."

Blakesley just nodded her head. She felt like bursting into tears at the moment for reasons she didn't quite understand. All she knew was that she felt lonely and abandoned already.

"That's too bad," she murmured, suddenly standing up and putting her napkin on the table. "I'm sorry, but I really need to go check on my girls. They're down on the beach and I should make sure they're okay. It was really nice meeting you both. I hope we get to have lunch or dinner again soon."

Beck tried to grab her but she pushed away from the table, out of his reach, as she made her way very quickly across the patio to the gate that led out to the walkway and the beach beyond. Before she could get to the gate, Beck was on her, putting his hand up and preventing her from opening the gate.

"Hey," he said softly, full of concern. "Where are you going?"

"Please," she whispered tightly, refusing to look at him. "Please don't make a scene. Just let me go."

He managed to wedge his body in between her and the gate. "I'm not making a scene," he stated. "Where are you going?"

Blakesley was verging on tears. "To check on the girls."

"The girls are fine. Nikki is with them."

"Please, Beck," she broke down into soft tears. "Please just let me go."

He put his big hands on her arms, feeling the warm, velvety texture in his grip. "Baby, tell me why you're crying," he begged. "Is it because I didn't tell you I was deploying tonight? I was going to, I swear, when the time was right. I just didn't want that to be the first thing you heard from me so it was hanging over our heads all afternoon. I swear I was going to tell you."

She sobbed deeply, her hand on her face, and he pulled her against his big chest, holding her tightly. But she resisted.

"No," she wept, pushing him away. "Don't hold me. People are watching."

"Screw them," he hissed. "I don't care who's watching."

"Please," she begged yet again, trying to open the gate. "I just want to see the girls."

Seeing that he wasn't going to convince her to come back to the table, he pushed the gate open and walked out with her, his arm around her shoulders. He held her as they walked back out onto the sand. She wept softly beside him.

"I want to talk to you about something," he said. "Can you walk with me a little bit before we go back and see the girls?"

She nodded, wiping at her nose with the back of her hand. "Beck, I know this is what you do for a living and I'm sorry I'm not tough about it yet," she sniffled. "I'm not tough like Gina is. She's almost jaded about it."

He hugged her gently as they walked across the warm sand. "She's not jaded," he told her. "Believe me, she gives Butch plenty of crap about it. But I would say that she has accepted the situation for what it is. She deals with it, using the other wives as a support group. A lot of military families do that. Actually, I'm glad you met her. I'll have her call you while I'm away so she can check in on you. Would you be okay with that?"

Blakesley nodded hesitantly. "I guess."

He hugged her. "Thanks. It makes me feel better, too, knowing you're not so alone."

Blakesley fell silent as they reached the water's edge and began strolling. There was a great deal on her mind. Beck felt her cuddle against him as they walked with her head against his chest and her arm around his waist. He kissed the top of her head, noticing Cadee, Crosby and Charlotte in the near-distance as they built their sand castle of pristine white sand.

"My team is deploying tonight at midnight," he said, his focus on the little girls in the distance. "I don't know when we'll be back."

Blakesley had nearly collapsed into him as they walked. "Can you tell me anything more?"

"I can tell you that I love you and that I'll miss you."

She came to a halt, facing him as the sea wind blew gently across her features. "I love you, too, and I don't want you to go," she said, "but I understand you have to. Can... can you tell me if this is going to be a really dangerous trip?"

He smiled faintly. "They're all pretty dangerous."

"But how dangerous?" she wanted to know. "Like, if you were to rate it like terrorist alert levels, would it be mild, moderate, serious or extremely serious?"

He sighed and shook his head. "If I tell you, you're just going to worry," he pointed out. "Does it make you feel better knowing it's extremely serious? Moderate? It doesn't matter what I tell you, you're still going to worry."

"Would you rather I didn't worry?"

He put his hands on her shoulders. "I would rather not frighten you unnecessarily," he said. "I would rather that you miss me every day but know that, in the end, I will come back to you. I swear I will always come back to you, Blakesley."

She could see his point. She sucked up the rest of her tears and squared her shoulders. "Okay," she said resolutely. "If that's how you want me to handle it, then that's the way I'll handle it. I don't want to make your job any harder than it already is and I don't want people to go around describing me as bitchy like they do your ex-wife."

He grinned. "Hell, toward the end of our marriage, Sharon would change the locks when I deployed and I'd come home and my key wouldn't work," he snorted. "Once, Butch broke into the house and she was there and clobbered him with a lamp before she knew who it was. I don't think Gina ever forgave her for that."

In spite of herself, Blakesley grinned. "I'm not sure I would have, either," she chuckled, sobering as she gazed into his green eyes. "I promise I won't change the locks. I'll be just where you left me and your key will still work."

His eyes glimmered warmly at her. "I don't have a key."

"I'll give you one."

He pulled her closer, his arms going around her as the waves swirled around their feet. "That's what I wanted to talk to you about," he explained. "Can you spare about an hour? I want to show you something."

———

With a sun dress pulled over the pink bikini and flip flops on her feet, Blakesley sat beside Beck in his big Chevy truck, watching the bay as they crossed over on the big Coronado Bridge. He held her hand but was, so far, tight-lipped about where they were going, but Blakesley didn't mind. She was just glad to be with him. It was such a lovely day, bright and warm, as the bridge dumped them out onto the California mainland.

They took the 5 Freeway north to the 19th Street exit, paralleling the freeway until they came to Market Street. On Market Street, they cut east through the older and more rundown section of San Diego, very bustling and full of businesses and people, until they came to 27th Street. Beck took a right and went south for a few blocks before he pulled the car over and parked it.

Blakesley was looking around with interest. There were older homes in the area, some rundown but some well-tended. It was an old and established neighborhood. They sat next to a park on the west side of the street while a line of older homes were on the east side. They were on a slight rise, as San Diego was rather hilly, and they could see the great, green Coronado Bridge in the distance.

"Come on," Beck said as he opened up his door. "I want to show you something."

He was swiftly out of the truck. Blakesley went to open her door but he was already around the truck, opening it for her. She climbed out, the long sun dress blowing in the breeze as she looked around the neighborhood. He took her hand and led her across the street.

There were two big, old Victorian homes sitting side by side. One was well lived-in and cluttered while the other one looked newly restored. The exterior walls were a medium green color while the gingerbread moldings all around the roof were bright yellow. It really was a lovely house and someone had taken the time to lovingly restore it. As they went up on the wide porch, Beck went to the door and tossed the combination on the Knox Box. The box popped open and he pulled out a key. Blakesley watched him curiously.

"What are you doing?" she asked.

He just grinned at her as he opened the door, one that had the original hardware from when the house was built. Blakesley stepped into an empty home with glossy, restored hardwood floors, newly painted walls, and all new or restored fixtures. She gasped with delight as she went into the living room with its enormous windows and deep brown floors, looking with pleasure upon the moldings and detail work on the ceiling. Beck stood next to her as she inspected the place before pulling her into the kitchen.

"Come take a look at this," he said.

The restored kitchen was gorgeous with a black-tile brick backsplash and new stainless steel appliances. In fact, the entire house was gorgeous, all five bedrooms and three bathrooms worth of it. The old Victorian staircase had been left untouched for some reason but it was in spectacular shape for its age. Beck followed Blakesley up and down the stairs, from room to room, listening to her talk about how she wanted to restore her home much the same way the old Victorian had been restored. When they were in the master bathroom with its new double sinks and deep-soak tub, she turned to Beck.

"So are you thinking about buying this place?" she asked.

He half-nodded, half-shrugged. "I've got a townhome on Coronado that I bought about twenty years ago," he said. "Sharon and I lived there while we were married and when we divorced, I had to pay her half of the equity accumulated during our marriage. Anyway, she ended up getting about forty thousand dollars from it, which she pretty much gave back over to me because we had a lot of credit card debt when we divorced. To make a long story short, the townhome is almost paid off because I've owned it for so long so I was thinking about selling it and buying something bigger."

She smiled as she looked around the bathroom, at the big, new, tiled shower. "This house is gorgeous," she said sincerely. "It would make a great home."

"Enough for you to live here?"

She turned to look at him, the smile fading from her face. "I... I already have a house," she said, suddenly seeing why he had brought her here. She felt cornered but under no circumstances did she want to hurt his feelings. "I think this place would be great for you...."

He cut her off. "It's got five bedrooms," he told her. "Cadee, Crosby and Charlotte can all have their own rooms and Lizzie can have her own room when she comes to visit. I picked this house because it was old, because you seem to like old homes, and it's across the street from a park, which would be perfect for the girls. Baby, I know you said you had to think about moving in together and all that, but I just can't stand the thought of living away from you. I also can't stand the thought of you living in that big, old house with secret tunnels under the floors and God knows what else. I just don't have a good feel for that place and, although I know you bought it, I just don't like it."

Blakesley stared at him. She wasn't sure what to say. She sighed faintly and averted her gaze, looking at the bathroom again before wandering into the master bedroom with the beautiful French doors that overlooked a new deck and new backyard. She put her hand on the window molding, absently running her fingers against it as she thought about what she was going to say. Finally, she turned to him.

"The truth is that I would like nothing better than to be with you, in the same house as you, like one big, happy family," she said. "I've known you all of a week and already I feel like I've known you a hundred years. I feel like I know your heart and soul, and I can see what a good and sincere man you are. But I have to ask you this; if you're already trying to push me into moving in with you, what are your long-term plans for us?"

He folded his big arms across his chest thoughtfully. "That's a fair question," he said. "The fair answer is that I don't see myself being with another woman, ever. You're what I've been waiting for my entire life, Blakesley. I want to be with you forever."

She thought on his statement. "You told me that you would never get married again."

He pursed his lips and looked at his feet, unable to look her in the eye. "I know," he admitted. "I still don't know how I feel about that. Sharon went through such hell and I just can't do that to someone else."

Her eyebrows lifted. "So what's the difference? You want to move in with me, with my girls, and make a life with us like we're a family. Do you think not being married to you is going to make it any easier when you deploy, or get injured, or God knows what else? Do you think the absence of a wedding band makes me magi-cally impervious to pain and suffering and worry? It doesn't, you know. Married or not, I'll worry about you and love you just the same."

He cocked his head, the green eyes intense. "You're right," he agreed. "Not marrying you isn't some magic wand against what I do for a living."

She leaned back against the windowsill, gazing out over the California sky. "Marriage wasn't any picnic for me, either," she said. "It was more like a business arrangement, really. Ed and I had a lot of the same goals and dreams of financial independence. But the fact that we were more business partners than anything hasn't soured me on the idea of marriage in general. I still want to get married to someone I love someday. I deserve to be happy again. So do you."

She could hear him moving closer to her, his boots making muffled noises against the hardwood floor. When she looked up, he was standing over her.

"I want to buy this house and move you and the girls in," he said sincerely. "They won't have to live in a hotel anymore and we will live here while that house is being renovated. If you want to get married, then we'll get married, because I can't even comprehend not having you with me for the rest of my life. The thought of you marrying someone else... God, Blakesley, you have no idea how that would destroy me. I'd explode into a million different pieces of heartbreak. I'd be in pieces forever."

She looked up at him seriously. "I'm not going to force you to do something that you're uncomfortable with. But I'm not sure I can move in with you if that's the case. It somehow cheapens what we have between us, like we're not committed enough to each other to get married and tell the world that we're proud to belong to each other. I think moving in with someone without marriage makes the whole relationship seem cheap and easy."

His jaw ticked as he thought on her words. Then, he slid down against the wall until he was sitting on the floor beside her, his back up against the wall. He pulled her down onto his lap, smelling the scent of suntan lotion on her sun-kissed skin.

"I never saw myself getting serious with a woman again, much less getting married," he said quietly. "I said that I'd never marry again before I really knew you or knew what you would come to mean to me. When I said I'd never get married again, I just meant that I wanted to spare a woman the uncertainties that being with me would bring. I didn't mean I was opposed to marriage in general."

She wrapped her arms around his neck. "I'll tell you what I told you yesterday," she said. "It's way too soon for us to talk about moving in together. For the same reason, it's way too soon to talk about marriage. We're really just starting to get to know each other but things are moving incredibly fast. My head tells me to slow down but my heart tells me to go for it."

He sighed knowingly, thinking of the mission he had before him, knowing the risk, wondering if he wasn't feeling these things because he was afraid, in spite of all of his assurances to the contrary, that he really wouldn't make it back to her. It was difficult to sort it out in his head, mostly because he'd never had to deal with these feelings before.

"Can you see yourself married to me, though?" he asked, his green eyes intense.

She smiled, nodding. "I can," she acknowledged. "Can you see a baby brother for all of these girls we have between us?"

He grinned. "I hadn't really thought about it, but I guess I can," he said. "I thought you said you didn't want any more kids."

"Just like you said you'd never get married again. The right person and the right circumstances tend to change your mind."

His smile grew and he pulled her closer. "In that case," he said, "I can see two or three baby brothers to balance out all of these girls."

She laughed. "Wait a minute, buster," she said. "You're getting ahead of yourself. I just said one."

"Me and Beck Jr. against five women?" he shook his head. "That doesn't seem like good odds."

Blakesley giggled. "The first time Charlotte puts a princess crown on him or paints his fingernails, you're going to come apart at the seams, right?"

"You're going to have to call an ambulance 'cuz I'm going to be having a fit on the floor."

They shared a laugh and he kissed her, growing more amorous until they were interrupted by a voice from the entry.

"Hello?"

It was a male voice and Beck stood up, putting Blakesley on her feet. "Hello," he called, heading for front of the house with Blakesley behind him. "Is that you, Kevin?"

"It's me," came the voice.

Beck and Blakesley came through the dining room to find a nice-looking man standing just inside the entry. He had dark blue eyes and a buzzed haircut. He smiled and extended his hand to Beck.

"Hey, Beck," he said. "I see you were able to get in the Knox Box."

Beck shook his hand. "Thanks for the combination." He turned to Blakesley and put his arm around her. "This is my girlfriend, Blakesley. Baby, this is an old friend, Kevin Robinson. He's a real estate agent."

Blakesley shook Kevin's hand. "Nice to meet you," she said. "Did you turn him onto this house?"

Kevin nodded. "He called earlier and said he was looking for something old and restored, with a lot of bedrooms," he replied. "Does this fit the bill?"

Blakesley just looked at Beck, who forced a smile at his friend. "It sure did," he replied. "We love it."

"Great," Kevin said. "Did you want to make an offer?"

Beck looked at Blakesley and she could see the yearning in his eyes. He really, really wanted them to all move in together, all one big, happy family. She could feel his eagerness, the green eyes silently begging her to consider it. She sighed faintly and looked at Kevin.

"What are they asking?" she wanted to know.

"Four hundred and ninety-nine thousand dollars," Kevin replied. "They bought it about six months ago for two hundred and twenty thousand, but they gutted it and renovated the entire thing."

"If we were to make an offer, what would you suggest?"

Kevin looked around, shrugging. "The market is sluggish right now," he said. "I'd offer them four hundred and forty thousand and see what they say."

Blakesley looked around also. She wandered back into the living room, the bathroom under the stairs, and into the kitchen. The men followed. She looked at the hot water heater, the fuse box, and flipped a few switches. She inspected walls and doorjambs.

Beck watched her, smiling at her inspection of the details, shrugging at Kevin when the man looked at him curiously. The woman obviously had something in mind and she clearly knew what she was doing. Finally, Blakesley turned to the real estate agent.

"The quality is good but they cut corners with things like paint." She pointed to the wall. "See the bubbles? They're tiny, but still visible. That means cheap paint. The drywall looks good and so do the restored floors, so I'd say all in all, they probably put eighty to one hundred thousand dollars into restoring this place. That brings them up to a three hundred and twenty thousand dollar investment, maximum. I'd really be surprised if they spent that much, but I'll give them the benefit of the doubt. They're asking four hundred and ninety-nine thousand, which is about an eighty percent profit once everything is paid off. That's kind of high. Offer them four hundred and ten thousand, they pay all closing costs, and see what they say."

Kevin was looking at her with some surprise. He looked at Beck, who was staring at Blakesley. Beck cleared his throat softly.

"Hold on, Kevin," he crooked a finger at Blakesley. "A word, please."

Blakesley followed him into the master bedroom. He stopped when he came to the French doors and turned to her.

"Baby, I'm not sure I can afford that," he said. "Kevin never told me what the list price was. He just sent me to an old house like I'd asked. We never even discussed price."

She put her hands on his chest. "You said your condo is nearly paid off, right?"

"Right."

"How much is left on the mortgage?"

"About twenty-five thousand."

"What did it appraise for?"

He shrugged. "The townhome next door the same size as mine sold for almost three seventy."

She lifted her eyebrows at him. "What are you worried about?" she wanted to know. "Worst case, your property lists for three sixty. It sells for three fifty. You pay off the remainder of your mortgage and still have three hundred and twenty five thousand dollars to turn over into a new home. Add a new mortgage of maybe one hundred and thirty thousand and you're talking about a house payment that's less than a thousand dollars a month. You can't afford that?"

He scratched his chin, listening carefully to her. "I'm not going to make an offer on anything unless you and I resolve the issue of whether or not you and the girls are moving in with me."

She backed off somewhat, gazing up at him with big, confused eyes. After a moment, she simply shook her head.

"I'm not ready to make that decision right now," she said. "It's just too soon, Beck. I told you that you needed to give me time."

"Then I can't make the offer."

"You'd better go tell your friend."

There was pain in his expression as he turned away from her and Blakesley felt about as bad as she possibly could. But she wasn't ready to make the decision yet. It was a subject they would have to delve in to deeply to resolve and he would have to understand they couldn't do it in a matter of hours. Still, she felt very bad about it. She didn't want him to be embarrassed in front of his friend. Quickly, she made her way out to where the men were.

Beck was just starting to say something to Kevin when Blakesley charged in. "Kevin," she interrupted them. "Beck and I need to talk about what we really want to do, so don't make the offer yet. Tell them you have an interested buyer but Beck is going away tonight and he's not sure when he'll be back, so we don't want to rush this."

Kevin looked at Blakesley, at Beck, and then back to Blakesley again. "Sure," he agreed. "Sounds good. Call me when Beck gets back and we'll go from there."

Blakesley smiled at him. "Thanks," she said sincerely. "And thanks for letting us see the house. We really love it."

She took charge of getting them out of the house, of making sure the door was locked, and then getting rid of Kevin. As he drove off, she turned to Beck.

"Look," she held up her hands in a supplicating gesture. "I appreciate what you're trying to do and I love you for it. But I don't want to make a rash decision that's going to make you wake up in a week and wonder what in the hell you've done, or worse, I don't want to wake up in a week and want to back out of it. You're so sweet and generous, and I know you mean well, but I'm going to stick to my guns on this one. I need to think about moving in with you so soon and I need you to decide just what, exactly, you want to do about the marriage issue. If you really don't want to get married, then you need to be firm about that so I know where I stand. But if you do... well, then we'll talk. I guess the bottom line is that I want us both to be very, very sure."

He reached out and grasped her hands. "I know," he said quietly. "I'm sorry I pushed. I know you're only concerned with what's right for you and the girls."

She put her palms on his cheeks, kissing him sweetly. "I'm concerned about what's right for you, too. You're a very big part of this equation, Beck."

He smiled, returning her kisses. "I appreciate that," he said, taking her hand. "Let's head back to the hotel and see what the girls are up to. Maybe we can go get an early dinner."

"I need to go over to the house because the City is going to be there at three o'clock." Her smiled faded as he led her back to his truck. "What time will you be leaving us?"

He opened her door. "Around six."

"Then I'll call them and postpone the meeting. I don't want to waste this afternoon with them if you're going to be leaving me tonight."

He winked at her, smiling when she did. He led her to the truck and opened the door, closing it behind her after she climbed in and then entering the truck from his side. He seemed subdued, disappointed, so she didn't say any more. She didn't want the subject to become an open wound, constantly being rehashed. It was better to let it go for now so they could both think about it in peace.

Beck turned the truck on and pulled out, silently driving back to Coronado.

TWELVE

HE'D MADE her promise not to move in to the house until he returned.

Blakesley had made the promise because she was so upset that he was leaving again that she was willing to promise him almost anything. He'd taken the whole gang out to dinner in the Gaslamp Quarter of San Diego, to another fun and lively restaurant that the girls had loved. Beck and Blakesley had sat next to each other, his arm around her most of the time or his hand holding hers, as Crosby and Charlotte provided great entertainment for them and those around them.

It had all started when Crosby had somehow gotten a hold of her mother's lip liner pencil and proceeded to draw on her baby sister's face when her mother's back was turned. Beck had caught sight of what she was doing before Blakesley did, but she quickly caught on and promptly took back her pencil, scolding Crosby. Crosby wasn't down and out for long as she went to sit on Beck's lap to hopefully garner some sympathy from the man. It had been difficult, but Beck had stayed strong against her whining, even when she pleaded for an ice cream only dinner.

Cadee and Charlotte were surprisingly well behaved, but it was Crosby who was the problem child. Beck thought it was all great fun to try and coerce her to sit, to eat her spaghetti, or to wipe her mouth. She seemed to respond to him much better than her mother, who had her attention diverted with the other two. Beck was coming to see that Crosby, the middle child, was only acting out for want of attention, which he gave to her. It really made him miss Lizzie and the times they had shared together when she had been small. Besides, Crosby was as cute as a button and genuinely sweet, so he didn't mind one bit that she was demanding all of his attention.

With dinner over, Blakesley had Nikki take the girls back to the hotel so she could spend some time alone with Beck before he had to report to base. They had less than an hour to spend with each other so Beck put her in the car and drove her to Imperial Beach, a stretch of sand on the opposite side of the bay from Coronado. They sat in the cab of his truck and watched the boats in the bay, cuddled up, talking about Beck's childhood and how, as the only child, he spent a lot of time with his dad fishing in the sea.

As the sun began to set, he laid the seat back and Blakesley ended up next to him as they reclined. Gentle kisses turned into a heavy make-out session, which turned into a lot of petting and Beck nursing hungrily at her breasts as his fingers probed her deep. Beck felt like a high school kid sneaking off to play grab-ass with his girlfriend because they almost got caught a couple of times as people walked past his truck. Blakesley had a great sense of humor about it but they always went back to doing what they were doing, more amorously than before.

Time eventually caught up with them and Beck was forced to drive her back to the hotel so he could make it to the base on time. They arrived at the hotel and sat in the parking lot, holding hands but not saying a word. Beck found himself wanting to tell her all about what was coming up but he refrained, simply because he didn't want to upset her any more than she already was. She held herself together admirably but he was sure it was just for show.

Time was growing short so he took her in his arms, kissed her and told her how much he loved her. It was really all he could do.

He promised he'd be back as soon as he could and she vowed to hold him to that promise. And with that, she climbed out of the truck and waved bravely at him as he pulled away.

She didn't cry until much later that night when the girls were in bed and no one could see her.

———

It was about eight thirty in the evening and Blakesley had just put the girls to bed. Closing the door softly, she wandered into the living room of her rented rooms, looking around at the vanilla surroundings, thinking heavy thoughts of Beck now that she was alone for the first time that day. It had been three weeks since she had last seen him and she was trying not to feel lonely or scared. Beck had told her he would come back and she clung to that thought, like it was the only thing saving her from deep depression.

Weird how she'd known the man all of a couple of weeks and already she couldn't remember what her life had been like before she had met him. So she poured herself a glass of wine and planted her butt in front of the television, suddenly thinking that she didn't even have a picture of him. If something happened to the man, she wouldn't have anything to remind her of one of the sweetest and most exciting times of her personal life. More depressing thought swamped her and she took a big drink of wine, hoping that would help ease the pain and uncertainty.

As she flipped the channels looking for something to watch, her cell phone rang. She looked at the incoming number but didn't recognize it. Hesitantly, she answered the phone.

"Hello?"

There was a brief pause. "Hello?" it was a woman. "Hi, this is Gina Aguirre. Can I please speak with Blakesley?"

Blakesley was pleasantly surprised. "Hi, Gina," she said. "It's me."

On the other end of the line, Gina let out a little laugh. "Hi there," she said. "Sorry to call you so late. I hope this isn't a bad time. Beck gave me your number and told me to give you a call while he was away to check up on you."

Blakesley laughed softly. "I'm glad he did," she said. "How are you?"

"Fine," Gina replied. "How are you doing? This is your first real separation from Beck, isn't it?"

Blakesley shrugged. "The second, but I didn't know him very well the first time," she said. "How many years have you been doing this?"

"Seven," Gina said with some distain. "I hate it every time but it's just the way it is. I make Butch take me to Vegas every time he's been gone longer than a month. Beck says Butch tries to speed things up whenever they're working because he's afraid of that one month mark. He says it costs him a fortune every time."

Blakesley laughed again. "I'll have to keep that in mind," she said. "I like the penalties that get tacked on for extended deployment. Who knows? Maybe I'll rack up a trip to Europe."

Gina laughed. "I like the way you think, girl," she said, then sobered. "Actually, I am calling for a reason. I didn't know what else to do, so I hope this is okay."

"What's up?"

"Well," Gina sighed and lowered her voice. "Beck's daughter, Lizzie, showed up at my doorstep a little while ago. She's looking for her dad."

Blakesley was both surprised and concerned. "Doesn't she live up in San Francisco?"

"Yes," Gina replied. "She said she flew down this afternoon to see her dad. Did you know anything about it?"

Blakesley shook her head. "No," she replied. "Beck didn't say anything before he left. I'm sure he would have told me had he known."

Gina lowered her voice further. "She seems really upset," she whispered into the phone. "It looks like she's been crying. What do I do?"

"I don't know," Blakesley admitted. "Have you tried to talk to her?"

"A little, but she doesn't want to talk to me. She wants to talk to her dad."

"And he won't be back until God knows when." Blakesley glanced at the clock; it was almost nine at night. She began to scramble around for a pen. "Give me your address. I'll come over and see what I can do."

"Thank you," Gina sounded relieved. "I'll tell her your coming."

"No, don't," Blakesley said. "I don't know how she feels about her dad having a girlfriend and I don't want her to hear it from someone else. I'll tell her when I get there."

"Okay," Gina said before giving Blakesley her address. "See you in a bit."

"Absolutely," Blakesley was already off the couch. "Thanks for the call."

"You're welcome."

Blakesley hung up the phone and scooted into her bedroom, quickly changing into jeans, a long sleeved knit top, and her sparkly flip flops. Sticking her head into the girls' room, she woke Nikki up and told her she would be back shortly. Fleeing down to the parking lot, she jumped in her car and took off for Gina's house.

Gina and Butch lived in a small house that was just over the bridge from Coronado. It was neat and plain, with a big driveway and cement patio with kids' toys all over it. Blakesley double-checked the address that Gina had given her before she turned the car off and got out. Her flip flops made clicking noises against the cement as she made her way to the front door and knocked.

Gina opened the door right away, smiling at Blakesley. "Hi there," she said. "That didn't take you long."

Blakesley smiled in return as Gina drew her into the house. "Thank God for my GPS," she said, looking around. "Your house is so nice."

Gina grinned. "Thanks," she said, automatically picking up a nearby toy truck on the floor. "It's hard to keep it clean with a three-year-old."

"Tell me about it."

Gina grinned, nodding, as a little boy in pajamas suddenly emerged from one of the rooms. He had dark hair and big dark eyes, grinning up at Blakesley shyly as he grabbed his mother's hand. Gina smiled down at her son.

"This is the mess-maker himself," she said. "This is Spike. Baby, can you say 'hi' to Blakesley?"

The little boy's grin spread and he began to chew his fingers nervously. "Hi, Bee."

"Her name is Blakesley, baby."

"Beebee!"

There was no way the kid could say her name. Blakesley giggled. "Hi, Spike," she said. "How old are you?"

Spike held up three fingers. "Free," he said.

Blakesley pretended to be impressed. "Three years old," she said. "You're such a big boy."

"I can write my name."

"That's great."

Little Spike giggled and ran back to his bedroom at his mother's prompting. Gina watched him go, making sure he actually went into the bedroom and not into the kitchen before drawing Blakesley into the living room. On the sofa, watching television, sat a beautiful young woman with long blond hair. Elizabeth Beatrice Seavington had her father's good looks and when she turned to look at Blakesley, Beck's features on the young girl were evident. She had his eyes and the big dimple in her chin. When she stood up, she was several inches taller than Blakesley with the lean body of a supermodel. She wasn't shy about extending her hand.

"Hi," she said. "I'm Lizzie Seavington."

Blakesley took the slender, warm hand in her own hand and shook it. "Hi," she said. "I'm Blakesley Thorne. I'm so happy to meet you."

Lizzie gazed at Blakesley, studying her, before cocking her head in a gesture that looked a good deal like her father.

"So you're my dad's girlfriend?" she asked.

Blakesley was caught off guard, letting loose an awkward chuckle as she looked at Gina. Butch's wife lifted her shoulders helplessly.

"Sorry," she replied. "It just slipped out."

Blakesley chuckled again, looking back at Lizzie with a rather embarrassed expression.

"I... I'm sure that's something he wanted to tell you himself," she said. "He's just been really busy. I'm sorry if he hasn't already told you."

Lizzie shrugged, her green eyes scrutinizing Blakesley. "That's okay," she said. "But... wow. You're really pretty."

Blakesley smiled. "Thanks. So are you."

Lizzie was still staring at her. "Gina said that my dad is really crazy about you."

Blakesley's smile grew. "The feeling is mutual." She was feeling somewhat awkward so she motioned for them to sit on the couch, turning to see where Gina was and noticing the woman had vanished. "I think we've been deserted."

Lizzie sat heavily on the couch. "That's okay," she replied. "I kind of barged in on her."

Blakesley's gaze lingered on the beautiful teenager who seemed much older than her fourteen years.

"Why did you come here?"

"Because my dad and Butch are good friends. This is the only place I could think to look for him. I'm sure she didn't know what to do with me."

Blakesley nodded faintly. "She called me because I guess she thought I could help," she replied. "Did your dad know you were coming?"

Lizzie sat back against the couch, averting her gaze and picking up a throw pillow. "No."

Blakesley watched Lizzie pick at the throw pillow. "You know, your dad and I had a conversation before he left that had to do with you. See, I have three little girls who have really taken a liking to your dad and he said that he hadn't seen you in a while, so I told him he should have you fly down. He really wanted to see you but with his schedule, he was afraid of what would happen to you if he had to leave all of a sudden. I told him I'd make sure you were safe, so right now, I kind of feel responsible to make sure you're okay since he's not around. You don't even have to tell me why you're here if you don't want to, but I promised your dad that I'd make sure you were okay if he wasn't around. Does that make sense?"

Lizzie was still picking at the pillow but she looked up at her. "It does."

"Good," Blakesley smiled at the young woman. "Is there anything I can do to help you?"

Lizzie shook her head. Then she shrugged. Then she started crying. "I just want my dad."

Blakesley put her hand on Lizzie's knee and rubbed gently. "I know, sweetheart," she comforted. "I just don't know where he is but I promise I'll help you however I can if you want to tell me what the trouble is."

Lizzie wiped at her eyes. "I... I don't know."

Blakesley patted her knee. "It's okay," she assured her. "You don't have to. But I'd really like to help if I can. Meanwhile, since your dad is away, why don't you come stay with me until he gets back? He'd be okay with that."

Lizzie looked at her, all watery-eyed, and shrugged. "I... I came down here to stay with my dad. I didn't plan on staying with anyone else."

"I know, but he's not here and I don't have a key to his house. You really can't stay with Gina."

Lizzie nodded; she knew that. She picked at the pillow, her jeans, before finally looking up at Blakesley again.

"I'm not trying to be a pain," she said. "I... I just flew down here today to be with my dad. I guess I should have called first but it all happened so fast, I just got on the airplane and came."

Blakesley nodded patiently. "Maybe we should call your mom and...."

"No!" Lizzie erupted. "Don't call her. I don't want to talk to her!"

That little outburst told Blakesley pretty much everything she needed to know. Whatever had chased Lizzie onto an airplane to San Diego obviously centered around her mother. Blakesley tried to be gentle. She was a teenage girl with a mother once herself.

"Okay," she said. "I won't call her. No worries. I ran away from home once myself, only I didn't have the money to take an airplane anywhere. I had this old beat up Volkswagen and it barely made it down the street. I just went to my friend's house. All my mom had to do was look out the front door and see that crappy car parked down the block. God, I hated that stupid car. I couldn't even make a good escape in it."

That drew a semblance of a smile from Lizzie. "I didn't have money for a plane," she said. "I took my mom's credit card and bought a ticket online. Then I took the cash out of her wallet and took a taxi to the airport."

Blakesley sighed faintly, thinking on the fact that she used a credit card to make her escape. "You know your mom can trace the purchase, right?" she asked. "She can find out what airline and where you went. When she finds out you went to San Diego, she's going to know you came to see your dad. Don't you think she'll head down here to look for you?"

Lizzie turned red in the face. "She can come down here," she said angrily. "I don't care if she does or not. But I'm not going home with her, no matter what."

"Why not?"

Lizzie burst out. "Because I'm not going back to that house where Dan jerks off outside my bedroom door and she doesn't give a damn about it," she snapped. "My mom married a pervert and all she cares about is protecting him. When I told her what had happened, she said I must have dreamed it. She didn't even believe me, not even when I told her again and again. It just kept happening. So I left."

Blakesley sat in shocked silence, feeling sick. It was more of an answer than she expected. "Oh, sweetheart, I'm sorry," she whispered. "Of course you don't have to go back. We'll wait until your dad comes back and he'll know what to do, okay?"

Lizzie was starting to tear up again, wiping at the moisture on her face. But she looked at Blakesley with some surprise. "You... you won't send me home?"

Blakesley shook her head. "That's between you, your dad and your mom. You can stay with me until your dad gets back, but on one condition."

"What?"

"You need to let me call your mom to at least tell her you're safe. If my daughter had run away, I would want to know that she's at least healthy and whole. I think it's only fair."

Lizzie thought on that, her expression dubious. "Well...," she said slowly. "You won't make me go back?"

Again, Blakesley shook her head. "No," she said. "I don't want you to go back, not if that crap is going on. You need to stay away from that until your dad gets back and figures out what to do."

Lizzie pondered all of that a moment longer before hesitantly nodding her head. "Okay," she said, fumbling around in her pocket and pulling out her phone. "You can call her. But just to tell her that I'm not lying in a gutter somewhere."

"Deal." Blakesley took the phone and brought up the contact list. "Is it under 'mom'?"

"Yes."

Finding the number, Blakesley pushed the dial button and put the phone on speaker. Someone answered on the second ring.

"Lizzie?" the woman on the other end sounded frantic. "Where in the hell are you?"

"Hi," Blakesley said. "This isn't Lizzie. My name is Blakesley and Lizzie is sitting next to me. Lizzie, tell your mother 'hi'."

Lizzie looked defiant and fearful at the same time. "It's me,

Mom," she said. "I just wanted to tell you that I'm fine and not in a morgue somewhere."

"Lizzie?" her mom sounded angry more than frantic. "What's going on? Where are you?"

Lizzie's defiance spread. "I'm with Dad," she said. "I'm not coming home, okay? I'm not going anywhere that Dan is. I told you what happened and if you don't believe me, then I'm getting out of there."

On the other end of the phone, there was an exasperated sigh. "Lizzie, cut this out," she snapped. "I talked to Dan and he says he never did anything like that. He swears he didn't and he has no idea where you came up with that. You're coming home, young lady, right now. Where's your father? Put him on the phone."

"No!" Lizzie shouted. "Will you listen to me for once and stop defending that pervert? I told you what I saw and you didn't believe me. I also told you that I saw him having sex with my friend Meggyn one night when she spent the night and you still didn't believe me. He wants to have sex with me, too, and I'm not going to let that happen. You're my mom; you're supposed to protect me and I don't feel safe with you!"

She was crying by the time she was finished. Shocked and disturbed, Blakesley put her hand on Lizzie's lowered head and spoke into the phone.

"Beck is away for a few days so it's probably best if you leave Lizzie with us until he gets back," she said calmly. "She's in good hands. We'll take good care of her."

That didn't ease Lizzie's mother in the least. "Who in the hell are you?" she demanded. "I don't know you. I'm not leaving my daughter with a stranger."

Blakesley understood that, somewhat. "My name is Blakesley Thorne and I'm Beck's girlfriend," she said evenly. "I have three small daughters and they'll get along just fine with Lizzie. We'll have a good time at the zoo and Sea World until Beck gets back. I just wanted you to know that your daughter is safe because I'm sure you're very worried about her."

Lizzie's mother wouldn't be soothed in the least. She was furious. "Listen to me, bitch," she snarled. "I don't know who you are and I don't care, but you'd better put my daughter on the next plane home or I'm calling the cops."

The woman's attitude had Blakesley's dander up. "I would encourage you to call them," she said. "Then we can also tell them about your husband who jacks off outside the bedroom of your fourteen-year-old daughter and apparently has sex with underage girls. I'll be happy to tell them all of that and I'm sure Lizzie will, too. So bring it on if you think you can."

On the other end of the line, Lizzie's mom was so angry that she was starting to screech.

"I'm coming down there and get her myself," she spat. "You'd better be...."

Blakesley cut the phone off and very calmly handed it back to Lizzie. "Does that phone have a GPS device on it?"

Lizzie looked at her phone, confused. "I... I don't think so."

Blakesley shook her head. "Just to be safe, you'd better turn it off," she said. "I'll take you to the store tomorrow and we'll get you a brand new one with a new number. You can pick out any phone you want."

Lizzie looked at her, shocked. "Any phone?"

Blakesley smiled. "Any phone."

Lizzie's shock grew. "Wow," she exclaimed. "I don't even know what to say. That's really nice of you."

Blakesley just smiled and stood up. "Well," she said. "Maybe we should head back and let Gina get some sleep. Do you have any luggage?"

Lizzie stood up, shaking her head. "Just a bag," she said, going to pick up the big, purple canvas bag next to the couch. "I just grabbed what I could and left."

Blakesley picked up her purse from the coffee table. "No problem," she said. "We'll pick up some stuff for you tomorrow if you need it."

Lizzie seemed a little stunned at the generosity of her dad's girlfriend. She eyed the woman closely. "Are you sure you don't mind me staying with you?" she asked. "I mean, it could be weeks or months until my dad gets back. I know how long he can be gone."

Blakesley waved her off, studying the tall, beautiful blond. "I'm looking forward to getting to know you. I'm honored to have you stay with us. I have three daughters – Cadee, Crosby and Charlotte – who are absolutely going to love you. I hope you like little kids."

Lizzie nodded, adjusting the bag on her shoulder. "I love kids." She lifted her pensive gaze to Blakesley. "Uh... my mom... she's kind of like that with everybody, you know, the way she talked to you. She used to talk to my dad like that all of the time. She wasn't very nice to him. I... I'm sorry that she was such a bitch."

Blakesley just smiled. "Trust me," she said, "she can't out-bitch me. I wasn't offended but it's sweet of you to apologize."

Lizzie just nodded as Blakesley called for Gina and somewhere in the back of the house, a response came.

"Wait," Lizzie said before Gina came out. "Are you really sure you want me to come with you?"

"Of course. Unless you don't want to. If you don't want to, then we need to figure out what to do."

Lizzie shook her head quickly. "I want to," she assured her. "I just don't want to be a pain."

"You won't be."

Gina started to come out from the kitchen but Lizzie was still focused on Blakesley. "Gina told me that you've been really good for my dad," she said. "I think that's really great because, you know, my mom and dad weren't happy when they were married. I've never seen my dad really happy or anything. I heard him tell my mom once that all he really ever wanted was a family and a good woman to come home to."

Blakesley couldn't help but feel saddened. "What did your mom say to that?" she asked.

Lizzie shrugged. "What she always says. She was mean. She just laughed at him."

Driving Lizzie back to the Extended Stay, they passed the freeway that she and Beck had taken when they had looked at the old Victorian. She kept seeing Beck's face when she told him she had to think about moving in with him, seeing the disappointment on his handsome features. She was disappointed, too. Maybe she shouldn't have been so hard on him. Maybe she was just over-thinking the whole thing. They loved each other and that was never going to change, wedding ring or no.

Lizzie had assimilated quite easily into the family. From the second Cadee, Crosby and Charlotte met her, they attached themselves to her. Cadee, ever stoic and sensible, liked the fact that she now had an older girl to talk to, but Crosby and Cadee hung all over her just like they had with Beck. The second night Lizzie spent with them on the fold-out couch in the living room, Crosby and Charlotte climbed out of bed and went to go sleep with her. Blakesley woke up the next morning to all three girls sleeping soundly on the fold-out.

After that, Lizzie and the girls were inseparable. More than that, it was increasingly apparent that the Extended Stay was just too small for Blakesley, her three girls, Lizzie and Nikki. They needed more space, and more bathrooms, and Blakesley kept rolling thoughts of Beck through her head, his wish to buy the old Victorian for all of them, and her resistance to the idea was waning.

The truth was that she wanted to be with him, too, forever, and maybe it was a foolish thought to dream of them all together living in that big old Victorian house, but it was a dream she was quickly succumbing to. She just couldn't help it. Beck wanted a family to come home to and she wanted the same thing. She wanted it with him. Almost four weeks after Beck's departure, Blakesley broke down and gave the real estate agent a call. Kevin Robinson was very glad to hear from her.

A month to the day after Beck's deployment, Blakesley took the girls up to the Earp homestead with her so she could meet with the people from the State of California and the City of San Diego. It had been a meeting to review the findings of the archaeologists about the pit and tunnel, among other things, but it turned into an argument over who had historical jurisdiction. As Lizzie and Nikki watched the girls play in the massive front yard, Blakesley grew increasingly disgusted with the bureaucratic rhetoric about her house, frustrated to the point of walking out on the meeting. She would let them hash it out without her.

So she and the girls returned to the Extended Stay and settled in for the evening. There were coloring books, Barbies and toys all over the living room as she prepared dinner, watching the news as she baked a pasta dish and cut up vegetables for the salad. Lizzie was trying to get Crosby and Charlotte to pick up their junk, helping them carry it into their bedroom, but Crosby just wanted to hang on to Lizzie's leg. Giggling, Lizzie struggled to walk as Crosby clung to her, dragging the little girl back into the bedroom.

Blakesley grinned at the antics, cutting up cucumbers, hearing her girls in the bedroom with Lizzie and half-heartedly watching the news. As she put salad in the bowl, she watched a story about a police chase and an illegal immigrant who was run over at the border crossing. Then came a story with a military helicopter as a graphic. Blakesley was putting the salad on the table and happened to be close enough to actually hear what they were saying.

"... and crashed into the sea. Early reports say that the heli-copter, a CH 47 Chinook model like the one shown here, lost its rear rotor and crashed into the sea off the coast of Panama. NBC News has learned that a Navy Special Warfare team detachment, or S.E.A.L.s, out of Coronado in San Diego was aboard the heli-copter and all hands were lost when the helicopter sank in two hundred feet of water. The Navy, however, has no comment at this time. Moving on to the other top stories, Bank of America has...."

Blakesley didn't hear any more after that. She had accidentally knocked the salad bowl over on the table and she scrambled with shaking hands to collect the vegetables and toss them back in the bowl.

As she grabbed for pieces of cucumber and tomato, it began to occur to her that fearful little sobs were escaping her lips. She tried to stop them but she couldn't. As she tossed the last cucumber back in the bowl, she hung her head and wept, trying very hard not to utter a sound.

She was so shaken that she could hardly breathe. She could hear the little girls making noise in the bedroom and Lizzie's laughter, struggling with every breath to stop crying. All she could see was Beck's face and feel his strong, yet tender, touch. She could hear his voice, deep and sexy, and she was shattered to think she might never hear it again. She had no way of knowing and the mere thought was killing her.

Hand over her mouth, she went from the table back to the oven, trying desperately to stop her tears. She didn't want her girls to hear her, or worse, Lizzie to hear her. She turned the water on full blast in case any sounds escaped her lips as she forced herself to calm. It wasn't easy.

Just as she was calming to a manageable level, her cell phone rang and she saw that it was Gina. She wasn't strong enough to talk to the woman, not at the moment, so she shut the phone off and called the girls to the dinner table. Cadee and Nikki came out, followed by Lizzie, Crosby and Charlotte. Blakesley remained stoic as she dished out pasta and salad, but inside, she was dying. She couldn't even look at Lizzie, fearful that the young woman would see that something was wrong.

The truth was that Blakesley didn't even know if anything was wrong. She could only hope and pray that it wasn't. Later that night, when the girls were asleep and the world was quiet, Blakesley summoned the strength and courage to answer Gina's call.

She stayed up all night on the phone with her.

———

"Beck, you okay?"

Beck had his head in his locker, emerging to see Captain Davis addressing him. He nodded wearily at his captain.

"Fine," he said, tossing some gear back into the locker. "I'm fine."

Davis, a youthful-looking man in his late fifties, came closer. "I know he was a good friend of yours."

Beck nodded, struggling against the grief that had been his constant companion for five long days. "He was," he said. "I'm going to miss him."

"How's Gina holding up?"

Beck shrugged and closed the locker. "As well as can be expected, I guess," he said. "I spent the past six hours with her, at least until her mother and sister could drive down from Los Angeles. She's a basket case, but I guess I would be too if I'd just lost my husband."

"We almost lost you, too," Davis said.

Beck looked at him. Then he shook his head wearily. "You know, I always thought I would get it in a firefight or go out in a blaze of glory," he muttered, leaning heavily against the locker behind him. "It never occurred to me that I'd get it in a helicopter."

Davis tried to be comforting. "There wasn't anything anyone could have done," he said. "That 'copter tipped off the deck and sank. You and Solis and the other three were lucky to get out alive. You can't blame yourself for the other nineteen that went down with it, including Butch."

Beck nodded his head although it was unconvincing. "I just happened to be in the right place at the right time," he said. "I was in the rear by the cargo doors. Had the cargo doors not been open, I would have drowned like the rest of them. As it was, I got sucked out when the chopper went over and started taking on water. Butch was up by the cockpit. He never had a chance."

Davis didn't have an answer to that. He slapped Beck on the shoulder and turned away. "You've got five days off," he told him. "Go someplace and relax. We'll talk about this next week."

"I just lost half of my team, Captain. I'm not sure I can relax anywhere."

Davis paused by the locker room door. "Try," he insisted. "I'm going to talk to Command and see what we can do about redistributing the teams for now. For now, your platoon is on R and R until we can figure this all out."

Beck just nodded his head, staring off into the darkness as he thought of the men he had lost five days ago in the chopper accident. He still couldn't believe it. As Davis left the room, Anthony came in, still wearing the same worn and dirty combat fatigues that Beck was. They were both oily and grimy, having not changed since the accident, subsequent rescue attempts, and the completed mission before all of that had happened. All in all, it had been hell.

They looked at each other, all dirty and sweaty and bloodied, reminders of the tragedy they had so deeply suffered. Nineteen of their forty-man team had gone down over the side of a carrier when the rear rotors on the Chinook Helicopter malfunctioned. The whole thing had spun out, tipped over, and crashed down into the sea just off the coast of Panama.

"How's Gina?" Anthony wanted to know.

Beck shrugged his big shoulders. "A wreck," he said honestly. "I'm going to go see Blakesley now."

Anthony suddenly produced a white envelope and handed it to him. "This was in your mail," he said. "I saw it on your desk and thought you might want it."

Beck sighed heavily and took the white envelope. "I haven't even been to my desk," he said, looking at the return address. He just stared at it. "It's from Blakesley."

Anthony nodded. "I know," he said quietly. "That's why I thought I'd bring it to you."

Beck continued to stare at the envelope, feeling the emotion he had tried so hard to suppress suddenly bubble up in his chest. He and Anthony were both thinking the same thing – that it was a Dear John letter from the woman Beck thought of twenty-four hours a day, seven days a week. When he wasn't talking about her, he was dreaming about her. After the past three weeks and the hell they had endured, Beck wasn't sure he could take any more heartache. In fact, he knew he couldn't. His hands started to shake as he slowly pulled open the envelope.

Anthony turned away and opened his locker. He had seen Beck's shaking hands and he muttered a silent prayer, praying for strength for them all. He pretended to busy himself in his locker although he was watching Beck from the corner of his eye. The man pulled out what Anthony originally thought was a card of some kind. It turned out to be a 3 x 5 photograph. Beck peered closely at it, flipped it over to read the back, and flipped it over again before shock registered across his face. He dropped the envelope but the photo remained in his grip.

Beck was up and running for the door before Anthony could ask him what had happened.

It was past midnight as Beck parked his truck at the curb and bailed out.

He could see the old Victorian house in the moonlight, outlined against the remarkably clear sky. His heart was pounding and his hands were shaking as he took the steps, the porch light the only source of light around the darkened house. Inside, it was dark and quiet.

Beck went to the old mailbox and stuck his hand inside, feeling around. He came across something stuck to the inside of the box and he pulled it forth. It was a small metal box with a magnet on one side that, when opened, revealed a house key.

I'll give you a key.

His heart was in his throat as he slipped the key into the lock and turned the old tumblers. Stepping inside, he could see that the place was completely furnished. He essentially stepped into an entry that was, from what he could see in the darkness, beautifully furnished with a giant piece of wall art and other knick-knacks, including a gorgeous rug at his feet. Peering more closely at the modern and edgy piece of wall art, he could see Blakesley's name on it.

Startled, he stuck his head into the living room to see the entire thing furnished with spectacular leather couches and other items that just made his head spin. There were more of Blakesley's beautiful art on the walls. When he stepped into the living room and noticed the dining room to his left, he seriously had to pinch himself. He thought he was dreaming.

Like a man in a fog, he moved back to the stairs, looking up to the second floor as he made his way up. He very carefully opened the first door he came to, poking his head inside to see Crosby and Charlotte fast asleep in twin beds. Toys were strewn all over the place.

Heart pounding faster, he silently closed the door and went to the next bedroom where he found Cadee sleeping soundly on a canopy bed, her room apparently all decked out in white and deep purple. There were unicorns and stuffed horses everywhere. Over in the corner was a futon and he could see Nikki curled up on her side. With a grin, Beck closed the door and moved to a third bedroom, a room with great northern exposure, to find Lizzie fast asleep on a beautiful double bed inside a fully decorated, very cool teenager's room.

Beck's eyes filled with tears as his gaze fell on his daughter, so incredibly glad to see her. He simply couldn't believe it. In fact, he couldn't believe any of it. He wanted to wake her up but he thought better of it. He would be content to see her in the morning and find out how she had come here. At the moment, he was more desperate to see Blakesley. Shutting the door softly, he went back downstairs to the master suite at the rear of the house.

The master suite had a grand, little entry off the dining room and he had to pause to look at the artwork in the small entryway. It was exquisite and a little overwhelming. In fact, all of this was overwhelming and he swore that if he were dreaming, he didn't ever want to wake up. All of his girls, living in the same house under the same roof, was his greatest and fondest wish. He had no idea what was going on or how Blakesley had accomplished it, but he was thrilled to death. With a quivering hand, he slowly opened the master bedroom door.

The curtains were closed against the big French doors that opened out to the deck and the backyard beyond, but there was enough light that he could see the layout of the room. An enormous California King bed was lodged against the north wall, a spectacular piece of furniture that was covered with some kind of luxurious bedspread. He couldn't really see what it looked like but he could feel it, and it felt soft and warm. As he put his hand on it, peering at the crumpled up covers on the bed, something heavy hit him across the shoulder.

Startled, Beck's training kicked in and he rolled away from the blow, over the bed, and landed on his feet. It was so dark in the room that he almost didn't see the baseball bat flying at him again until it was too late but he was able to duck at the last minute, grabbing the bat and yanking it away from the assailant. He tossed it aside, hearing a very female-sounding yelp, and realized that his attacker could only be one person. In the darkness, he reached out to grab her.

"Blakesley," he said sharply. "Baby, it's me!"

Blakesley could barely see his face in the darkness and, truth be told, she was still in panic mode. She had been ever since she heard the floorboards creaking in the dining room. As she struggled to focus in the darkness, she thought for a moment that she might be dreaming. She could see Beck's features but they truly didn't register for several long moments. But when realization finally dawned, she came apart.

"Beck!"

She threw herself on him, all arms and legs wrapping up around him. Beck held her tightly and she broke into hysterical sobs, her face buried in his neck and her legs wrapped around his waist. He just held her, rocking her tenderly.

"It's okay, baby," he murmured. "I'm here. Everything is okay."

Blakesley was sobbing so heavily that she couldn't speak. She just held him, refusing to let him go even when he tried to kiss her face. She had spent the last five days in utter and complete terror, wondering if she was ever going to see him again, so his midnight appearance had her shaken to the bone. It was the best shock in the world.

"Is it really you?" she sobbed.

He chuckled, rubbing her back soothingly with one hand. "It's really me."

"Swear it?"

"I swear."

That brought on a new round of hysterical tears and Beck laughed again before sitting on the bed and trying to peel her off of him.

"Baby," he tried to get her to loosen her hold on his neck. "Everything is all right. Why are you crying like that?"

Blakesley eventually pulled back to look at him, putting her hands on his face and gazing at every inch of his grimy, dirty features. He was absolutely filthy but she didn't care in the least. He was the most gorgeous thing she'd ever seen.

"Are you real?" she asked, lips trembling as she ran her hands over his face.

He kissed the hands that came close to his lips. "I'm real," he confirmed. "I promise. I'm real. Why are you so shook up?"

She started crying again. "I thought you...," she sobbed. "The news said... it said that a bunch of S.E.A.L.s were killed in a helicopter accident. Beck, I thought you might be dead."

She sobbed deeply, her face on his shoulder. He sighed heavily and wrapped her up in his arms. He hadn't heard about the event being on the news, not even from Gina. No wonder Blakesley was so shaken. She must have been living in the same hell he had been since the accident happened. Gently but firmly, he lifted her head from his shoulder and wiped at her wet cheeks with his big fingers.

"Listen to me," he commanded firmly. "I'm completely fine. Not a scratch. Please stop crying, okay? You're breaking my heart."

She let him wipe at her face, nodding even though the tears were still falling. "I'm sorry," she whispered. "I'm such a baby. But

I seriously thought... I didn't think I'd ever really know if anything happened because I'm not your next of kin or anything. How would they know to tell me?"

He shushed her, kissing her salty lips. "You're on my emergency card," he told her. "I added you before I left. Someone would have come to tell you. I don't want you to worry about that ever again."

She swallowed hard, struggling to stop the tears. "Okay," she wrapped her arms around his neck and he nuzzled her damp cheeks. "So you're all right, then?"

"I'm fine."

"It wasn't your team on the news?"

He sighed heavily and pulled back, looking at her watery eyes. She looked so adorable with her hair in two ponytails, all mussy like a little girl. He stroked her hair with one big hand, taking a moment just to get a good look at her. He felt like a starving man being given his first meal in weeks, so great his satisfaction simply to gaze upon her.

"It was my team," he replied with anguish. "I lost nineteen men, including Butch."

Blakesley's eyes widened. "Oh, my God," she breathed. "Poor Gina. Does she know?"

"She knows. I just spent the past six hours with her."

Blakesley struggled against the tears again, thinking of Butch and Gina, and little Spike who would never really get to know his father. "What happened? Can you tell me?"

He drew in a deep breath, thinking. Then he cuddled her all up against him and lay back on the bed with her lying on his chest. It was heavenly and for the first time in five weeks, he could feel himself truly relax.

"We were preparing to lift off in a Chinook helicopter and a piece of metal or something flew up from the flight deck and lodged in the rear rotors," he said softly, stroking her back. "We were about fifteen feet off the flight deck and the whole helicopter just tipped over and crashed into the sea. The cargo doors were open, which was where I was sitting, and I got sucked out as the water rushed in through the open doors. Next thing I know, I'm on the surface and the helicopter is going down with my men inside. Only five of us made it out before the thing sunk into the Pacific."

Blakesley's head was on his chest. She closed her eyes tightly, tears running out onto his shirt, as she realized how close he came to drowning with the rest of them. She could hear his heart beating strongly in her left ear, the thought of never hearing that heart again making her feel weak and hollow.

"So you were on the helicopter that went down," she whispered.

His arms tightened around her. "Yes, I was," he said. "But I'm fine. I lived. I made it back in one piece and came back to you just like I said I would. Okay?"

"Okay," she whispered, her throat tight with sorrow.

He could hear the emotion in her voice. "I don't want you dwelling on this, please?" he was very nearly begging her. "I have enough to deal with over next few days without worry about you, too. I need for you to be strong, baby. Please. I really need it."

Her eyes came open as she listened to his serious plea. He was right, about everything. It wasn't her luxury to feel grief, but he had every right. Swallowing her tears, her head came up and she wiped what moisture was left on her face. She was straddling him intimately and she crawled up on his body so she was eye to eye with him.

"No more tears, I promise," she whispered. "I'm just so glad to have you back. I love you and I've missed you so much."

He smiled wearily at her. "I love you and I've missed you, too," he reached up and tugged gently on a ponytail. "Now, can I please ask a question?"

She nodded. "Of course."

He sighed heavily, his smile fading. "What's going on?" he wanted to know. "I got the picture with you and all four girls in front of the house."

Her eyes twinkled. "So you figured it all out, did you?"

"That, and the note you wrote on the back of the photograph helped. I figured out where to find the key."

"I told you I'd give you one."

He smiled faintly, his hand wrapped up in a ponytail. "Yes, you did," he agreed. "It looks like you've moved into this house and, more than that, Lizzie is upstairs. What in the hell is going on?"

She smiled and leaned down to kiss his cheeks, his nose. When his arms tightened around her and he prepared to swoop in for a more passionate kiss, she stopped him.

"Do you want to know?" she asked, hand over his mouth. "If you start kissing me like that, you won't know anything for a few hours at least."

He sighed dramatically and nodded his head, loosening his grip. She removed her hand from his mouth.

"I bought the house," she whispered.

His eyebrows rose. "You bought it?" he repeated. "But what about all we talked about before I left? You said you didn't want to rush in to anything."

"I didn't," she said. "But I realized something after you left. I guess I really don't care if we're married or not. I want to be with you as much as you want to be with me, and we love you because you belong to us. I shouldn't have pushed the marriage issue or have been so stubborn about it. Ultimately, it matters what's in our hearts and not what's printed on a piece of paper. So I bought the house and wanted to surprise you with it. We're all moved in and we're all going to live here together. That is, if you still want to live with us. You may have changed your mind."

He had a fairly amazed expression on his face. "Are you joking?" he asked, incredulous. "I haven't changed my mind. It's all I could think about during the time we were apart. Hell, I was rushing over here tonight to ask you to marry me. Are you saying you don't want to get married?"

She smiled broadly. "I'd be so proud to be your wife," she whispered. "But I don't want to force you into something you don't want to do."

He shook his head. "I was crazy to say that." His arms began to tighten around her again. "All I could think about was being Mr. Blakesley Thorne and how proud that would make me. Will you please marry me?"

Her smile couldn't get any bigger. "Are you sure?"

"Hell, yes."

She laughed. "Then I'd love to. Yes, yes, yes."

He grinned, pulling her down for an amorous kiss. Blakesley collapsed against him completely, holding on to his neck as he rolled her over onto her back and took the dominant position over her. Before things got out of control too much, he put his big hand on her jaw, cupping her face as he pulled back to look at her.

"Before we get too far into this and I lose the ability to think," he began, "tell me what Lizzie is doing here."

Blakesley gazed up at him, her head rather dwarfed by his big hand. "It was really strange," she said. "Gina called me at the Extended Stay a couple of weeks ago to tell me that your daughter was at her house. Apparently, Lizzie had a big blow up with her mother and ran away. She took a flight down here, went to your townhome but you weren't home. She knew where Butch and Gina lived so she went there looking for you."

"So what happened?"

"I went to Gina's house and sat with Lizzie for a while to try and figure out what was going on with her," she said. "She's such a sweet girl, Beck. She ended up coming back to the hotel with me and she's been with me ever since. My girls are enamored with her. I... I don't want her going back to her mother."

His brow furrowed. "Why not?"

She put her arms around his neck. "You have to promise me you'll stay calm. If you can't swear to it, then I won't tell you."

"You need to tell me what you know if it's involving my daughter."

"I understand that, but I'm saying this on Lizzie's behalf. She came to you for comfort and your anger isn't going to help her at all. She's pretty traumatized."

His concern grew. "Traumatized with what?"

Blakesley shushed him because his voice was growing louder. "According to Lizzie, her stepdad made a pass at her," she whispered. "He didn't actually touch her from what I can gather, but Lizzie was so upset by it that she stole some money from her mother and bought a plane ticket down here. The poor kid's very upset by everything and it took me some convincing to get her mother's phone number so I could call her and tell her where Lizzie was. It's just a big mess. Oh, and by the way, your ex-wife was really a bitch. I told her we were going to have Lizzie for a while and she didn't like that very much."

Beck sighed faintly, his hand moving from her jaw to her hair, stroking it. "Sorry," he muttered. "Sharon was always kind of high-strung and mean at times. Her family was really well off and she just grew up with everything she ever wanted, so... well, it doesn't matter, but I'm sorry if she was rude to you. I'll talk to Lizzie in the morning and then give Sharon a call."

Blakesley watched his face, seeing how weary he was, now with the added burden of child issues. "You're such a sweet man," she told him. "How in the world did you end up with a woman like that?"

He shrugged. "Easy," he said. "She got pregnant so I did the right thing and married her."

Blakesley laughed loudly. "So you have a history of women forcing you into marriage?"

He grinned, the hair stroking moving to her shoulder and arm. "You didn't force me," he denied, leaning over to kiss her neck. "Besides, think about it; Lizzie just turned fourteen. I was married to Sharon for fourteen years and that ended four years ago. Sharon and I got married right away but she miscarried the baby. It took her another four years to get pregnant with Lizzie but the doctor told her after that she couldn't have any more kids."

Blakesley closed her eyes as he nuzzled her neck and shoulder, peeling back the pajama top to get at her cleavage. "I'm sorry about that," she whispered. "You're great with kids. You deserve to have a dozen."

He snorted, a hand cupping her left breast as he rooted around for a nipple. "I wouldn't know what to do with them all," he confessed. "We've got four girls between us. That's good enough for me."

"What happened to that baby brother? Still want him?"

"Sure, if we're lucky enough."

Blakesley shifted so she was wrapped up around him again, her legs around his waist, pulling him down on top of her. "Let's practice, okay?"

He found a warm nipple and suckled hard, feeling her squirm beneath him. "Absolutely," he breathed. "But I shouldn't even be touching you right now. I'm filthy."

Blakesley responded by grabbing his tee shirt and pulling it over his head. He was dirty, sweaty, beaten and bruised, but she didn't care. She just wanted to feel him against her, in her. In little time, they were naked between the sheets, practicing for that baby brother to balance out all of the girls.

They practiced most of the night.

THIRTEEN

BECK WOKE up the next morning to a wriggling bed. At first, he thought it was an earthquake until he heard giggling. Earthquakes don't giggle. Flat on his stomach, he peeped an eye open to see two big blue eyes looking back at him. Charlotte squealed when she realized he was awake and suddenly, the bed was alive with giggling girls.

He roared sleepily and grabbed Charlotte and Cadee, who happened to be closest. He tickled them as they screamed, rolling over onto his back and yawning as someone ripped back the curtains. Bright white light streamed into the room and he felt like a vampire trying to cover his eyes. As Charlotte tried to tickle him back, he looked to his right to see Lizzie sitting on the edge of the bed.

He grinned broadly at his daughter, sitting up and throwing his arms around her. "Hi, baby girl," he kissed the side of her head. "It's so good to see you."

Lizzie hugged her dad tightly. "Hi, Dad," she murmured.

Beck let her go enough so that he could look her in the face; she was tall, blond and beautiful and looked more like him every day. He opened his mouth to say something but Crosby charged him and wrapped her little arms around his neck as Charlotte jumped on Lizzie's lap.

"Beck!" Crosby was yelling. "We made you cinnamon rolls!"

She was shouting excitedly in his ear and he gave her a squeeze, watching Lizzie laugh. "Thanks, baby," he stuck his finger in his ringing ear. "I'll get dressed and eat them."

"No!" Crosby hurled herself off the bed. "We're going to bring you breakfast here. You stay here!"

She flew out of the bedroom with Cadee behind her. Charlotte stayed on Lizzie's lap as Beck took a moment to drink in the sight of his only child. There was such joyful chaos going on around him and although he didn't want to ignore the little ones, he really wanted to focus on his daughter.

"You're so beautiful," he said wistfully. "I feel like it's been years since I saw you last."

Lizzie cradled sweet Charlotte. "It's been four months," she said, hugging Charlotte. Her smile faded. "I guess Blakesley told you why I'm here."

Beck nodded. "She did," he started looking around the room. "I want to talk to you about it. But do me a favor, baby girl – step out for a moment and let me take a quick shower and get dressed."

"Sure, Dad."

Lizzie stood up with Charlotte in her arms. Beck watched his daughter cuddle Blakesley's youngest. It warmed his heart to see the sweet interaction.

"Hey," he added. "It looks like you have a friend."

Lizzie grinned, looking a good deal like her father. "They're sweet," she said. "I always wanted a little sister. I guess I'm going to have three."

He wasn't sure how much she knew but he didn't want to insult her intelligence. Since she had been staying with Blakesley for a while, he assumed she knew almost as much as he did. What she hadn't been told, she could figure out. She was a smart girl.

"Are you okay with that?" he asked as she headed for the door.

Lizzie paused at the door, turning to look at her dad as Charlotte reached up and tweaked her nose. "Totally," she grinned. "I like Blakesley, Dad. She's really awesome. I know she cares a lot about you and you deserve that."

"So you approve?"

"Yes."

Beck smiled as she exited the room and closed the door behind her. Tossing off the covers, he went into the bathroom with the big double sinks and turned on the shower. He was still grimy and sweaty and filthy, dying to get clean. He stepped into the big tiled shower, noticing that Blakesley had even set aside a "manly" section of the shower that had green soap, man-scented body wash, a couple of disposable razors, and man-shampoo. He grinned at her thoughtfulness and began to scrub down.

The hot water felt spectacular. He scrubbed himself from head to toe before standing there and just letting the hot water beat down over him. He actually felt pretty good, happy that he was with Lizzie, Blakesley and the girls, trying not to let the horrific grief that had gripped him for days seep back into his mind. Then he started to feel guilty that he was happy when Butch was lying in a pine box at Coronado. He told Gina he'd go with her to claim Butch's body at noon, thoughts of which began to drag him down into despair again. But his thoughts were interrupted when Blakesley knocked on the bathroom door and let herself in.

She smiled broadly at him as she came into the bathroom. "Hi, baby," she said. "I'm sorry the girls woke you. I tried to keep them out but it was tough. They were so excited to see you."

He just grinned, leaning out of the shower so he could kiss her good morning. "No worries," he told her. "I have no problem waking up every morning like that for the rest of my life. The only thing missing was you."

She chuckled softly and it was then he noticed what she had in her arms. She set a big fluffy towel on the counter by the shower but he saw that she still had more items draped over her arm. She held up a pair of jeans.

"Since I couldn't move your stuff in while you were gone unless I wanted to break into your condo, I winged it by getting you a few things to wear just until we can get your stuff," she said. "Gina and I guessed that you were about a thirty-two waist, so I got you a pair of jeans that I think might fit you. I also got you some underwear, some pajama bottoms, and a couple of shirts. If you don't like them, that's okay, but I wanted you to have something to wear until you could get to your clothes."

By this time, he had turned off the shower and grabbed the towel, drying his muscular frame as he looked at the items she had laid out on the bathroom counter. He fingered the jeans with great interest.

"You did this?" he asked, almost incredulous.

She was uncertain. "Yes."

He looked at her. "Just for me?"

"Of course."

He looked back at the clothing. "Baby, that's about the sweetest thing anyone has ever done for me," he said sincerely, giving her a sweet kiss. "That was really thoughtful of you."

She was relieved as her smile returned. "I just wanted to make sure you were taken care of," she said. "I also got you soap and razors and stuff. If you don't like any of it, I can get you something else or...."

He bent over and kissed her again, mid-sentence. "Baby, seriously, that's the sweetest thing anyone has ever done for me," he said again. "Thank you. I love everything, even the soap."

She was flattered and pleased. "I hope the jeans fit," she said, gathering everything back up and carrying it out of the bathroom, back into the bedroom. "The shirts are out here."

He dried off completely and wrapped the towel around his waist before following her out into the bedroom. In the light of day, he could see just how gorgeous the bedroom was with its white walls, white bedspread and wrought iron bed frame. Black and white pictures with gold and pale green accents lined the walls strategically. It was the most gorgeous bedroom he had ever seen and he wriggled his eyebrows when he saw the flat screen television bolted to the wall across from the bed. He hadn't noticed it until this moment and he suddenly looked at her, torn between delight and exasperation.

"Look at this room." He began to point. Then he stopped pointing, grabbed her hands, and set her down on the bed next to him. "Baby, we need to talk about this before we go any further. Last night you said you bought the house."

Blakesley thought he seemed upset. "I did," she nodded. "I offered them four hundred and forty two thousand for it and they took it," she said. "Your friend Kevin did the deal for us. Because the house was empty and I paid cash, they closed escrow in two weeks. It was just a matter of completing the paperwork. We only moved in five days ago."

He stared at her. "You paid cash?"

She nodded. "It was a good investment and I had the money." She winced when she saw his expression. "You're not happy about this, are you?"

He shook his head. Then he nodded. "Of course I am," he said. "But I guess I'm just a little hurt. I wanted to buy it for us."

"It is your house," she said. "I'm transferring the title to you. It's a gift."

"I don't want you to give it to me," he tried to explain without hurting her feelings. "I wanted to buy it myself."

"So you can buy it from me, then. I'll give you a good deal."

He didn't know what to say. As he watched, she stood up and walked to the French doors that faced outside to the big backyard with the perfect landscape. She pointed.

"I got you that, too," she said as if she wasn't sure she should tell him.

He didn't see what she was pointing at until he stood up and went to the door. Parked outside on a big cement area was a brand new Ford F-350 Lariat Super Duty crew-cab pick-up truck, complete with massive chrome accents, after-market chrome wheels, jet black in color with dark tinted windows.

It was the most beautiful truck he had ever seen and he just stood there at the door like an idiot, gaping at it. He also noticed a very big dog lying next to it and when the dog shifted, he could see that it was a German Shepherd. Off to the right against the fence that ran along a small alley, he could see a brand new doghouse painted just like the big house. His gaze inevitably moved back to the truck. He was stunned.

"Do you like the truck?" Blakesley asked hesitantly.

He looked at her as if she had lost her mind. "Do I like it?" he repeated. "You seriously bought that?"

"For you."

"For me?"

"Yes,"

"Why?"

She shrugged, looking back at the truck. "Because I was feeling bad after we left the house the first time we saw it," she said. "You were trying to do something so sweet for all of us and I was stubborn about it. I just wanted to do something nice for you. Plus, your truck is several years old and the brakes grind. I thought you needed a new truck."

Beck was speechless. He looked around at the house, the clothes laid out on the bed, the new truck in the backyard, and just shook his head. It was like a perfect life, a perfect house, all packaged up for him. It was something he had dreamed of his entire life.

"I don't even know what to say," he said, looking at her with shock. "I feel like this is a dream. Am I going to wake up from this?"

She smiled timidly. "No," she said softly. "I love you, Beck. I'm just so happy we found each other. Maybe I went overboard, but I just wanted to show you how happy I was and maybe when you drive the truck, you'll think of me just a little. Do you think it's creepy for me to give you all of this?"

He had to laugh. "Creepy? Why?"

She shrugged, smiling because he was. "I don't know," she said. "Maybe because it looks like I'm trying to buy you or something. I really wasn't trying to, you know. I just wanted to show you how much I appreciate you."

He frowned and smiled at the same time, as if she was saying funny, crazy things. He put his arms around her and kissed her forehead, gazing out at the truck and shaking his head again. He was in shock.

"I just can't believe it," he said. "No one has ever cared about me enough to do such nice things for me."

"So you like the truck?"

He rolled his eyes. "Oh, my God, I can't believe you even asked that," he said. "I love it. It's the most amazing truck I've ever seen. I can't thank you enough."

She grinned happily. "I'll turn the title over to you today," she said. "I didn't have any of your vital information so I had to purchase it in my name."

He just hugged her, feeling humbled and stunned by the whole thing. "Baby, you spent so much money on that truck," he muttered. "I already know you love me. You didn't have to buy me a forty thousand dollar truck to prove it."

"I know," she insisted. "But I wanted to. Now, go get dressed so you can take us all for a ride."

He laughed, kissed and hugged her again, his gaze lingering on the truck. The dog, resting next to the truck, suddenly stood up and shook itself before trotting to the corner of the yard where a child-size pool was sitting with a hose dripping into it. He pointed to the dog.

"Where'd you get him?" he asked. "That's a fine looking animal."

She grinned, watching the nearly all-black Shepherd splash in the pool. "That's Alfie," she said. "He's three years old. We got him from the San Diego dog rescue a couple of days ago. He seems to be a great watchdog and he's really good with the girls. They love him."

"He's really big."

"Really big and really sweet. He'll lick you to death. Besides, I thought he'd look great in your truck, like a mascot."

He just shook his head again, for the tenth time that morning, amazed at everything he had come home to. "You really did all this?"

"I did."

"Is there anything you didn't think of?"

"I don't think so. But if you think of something, you let me know."

He laughed again, watching the big dog splash around for a moment before heading back over to the bed and dropping the towel. He pulled on the boxer briefs she had bought for him, looking around the room and shaking his head at the expensive flat screen television again as he pulled on the jeans. They fit him extremely well. Blakesley picked up the towel he had dropped, watching him get dressed. She cocked an approving eyebrow.

"Those jeans make your ass look great," she told him.

He grinned, winking at her as he held up one of the shirts lying on the bed. It was a button-down long sleeved white shirt with crinkly material and a black design on it, making it kind of hip and cool. It wasn't something he normally wore, being rather conservative, but he hesitated to say anything.

"Lizzie picked the shirt out," Blakesley said helpfully. "If you'd rather just wear a tee shirt, there are some clean white ones in the drawer over there."

He shook his head and pulled the shirt on, buttoning it over his broad chest. "If my girl picked it out for me, I'm going to wear it," he told her firmly. Then he glanced at the clock, noting it was after ten in the morning. He sobered. "I told Gina I would go with her to claim Butch's body over at the base. I'd like it if you'd come with me."

Blakesley immediately sobered. "She hasn't gone already?"

He shook his head. "The team came back yesterday but the casualties didn't come back until early this morning," he replied.

"They have to be prepared and all that. The soonest she can get him is noon. Will you come?"

"Sure," she said. "If you don't think I'll be in the way."

"I don't," he replied. "Besides, I need you there."

"Why?"

"Because I do."

She could sense that he needed her support and she stopped asking questions. Putting the towel back in the bathroom on the rack, she opened up the bedroom door to find four girls standing outside. They had a big plate of cinnamon rolls and Lizzie had a mug of coffee. As soon as the door opened, Blakesley slipped out and they all slipped in. They swarmed around Beck.

"Wow," he said as Crosby shoved a plate of freshly made cinnamon rolls at him. "Those look really good. Did you make them yourself?"

Crosby and Charlotte nodded as Lizzie handed her dad his coffee. "Blakesley put them in the oven but they frosted them," she said, catching sight of the truck outside in the yard. "So how do you like your new truck?"

Beck looked at it, still shaking his head with wonder. "I love it," he said sincerely. "I'm really shocked."

Lizzie watched her dad as he sipped his coffee, staring at the truck. "It's about time you found someone to be nice to you," she said.

He looked at her, surprised. "Why do you say that?"

Lizzie shrugged and looked away. "Because Mom sure wasn't," she said frankly. "She still isn't. She's just a big, fat bitch."

Beck had never heard Lizzie talk that way. The little girls were still clamoring at his feet and he took a roll just to make them happy, catching Blakesley's attention when she came back in the bedroom. He silently begged her to take the little girls out and she caught his subtle gestures. She could also see the expression on Lizzie's face and knew the subject of her appearance had been broached. She turned for the chest of drawers and picked up the truck keys from the surface.

"Hey," she tossed the keys at Beck. "I...I, uh, need some milk. Will you and Lizzie go to the store and get some?"

Beck deftly caught the keys. "Sure, baby," he said, already moving for the door. "Where did I put my shoes?"

"Here," Blakesley collected his work boots from a spot over by the television. Beck took them from her.

"Thank you," he set the coffee down and sat on the bed as Crosby got in his face.

"Do you like my rolls?" she wanted to know.

He was busy pulling on his boots. "I love them, baby girl," he told her. "Save them for me. Lizzie and I are going to go to the store and get some milk. We'll be right back."

Crosby started whining about wanting to go with him, which set off Charlotte, but Blakesley herded them out of the bedroom and back up the stairs. Cadee was already upstairs getting dressed while Nikki was down in the kitchen cleaning up. Blakesley and the two youngest girls were halfway up the stairs as Beck popped in from the living room.

"Lizzie and I will be right back," he told her. "Will you be ready to leave by eleven?"

Blakesley was pulling Charlotte up the stairs. "I'll be ready," she said. "You and Lizzie take your time."

He winked at her. "Thank you," he said with soft sincerity. "Love you. We'll be right back."

Blakesley waved him on, taking the girls up to the bathroom for a quick bath. But before she turned the water on, she heard Beck fire up the new truck, gunning the engine. She grinned as he revved it and peeled off down the alley next to the house.

It was good to have him home.

FOURTEEN

"SO WHY DID you call your mom a bitch?" Beck asked as he took Market Street back over to the 5 Freeway.

Lizzie was watching the scenery go by. "Did Blakesley tell you what happened?"

"I want to hear it from you."

Lizzie shrugged as she thought on her father's question. "Dan's been getting really weird with me," she said. "Especially when my friends come over. I've caught him spying on us."

Beck shrugged. "That's not a crime."

Lizzie looked at him, indignant. "No, it's not, but when he stands in the hallway outside of my door and masturbates, that's just sick."

Beck looked at her, feeling his control slip and struggling against it. "How do you know?"

Lizzie threw up her hands. "Because I've caught him," she exclaimed. "It started about six months ago. I told Mom but she didn't believe me. When Dan came into my room three weeks ago when I was reading in bed and tried to touch me, she still didn't believe me. So I left."

Beck could feel his body tensing as he tried to control his rising anger. "Where did he try to touch you?"

She sighed, looking out the window. "At first he told me how beautiful I was getting and tried to touch my hair," she said, feeling dirty like she had the first time she had told the story. "I pushed his hand away and he laughed. Then he tried to touch my arm but I swear he was going for my boob. It was just gross, Dad. I'm never going back there ever again."

He took a deep, thoughtful breath. "You won't have to when I call my lawyer and tell him what you told me," he said. "If your mom fights me on it, I'll press charges against Dan for sexual battery and lewd acts on a minor. In fact, I'm going to do it anyway. That sick bastard isn't going to get away with this."

Lizzie looked at him. "So you believe me?"

"Are you lying?"

"No."

"Then I believe you."

She sighed heavily. "Thank you," she said. "Mom didn't. She told me I must have been mistaken because Dan wouldn't do something like that. He's a teacher, you know. I think she's just afraid he could lose his job."

Beck grunted. "He's not only going to lose his job but his teeth when I get finished with him," he grumbled. "The guy makes a pass at his stepdaughter whose father happens to be a trained killer? What an idiot. Dan's living on borrowed time."

Lizzie was watching him, silently. When he turned to glance at her as they sat at a red stoplight, he could see her eyes full of tears. Beck reached out and put a comforting hand to her cheek.

"No worries, baby girl," he said softly. "I'll take care of it. I don't want you to worry."

She burst into tears. "But there's more, Dad," she sobbed.

He looked at her with concern. "What?"

She wiped at her eyes. "My friend, Meggyn, thought Dan was hot. She told me to tell him but I wouldn't. One night, she was spending the night and I woke up really late to go to the bathroom and saw she wasn't in my room. Dad, she was with Dan."

The light turned green but Beck was hanging on every horrifying word. "What do you mean she was with him?"

Lizzie wept. "I mean she was with him," she whispered. "They were in the living room on the floor. He was on top of her."

"They were having sex?"

She nodded, turning away and sobbing softly. Beck was through the intersection but pulled over. He couldn't drive and deal with this. He was stricken.

"What did you do?"

Lizzie wiped at her eyes. "I told Mom," she said. "She and Dan had a big fight but in the end, he told Mom it wasn't true and I must have been dreaming. She believed him, Dad. She believed him over me, so then Mom thought I was trying to break them up. She started being really hostile towards me and that's when Dan started hanging around outside my bedroom and jacking off."

Beck hissed. "Jesus Christ," he struggled not to explode as he looked at his crying daughter. "I don't want you to worry about this, okay? I need to take care of some things today, but tomorrow, I will resolve this. In fact, I'm calling my lawyer today and we'll get the ball rolling. Dan is going down and you're going to live with me from now on. All right?"

Lizzie nodded, sniffling. "Thanks, Dad."

He put his arms around her, kissing the side of her head. "I'm so sorry you had to go through this, baby girl," he murmured. "But I'll take care of it, I promise."

"Blakesley says she's going to hire thugs to break his legs."

Beck laughed. "She won't have to hire anyone," he said. "She'll go break his legs herself."

"I think she would, too."

They shared a giggle and he kissed her cheek again before putting the car into gear and resuming their drive.

"I'm going to call your mom and talk to her about this," he said, picking up his cell phone. He had no idea how to work the Bluetooth on the new car so he opted to just use his phone for now. "Just sit and listen. I want you to hear what I tell her."

"Sure, Dad."

Beck made the call as he and Lizzie continued on to the market. They returned to the house about forty minutes later with a gallon of milk and a box of ice cream bars. Cadee, Crosby and Charlotte were in the small room off the entry that had been turned into a children's play and television room, so they had a full view of Beck and Lizzie coming in the front door with treats. Crosby went crazy, begging for ice cream at eleven in the morning, as Blakesley emerged from the master bedroom.

She was dressed in a black wrap-around dress that showed off her spectacular figure. She wore five inch platform heels, something Beck had come to expect from her, but as he looked at her walking into the kitchen fixing an earring, all he could manage to feel was wild, unadulterated love and attraction. She looked stunning.

"Wow," he said as she walked past him. "You look amazing."

She smiled as she finished with the earring and told Crosby she couldn't have any ice cream until she ate lunch. Someone had let Alfie in and the big dog came right up to Beck, wagging his tail and cocking his big head curiously. Beck held out a hand, making friends with the dog, as Crosby put her arms around the dog's neck and hugged him.

"Do you like Alfie?" she demanded.

Beck let the dog sniff him and get used to his scent before petting the animal on the head. He was rewarded with big licks.

"He's very nice," he told her. "Do you like him?"

Crosby had her head on the dog's back. "He's my best friend," she said sincerely. "Mama, can Alfie have some lunch with us?"

Blakesley shook her head. "Honey, he needs to eat his own food," she said. "Remember what I told you? We feed him in the morning and at the night. That's all he gets. And no treats for him; they'll make him sick."

Crosby wasn't happy and she hugged the dog, talking silly baby-talk to him. Beck was convinced she was trying to talk the dog into a mutiny against a treat-less existence when Blakesley got his attention.

"Baby, do we need to go?" she asked him. "You wanted to leave around eleven and it's that now."

He looked at his watch. "Yes," he said after a moment, sounding reluctant. "Are you ready?"

"I am."

"I need to swing by my townhouse and change."

"Then let's go."

Blakesley relayed instructions to Nikki, who was standing near the sink holding Charlotte. Charlotte didn't take too kindly to her mother leaving and started to whine. Crosby, yelling her farewells, suddenly bolted through the kitchen and out through the back door with the dog running after her. Cadee followed the dog and her sister, racing out to the backyard to play.

It was sweet and normal, and a million times better than the hotel or a rundown old home with tunnels under the floor. Blakesley knew now as she had known when they had moved in, that it had been the right decision. She kissed weepy Charlotte, waved goodbye to Lizzie, and quit the kitchen with Beck on her heels.

He took her hand as they left the front porch and made their way down to his truck parked at the curb. It really was a magnificent vehicle and Beck took a moment to inspect it again, grinning as he ran his hand over the chrome around the dark-tinted windows. Blakesley stood there and watched him.

"I think you like your new toy," she said with a grin.

He nodded sincerely and turned to kiss her as he used the key fob to unlock the door. "My new toy and my new girl," he said, helping her in. "Thank you for everything, baby. I've never known anyone so thoughtful or generous. I'm just really humbled by it all."

"I was happy to do it. You deserve it."

He smiled as he closed the door and went around to the

driver's side, climbing in. He puffed out his cheeks as he went to engage the ignition.

"I feel like I'm driving the space shuttle," he commented. "Did you know this thing has keyless ignition?"

"I do."

"The dashboard talks back to me."

She giggled. "I know," she said. "I tried to get them to program it with my voice, but they couldn't do it. Sorry."

He snorted as he started the car and revved the diesel engine. Pulling away from the curb, they headed off to the Martin Luther King Freeway about a mile and a half to the north.

"Did you and Lizzie talk?" Blakesley asked as she dug in her purse for her lipstick.

He nodded. "Thanks for giving us some alone time," he said quietly. "I'm assuming she told you everything."

Blakesley looked at him with some distaste in her expression. "Yes."

He sighed heavily. "I called her mom while we were out getting milk."

"And?"

"And I told her that Lizzie would be living with us from now on and that I was going to file charges against her stepdad." He glanced at Blakesley. "Needless to say, she was upset. She's got a lot to deal with, having a husband who's sleeping with underage girls."

"How does Lizzie feel about everything?"

"She's thrilled to be with us and not her mom. She loves the girls and seems very happy about the arrangement. I'm just thrilled to have my baby girl with me, you know? I've hardly seen her the past four years."

Blakesley smiled and touched his cheek sweetly. Then she touched up her lipstick as Beck started messing with the dashboard, the radio, and any other knobs he could find. She watched him from the corner of her eye, grinning when he accidentally turned on the windshield wipers. He was particularly fascinated with the satellite radio and he fooled with it until he found something he liked. Alice in Chains blasted over the Bose speakers.

"God, this is amazing." He settled back as the music played. "You have no idea how much this helps me face what's coming. I mean, it's not like you needed to do any of this. Just to see your smiling face when I got back would have accomplished the same thing."

She reached over and took his hand. "So you're telling me that I didn't need to spend a half million dollars to reel you in?"

He cocked an eyebrow at her but he was grinning. "You reeled me in the day I met you – you know that." He was almost scolding her but not quite. "It's just like I told you earlier – I've never had anybody be so generous towards me. It makes me feel like maybe I'm something special. I still feel like I'm going to wake up tomorrow and this will all have been a dream."

"It's not a dream," she said as she squeezed his hand. "Maybe you just never let anybody get close enough to you to be generous. I just want you to be happy."

"I am happy." He looked at her. "Happier than I've ever been in my life. You did that the night you let me barge in on you over at the Del and have dinner with you. That was the luckiest night of my life. Now, the question is: are you happy?"

She sobered. "I wouldn't be here if I wasn't," she confessed. "Can I tell you something?"

"Anything."

She sighed and turned to look at the passing urban-scape as they took the on-ramp to the freeway. It was a bright, beautiful day outside as if unaware of the sad thing they were about to do.

"When I saw that story about the accident and the dead S.E.A.L.s, I cried all night," she said. "It made me think so many things, but it mostly made me realize that life is short and you can't put things off. There may not be a tomorrow. I had already purchased the house at that point and mailed the picture to you at the base, but it just made me realize that you're such a special guy. I need to show you how much I love you every single day because you could deploy tomorrow and I'd never see you again. So I bought the truck, and the dog, because I wanted to make a home for you. Does that make any sense?"

He nodded, squeezing her hand. "Sure it does," he murmured. "Butch's death made me realize a lot of things, too, the same things you realized. Life is very short and we need to make the most of it while we can. That's why the first words out of my mouth when I saw you were going to be a marriage proposal. You're the woman I want to spend the rest of my life with and I don't want to waste any more time. I'm yours, body and soul, and not because you bought me a really cool truck."

She laughed as he winked at her. "So you're really not freaked out by all of this?"

He shook his head. "I'm flattered and touched that you would think enough of me to do it," he said. "I can't tell you enough how much I love it, or you, which brings me to something I was thinking this morning – what are you doing to do with your house? What's going on with that?"

Blakesley sighed. "That's such a big mess," she breathed. "The City came in the day after you left and basically declared the entire thing unsafe and off-limits until they can determine the extent of the tunneling. Then the State of California came in and told the City to get their hands off it because it was a State Historic Landmark, so the State of California has taken it all over and the entire thing is being roped off and studied. It's turned into a pissing match between the City of San Diego and the State of California. They can't give me a date as to when I can resume restoration, much less when I will be able to move into it, so that's why I bought the old Victorian. I wanted some place for all of us to live."

He took the off-ramp that lead up the Coronado Bridge. "So what happens when the house is restored? Do we move out of the Victorian?"

She shrugged. "I'm not sure," she said. "I really like the Victorian and I love the way it's so kid-friendly. I'm not sure about the

Earp homestead anymore. It... it's almost like that curse old Mike talked about just hovers over it."

"Have you seen old Mike since all of that started?"

"No," she shook her head. "Not at all. I'm kind of worried about him."

"Why?" Beck wanted to know. "He can take care of himself."

She just shrugged, looking out over the bay as they traveled up and over the bridge. "Because he's an old man living in a cave." That's the best she could do to describe why she was worried. "Oh, well, I guess it really doesn't matter. The State of California has probably already found him and kicked him out."

"Have you been out to the house lately?"

"I try to go every day. They're coming up with some pretty fascinating stuff from the tunnel." She turned to look at him. "Did you know there was a body down there?"

He scratched his chin, hoping she wouldn't become upset with his answer. "I saw it," he said quietly. "I didn't want you to see it, which is why I herded you out of there so fast. Don't you remember?"

She shrugged. "Not really," she said. "Anyway, the people from the state said it's got to be a hundred years old. They have no idea who it is."

"Maybe it's that Mexican guy that Mike told us about, the one that old Ben Earp held for ransom."

She wriggled her eyebrows. "Could be," she said. Then she shook her head sadly. "He sounds like a really bad guy. I'm kind of ashamed to be related to him."

He lifted her hand, kissing it as the bridge dumped them out onto Coronado Island. Beck continued driving straight for about a mile until he came to G Street and hung a left. It was a tree-lined street clustered with townhomes and condos, and Beck eventually pulled up next to a well-kept series of buildings about halfway down the block. He turned off the truck.

"Welcome to my former home," he said as he opened the door. "Come on in and make yourself comfortable."

She opened her door but he fast-stepped it around the truck and helped her exit. He couldn't keep his eyes off her lovely legs, looking great in the high-heels, and the silky wrap-around dress showed every curve. He put his arm around her, possessively, as he walked her back to his townhome.

He had a unit about midway down the building. He opened the door and ushered her inside. It was dark, the blinds closed, and Blakesley looked around as her eyes adjusted to the darkness. Beck opened up a couple of blinds and white sunlight streamed in. It was a Spartan place with just the bare necessities, neat with its carpeted floors and blue-fabric couch, but it didn't looked lived in at all. As she looked at the pictures of military men on the walls, he called to her from the stairs.

"Come up here with me, baby," he said.

Gaze lingering on the picture of a very young and very hand-some Beck in his academy graduation photo, she followed him up the stairs. There were two bedrooms on this level, a master bedroom with a bath and a smaller bedroom and bath. She trailed after him into the master bedroom.

The master bedroom wasn't much better than the rest of the house. There was just a big bed, a television and a chest of drawers. Blakesley stood in the doorway and looked around.

"How long have you lived here?" she asked.

He was in the big walk-in closet. "About twenty years."

"It looks like you haven't spent twenty minutes here."

She heard him snort. "Sharon took pretty much everything when we divorced," he said. "Couches, beds, furnishings, that kind of thing. I just have the bare necessities. I'm on base so much of the time that it really doesn't matter."

"What are you going to do with it now that we've got the Victorian?"

"Rent it out or sell it," he said. "You're the real estate whiz. What do you think?"

She looked around some more, inspecting the bathroom. "You could rent it out and glean the income," she said. "You said you don't have that much more to pay off. Why not just rent it out? Property on Coronado demands a premium. You could make a nice chunk of change monthly."

"Good idea." He suddenly came out of the closet with his arms full of clothing. He tossed it on the bed. "This can all go back to the house. I don't have any boxes to put it in."

She went over to the bed, shrugging at the pile. "We can just carry it down and throw it in the truck."

He nodded, hands on hips as he studied the clothes. Blakesley studied them, too, until she looked up and noticed he was only wearing a pair of dress khakis. His bare chest looked magnificent and her gaze drifted over him with appreciation. He made her feel all hot and bothered.

"Are you going like that?" she teased.

He had no idea what she was talking about until he looked at her and noticed what she was referring to. He looked down at himself, half-dressed.

"Would you like me to?" he teased back.

She grinned and ran her hand across his chest, sensually, before falling into his embrace. "You better believe it," she purred.

He wrapped her up in his arms and went in for a big kiss but she stopped him. "You'll mess my lipstick," she said, putting her hand over his eager mouth. "Besides, you need to finish dressing. We have to go."

The smile faded from his lips and he sobered. "I guess." He let her go and went back in the closet. "I'm really not looking forward to this."

She sobered as well, sorry she had put a damper on things. She sat on the bed next to his clothes.

"I know, baby," she said. "I'm so sorry. I know he was your friend."

Beck didn't say anything. She could hear him moving around in the closet and when he finally emerged, it was in his service dress khaki uniform. He looked quite impressive but Blakesley wasn't sure if she should tell him. He was getting dressed up for a somber occasion and she wasn't sure flattery would be well met.

"I'm not sure if it's appropriate to tell you that you look great, but you do," she said. "You do that uniform justice."

He smiled weakly at her as he went to his dresser, opened up the drawer, and pulled out a box which he took over to the bathroom with the big mirror. Looking at himself in the mirror, he began pinning things on his crisp khaki shirt, bars and stars and other colorful things. As she sat and watched, he just kept pinning more and more on his chest, on his collar, and then he pinned on what looked like two medals. Everything was neat and orderly as she watched, entranced.

"What are all of those bars you're pinning to yourself?" she asked.

He finished with the second medal. "They're rank insignia, various service awards, things like that," he said, turning around and pointing to the different bars on chest. "This one is the Presidential Service Citation, this one is the Navy Unit Commendation, and this one is the Meritorious Unit Commendation."

She stood up from the bed and went to him to take a closer look. She pointed to the two medals hanging below all of the colorful bars.

"What are those?"

He glanced down at them. "The Navy Cross."

"What are they for?"

He stroked her arm affectionately as he walked around her to go get his shoes. "For extreme gallantry and risk of life in actual combat with an armed enemy force and going beyond the call of duty." He disappeared into the closet and emerged a few seconds later. "That's what it says in the Navy Manual, anyway. I got one in Afghanistan and the other in a very dicey situation that I'm not at liberty to discuss."

She watched him sit on the bed to pull his brown Navy regulation shoes on. As he was fussing with the laces of one of the shoes, she sat down next to him and watched. Her expression was pensive.

"You've risked your life a lot," she said.

"That's my job."

"Why can't you tell me what you did to earn them?" she asked. "I'm not going to tell anyone."

He looked at her, cupped her face, and kissed her cheek. "Because I don't want to freak you out," he said frankly. "Does it matter?"

She half-shrugged. "Probably not, but I'd just like to know. I already think you walk on water. I just want to know how often you do it."

He laughed and pulled on the other shoe. "Too often," he said, putting his hand on her arm when she opened her mouth to press him. "Baby, it's not that I'm withholding information or being deliberately evasive, but now that you're with a military man, you should know that most of us don't like to talk about these things. To talk about it is to relive it again and, trust me, I don't want to relive the events that are represented by those medals. I lost very good friends and did things that a movie writer couldn't even imagine. Some things are just better left unsaid."

She nodded in understanding. "I'm sorry," she said. "I'm not trying to pry. I'm just proud of you and I want to know all about you, even the awful things."

He looked at her, seeing that she really didn't have a clue what he meant. It wasn't her fault; she just wasn't used to being with a man who risked his life every time he put on the uniform. He sighed faintly, cupped her face, and kissed her cheek again.

"I'm going to tell you this just once so you understand where I'm coming from," he said quietly, "and then I'd appreciate it very much if you didn't press me about things I don't want to talk about. If I want to tell you, I will, but if I don't, just let it go. Deal?"

She nodded seriously. "Deal. I'm sorry."

He shook his head. "Don't apologize," he said softly, pointing to the first of the two Navy Crosses. "I was in Afghanistan and my troop and I had just finished reconning a Taliban outpost because we had good information that they were holding two U.N. workers hostage. This outpost was high in the mountains and we scaled slopes like Spiderman to check it out. To make a long story short, we were ambushed. My troop got split up in the firefight and about half of my men were caught in very bad crossfire in a canyon. I managed to get the other half of my men to safety before returning for the rest who were pinned down and receiving heavy fire. Butch and I figured out that there were about twelve insurgents firing on my men so he and I systematically picked off one insurgent at a time until there were four left. We captured those four."

She was listening intently. "So you received the medal for that?"

He shook his head. "I received the medal when I went into the canyon in spite of the gunfire, sheer cliffs and nasty conditions to carry out two men who were badly wounded. I carried one guy twelve miles on my back to an LZ to be medevacked."

"What's an 'LZ'?"

"Landing zone."

By the time he was finished, she was looking at him with great warmth and respect. She kissed him gently on the jaw. "You're so brave," she whispered. "Thank you for telling me. I'm so proud of you."

He smiled. "Thank you," he replied, his smile fading. "But I also lost seven men in that little adventure, kids hardly older than Lizzie, kids that showed bravery and skill like experienced men in the face of great adversity. Butch and I collected each and every one of those brave young men and carried their bodies to safety. I'll tell you something that I've never told anyone – it felt like my kid brothers were killed. I know every one of those boys and their serial numbers. I've memorized them because I don't ever want to forget how brave they were for their country and every day on the anniversary of their death, if I'm able, I lay a wreath on every one of their graves. I never let that day pass without some kind of remembrance."

Her smile was gone and her eyes were moist. "That's very noble," she said. "It just confirms what I already know. You're a man of great character and honor."

He stood up and took her hand, squeezing it. "That may be," he said quietly, "but I will tell you that I'm just hanging on by a thread right now. Butch was closer to me than a brother. I'm not sure how I'm going to get through this today."

Blakesley's first reaction was to cry for him, to hurt because he was hurting. But she realized that was the wrong thing to do. He needed support and encouragement, not tears. It wasn't her right. She put her arms around his neck and kissed his jaw again, leaving red lip prints that she gently wiped away.

"I'll be there for you, whatever you need," she said confidently. "If you need your hand held, or a cup of coffee, or a hug, I'll be there for you. I'll always be there for you."

He appreciated her support more than she would ever know. He hugged her gently and, taking his khaki head cover, led her back to the truck parked beneath the gently blowing trees. He held her hand the entire time, not saying a word. He didn't have to. He knew they were coming to understand each other very, very well, reaching a place where words were no longer necessary. He never had that with anyone in his life, not ever.

Pulling his new truck out into the street, he felt extremely fortunate as they headed for Gina Aguirre's house.

FIFTEEN

THEIR ARRIVAL at Gina's house had been an odd and sickening experience.

Gina's entire family was down from Los Angeles, a big Mexican-American family with a mother, father, sister, brothers, brothers' wives, aunts and various children running around. The house was absolutely packed with people and everyone but Gina's father was weeping steadily. It sounded horrible and Beck and Blakesley paused at the front door, hearing all of the noise and looking at each other with trepidation. Beck fought his down while Blakesley swallowed hard, took his hand, and followed him inside.

Gina, oddly, wasn't crying. She was sitting on the couch with her son in her arms, her eyes red-rimmed and swollen, as the women sitting around her howled and wept. She seemed to be in some kind of trance, perhaps remembering days gone by or thinking on her future without Butch. Whatever the case, she noticed Beck immediately when he came in the house. Like no one else in the world existed, she got up from the couch and walked straight to him.

"Beck," she sounded exhausted. "I'm so glad you're here."

Beck smiled at her, putting his hand on Spike's head when the boy looked up at him. "I told you I'd be here at noon," he said, firmly. "Are you ready to go?"

Gina nodded, noticing Blakesley for the first time. She smiled wanly. "Hi, Bee," she said. "I'm glad you came with him. I hoped you would."

She looked absolutely strung out and exhausted, and Blakesley swallowed the lump in her throat. Her heart ached for the woman.

"You knew I'd come," she put her hand on Gina's arm comfortingly.

Gina's smile was grateful. "Thank you."

Blakesley noticed that Gina was still in her pajamas, all wrinkled and stained. Looking at the weeping women strung throughout the house, she suddenly felt angry that these people weren't taking care of Gina. Instead, they were apparently competing to see who could cry the loudest. She put both hands on Gina's shoulders.

"Let's go get dressed, okay?" she said, turning her back towards the bedrooms. "I'll help you. Beck, can you watch Spike while Gina gets dressed? We won't be long."

Beck reached out and scooped the boy out of his mother's arms. "Come on, buddy," he said. "Let's go in the kitchen and get something to eat."

As Blakesley directed Gina to her bedroom, she watched Beck over her shoulder. He had been cornered by a couple of crying women near the kitchen door and she could hear him speaking to them in low, calm tones. But Blakesley lost sight of him as she and Gina entered the dark hallway and filed back into the rear master bedroom.

Gina walked into the room and just stood there. She really couldn't even move. Blakesley could see that the woman was having difficulty functioning so she took charge, going into the bathroom and turning on the shower.

"Come on, sweetheart," she said gently, taking hold of Gina's shoulders and pushing her into the bathroom. "Let's get showered so we can go."

Gina fumbled with her pajamas like she was trying to remove them but she wasn't doing a very good job. Blakesley ended up pulling her pajamas off and clipping her hair on top of her head so she could keep it dry in the shower. Gina was able to get in on her own and make a half-hearted attempt at soaping down, but it was really all mechanical in motion. Her mind was elsewhere and her movements were weary. But it was enough to get her reasonably clean and Blakesley turned off the shower, pulled the woman out, and dried her off.

Blakesley then directed her over to the bed, where she sat heavily. Blakesley went into the closet and began digging around.

"Let's find something nice," she said, pulling out a pretty black and white dress. "Oh, I love this. You can wear this."

Gina just sat on the bed, looking forlorn and beaten, as Blakesley got her dressed. The woman moved so slowly that Blakesley had to help her with everything; bra, underwear, jewelry. Blakesley turned the flat iron on and quickly ran it through Gina's hair as the woman fiddled with her wedding rings. Then she found Gina's makeup stash and put some color on her face. Gina just stood there and did as she was told; lift her head, stand up, sit down, look up, and pucker up her lips. Blakesley bossed her around and Gina let her. When all was said and done, Blakesley had pretty much transformed the woman into something sleek and lovely. Gina just stared at herself in the mirror.

"I don't even know what I'm going to do," she whispered, staring at herself. "I'm a widow. Butch is gone. I'm only twenty-nine years old. What am I going to do without him?"

Blakesley looked at her in the mirror, feeling saddened. "I don't know," she said. "I honestly don't know. But Beck and I will help you however we can, I promise."

Gina continued staring at herself. "Beck," she murmured. "He loved Butch and Butch loved him. Poor Beck."

Blakesley didn't know what else to say. Quietly, she took Gina by the hand and led her out into the living room where her family was gathered around, still crying, still carrying on. Blakesley found

Beck in the kitchen with Spike, feeding the boy a peanut butter sandwich. He looked up from the child, smiling when he saw her standing in the doorway.

"Is she ready?" he asked.

Blakesley nodded. "She's dressed but I don't know if she's ready."

His smile faded as he thought on that statement. He picked up a napkin and wiped his hands of any remaining peanut butter. "I heard her call you Bee," he said. "Where did she get that?"

Blakesley smirked and went to the table where Spike was stuffing his face with peanut butter. "Spikey," she smiled at the boy. "Who am I?"

The little kid grinned broadly, bread hanging out of his mouth. "Bee!"

Both Blakesley and Beck laughed. "See?" she looked at Beck. "He can't say my name. It kind of stuck."

Beck put his hand on the kid's dark head. "I like it," he said, stroking the boy's hair and thinking how much he looked like Butch. But that was too painful so he focused on Blakesley instead. "Ready to go?"

Her smile faded. "Let's get this over with."

Beck lifted Spike up from the table, setting him on the floor and taking the little boy's hand as they made their way back into the living room. He turned the child over to his grandmother as he collected Blakesley and Gina. Some of Gina's family wanted to go but Gina waved them off. She wanted to do this alone even though her mother strongly argued with her. Still, Gina remained resolute, insisting that they needed to stay with Spike. Beck pulled her out of the house while Blakesley practically slammed the door in the face of her family.

The whole experience at the base was surreal. That's the only way Blakesley could describe it.

On their way to the base, Beck got on the phone to someone to let them know he was bringing Gina to claim Butch's body. Although Beck tried to speak quietly, Gina heard what he was saying and the tears came. The closer they got to base, the more she cried. By the time they reached the first set of guard gates leading onto the NAB, Gina was working herself into a state no matter how hard Blakesley tried to keep her calm.

They arrived on base at the northwest end of Coronado Island, a massive expanse of base that seemed to go on and on. There were buildings and warehouses and jets and all sorts of military paraphernalia. Beck went through three guard posts to admit them to the area of the base where the teams were housed.

Winding his way through the base, he ended up in front of enormous building that looked like an airplane hangar. It was big and metallic looking, with double doors to admit entry. It looked like a vault. Blakesley peered at the tall and somewhat foreboding building, holding Gina's hands as the woman sobbed.

As they drew closer, they noticed three hearses parked neatly off to the southwest side of the building. There was also a big, dark blue Navy truck. Beck parked his pickup near the doors to the building and turned the vehicle off, turning to look at the women in the backseat. His gaze locked with Blakesley's and the two of them exchanged concerned and sorrowful glances as Gina continued to sob. As Beck climbed out of the truck, a few men spilled out through the big double doors on the side of the building, loosely gathering but not approaching the truck. Beck opened up the back door of the crew cab and held out a hand to Gina.

"Come on, honey," he said. "Let's go do this."

Gina suddenly came apart. "I can't," she shrieked. "I can't do it. I can't see him. If I see him, then he's really dead."

Beck grasped her by the arm to gently pull her out but she clung to Blakesley as if the woman could stop the progression of what was about to happen.

"Gina, please," Beck begged. "I know you don't want to do this but you have to. Butch deserves that."

Gina was practically throwing herself against Blakesley, who had her arms around the woman. "Please," Gina wept. "I can't do it. I can't see him."

Beck tugged more firmly but Blakesley stopped him. She touched his hand as it grabbed the woman, gently pushing it away. Beck backed off. Then Blakesley put her hands on Gina's face and forced the woman to look at her. Gina was a mess, with tears and snot and hair everywhere.

"Gina," she said. "I want you to listen to me because this is important. Okay?"

Gina had a hard time complying. "Uh... uh...."

"Okay?"

After a moment, Gina nodded hesitantly. "Okay."

Blakesley's facial expression was calm. "Honey, I don't know what you're going through but I will tell you this," she said, "about two years ago, I went through just about the worst thing anyone can go through. My husband killed the woman he was sleeping with and I spent months going through a trial where my whole life was laid out for strangers to judge. I saw pictures of this woman who had slept with my husband, pictures of them having sex, pictures of her dead, pictures of her wearing my jewelry and my clothes. There were even pictures of her with my girls. I found out that because of this woman, my husband started working with a Colombian drug lord and when it came time for me to testify against him, someone slit my brake lines in an attempt to kill me and also took a shot at me one day when I was picking my girls up from school. I went through hell for months and months, like my whole life was destroyed, which it was. But my point is this; I was stronger than I thought I was. I had three girls who needed me just like you have Spike who really needs his mom. You're stronger than you think you are, Gina. You need to make Butch proud of you and go in there and do what you need to do. Stop overthinking it and just do it. You're better than that. Okay?"

By this time, Gina was staring at her with big eyes. The tears were still there but they had stopped flowing.

"Poor Bee," she whispered mournfully. "What did they do to you?"

Blakesley shook her head. "Nothing," she assured her, patting her cheek. "I'm fine. You'll be fine. Beck and I are here and we're not leaving you. So let's go in and do what needs to be done. You're not alone, okay? I know you can do this."

Gina digested what Blakesley had said, her muddled mind able to focus enough to realize that there was some good advice there. She didn't want to claim her husband's body but she knew she had to. She was a Navy wife and she had always known this moment could come, especially in the line of work Butch was in. She owed it to him.

After a moment, she nodded. "Okay."

"You good?"

"I'm good."

Blakesley smiled at her and pulled a tissue out of her purse, wiping off Gina's cheeks and handing her the tissue. She helped Beck get her out of the truck and climbed out after her, into the bright California sunshine. Beck had Gina by the arm but he held out his hand to Blakesley, who clasped his hand tightly. The expression on his face told her more about his love and respect for her than words ever could.

A trim man with blond-gray hair and dressed in an impeccable uniform joined them, and Blakesley was introduced to Captain Davis. He took charge of Gina and escorted her into a giant hanger-like section of the building where nineteen flag-draped coffins were neatly lined up. Blakesley stood back by the door respectfully as Beck, Gina and Captain Davis did what needed to be done with Butch. The mortuary was already there to take him away, the men standing in the shadows as Gina said her goodbyes.

Blakesley watched it all from a distance, not wanting to intrude and thinking that it was all incredibly sad. She also couldn't help but wonder if she would be able to pull herself together half as well if Beck had been lying in one of those boxes. She couldn't bear the thought. As she was standing there wallowing in her dark thoughts,

Captain Davis broke away from Beck and Gina and slowly wandered back towards the area where Blakesley was standing. She smiled at the older man when their eyes met. He smiled back.

"It's nice to finally meet you." Davis came to stand next to her. "I'm just sorry about the circumstances."

Blakesley nodded faintly, her gaze moving to Gina and Beck standing over by Butch's coffin. "I know what you mean," she said. "This is really the only time I've been on base. Beck doesn't talk much about his work."

Davis looked at her. "Did you know Butch and Gina before this?"

She nodded. "Gina and I became friends while Beck and Butch were off on their latest deployment."

Davis' gaze moved back to the coffins in the big, cavernous hanger. He sighed heavily. "This is going to be hard on Beck." He turned to look at her again. "Just so you know, you're getting a good man, young lady. Most of what I've heard about you has been through the rumor mill, so it's good to finally meet you in person."

She looked at him, a smile playing on her lips. "What have you heard?"

Davis grinned, unusual for the usually serious man, and looked away. "Things."

She laughed. "You're not going to get off so easily. You brought it up."

He shrugged, getting swept up in her charm and coming to see what had attracted Beck. She was a stunningly beautiful woman.

"All I heard was from the men who pulled you out of the surf," he said. "They said Beck pulled your daughter out of the water and then never left your side. That's unusual for a man whose natural state is the command and control mode."

"It's unusual that he paid attention to me?"

"It's unusual that he paid attention to a woman, period." He turned to look at her again. "I've known Beck for ten years. I knew his ex-wife. I saw him go through that hell with her but it never reflected on him personally. The man never brought it to work with him. I guess I just want you to know that in the short time you've known him, I can already see the impact you've made on him. He seems so much happier. He deserves it, you know. There's no one in the Navy I respect more than Beck Seavington."

Blakesley was genuinely touched. "Why is that?"

Davis' gaze moved back to Beck and Gina. Beck now had his arm around the woman as she ran her hand over the top of Butch's casket.

"I'm going to tell you something that you probably shouldn't repeat to him," he lowered his voice. "It's not that he wouldn't want you to know, but more that he doesn't like to be recognized for heroics. He's too humble that way. He's uncomfortable in the spotlight. You saw those Navy Crosses on his shirt?"

Blakesley nodded. "I did," she said. "It was like pulling teeth to get him to talk about what he did to earn them."

Davis grunted. "I'm not surprised," he said, still speaking very softly. "We practically had to tie him down when they were awarded to him. Did Beck tell you he was on the chopper that went down?"

Blakesley shuddered. "He did."

"Did he tell you that he saved four of his men before the thing sank?"

She looked at him, shocked. "No."

Davis nodded. "I was on the deck of the carrier watching the entire thing," he said. "The helicopter was about fifteen feet off the deck when debris from the flight deck destroyed the rear rotors. The aircraft rolled over onto its side and fell like a rock into the sea. The rear cargo bay was open so water just started pouring in. The men were strapped into their seats for take-off and with the water rushing in the way it was, I was sure we were going to lose all of them just from the force of the water. But suddenly I see Beck on the surface and he's pulling shit, excuse me, stuff off of him. Packs, whatever else he was wearing to weigh him down. Then he went under and I saw him swimming into the back of the 'copter as it was sinking. After about thirty seconds, I see two other heads pop up and then a third. Then a fourth. By this time, the entire heli-copter is covered with water and sinking fast. I didn't see Beck until a couple of minutes after I saw him go back in. He and four other guys were on the surface and that's all of the twenty-four men that were in that 'copter. He saved them. He tried to save more and nearly drowned doing it."

By this time, Blakesley was looking at him with watery eyes. "Oh, my God," she whispered, trying to swallow away the lump in her throat. "He didn't tell me that."

"He wouldn't. I've put him in for a commendation and he's going to kill me for it." Davis looked at her. "Seavington is an American hero, ma'am. Movies and stories wouldn't do the man justice. He's a real-live G.I. Joe, bigger than life, and he runs from any recognition you want to give him. I know he won't tell you, so I will. He's the best man in the Navy. Treat him right or you'll have to answer to me."

He was smiling when he said it but Blakesley understood. She stood there, stunned, as he moved away from her and went back to Beck and Gina. She continued to stand there, struggling to come to terms with what Beck's commanding officer had told her, when Beck broke away from Gina and came back over to her. She smiled at him, perhaps seeing him through new eyes, as he grasped her gently by the arms and kissed her cheek.

"Gina is about ready to go," he said quietly. "She's going to ride in the hearse with the casket and I'm going with her. Can you follow us in the truck?"

Blakesley nodded. "Sure," she answered. "How is she doing?"

He shrugged. "Okay, I guess. Better now than she was in the truck. Thank you for that, by the way. That meant a lot."

She smiled modestly. "You're welcome," she whispered. "Can I get either of you anything? A bottle of water or something?"

Beck glanced back at Gina. "She might like something," he said. "I'll take whatever you get her. There's a vending machine if you go back out the door behind you. You'll see it on the left."

Blakesley nodded, kissed him, and went to get three bottles of water. She proceeded to follow Gina, Beck and Captain Davis out into the warm sunshine as the people from the mortuary loaded the casket into their car. Following the hearse back across the bridge in Beck's new truck, she was glad that Davis had told her what he knew of Beck from his perspective. It gave her a better view of the man she was coming to know, the strong and honorable person he was. It also made her realize why she loved him so much.

The man was a keeper.

SIXTEEN
THREE WEEKS LATER

"DO YOU LOVE IT?"

Blakesley was so happy that she was literally twitching. Beck just grinned at her, his fists resting on his hips as he looked around the big, cavernous space that she was showing him. It was a storefront in the Gaslamp Quarter down by the convention center, in an old building that was near the corner of the Hard Rock Café. It was pricey real estate but Blakesley was happy and that was all that mattered. She finally had her gallery.

"Baby, if you love it, I love it," he said. "I'm happy for you."

Blakesley giggled, turning to look around the space happily, which was now a little more than eighteen hundred square feet of whitewashed walls. She began to pace around, outlining her plans with her arms outstretched.

"I've been really thinking about this and it's going to be more than a gallery for my paintings," she said. "I want to turn it into a wine and dessert bar."

He lifted his eyebrows at her. "You do?"

She nodded eagerly. "I've got a hell of a lot of experience with restaurants so I may as well put it to good use," she said. "I'm going to paint up in the loft and my paintings will be displayed all throughout the bar. People can come and enjoy a glass of wine and a cupcake, and look at all of my paintings. They can buy the ones they like."

His smile returned. "Sounds good," he said. "What are you going to call this magical place?"

She giggled. "The Art Bar, what else?"

"Perfect."

She was full of excitement and ideas as she paced around. "We'll serve a full complement of fine wines and champagne," she said, "but no beer. I don't like beer and unless it's imported and very exclusive, I'm not going to carry it. This isn't going to be a sports bar."

He fought off a smirk. "You're a beer snob."

"Yes, I am," she said firmly. "I know a lot of pastry chefs that would be dying to come down to San Diego and help me run this place. I think it will be really successful if we have good food, good product, good prices and make this into kind of a high-end gallery with booze and food."

He watched her prance around as she described her idea. "So who are you going to get to help you with this thing?"

She grinned. "You," she said, batting her eyelashes coyly. "You'll be my headwaiter. One look at you and we'll have every woman in San Diego in here every single night."

He laughed. "That's not what I meant."

Her face fell. "You're not going to help me?"

He shook his head and moved in her direction, hands out to ease her. "Of course I will, baby, that's not what I meant. Don't you need a contractor? A designer? That kind of thing?"

"Sure I do, but I know a ton of them from Los Angeles so that won't be an issue. I'm just excited to get started."

He reached her, putting his hands on her arms affectionately. "It's going to cost a lot of money."

She shrugged and looked around the space. "I have a budget I'll stick to. I know how much something like this should cost."

"Don't you think you should be saving for a wedding?"

She looked at him, surprised, as if she had completely forgotten about that. "I don't know," she stammered somewhat. "We're all so happy living at the Victorian that I haven't really thought about it. There's been so much going on."

His expression grew serious. "I realize that," he said. "But I want you to think about it. I don't want to put the wedding off too much longer. I'd like to be able to refer to you as my wife and not my girlfriend. Have you even thought about a date yet?"

Truth was, she hadn't. She shook her head. "No," she said honestly. "But you know what would be fun? To get married at Christmas and have it up at Lake Tahoe in the snow. The girls would love that."

He smiled and pulled her into his arms. "I don't want to wait that long," he murmured, nuzzling her cheek. "But if you want a Christmas wedding, then so be it."

She snuggled against him. "We could just go to the courthouse on Saturday. I'm fine with that, too."

"If you're fine with it, I'm fine with it."

She grinned up at him. "How soon do you want to do it?"

He shrugged and then dug into the pocket of his jeans. Blakesley's heart jumped into her throat when she realized he was pulling out a small ring box. She could see that it was covered in dark blue satin with gold script on the top. He held it up to her.

"How soon do you want to wear this?"

She shrieked and went to snatch it but he pulled it back, moving away from her and putting it back in his pocket. She stomped a foot, frowning.

"Beck," she pouted obviously. "Don't tease. That's mean."

He tried to look stern but it wasn't working; his grin kept breaking through. "You're teasing me with ideas of snow weddings and city hall dates," he said. "I don't hear anything firm."

She sighed heavily and pulled out her smart phone. She began pushing the touch screen and scrolling around. Beck watched her curiously.

"What are you doing?" he asked.

She held up a hand to him as if to silence his question, pushed another button, and put the phone to her ear. He continued to watch her curiously, meeting her gaze as she apparently waited for someone on the other end to answer the phone.

"Hi," she said when the party answered. "I'd like to know if you have any appointments open on Saturday for a civil ceremony and a marriage license."

Beck grinned as he watched her turn away from him, phone to her ear, listening to what she was being told. Every once in a while she would say yes, or no, or answer a question with a few short words. He watched her pace across the floor, studying her sexy backside and thinking dirty thoughts. But more than that, he realized he was excited about the possibility of getting married on Saturday. She finally hung up the phone and turned to look at him.

"The soonest appointment they had was next Saturday at ten in the morning," she said. "I took it. Can I have my ring now?"

He smiled broadly and pulled the box out of his pocket. She scooted over to him, excited, but before he could open the box, she threw her arms around his neck and hugged him.

"I wasn't deliberately putting off our wedding," she murmured into his ear. "Honestly, there's so much going on and we're so happy just where we're at right now that I didn't see any rush. I'm sorry if you thought I was trying to put it off."

He hugged her tightly. "I didn't think that at all," he said. "I'm just really excited that we're getting married next Saturday."

"Will you wear your white dress uniform?"

"Hell, yes. I guess now you have to go shop for a dress."

She kissed him sweetly. "Come with me."

"I wouldn't be any help with that, baby. Take Gina and the girls."

She shook her head. "I'll take Gina, Lizzie and Cadee, but you have to watch the little girls and Spike."

He nodded. "I can do that."

She grinned, full on, gazing into his handsome face. "I swear I'm the luckiest girl in the world. I'm so lucky to have you."

He pulled her against him, echoing her sentiment. He felt like the most fortunate man on the planet. He kissed her a couple of times, feeling the excitement of their coming wedding full-bore.

"Can I have my ring now?" she asked again.

He laughed as he let her go, presenting her with the box that was still in his hand. Thrilled, Blakesley opened it up and her face went from grinning to tearful in a matter of seconds. He looked at her, concerned.

"Baby, what's wrong?"

Her smile returned to let him know she wasn't upset. "This is so beautiful," she said, pulling it out of the box. "You have amazing taste."

He smiled as he watched her inspect the nearly one carat solitaire, held in place by an intricately beautiful pave diamond band. It was truly a spectacular ring and he took it from her, slipping it on her left hand. It fit snuggly and she admired it, teary-eyed and smiling.

"My God, Beck," she breathed as the light caught it. "This is really gorgeous."

He watched her reaction. "I did it all by myself," he told her proudly. "I was going to have Lizzie go with me, but I wanted to do it alone. I wanted to give you something I picked without any help."

She took her gaze off the ring long enough to put her arms around him and kiss him. "You did a beautiful job."

"So you like it?"

"I love it."

Pleased with himself, he hugged her for a few moments, feeling her against him, feeling a lot of excitement for the next chapter in his life with her by his side. Six weeks ago, he would have never believed such a thing possible. He still felt like he was living a dream. He was going in for another kiss when his phone buzzed. Noting that the caller I.D. was Lizzie, he answered accordingly as Blakesley went over by the window to admire the glitter of her new ring.

"Hi, baby girl," he said pleasantly. "What's up?"

"Dad, I'm sorry!" Lizzie cried. "Mom was trying to get me to come home and I told her no and...."

"Slow down, baby," he said softly, firmly. "What happened?"

Lizzie was frantic. "She was being so mean, Dad. She was saying how you stole me and you're not getting away with it. She made me so mad."

Beck remained cool. "What did you say?"

Lizzie was verging on tears. "She was just yelling at me and telling me I'd better come home or else. I told her to screw off."

He sighed heavily. "Is that what you really said?"

"No," Lizzie said reluctantly. "I told her to fuck off."

He grunted with regret. "Lizzie, you know better than that," he said quietly. "I don't care how mad you are. You don't say things like that."

"I know," Lizzie tried weakly to defend herself. "But she threw something at the door. I think it was a...."

"The door?" Beck's brow furrowed. "What are you talking about?"

"Mom threw something at the front door. I think it was a soda or something."

"Was she at the house?"

"Yes," Lizzie said. "Dad, I don't know how she got our address but she showed up and wanted me to come home. I told her to fuck off and she wanted to talk to you. I'm sorry, Dad, but I told her where you were. I just wanted her away from here."

Beck was not only shocked at Sharon's appearance, he was also very concerned. Unfortunately, he could see that he had Blakesley's attention and he hastened to cut the conversation short.

"What did you tell her?" he asked steadily.

"At Blakesley's new gallery," she said. "I told her it was downtown by the Hard Rock. Dad, I just wanted her away from the house. She was yelling and the girls were scared."

"It's okay," he assured her. "I want her away from the house, too. I'll take it from here, baby girl. Just keep the house locked up and don't open it for anyone but me or Blakesley, okay?"

"Okay," she replied, sounding afraid. "Are you mad?"

"No, baby, I'm not," he told her. "I'll call you later."

He hung up the phone and put it back in his pocket, taking a deep breath and wondering what he was going to tell Blakesley. He opted for the truth simply because he wasn't in the habit of lying to her. She was still standing over by the window, admiring her ring, as he approached her. She smiled when she saw him coming.

"I think we have a bit of a problem," he said.

Blakesley's smile faded when she saw the look on his face.

Sharon Du Pont Seavington Tracy was a beautiful woman. She was tall, lean and elegant, with long brunette hair, a well-cultivated California tan, and brilliant white teeth. She wore expensive designer jeans and was very well dressed, like she had just walked out of Nordstrom's. When the woman pushed open the gallery door, Blakesley could smell her expensive designer perfume.

Upset and apprehensive, Blakesley sat by the front window near the door so that when Sharon came in, she didn't see her tucked back against the wall. Beck had specifically put her there so she wouldn't instantly be the target of Sharon's venom and he had no doubt that the woman was out for blood. An unexpected appearance had him very edgy. Before she could even speak, Beck set the ground rules for the conversation by taking the offensive.

"If you ever show up at my house again uninvited, I will file a restraining order against you," he spoke in a deadly tone that Blakesley had never heard before. "Are we perfectly clear on that?"

Sharon came to a halt about ten feet inside the door, pulling off her expensive designer sunglasses. "You have a lot of nerve to threaten me," she fired back. "You stole my child. I've come to take her home."

"I will not continue this conversation unless you tell me how you got my address."

"I'm not telling you anything."

"Then you can walk right out of here because I have nothing more to say to you."

Sharon just stood there and glared at him. "Since when have you become so aggressive?"

Beck didn't say anything. He just folded his big arms across his chest and stared at her. Sharon grew frustrated. "Very mature, Beck," she said. "The silent treatment always works wonders."

Beck shifted on his muscular legs, waiting. Finally, Sharon rolled her eyes in surrender because she knew how stubborn he could be. She knew he wouldn't talk to her unless she told him what he wanted to know.

"Lizzie's boyfriend gave it to me," she said. "It wasn't his fault. I tricked him into it, so don't get mad at him or at Lizzie. She doesn't know."

Beck cocked an eyebrow. "Tricked him?"

She nodded curtly. "I told him I had accidentally deleted it from my contact list and I needed to mail her some stuff. He gave it to me."

Beck was coming to understand now. "So you just show up down here? I told you that Lizzie is going to live with me from now on. She's not going to live in the same house as a pedophile."

Sharon went into furious mode in an instant. "Screw you," she hissed. "He is not a pedophile."

"He's jacking off outside of your fourteen-year-old daughter's bedroom, Sharon," Beck fired back. "He also had sex with one of her underage friends. What the hell would you call it?"

Sharon was livid. "He says it didn't happen and so far, I don't have any proof that he did anything wrong other than Lizzie's testimony."

"She saw him."

"She could have imagined it or maybe she just made it up. Dan says he didn't do anything wrong."

"So you believe your husband over your own child?"

Sharon jabbed a finger at him. "At least he's home," she hissed. "He's home more than you ever were. He cares for Lizzie and is good to her."

"He wants to sleep with her, Sharon. What's it going to take for you to believe your own child? A rape?"

Sharon's jaw ticked. "He would never do that. I resent you for suggesting it."

Beck was struggling with his temper. "A police report was filed by your daughter," he rumbled. "Dan has been accused of lewd acts upon a minor and statutory rape among other things. Lizzie has already spoken to the San Francisco police and they've taken her statement, but you already know all of this; otherwise, you wouldn't be here. Based on the lawsuit, my lawyer has said that no judge will allow Lizzie to go back into that environment. She's with me now and she's staying with me. If you came down here to talk me out of it, then you're crazy. Go back up to San Francisco and your pedophile husband because Lizzie is never going to be around him again."

Fury wasn't working so Sharon resorted to tears. "God, you're such an asshole," she hissed, turning away to wipe at her eyes and catching sight of Blakesley sitting near the window. Her eyes widened. "So this must be Blakesley? She's beautiful, Beck. Very beautiful. You did well for yourself."

Beck's eyes narrowed. "You're talking to me, not her. Leave her out of it."

Sharon swung around. "Leave her out of it? I think not," she pointed in Blakesley's direction. "Her husband murdered his mistress and you have the nerve to lecture me on Dan? You'd rather have our daughter around... around that?"

Blakesley wasn't surprised she knew all of that. It was public knowledge and, apparently, Sharon had done her homework. Blakesley remained cool but Beck didn't. He marched up to his ex-wife, putting himself between Blakesley and Sharon. Before Blakesley could stop him, he towered over his ex-wife, posturing angrily.

"If you ever talk about her like that again, you'll be very sorry," he rumbled. "You leave her the hell out of this. She loves Lizzie and Lizzie loves her, and she's been extremely good to my daughter. She's been more of a mother to her in two months than you've been in her entire life. You back the hell off of Blakesley."

Blakesley came up behind him, putting her soft hands on his arm and pulling him away from Sharon before the confrontation went to the next level. She knew that Beck wouldn't physically assault the woman in any way, but he wasn't so sure about Sharon. If she threw a punch, Blakesley would be forced to throw one back.

"Back up, baby," she whispered pleadingly. "It's okay. I'm a big girl. She can't hurt me."

Beck was as furious as Blakesley had ever seen him, which was an unusual state for him. He was usually supremely cool and calm. He backed away but he didn't move away completely as Blakesley put herself between Beck and Sharon. Her focus was on Beck's ex-wife.

"Sharon," she said. "I wish we had gotten to meet face to face under different circumstances, but I guess it is what it is. I just want to tell you that you have raised an extremely sweet and beautiful girl. Lizzie is wonderful and I love her very much. You've done a good job with her."

Sharon was startled by Blakesley's kind words. She had been geared up for a catfight and was rather surprised to see that Blakesley wasn't rising to her. It threw a monkey wrench into her attack and she scrambled to come up with something to say.

"I want her to come home with me," she said, rather guarded. "She needs to be with her mother."

Blakesley nodded patiently. "I know you think so," she said. "Any mother would and I sympathize. But I have a problem with the fact that Lizzie came to you with concerns over Dan and you just blew her off. She's your daughter and you needed to listen to her."

Sharon started to flare. "Don't you tell me how to deal with my daughter," she hissed. "What the hell do you know, you and your screwed-up family? I read all about you and how your husband murdered his whore. I don't want my child exposed to a murderer."

Blakesley's brow furrowed. "My ex-husband is in jail," she said evenly. "He's not around my family at all. He's gone for good. But at least he didn't have sex with one of my daughter's friends and masturbate outside of my daughter's bedroom. Dan is a pedophile, Sharon. What in the hell is wrong with you that you would expose your daughter to that? Are you that desperate for a man that you'll stay married to one who banged a fourteen-year-old? He's going to jail, by the way. That's what happens to pedophiles, so in that sense you're no better than I am with a husband in jail."

Sharon took a step back; she had to, otherwise, she would start throwing punches. "This is not over," she said forcefully. "My lawyer has all the information about you and we're going to pursue this."

"Pursue what?" Blakesley wanted to know. "I haven't done anything wrong."

Sharon was back to furious tears by this time. She turned like she was heading out of the door but instead she ended up pacing around like a caged animal.

"You have no idea." She was gearing up dramatically. "You have no idea what you're doing. You can't steal my daughter. Lizzie belongs with her mother. You can't just take her."

Blakesley knew they had the upper hand from the way Sharon was acting; she'd already lost control.

"First of all, it took you six weeks to come for her?" Blakesley asked. "If you really wanted her back, you would have come to get her the day I called you. Why did you wait so long?"

Sharon stopped pacing and glared at her. "Fuck you."

Blakesley sighed heavily. "Is that the best you can do? Really, Sharon?"

Sharon postured angrily. "That's what you deserve for taking my child," she hissed, then looked at Beck. "I hope you like court because we're going back. I'm getting my daughter back."

Beck stood behind Blakesley, much calmer than he had been a few moments before. "No, you're not," he said frankly. "You also seem to be forgetting that Lizzie can decide for herself where she wants to live. She's fourteen years old and any judge will side with what she wants. In any case, she's not coming back to live with you and the pedophile. Oh, and one more thing; if I ever see Dan again, you can tell him for me that I'll kill him. I can do it twenty different ways and he'll never know what hit him. He's a dead man if he ever comes near Lizzie again."

Sharon paled. "Oh, my God," she breathed. "I can't believe you just threatened him."

"It's not a threat. It's a fact."

Sharon jabbed a finger at him. "My lawyer's going to hear about that, too."

Blakesley lifted her eyebrows casually, turning to look at Beck. "Hear about what? I didn't hear anything."

He wriggled his eyebrows at her as Sharon gasped in outrage. "I'd like to see you deny it under oath."

Blakesley couldn't help it; she grinned because Sharon was so incredibly dramatic and ridiculous.

"I can't testify against him," she said. "We're getting married next week and a wife can't testify against her husband. But even if we weren't married, I still wouldn't testify against him."

"You'd lie? To a judge?"

Blakesley just lifted her shoulders as if to say "oh, well". Infuriated, Sharon grabbed her sunglasses and shoved them on her head.

"Fine," she hissed. "If you want to play hardball, that's your choice. See you both in court."

She blew out of the empty shop, stomping along the street until she disappeared from view. Blakesley turned to Beck.

"So now what?" she asked. "Do we need to get a restraining order? I don't want her near our house."

Beck just shook his head and put his arm around her. "She's fired up but she's not stupid," he said. "She'd rather pay people to do her dirty work, like a lawyer. I would be surprised if she came around to the house again, but I am concerned that she might try to make a grab at Lizzie."

"Kidnap her?"

He shrugged. "Maybe," he said, looking around the space. "Are we done here?"

"I think so."

"Let's get home to the girls, then. Lizzie was pretty shook up with her mom's appearance."

Blakesley nodded and went to the staircase to collect her purse. Beck turned off the lights and they left the building, locking the door behind them. He put on his sunglasses, taking her hand as they walked down the street towards his truck. Although it was small talk all the way home, Beck was coming to wonder if, in fact, he might have to get a restraining order against Sharon at some point.

It was just a feeling he had.

SEVENTEEN

BECK WAS SITTING on the couch in the living room after sundown, the Batchelder-tiled fireplace cracking softly in the early evening as he watched the San Diego Padres obliterate the St. Louis Cardinals. Charlotte lay with her head on his lap, sucking her thumb and falling asleep as Blakesley and the older girls cleaned up the kitchen.

Lizzie came barreling down from upstairs, her laptop computer in her hands. She plopped on the sofa next to her dad and got comfortable as she flipped open the laptop.

"Dad," she said as she booted up, "can I invite Jamie and Ashley down to visit? I really miss my friends."

Beck tore his eyes away from the game to look at his daughter. "I know," he said softly, putting a hand on her foot. "Let me check with Blakesley but I'm sure she won't mind."

"Won't mind what?"

Blakesley came out of the kitchen with Crosby and Cadee on her heels. She had a beer in one hand and a glass of red wine in the other. She handed Beck the beer as she sat down beside him.

"Lizzie was wondering if she could invite a couple of friends down to visit," Beck said. "Do you mind?"

Blakesley shook her head. "Not at all," she looked at Beck. "But the bigger question is if you mind. You're already outnumbered in this house six to one. You want to add two more girls on top of that?"

He grinned and put his arm around her, snuggling down with her in front of the television. "I like girls," he kissed her temple. "I spend too much time around a bunch of guys. It's good to come home to nail polish and Barbies and the bathrooms all hogged up."

Blakesley laughed softly. "You're a big pushover."

"You better believe it."

Alfie suddenly charged into the living room, courtesy of Crosby letting the dog in. He jumped up on the couch, knocking over Lizzie, who yelled at the dog. Crosby was chasing the animal around trying to control him and the noise woke up Charlotte, who started crying. Blakesley set her wine down and picked up Charlotte, cradling the little girl as Beck got off the couch and collared the dog.

Crosby pleaded for leniency for her best friend but Beck wasn't feeling too generous considering the chaos the big animal had just caused. But he looked at Blakesley for the final word, and she granted the dog a reprieve. Crosby and Cadee took the dog across the entry and into the small room they used as their playroom. Lizzie, insulted by the dog slobber on her arm, retreated back upstairs to her room.

Beck plopped back down on the couch, collecting his beer and his girl. "Whew," he blew out his cheeks. "That dog needs some obedience training."

Blakesley was cradling Charlotte. "I was thinking about that," she said. "I'll look in to it next week."

"You've got a wedding to plan next week."

"I know," she nodded. "Oh, which reminds me; I called my lawyer earlier today about a prenup. He said he could draw one up in a couple of days providing we agree on everything."

Beck was watching the game, focusing on the action so her statement didn't sink in right away. When it did, he looked at her curiously.

"Prenup?" he repeated.

She nodded, watching the game on the fifty-two inch plasma screen on the wall. "Especially with the Art Bar opening up at some point, I just want to make sure everything is spelled out."

He was staring at her. "What do you mean spelled out?" he said. "Why in the hell do we need a prenup?"

She realized there was some anger in his tone and turned to look at him, seeing that his expression was surprisingly tight. Her brow furrowed.

"To make sure we're both protected," she said patiently. "It makes total sense. Like, if something goes wrong with the Art Bar, if I have it listed as my asset, the IRS or lawyers can't go after you for any financial liability. We'll make sure that the truck and the house are your assets, but anything we gain during the course of the marriage will be ours equally. Does that make sense?"

His expression darkened. "Look," he said, trying not to become angry. "I know that your mind thinks that way and I know that it protected you from Ed's bullshit, but I'm not Ed. I'm not going to cheat on you, or go on a murder rampage, so there's no reason to protect yourself from me."

Blakesley could see that he didn't have a clue what she was talking about. He was offended by the mere suggestion.

"Baby, it's to protect you, too," she insisted. "We have a lot of assets and it's just smart to spell everything out so there are no surprises."

His jaw ticked. "It's insurance against a divorce," he said in a low voice. "It's an insurance policy so you can walk away from a marriage whenever you want to and know you're safe from giving up anything."

He was rightfully angry and Blakesley shushed him so he wouldn't wake up Charlotte, now dozing on her shoulder. His rage was starting to fire her up.

"That's not true," she replied, losing her cool. "Most people do prenups to a certain degree. It just makes good business sense. It's like a will when you die – it just spells out your wants in case something happens."

His jaw was ticking furiously and he turned to watch the television. "It's an easy way out," he muttered. "You're assuming the marriage is going to fail simply by suggesting a prenup. You don't have any faith in this marriage, do you?"

"That's totally not true. Now you're just being ridiculous."

He just waved her away. "Do whatever you want. I'll sign it."

Blakesley was verging on tears. She got up with Charlotte sleeping on her shoulder and carried the little girl upstairs and put her to bed. Nikki was in Cadee's room reading while Lizzie was talking to someone on her cell phone in her bedroom. Heading back downstairs, Blakesley went into the master bedroom, pulled her shoes on and collected her purse.

The cars were parked in the backyard and she went out the French doors from the master bedroom to the big cement area towards the back of the yard where the cars were kept. She was starting to lose the battle against the tears and they streamed down her face as she unlocked her car and climbed in. She fumbled with her purse, setting it down on the passenger seat, turning the car on and reaching into the side panel for the box of tissue she always kept there.

The moment she lifted her head to put the car into reverse, she caught sight of Beck standing next to the car. She yelped, startled, as their eyes met. His expression was impassive.

"Open the door," he said.

She burst into soft sobs and shook her head. "Why?" she yelled, muted through the closed door. "So you can tell me I don't have any faith in us? Leave me alone. I'm going for a drive. I need to clear my head."

Her car door suddenly opened and she gasped, surprised, until she remembered that Beck had a second set of keys to her car. She tried to yank the door shut but he was stronger and pulled it open. He ended up pulling her right out of the car.

Blakesley stumbled out of the car but Beck caught her before she could fall to her knees. But she pulled herself away, roughly, staying out of his arm's reach.

"Just... leave me alone," she said, walking around the other side of the car. "I don't want to talk to you right now."

He followed her. "Why?" he wanted to know. "I told you I'd sign the prenup. Why are you so upset?"

She sobbed. "How can you be so mean to me? How can you say I have no faith in our marriage?"

He sighed, showing some regret for the first time. "I just don't believe in prenuptial agreements. You have never, in the time I have known you, said anything about us having a prenup. They're an easy way out."

"They're smart business sense!"

Their last statement was choppy and overlapping, full of emotion. Beck could see how upset she was but the truth was that he was upset, too. He struggled to calm down, otherwise, they would never settle this.

"I understand that you look at them that way," he said, his voice considerably softer as he tried to be reasonable. "I guess... I guess you hurt my feelings by suggesting one. It's like you don't have any faith that our marriage is going to last forever so you need this agreement to make sure that everything is fair and equal if we divorce. Baby, do you have any idea what it would do to me if we divorced? It would kill me. It would literally kill me. When I hear prenup, I hear –pre-divorce. I can't even hear that word without feeling nauseous."

She was coming to understand where he was coming from and she, too, eased up. He was trying to be reasonable so she tried, too.

"But that's not what it means at all," she insisted. "Let me see if I can give you an example of what I mean; let's say that you sell your townhome and have three hundred and fifty thousand dollars in the bank from it. Now, let's say we open the Art Bar and the business isn't a success. We lose money, we go into debt, and suddenly creditors are filing lawsuits to get their money. We have to file bankruptcy. Baby, if we don't divide the assets with a prenup, then that money you have sitting in the bank from your home sale becomes my asset as well and the creditors can take it all. That's your money and I want you to keep it safe. That's why I suggested a prenuptial agreement, and for no other reason than that."

He understood what she was saying perfectly. He sighed heavily, thinking that maybe he had done something terribly wrong in reacting the way he had. He hung his head.

"I'm sorry," he muttered. "I thought the worst and I shouldn't have. That was really unfair and wrong. I have more faith in you than that and I'm sorry I didn't show it. You're so much smarter than I am... I should just listen to you."

Blakesley wiped the last of the tears from her cheeks. "I can get over you thinking that a prenup is an easy out to a marriage," she said as she walked around the car. "But I really need to come to grips with the fact that you thought I was trying to bamboozle you somehow or had a lack of faith in our relationship. That just really hurts."

He was starting to feel desperate and deeply repentant. "I said I'm sorry," he said, watching her walk towards the house. "What do you want me to do? I'll write it in blood if I have to."

She took the steps up to the deck that led to the master bedroom. "Next time, don't think the worst of me," she looked over her shoulder at him. "I wouldn't do that to you."

He watched her walk into the house with a hugely heavy heart. He couldn't remember ever having hurt so badly about anything. There was a lump in his throat and tears in his eyes. Feeling his keys in his right hand, he went to his old Chevy truck, parked up against the big four-car garage and started it up.

Sliding out onto the street, he drove off into the deepening evening.

He wasn't sure where he was going, only that he had to clear his head. Maybe he was making too much out of this. Self-doubt swamped him, as did confusion. When his phone began to ring he grabbed at it, thinking it might be Blakesley, but it wasn't. It was an old friend, but he wasn't sure he wanted to be social at the moment. Still, it would be good to hear a friendly voice.

He answered on the sixth ring.

"What's up, Ethan?" he said. "Long time, no see."

Ethan Serreaux chuckled quietly. "Hey, Beck," he said. "You must be stateside if you're answering the phone."

"I am," Beck replied. "But who knows about tomorrow."

"Still loving the Navy?"

"Still loving it."

"Can't talk you into coming to work with me?"

Beck grinned. "What would I do in a cushy office all day long?" he said. "Getting soft and fat like you? That would drive me crazy."

Ethan's good humor faded. "It hasn't been so cushy lately."

"Really?" Beck said with some interest. "What's going on?"

Ethan seemed hesitant. "So much," he finally said. "Things are... weird. Let's just leave it there for now. But I think I have a problem and I need some advice."

"Sure," Beck said. "What kind of a problem?"

"Woman problems."

Beck grunted softly. "I think I'm the last person to give you advice on women," he muttered. "I've got some of my own."

"Oh, God," Ethan said with distress. "Sharon again?"

"Surprisingly, no," Beck said. "I've met someone. It's been a hell of a whirlwind and to say I'm crazy about her is an understatement."

"Seriously?" Ethan said. "Beck, I'm happy for you, man. That's great."

Beck sigh heavily. "It is," he said. "Really, it is, but tonight I did something... I was way out of line. I'm out driving around trying to clear my head about it."

"Oh," Ethan said, less enthusiastic in his reply because Beck seemed upset. "What happened?"

"I don't really know," Beck said. Then, he paused. "Yes, I do. I was an ass. We want to get married and she has assets. A lot of them. She asked me to sign a prenup. For protection, she said. It would keep our finances separate and protect me if anything happened on her end. And it would protect me if anything happened on her end. I don't know, Ethan... every time I hear prenup, I hear pre-divorce."

"You can't look at it that way," Ethan said. "She's right – it makes smart financial sense to protect everyone's assets. You've worked hard for what you have and it sounds like she wants to make sure that's all protected. It's no big deal. But you should have your lawyer look it over."

Beck grunted again. "Not you, too."

"What?"

"That's what she said."

"She sounds like a smart lady, Beck. You might want to listen to her."

Beck sighed heavily again. "Like I said," he said. "I was an ass about it. The last time I had trouble with her, I had to have Cord talk me down from the ledge."

"How's the witch?"

"Warlock."

"Sorry – *warlock*."

"Seems to be good," he said. "Anyway, enough about us. What about you? You've got woman trouble and I want to hear about it."

"I met her on the job," Ethan said. "There's a lot of crazy stuff going on that involves her, stuff I really can't talk about, but the truth is that my boss is starting to catch on that there's something there."

"No fraternizing, eh?"

"Exactly."

"Well," Beck said slowly, "it's not a fling, is it? Like, the woman is crazy-hot and you just want to sleep with her?"

"No, nothing like that," Ethan said with soft sincerity. "I feel like... like this is the real deal, Beck. It's not a whim. I don't work that way."

"I know you don't," Beck said. "But I have to be honest, Ethan – when it comes to women, you are one of the most closed off people I've ever seen. I've seen you get downright nasty with them. I'd be shocked if this was just an impulse."

"I know," Ethan said. "But not with her. Not with Cydney."

"You feel like this could go somewhere?"

"I really do."

"Then I suggest you take it slow," Beck said. "You can't take another Kimberly."

He was referring to Ethan's ex-wife, who had ripped Ethan's heart out when she divorced him and took their son to live with her. "I think it might kill me if it was with Cydney," Ethan said quietly. "But I really do want to explore whatever's happening."

"Then you should," Beck said. "Hell, I met Blakesley when I saved her daughter from nearly drowning. In our professions, sometimes we don't always meet people in the best of circumstances. But it's what arises from those circumstances that count, no matter what your boss says about it. If it's real, it's real. You can't deny it."

"Says the man who calls himself an ass when it comes to women."

They shared a chuckle until Ethan muttered. "Speaking of bosses," he said. "I need to go. But thanks. You've given me something to think about."

"Good luck," Beck said. "And whatever's going on with your job, I wish you well."

"Thanks," Ethan said. "As for your lady – just grab her some flowers and apologize. You're not an ass by nature, Beck. If she loves you, she'll forgive you."

"I hope so."

They said their farewells and hung up. Beck was coming to think that Ethan's phone call was fortuitous, like a sign from God. Talking to the man helped reinforce the situation, the conversation, and the path he needed to take, more than ever.

If she loves you, she'll forgive you.

Hopefully she would, but Beck had to make a couple of stops first to ensure that would happen.

He honestly couldn't take it if it didn't.

———

Blakesley was keenly aware that Beck had left. Part of her wanted to go running after him but part of her was glad. She needed some time to breathe, away from him, and ponder his reaction to her suggestion of a prenup. She saw his point after he had calmly explained it, but to immediately assume the worst had hurt her deeply. It just showed that they really didn't know each other as well as they hoped. It wasn't his fault. It was her fault for assuming he could read her mind.

So she calmed down and settled in to her evening routine with the girls. All three little girls got into the bathtub at eight o'clock and bath time ensued until eight-thirty, whereupon she got the girls out of the bathtub with Nikki's help and got them ready for bed. Then it was story time for Crosby and Charlotte, and Alfie, too, because he ended up lying on Crosby's bed.

As Blakesley lay on Charlotte's bed and read them the story of the Velveteen Rabbit, Blakesley heard Beck's truck pull down the alleyway next to the house. She heard the electric gate at the back of the house open and continued reading distractedly until she heard the back door open downstairs. Feeling relieved he was home, she finished off the book but Crosby demanded one more. Blakesley rolled over onto her side to finger through the stack of books on the bed stand between the beds when Crosby suddenly yelled.

"Beck!" she flew off the bed and raced to Beck, standing in the doorway. "Will you read us a story? Please?"

Blakesley turned to look at him. He was holding Crosby's hand as she yanked him in the door but his eyes were on Blakesley.

"Sure," he told Crosby. "If it's okay with your mom."

Blakesley nodded, her eyes riveted to him and trying to glean some feeling off of him, good or bad. "It's fine," she said quietly.

He smiled at her and she smiled back, feeling a huge sense of relief. There was warmth in his eyes; she could see it. Beck picked Crosby up by both arms, dangling her over Blakesley and Charlotte's head before depositing her gently onto the bed. As Blakesley held up the book for him to read, he took it and climbed onto the bed beside her. It was a twin-sized bed, rather snug for two grown adults and two small children, but he snuggled in right behind Blakesley and pulled her tightly against him. Blakesley held Charlotte and Crosby, all three of them wrapped up in Beck's big arms as he read Good Night Moon.

It was sweet and heavenly and cozy. Blakesley relished the feel of him against her and she closed her eyes, listening to his deep and sultry voice read the children's book. When he was finished, he put Crosby in her bed and tucked her in while Blakesley tucked in Charlotte. He left the dog because Crosby had begged him to and, being a sucker, he couldn't refuse. He would leave the mutt until the girls fell asleep, at any rate. As they both walked from the room together, Blakesley softly shut the door.

"Baby," Beck didn't even wait until the door was completely shut. "I'm so sorry I said those things to you. Please don't be mad at me any...."

Blakesley put her fingers to his lips, silencing him. "It's my fault," she admitted. "I just assumed you knew what I was thinking and why, and I shouldn't have done that to you. I blindsided you and that wasn't fair."

He pulled her into a fierce hug, holding her tightly. "I shouldn't have reacted the way I did," he whispered, kissing her ear. "I love you so much. I'm nothing without you. If you think a prenup is the right thing to do, then go right ahead. We can do it however you want. I know you're just trying to be smart about things and I respect that."

She put her hands on his cheeks, looking him in the eye. "Are you sure?"

"Absolutely."

"My lawyer said he can write it up any way we want, but you should have another lawyer look it over. Just like a second opinion."

"Sure, baby. Anything you want."

She kissed him and he responded fiercely, soft touches and gentle tastes reaffirming their love and commitment to each other. Lizzie picked that moment to come out of her bedroom and she groaned at the sight of the two adults in a tight clinch.

"Geez, Dad," she sneered, pushing past him on her way to the bathroom. "Don't do that around the kids. Go downstairs and do that stuff in your own space."

Beck grinned, looking at Blakesley, who was also smiling. Blakesley gently pulled from their embrace and headed downstairs as Beck had a few words with his daughter. Blakesley closed the blinds in the small playroom off the entry and turned off the light, turned on the porch light, and made her way through the house closing blinds, curtains, and turning off lights.

By the time she reached their bedroom, she opened the door to find the entire room lit with a dozen or more candles and a gigantic bouquet of flowers lying on the bed. As she gasped, she felt a body walk up behind her.

Beck bent over and scooped her into his arms, carrying her into the bedroom and kicking the door shut behind them. Blakesley's arms were around his neck, looking around the room at all of the candles.

"Baby, what did you do?" she asked.

He kissed her on the cheek. "I'm trying to make up for being an ass," he told her, setting her gently to her feet. He pointed to the nightstand on his side of the bed. "I got a bottle of the best champagne I could find. The guy at the liquor store said that brand is guaranteed to get me laid."

Blakesley looked at the bottle of Veuve Clicquot sitting in a blue plastic bucket with ice. She giggled as she turned to him.

"You didn't have to do all of this," she said. "I forgave you the moment you drove out of the driveway."

He sighed and made his way towards her. "I couldn't count on that," he said quietly. "I just wanted to say how sorry I was. I was a jerk."

She smiled at him. "You're forgiven." She stood on tiptoes to kiss him. "Now, are you going to get me drunk and take advantage of me?"

His eyes twinkled. "Can I?"

"Sure."

Beck did just that. He came to discover that Blakesley had a very low tolerance for alcohol and by the third glass of champagne, she was quite literally wasted. She was a happy, funny drunk and very horny, and he had some of the best sex of his life that night before she passed out. The unfortunate part was that he awoke to a grumpy fiancée with a very bad hangover.

EIGHTEEN

MARSHALL THORNE CAME DOWN from Los Angeles a couple of days before the wedding to meet his future son-in-law and spend some time with him. Beck had been a little nervous meeting Blakesley's father but discovered that Marshall was one of the nicest guys he'd ever met. He had a quirky sense of humor and walked around with an unlit cigar hanging out of his mouth. Blakesley wouldn't let him smoke it around the girls so he would go outside and sit with Alfie, who happily followed the man around in the yard.

Beck's parents also came down from Santa Rosa and he had the privilege of introducing Blakesley to his father, Rear Admiral Beckham Raymond Seavington the Second, retired, and his mother, Elizabeth. Blakesley was surprised to know that Beck's father was a retired admiral, but she remembered that Beck said his father had been in the Navy, so it really wasn't that much of a surprise in hindsight. Tall and blond like his handsome son, Beck Sr. was a quiet and kind man, and Blakesley liked him immediately.

Beck's mother was a sweetheart, too. Everyone called her Betty. Betty was a warm and gracious woman who took to Blakesley and her girls right away. She only had one son and one granddaughter, so the introduction of a new daughter-in-law and three new granddaughters was thrilling for her. Beck noticed that it took all of five minutes before Crosby and Charlotte were sitting happily on his mother's lap. His mother ate it up.

Sometime around mid-afternoon on the day before the ceremony, Blakesley's best friends from Los Angeles had driven down and Beck found himself introduced to a horde of beautiful and feisty women. Sophia, Kimberly, Barbi, Cyndee and Terri were sweet, friendly, happy, funny as hell and incredibly protective of Blakesley. Beck found that out when Blakesley introduced him to the group of ladies and then was called away because Charlotte had awakened from her nap.

Alone with the group of women, Beck smiled at the women as he thought on how to continue the conversation without Blakesley but the group had other ideas. They literally ganged up on him in the kitchen and told him in no uncertain terms what their expectations of him were. He fought off a grin as Sophia, the most beautiful but most outspoken of the group, stopped short of threatening his manhood should he do anything to hurt Blakesley. Beck understood and was touched by their loyalty and softened them up with his honesty and charm. Within the first twenty minutes of knowing the ladies, he'd won over most of them except for Sophia. She was still the hard-sell but she was fading fast.

The women hit the beauty salon on Friday afternoon, with Blakesley and Betty going on Saturday morning. Beck dropped them off at the salon before heading out with his dad and Blakesley's dad, picking up the flowers and running last minute errands. When he returned an hour later to pick the ladies up, he was astounded at Blakesley's transformation.

She had an elaborate up-hairdo with a tasteful, small tiara artfully woven into her honey-colored hair. From the neck up, she looked like a goddess but from the neck down, she wore yoga pants and an oversized shirt, so he ran the women home so they could get dressed. Time was growing short.

Nikki and Lizzie had dressed the girls while Blakesley had

retreated to the master bedroom to put on her wedding gown. It was a beautiful, casual wedding gown made of chiffon and satin, with bejeweled spaghetti straps, an empire waist, and a jewel-encrusted band embracing her torso just below her breasts. It was sweet and gorgeous and flowing, and it took Beck's breath away when he saw her emerge from the master bedroom. She was the most beautiful thing he had ever seen. He took her hand, kissed it, and struggled not to tear up. He had no idea that Blakesley was doing the same, looking at him in his sharp dress white uniform. He was the handsomest man in the world.

Charlotte and Crosby looked like little angels in their pretty, white dresses. Cadee also had a pretty, white dress that was a little more grown up than her sisters' clothes, while Lizzie had a gorgeous, silky, white dress that made her look like a super model. All of the girls had bouquets of orange-yellow roses with orange lilies and yellow irises mixed in. With everyone dressed and ready, Beck herded everyone into three cars and they headed off to the county clerk's office.

Captain Davis, Anthony Solis, Gina and several other men and their wives from Beck's troop were waiting for them at the main San Diego county clerk's office in the heart of San Diego, along with a photographer Blakesley had hired. Truthfully, it was a bit of a circus as they all filed into the country clerk's office for the five-minute ceremony, but when all was said and done, Beck and Blakesley were married and that was all that mattered. Blakesley had her gorgeous ring on, plus a matching slender wedding band with pave diamonds and Beck had a big, sleek, titanium wedding band. He'd never worn one before but he was very proud to wear one now. He kept touching it, hardly believing it was real.

When the ceremony ended, Crosby and Charlotte had had enough pomp and circumstance, and Beck found himself carrying Crosby out of the building because she was very unhappy about nearly everything. Sophia had Charlotte while Cadee followed her mom, holding her hand, and somehow they made it out to the grassy area outside of the building to take pictures. Now they had two crabby little girls on their hands, but Beck and Blakesley got some spectacular shots with San Diego harbor as the backdrop. When the picture-taking was over, Captain Davis had made lunch arrangements at the Grant Grill at the U.S Grant Hotel in downtown San Diego, which was a local icon built in 1910 and very upscale. Davis knew the general manager and had set up a fabulous lunch reception.

It was a happy group that celebrated the marriage of Beck and Blakesley. Blakesley's friends integrated nicely with Beck's men and everybody seemed to be having a good time, especially Sophia and Kimberly, who were ragingly drunk by early afternoon. While Kimberley sat on Anthony Solis' lap and flirted, Sophia zeroed in on Captain Davis, a divorced and very eligible man who was very flattered and a little frightened at the attention from the beautiful blond. Beck and Blakesley watched it all, enjoying the moment and laughing between themselves at the antics going on.

The restaurant manager managed to pipe in a mix of dance and ballads into the restaurant's sound system, meant to be a background accompaniment to a fine meal, but it turned into a dance party when Kimberly got a hold of a couple of wax bananas from a display and shook them around like they were maracas. It started to get out of control so Beck sent Nikki home with the little girls and with Spike Aguirre, while Lizzie stayed on, hanging out with her grandparents and enjoying being included with the adults.

Blakesley tried to convince her drunken friends to ease up, but the Navy men in the group circumvented her attempts and soon, there was a full-blown party going on. Beck sat with Captain Davis, smirking at the craziness and sipping Seven and Seven with his captain. Truthfully, it wasn't often they got the opportunity to relax and cut loose, so Beck wasn't inclined to cut their fun short. They deserved it. Even Gina was up and dancing, enjoying a few moments of joy in the past few weeks of hell.

Blakesley had been particularly concerned about Gina throughout the wedding and reception, acutely aware of her fragile mental status. She told her girlfriends and they made sure they were very sweet to Gina and made her feel included. So they sat and watched as Gina let her hair down with some of the men, Butch's men, and it seemed to be very therapeutic for her. The woman was not only coping with her husband's death, but she was also starting to heal.

Although the group had only intended to stay a couple of hours, they ended up hogging a good section of the restaurant all afternoon and into the dinner hour. Beck wasn't a dancer but he couldn't resist dancing a slow, romantic ballad with his new wife, something that softened even Sophia has she watched. It was sweet and deeply romantic. Any man who made her friend so happy couldn't be all bad, so she had a little fun with him. After the slow dance was over, she made sure something fast and very 1980's was played so all the women could jump up and dance with Beck. Blakesley laughed as Beck found himself surrounded by seven aggressively dancing women, including his wife, so he just sucked it up and put on his best John Travolta moves. It was hilarious to watch.

By five in the afternoon, the group finally called a halt to the festivities and cleared out of the restaurant. Beck caught Blakesley giving the restaurant manager her credit card to pay for everything, which he gently argued with her about, giving Marshall time to slip in and pay for the tab. Covert operation complete, Blakesley argued with her dad all the way out to the front driveway, prompting Marshall to threaten her with a spanking if she didn't shut her mouth. As the entire group filtered to the front of the hotel to wait for the valet, the general manager from the hotel caught up to them.

"Mr. and Mrs. Seavington," the Hispanic man was beaming. "I have something for you."

It was the first time Blakesley had heard her new title. She grinned with pleasure as the general manager handed Beck an envelope. Looking curiously at Blakesley as he opened it, Beck discovered that someone had paid for a night in the U.S. Grant

Presidential Suite for them. Shocked, Beck handed the card over to Blakesley who, after reading it, looked equally shocked.

They looked around to see who was guilty but apparently the entire group was, because everyone was smiling and laughing. Marshall slapped Beck on the shoulder.

"Congratulations," he beamed. "It's a gift from your parents and me. You've got five hundred kids waiting for you back at that house and we figured you'd like one evening just to yourselves."

Beck smiled at his father-in-law. "That's really thoughtful, thank you." He looked at Blakesley. "Are you okay leaving the girls for a night?"

Blakesley nodded without hesitation. "Absolutely," she said eagerly. "Nikki's with them. But I don't have any of my stuff...."

"We're going to go pick it up," Sophia announced, still hammered. "We're going to pack for you and bring it back."

Blakesley cocked an eyebrow at her. "No driving for you," she looked at Kimberly and the rest of the happy group. "None of you, okay?"

Marshall put his arm around his only child and hugged her. "I'll take care of them," he told her. "We'll make sure everything is taken care of."

Blakesley hugged her dad. "Thanks, Dad," she said, looking him in the eye. "For everything."

Marshall kissed her cheek and began to move off with the group, issuing directives and hailing the valet. Sophia and Kimberly staggered their way back to Blakesley, big grins on their faces as they looked at her and Beck.

"We'll pack for Beck, too," Sophia announced. "Little satin underwear, French maid's outfits and all that."

Beck rolled his eyes. "Great," he grumbled, although it was in good humor. "Just what I need. Do me a favor, okay? Don't do me a favor by packing for me."

The women laughed, hugging Blakesley and Beck before staggering back towards the valet stand. "No promises," Sophia called over her shoulder. "You married Blakesley. Now you're going to have to deal with us. We're family, too."

He smirked, looking at his wife. "Seriously? They're going to pack for me?"

She fought off a grin. "There won't be clothes in the suitcase, just piles and piles of condoms and sex toys. Trust me. I know those two."

He laughed softly, shaking his head as he watched the women pointing and laughing at him. "Look," he said. "They've got Gina with them now. Is she going to be okay?"

Blakesley watched Gina as she laughed and chatted with Barbi and Cyndee. "She'll be fine," she said, softening. "They'll take care of her. I think they're exactly what she needs right now."

Beck sobered as he watched Gina, also. "I'm sorry Butch missed this," he said quietly. "I miss him."

Blakesley turned to him, patting his cheek with sympathy. She knew he was still hurting for Butch although he wouldn't admit it except in times like this, almost in passing. It was a happy day minus his good friend but he was carrying on nonetheless. Life went on.

The valets started bring the cars around so hugs and kisses went all around as Beck and Blakesley left their friends and headed back into the hotel. The General Manager was waiting just inside the door to escort them to their suite. As Beck carried his new wife over the threshold into their bridal suite, he knew for a fact that he had never been happier. Every time he looked at Blakesley, he felt like pinching himself because he still couldn't believe any of this was real. It was as sweet and thrilling and wonderful as he could have imagined it.

They stayed up to watch the sunrise together.

NINETEEN
EARLY AUGUST

"SERIOUSLY?" Blakesley was bordering on livid. "You guys are seriously telling me that this entire property has to be re-surveyed? That's a bunch of crap."

The archaeologist from the State of California could see how upset she was. He was just trying to be truthful.

"I'm just telling you what our engineers are saying," he said. "There are all kinds of blocked-off tunnels underneath the public wing and then we've come across some big voids underneath the family wing that the ground penetrating radar is picking up. The records on this property indicate it has never been properly surveyed since it was built in 1847. For the historical value, and for your safety, we're going to have to keep it sealed off."

Blakesley sighed heavily. "But I've got one hundred and sixty years of family artifacts and heirlooms in there. Can we at least clear out the family wing? I've got to pay for twenty-four hour security for this place to protect the contents and it's really becoming expensive."

Dr. Nate Welton had been a State of California historian for thirty years. He knew the historical details of the entire state intimately and particularly the details of Southern California. He knew how valuable the Benjamin and Dulcinea Earp house was to the State. He'd been on-site since the beginning and the more he studied the house, the more valuable it became.

"I apologize if this is a bad suggestion, but I really have to ask," he said. "Have you thought about selling it to the State of California? I can't tell you how valuable this place is from a historical standpoint. The artifacts, the mine shafts, the structure itself are just remarkable and really integral to the history of the state. Would you consider selling it or donating it?"

Blakesley's gaze drifted over the whitewashed structures. "I'm not sure," she said, no longer angry but more thoughtful. "It's my family's history. I'm not sure I want to part from it even though it's becoming a pain in the ass. I'd really hoped to live here someday."

Welton looked at the structures as well, now pulled apart as engineers and historians went through it.

"You need to look at this like an old castle," he said. "Castles are great to look at and very historical, but financially, they're just not feasible to live in. The upkeep costs are enormous, as they are with any historical structure. Didn't you say you have children?"

Blakesley nodded. "Four girls."

Welton wriggled his eyebrows. "I'm not sure I'd want my kids roaming around this place," he motioned to her and began to walk. "Come over here. I want to show you something."

Blakesley followed. She was in flat shoes and jeans, making it much easier to traverse the uneven ground. She and Dr. Welton crossed the driveway and ended up over by the public wing. Welton pointed to a yellow-taped off area a few feet away.

"See that?" he jabbed a finger at what appeared to be a small sink hole, overgrown with weeds. "That's an old well. We've found four of them but there are probably more. Not a safe set-up for kids or animals."

Blakesley peered at the well without getting too close. She was coming to feel a sense of foreboding and disappointment. "Three of my girls are small," she said. "They'd fall right in those holes."

Welton nodded. "They'd get swallowed up," he said. "In fact, this entire area is a landmine of stuff. We've found old railroad spikes, buried wagon wheels, stuff like that. But that tunnel under the public wing has been a time capsule. We'll be pulling stuff out of there for years to come."

Blakesley looked at him. "What about that old man who was living in the tunnel? What happened to him?"

Welton snorted. "That old guy?" he said. "The cops had to come and get him out. He was really dug-in down there. I don't know what happened to him after the cops removed him. Did you know him?"

She shook her head. "Not really," she said. "He seemed to know a lot about the history of the area, though. Maybe you should talk to him."

Welton half-shrugged and half-nodded, not particularly interested in that suggestion. Blakesley was feeling more and more disappointed as she looked around the property again, fighting off the impending sense of doom. She was coming to think that this place was never meant to be hers because since the beginning, fate or curses or whatever witchcraft one might believe in seemed to be preventing her from moving in. Looking at the structures made her remember everything Old Mike had told them. She sighed heavily.

"So you don't think it would be safe to move my girls in here?" she asked.

Welton shook his head. "If it were me, I wouldn't do it," he could see she was depressed. "Look, this is a very old house. Even if you were to rewire and re-plumb, the State of California and the City of San Diego would fight you on every turn because you'd be disturbing original walls to do those things. You can't mess up the old adobe because people are going to have a fit. You wouldn't be able to remodel or add on or change the roof. The State would file lawsuits to prevent you from altering the structure in any way. See where I'm going with this? You own, unfortunately, one of the last great true and untouched historical structures in the State of California and the State is going to be hugely protective of it. There's not going to be a lot you'll be able to do with it."

Blakesley was starting to see the light, however reluctantly. "Do you think the State would buy it from me?"

Welton nodded. "Given the historical significance of this place, I would think they'd be very interested," he replied. "What did you pay for it?"

"Three point one million," she replied. "I wouldn't take a penny less."

"Let me talk to some people, then."

"Have them give me a call."

"Do you want to talk to your husband first?"

She waved him off. "He'll do whatever I want to do," she said. "Besides, he's away on business."

"What does he do?"

"Navy." She didn't want to get into Beck's absence so she started to walk. "Can I just look around?"

Welton nodded. "Watch your step."

Blakesley nodded her acknowledgement and continued walking around the rear of the public wing. It was a hot day, dusty and dry, and she fanned herself as she walked back to the edge of the yard where the slope disappeared down into the wooded canyon. She turned to look at the rear of the house, the same door that she and Beck had charged through the first time they had made love. This house had some deep memories for her in spite of the fact that she had never lived in it. It didn't look like she was ever going to.

She began to pace around the perimeter of the public wing, into an area that they were doing some external surveying on. There were areas sectioned off with yellow caution tape. As she wandered, her cell phone rang. Caller I.D. showed it to be Sophia and she answered accordingly.

"Hey, chickie," Blakesley said, phone against her ear. "What's shaking?"

"Hi, Doll," Sophia sounded happy. "I was calling to see if you and Beck wanted to join Curtis and me for a fundraising gig for

Curtis' hospital. Lots of big-wigs will be there. It's on September first."

"That sounds like fun," Blakesley said earnestly. "But I don't know when Beck will be home. He's been gone for a couple of weeks now."

Sophia sighed. "Long time for a newlywed, honey. I'm sorry."

"Long time for anyone," Blakesley said softly, fighting off the feelings of sadness, loneliness and worry. "This is the third time since I've known him that he's been called out. Three times in two months. I promised him I wouldn't worry, but I just can't help it. It just eats at me and he knows it."

"How does he know?"

"Because I always lose weight," she said. "He comes back and thinks I look skinnier. Boy, is he in for a surprise this time."

"Why?"

Blakesley smiled. "Because I think I'm pregnant. I've been eating like a pig."

Sophia screeched into the phone. "What?" she howled. "Oh, my God! Blakesley, are you serious?"

Blakesley nodded. "Pretty sure," she said. "All I've done over the past couple of weeks is eat. I eat constantly and I've got that ravenous feeling all of the time. Remember when I was pregnant with the girls?"

"God, yes," Sophia snorted. "We couldn't keep you fed. You were an eating machine. So I can see that case of condoms we sent to your honeymoon suite weren't used."

Blakesley giggled. "No, but the lubricant was," she teased. "Thanks for that. It made everything work like a well-oiled machine."

"Gross," Sophia chuckled as Blakesley laughed loudly. "Well, at least you were all lubed up. That's what counts, especially on your honeymoon."

Blakesley was still laughing. "It wouldn't be a good thing to get chaffed, not with all the screwing we were doing."

"Too much information!" Sophie exclaimed. Then she sobered. "What does Beck think about a new baby?"

"He doesn't know," Blakesley sobered as well. "I only really started putting the pieces of the puzzle together since he's been gone. I'm sure he's going to be happy. I hope so, anyway."

"Sure he will," Sophia assured her. "Maybe you'll have a boy this time."

"That would be nice, but I'll take a healthy baby of either sex."

"No worries," Sophie said. "You always have beautiful, healthy kids. So, do you know where Beck is?"

Blakesley shook her head. "No," she said. "He never tells me. He could be on the moon for all I know. I guess that's the scary part, not knowing. He left the day after our wedding and I haven't seen or heard from him since. That's so damn hard."

Sophie grunted in agreement. "Maybe, but knowing the way his job works didn't stop you from marrying him. Not that I blame you; he's a keeper."

Blakesley's smile returned. "Absolutely," she said. "Anyway, I was just heading out to pick up the girls from summer camp, so I'll let you know about the fundraiser, okay? As soon as I know something about Beck's schedule."

"Okay, Doll. Have a good day. Love you."

"Love you, too. Talk to you soon."

Blakesley turned off the phone and headed back to her car, parked in front of the family wing. She wound her way through the overgrown courtyard between the two wings, looking at the dry fountain and hoping they could get that restored soon. It really was a lovely fountain. But her thoughts were also lingering on possibly selling the estate to the State of California, something that didn't sit well with her but something that was increasingly of interest. Maybe it was the thing to do. She'd give her dad a call to see what he thought.

Blakesley looked at the clock in the car as she turned it on, seeing that she was going to be late to pick up the girls if she didn't get moving. Putting the car in gear, she pulled out of the long driveway and out onto the street beyond. The roads were narrow in these hills, winding, with plenty of blind curves.

Blakesley was thinking of the Beck, of the girls, and of what to feed them for lunch when she came around a corner and an old man in a big car who wasn't paying attention came shooting through the intersection and hit her broadside on the driver's side. He had been traveling at such a high rate of speed that he nearly cut Blakesley's car in half when he drove it clear across the intersection and into a big Eucalyptus tree.

Blakesley never knew what hit her.

————

Night ops were the worst. In heavy seas and driving rain, under the cloak of darkness, Beck and his troops had made their way onto a Los Angeles Class submarine en route from their successful mission to a very small island in the Philippine archipelago. Two sailors from Subic Bay had been kidnapped by a local warlord and Beck's team had spent two weeks scouting the place out before making their move.

It had been jungle warfare, down and dirty. Beck had a bullet burn on his forearm but wasn't any worse for wear as he had freed the two young and terrified sailors. All insurgents had been killed in the procedure before the team had faded back into the jungle and headed back for the coastline where their transport waited.

It was the end of a very long three weeks and it would take them another few days to get home. Beck could already taste Blakesley, his mind full of her for the past two days. When he was operating, he tried not to let his thoughts linger on her because a distraction could be deadly, but since their op was over, he let her flood his mind. He couldn't wait to get home.

The transfer to the sub had been tricky and dangerous, and one of his men had come away with a broken ankle because the sub had been rolling so much. But once the submarine went deep, the ride was smooth and the men were able to decompress and debrief.

When the reports were written and every round, every weapon was accounted for, Beck fell into a heavy sleep on one of those narrow little beds that weren't built for a man his size. Still, it was better than the beds that had slept on for the past several days. At least this one had a mattress.

He was in a deep and dreamless sleep when he heard Davis' voice. Groggy but alert, he rolled up at the sound of his captain.

"I'm up, I'm up," he muttered, rubbing his eyes. "What's up, Captain?"

Not only was Davis in the small cabin, but so was Anthony Solis and another veteran S.E.A.L., Commander Bill Hudson. Hudson, in fact, commanded the second of the three troops in S.E.A.L. Team 3, and was a very seasoned and experienced sailor. Beck had known him for ten years. When Anthony quietly closed the cabin door, Beck knew it must be serious. He struggled to shake off the sleep.

"Beck," Davis said quietly. "The sub just received a transmission from San Diego. We've been out of range for about a day so it just now came through the ultra-low frequency exchange."

Beck nodded. "What's going on?"

Davis tried to soften the blow. He had debated whether or not to tell him anything at this point, but he couldn't, in good conscience, withhold that kind of information. He knew it was going to tear Beck up, more still because they were at least three days out of Hawai'i, where they would catch a transport home. It would be at least ninety-six hours before they could get Beck home. He braced himself as he delivered the news.

"The message was for you," Davis said, his voice surprisingly gentle for the usually brusque man. "Blakesley has been in an accident."

The news didn't register with Beck at first. He was still waiting for some secret missive to come forth, something that would prevent him from getting home to see his wife. But when he realized what Davis was saying, his eyes widened and his pallor went from a healthy pink to an ashen white.

"Accident?" he breathed. "What... what accident?"

Davis put his hand on Beck's shoulder. "A car accident," he said as gently as he could. "We don't know any more details other than she was badly injured. Your father sent you the message, Beck. The admiral has ordered you home."

Admiral Seavington. Beck hadn't heard his father referred to as that in a couple of years, at least since the man retired as admiral in charge of a carrier group. Beck just stared at his captain. He wasn't sure how to react. In fact, he was afraid to move because he was afraid he would lose all semblance of control. He just sat there, frozen, his mind whirling with disbelief.

"He didn't say what happened?" his voice sounded oddly weak.

Davis shook his head. "Just that she was in a car accident. The captain has ordered full steam ahead so we should make Hawai'i in a couple of days. We'll get you back to her, I promise."

Beck sat on his bunk as if unable to function. He just sat there, staring at the captain. "What about the girls?" he asked, his voice now trembling as the news began to settle. "Did he say anything about the girls?"

Davis shook his head again. "Just Blakesley," he patted his shoulder. "I'm sure if the girls had been involved, your father would have said so. I'm sure they're fine."

Beck continued to stare at him as the others watched with tense anticipation. Beck wasn't an emotional man, nor was he known to show much variation from his steady demeanor. But they could see that the news had him reeling. As they watched and waited for some kind of explosion, Beck reached over into his big, black pack, the one that followed him everywhere, and pulled out what looked like a small, leather notebook.

However, when he opened it, they could all see photographs inside. There were photos of blond girls and women, and he flipped the pages until he came to one particular photograph. It was a picture of Beck and Blakesley on their wedding day, arms around each other, cheek to cheek as the blue waters of San Diego bay glistened in the background. Blakesley looked happy and gorgeous, and Beck stared at the picture for several long moments.

"Oh, my God," he breathed. "This can't be happening."

Davis was deeply sympathetic. "We'll get you home as fast as can, Beck."

Beck acted like he didn't hear him. "It was supposed to be me," he muttered. "I was the one who put my life on the line, the one who always had the odds of never making it home. Not her. It was me."

Davis sat down on the chair next to Beck's bunk. "She's not dead," he said softly, insistently. "The message just said she had been in an accident and was badly injured. She's not dead, Beck."

Beck didn't say anything. He just continued to stare at the picture. Then, small splashes of water hit the plastic covering the picture as tears popped from Beck's eyes. Davis and the other men in the room couldn't have been more astonished, which made the sympathy they felt for Beck all the more painful. The man was shattered.

"I don't want to do this anymore," Beck suddenly whispered. "I don't want to leave my family anymore. My wife. I don't want to be away from home anymore. I want out of this."

Davis cast a concerned glance at Anthony, at Bill, as he replied. "Beck, I don't want to lose you but I understand. You're a man with a family and a lot of responsibility, but don't do anything rash. I'll see if I can get more information on Blakesley's condition for you, all right? Just hold it together, son."

He stood up and left the room, giving Anthony and Bill silent instructions to remain with Beck. When the door closed behind the captain, Anthony took the chair the man had vacated. Beck was still staring at the picture with tears all over his face. Anthony was all torn up about it. He hated to see such a strong and noble man in such pain.

"She'll be okay, Beck," he assured him. "I'm sure she's fine already. It takes time for those messages to get out, so I'm sure that's old news. She's probably up and around already."

Beck was still looking at the picture. "She's strong," he muttered. "She's strong and beautiful and perfect. She was probably driving that damn car too fast like she always does and... oh, God, what am I saying? I'm sorry, baby, I didn't mean it."

The picture book fell to his lap and his head collapsed into his hands. His low, mournful sobs filled the still air, driving Anthony to tears simply because Beck was so upset. Only Bill seemed in control and that was only because he'd never met Blakesley. He'd never had the chance to see the two of them together. Still, he hurt deeply for his friend.

As Bill went down to the mess to get Beck a cup of coffee, he found himself hoping that Blakesley Seavington would pull through, or at least wouldn't pass away while her husband was at sea. What a horrible thing that would be for Beck. From what he had heard, Beck and his wife had only known each other a couple of months, yet they were hopelessly and deeply in love with each other. He'd heard Anthony comment that the relationship between Beck and his wife was the thing all men hoped for in their life but seldom got. Beck had it all and now, it threatened to slip away.

Bill didn't even know the woman, yet he prayed for her.

Beck had probably gotten a total of four hours of sleep in the past three days and he was so strung out on caffeine and adrenalin that his entire body was twitching. He hadn't showered or shaved in days and once the transport from Hawai'i landed at Coronado, he was the first man off the plane. He bolted as if an invisible lasso had lashed in through the hatch and yanked him out. Anthony and Captain Davis were right behind him.

It was a bright and sunny day outside, the California sky a brilliant blue, but Beck didn't notice. He was more concerned about dumping his gear, getting to his truck and heading to the hospital. But a sight on the edge of the dusty tarmac stopped him in his tracks.

Beck Sr. was waiting for him. As Beck disembarked the plane with his bags slung over his shoulder, he could see his father standing next to his car about a hundred or so feet away. Beck came to a jerky halt about halfway across the tarmac, unable to walk any further, terrified that his father had come for him bearing bad news. He just stared at his dad, his heart in his throat, knowing that his father's appearance was not a good thing. He tried to take another step but his knees buckled and he went down hard on his right knee. That brought his father and several other men, running in his direction.

"Son, it's all right," Beck Sr. moved fast for an old man; he was at his son's side quickly, pulling off the heavy bags and gripping his son by the arm to pull him to his feet. "Let's get over to the hospital."

Beck was feeling weak and dizzy as his father and Captain Davis walked him towards the car. He staggered like a drunken man.

"Is she dead?" he asked, trying to pull away from their steadying grip. "No one would tell me a goddamn thing when we got to Hawai'i. Dad, how is my wife?"

"I asked them not to," Beck Sr. said steadily. "I wanted to tell you everything, the truth, so you wouldn't get information in pieces. First of all, Blakesley's not dead at all. Secondly, the girls are fine. They weren't in the car with her when it happened."

Beck was having a good deal of trouble composing himself. They reached his dad's car and Davis yanked open the passenger door.

"I'm glad the girls are okay," Beck muttered as he practically fell into the front seat. "Where are they?"

"Your mother is staying at the house with them," Beck Sr. said. "Lizzie is there and so is their nanny. They're fine. But they're understandably scared and they miss their mother."

Davis shut the door on Beck as Beck Sr. ran around the front of the car and climbed in the driver's seat. Beck put his hand on his dad's arm before the man could start the car.

"Dad," he begged in a hoarse whisper. "Please tell me how Blakesley is. Please."

His dad sighed faintly and looked at his son; he'd never seen him look so run down or stressed out. The man looked like hell and his heart ached for him.

"She was hit broadside on the driver's side," he said softly. "The guy who hit her was just some old man going too fast to control his car. He plowed into her and knocked her into a tree. She never saw it coming. I don't know if that's a blessing or not. Anyway, she's been in a medically-induced coma for about six days now."

Beck's eyes widened. "Medically induced coma?" he repeated, horrified. "Why?"

Beck Sr. started the car and pulled out. "Surprisingly, she didn't suffer any major broken bones other than a few cracked ribs and a cracked collar bone," he replied, pulling out of the airfield and heading off base. "But she's banged up, son. Her lungs are bruised and her spleen was ruptured. They had to do emergency surgery on the spleen to remove it. They put her in a coma to help her heal faster because she was fighting the intubation tube so much. She kept trying to pull it out so they just knocked her out."

Beck listened to his wife's injuries, horrified and frightened. He watched the landscape pass by, tears rolling down his cheeks.

"Is she improving?" he asked, his voice hoarse. "What do the doctors say?"

"They say she's getting better," Beck Sr. replied. "She's going to be okay, son. They're weaning her off the respirator today and she should regain consciousness soon. I wanted you to hear all of this from me directly and not pieces of messages that told you how badly she had been injured. I'm sorry if that scared you, the not knowing. But I felt it was best to tell you everything all at once. The main thing is that she's going to be all right."

Beck sighed heavily, struggling to get a grip on himself. "Thank God," he muttered, wiping the tears that were coursing down his face. "You can't even imagine what hell it's been the past few days. I didn't know if she was dead or alive."

"She's very much alive." Beck Sr. took the road out of the base, heading for the Coronado Bridge. He glanced at his son. "But...

well, there's something else you should know. Maybe you already knew. The doctors said she was pregnant."

"What?" Beck looked at his father, shocked. "She is?"

"Was," Beck Sr. stressed softly. "The accident caused her to miscarry. You didn't know about the baby?"

Beck stared at his father, absorbing the news. He put a hand over his mouth as if to hold back the horror he felt. "No," he breathed. "She didn't tell me. Why didn't she tell me?"

Beck Sr. shrugged. "The doctors said it was a very early pregnancy," he said quietly. "Maybe she didn't know yet herself. I'm sure she didn't deliberately keep it from you."

Beck closed his eyes and looked away, more tears rolling down his cheeks for the baby she had lost. But he comforted himself with the knowledge that she was going to be all right. That was the most important thing in the world. There would be more babies, but there would only be one Blakesley. Still, he was feeling everything down to his very bones and his emotions, so carefully controlled, were all over the place.

He wept the entire way to the hospital.

TWENTY

SCRIPPS MERCY HOSPITAL was a state-of-the-art medical facility with a nationally recognized trauma center. It had been instrumental in saving Blakesley's life. As Beck made his way into the hospital with his father holding on to his arm, he realized that he was resisting the urge to run. He kept walking faster and faster but Beck Sr. kept a firm hold on him. By the time they entered the hospital, Beck was pulling his father along.

Beck Sr. took his son to the elevators and up to the third floor ICU ward. It was a very nice hospital, one of the top in the nation, and Beck took comfort in that. Still, he was overwhelmingly anxious to get to Blakesley. He didn't even know where he was going; he just charged off the elevator and kept walking. Beck Sr. had to turn him around and direct him into the ICU.

It was a nice unit as far as ICU wards went, pristine and shaded in elements of blue and white. Each patient had their own glass-enclosed room and Beck and his father stopped at the nurse's station first. The nurse on duty recognized Beck Sr. and shook hands with Beck. Gabrielle Johnson was a very pretty, motherly African-American woman with a big smile.

"So you're Miss Blakesley's husband," she said, visually

inspecting the big, blond man with the growth of beard and the dirty clothes. "I've heard a lot about you."

Beck was pale, exhausted, struggling not to make an emotional mess of himself, but he still managed to be somewhat polite.

"From who?" he smiled weakly.

Gabrielle pointed to Beck Sr. "Your father has been here every day," she said. "So has Gina Aguirre and Blakesley's father. Marshall is in there with her now, in fact. He hasn't left her since this happened. I'm sure she'll be very happy to see you."

Beck perked up. "Is she conscious?"

Gabrielle shrugged. "She's trying." She waved him to follow her. "We took her off the respirator this morning and have been weaning her off the drugs. She's starting to twitch around so I'm guessing she's going to come out of this at some point soon."

Beck put his hand on the woman's arm, stopping her. "Please tell me how she is," he begged. "My dad told me what happened, but how is she now?"

Gabrielle could see how distraught the man was. It was touching, really. She patted the hand that was on her arm.

"She's a fast healer," she assured him. "She came through surgery like a champ and she seems to be healing very well. The doctor will be around later, but he's confident she'll make a full recovery. Don't worry so much."

She smiled and pulled him in to the nearest glass-enclosed room. Beck stepped inside the door, his eyes falling on the bed in the middle of the room. Blakesley lay there with an oxygen mask on her nose and mouth and as he drew closer, he could see the bruising on her face and a cut above her right eyebrow. Her long hair was dirty and stringy, all wrapped up in a surgical cap to keep it out of the way. The shock of seeing her suddenly brought everything down around him and he grasped her hand, the one that didn't have all of the I.V.s sticking out of it, and burst into tears. His soft sobs filled the room.

Marshall had been sitting in a chair next to the bed but Beck hadn't seen him. When Beck broke down, Marshall jumped up from his chair and shoved it at Beck as Beck Sr. lowered his son into the seat. They stood there with their hands on Beck as the man wept, their comforting grips willing strength and support into his body to help him face what he must. Beck lay his head down on the bed next to Blakesley and sobbed.

Gabrielle stood by the door, watched the man break down and felt deeply sorry for him. Sometimes words just couldn't bring comfort so she quietly slipped out to allow the family time alone. Marshall, too, had tears in his eyes and thought it would be better if he left Beck alone with his wife. The man deserved some privacy in his weakest moment. So he slipped out, followed shortly by Beck Sr., who didn't like seeing his proud, heroic son so distraught, especially when he couldn't do anything to help him. There was nothing any of them could do. He went outside of the room to stand with Marshall, struggling not to tear up.

Beck didn't even realize he was alone with Blakesley. He was struggling with his grief, of seeing Blakesley so badly injured. It was tearing him apart. He turned his head so he could see her, tears still streaming down his face.

"Hi, baby," he whispered, gently rubbing her arm. "I'm here. Everything is going to be fine, okay? I'm here and I swear I'm never going to leave you again, not ever. Can you hear me?"

She twitched a little but he was mostly met with silence. He stood up from the chair, taking a very close look at her face to see the damage. He ran a gentle hand over her forehead, inspecting the big bruise on her left cheek and the cut above her eye. No matter what her injuries, he still saw the most beautiful woman he had ever seen. Very tenderly, he kissed the tip of her nose, her right cheek.

"I'm here, baby, I'm here," he whispered, tears popping from his eyes and falling on her pale cheek. "I'm never leaving you again, I swear it. I love you so much. I need for you to wake up and talk to me, okay? Please, baby. Can you hear me?"

She remained still and silent. Beck reclaimed his chair and pulled it up close to the bed so he could put his arm around her and lay his head down on the bed beside her. He just wanted to touch her, to be near her. The man was so exhausted and emotionally tapped out that in little time, he was sound asleep, snoring loudly next to his wife.

———

Blakesley could hear the snoring. It was Beck; she knew that because he snored so hard sometimes that his chest rattled. She went to pat him to tell him to roll over but she found that she couldn't move. Her arms seemed very heavy. It was strange so she tried to roll over, but searing pain shot through her body and she awoke into a harsh world of bright light and glaring agony.

Beck woke up to Blakesley's painful gasping and his head shot up, his focus on her in an instant as she struggled to move around on the bed. He put his hands on her shoulders to still her.

"Take it easy, baby," he soothed. "You're okay. Everything is going to be okay."

Blakesley was incoherent, half-awake, and had no idea where she was. She began crying. "B-Beck," she wept. "Wh-what's happening?"

He was hovering over her, his lips against her face, his hands on her shoulders to keep her from moving around too much.

"It's okay, baby," he soothed her softly, catching Gabrielle and Marshall out of the corner of his eye as they entered the room. "You're okay. You're going to be fine. Just calm down, okay? Calm your breathing. That's right; slow down."

Blakesley was trying to listen to him but she was in a great deal of pain. "It... it hurts," she sobbed. "Everything hurts."

Gabrielle came up on the other side of the bed, checking the I.V.s to make sure Blakesley hadn't dislodged anything.

"Miss Blakesley." She put her face next to Beck's. "My name is Gabrielle. I'm a nurse. You were in an accident, honey. You're at Scripps Mercy Hospital."

Oddly, that seemed to calm her down. At least she knew where she was now. The tears stopped abruptly as she looked at Gabrielle, struggling to clear the cobwebs out of her mind. She looked around the room a bit without moving her head, her frightened gaze coming to rest on Beck. She focused on him.

"You look so tired," she whispered. "Are you okay?"

He smiled at her, fighting off the tears. "I'm fine."

She stared at him, fighting the confusion. "Where are the girls?"

"They're fine," he assured her. "They're at home with Lizzie and Nikki."

"I was in an accident?"

He nodded. "Your car was hit."

She blinked, thinking back to the last thing she remembered. It was all so muddled. "Is my car okay?"

Beck glanced back at Marshall, who stepped forward so his daughter could see him. He smiled at Blakesley when she focused on him.

"We're going to have to buy you a brand new car," he said. "I was thinking about a nice, big, heavy Cadillac."

Blakesley digested the statement, lucid enough to know that her father was teasing her. She hated Cadillacs. "I don't want your old man car, Dad," she muttered. "Those are for old farts."

Beck snickered, kissing her cheek just because he was so happy she was conscious and moderately coherent. At least she was clear enough to joke. He felt better than he had in five days.

"We'll get you whatever you want," he assured her. "I'll keep your dad away from the Cadillac dealer."

A flash of a smile crossed her lips as she looked at Beck again. "Where are my girls?"

His smile faded, thinking maybe she wasn't as lucid as he thought if she was repeating questions. "At home, baby. They're fine."

"Can I go home?"

Gabrielle shook her head. "You've got a little recovery time to do here and then you can go home," she said. "Now, can you tell me how you feel?"

Blakesley thought on that question, taking a deep breath and gasping with pain as she did so.

"My body hurts," she grunted. "My ribs. My belly. My throat really hurts. What happened to me?"

Gabrielle glanced at Beck to see the man's reaction to his wife repeating questions when they already told her the answer. She could see the distress in his face.

"You were in a car accident," she said evenly. "You need to sleep now and recover. You're going to be fine."

Blakesley looked at the woman, hearing her words, but the cobwebs were still there. They had cleared as much as they were going to clear at the moment. She gripped her husband's hand and closed her eyes. She didn't want to deal with any more at the moment, too exhausted and muddled to care.

Beck watched her eyes close and he kissed her cheek. "Go to sleep," he murmured. "I'll be here when you wake up."

"Don't leave," she whispered.

"I won't, I promise," he told her, kissing her cheek again. "I love you, baby."

Gabrielle checked her monitors, checked the I.V. bag again, and gave Beck a nod before quitting the room. Beck gently pulled his hand free from Blakesley's grasp and followed the nurse. He caught her before she got to the nurse's station.

"Why was she repeating questions like that?" he wanted to know, stressed. "Is there something wrong with her brain?"

Gabrielle shook her head. "That's normal," she said. "She's still fighting off the effects from the drugs. Remember that she's been unconscious for six days. It's going to take a little while for everything to start working normally again."

Beck sighed heavily and squared his shoulders, forcing himself to believe what the woman was telling him. "Okay," he said, turning for Blakesley's room. "Thank you."

Gabrielle stopped him. "She's going to sleep awhile," she said, eyeing the very dirty and exhausted man. "Why don't you go home and clean up? Get something to eat. She'll be fine until you get back."

"I don't want to leave her. I haven't seen her in three weeks."

"And she's not going anywhere," Gabrielle stressed to him. "Go home and see your girls. Come back in a couple of hours. She's going to sleep at least that long and you need to take care of yourself. You won't do her any good if you collapse."

Beck almost refused again but he took a good look at himself, realizing he really was a sight. He could smell himself, too, and it wasn't pleasant. With a reluctant nod, he agreed.

Beck had his dad drive him back to the base so he could pick up his truck. He stopped to tell Captain Davis what was happening and Davis immediately put him on Family Medical Leave. It would free Beck up for at least a month regardless of what went on with the team, and Beck was grateful. Now he could focus on Blakesley and her recovery, at least for the next three weeks. There was nothing else more important.

He drove his brand-new truck that Blakesley had given him through a burger drive-thru and wolfed the burgers down as he drove home. He spilled something on the seat and knew Blakesley would kill him if she ever found out. He found himself laughing and tearing up at the same time, thinking of his wife now asleep in her hospital room. He was so relieved that he couldn't verbalize it, but his concern for her hadn't abated. He wouldn't believe she was going to be all right until she literally walked out of the hospital. Until then, he would be perpetually on edge. He simply couldn't help it.

It was early afternoon by the time he pulled up to the house, traversing the narrow alley that ran perpendicular to the house and pulled into the backyard as the big, automatic gate opened up. Alfie was up on the deck, barking furiously as Beck parked the truck, and he opened up the car door and called to the dog. The dog flew off the porch and raced towards him. As he climbed out of the truck and petted the excited dog, the back door flew open and girls began pouring out.

"Beck!" Crosby was yelling as she raced across the yard. "You're home!"

Charlotte was right behind her and the little girls ran at him, jumping into his arms. He picked them up and kissed soft cheeks in greeting. Cadee, Lizzie and his mother were still by the back door as he made his way towards them.

"Hi, Dad," Lizzie hugged her father tightly. "I'm glad you're home. Grampa called and said you were on your way. How's Blakesley?"

Beck set Crosby and Charlotte down, almost tripping when Charlotte cut him off as he took the steps to the back door. He caught himself on the rail, holding on as the dog bolted past him and up into the house after the girls. He was home, thrilled with the instant, happy chaos. It comforted him like nothing else.

"She's awake," he said. "She knew who I was, she carried on a conversation, so I'd say she's doing much better."

Lizzie simply nodded, relieved, but Cadee was watching Beck with big eyes. She was the quiet one, the introspective and deep-feeling one, so Beck paused to pay special attention to her.

"Hi, baby girl," he kissed her forehead. "How are you doing?"

Cadee gazed up at him with eyes that looked exactly like her mother's. "Mom is awake?"

He nodded. "She is. She asked about you. She really misses you but she'll be home soon."

Cadee thought on that. Then, she turned and ran into the house. They could hear her running up the stairs. Beck looked curiously at Lizzie and his mother.

"Is she okay?" he asked.

Elizabeth hugged her son in greeting as he came in the back door. "I don't know," she said honestly. "She's hardly spoken since her mother was hurt. I think she's really scared but afraid to show it. She's very stoic, that one."

Beck's jaw ticked faintly. "She's been through a lot the past couple of years. She's the only one out of the three old enough to understand everything."

Beck went into the kitchen with his mother and Lizzie on his heels. He opened his mouth to say something to his mother but Crosby and Charlotte suddenly ran at him from the dining room, handing him multiple pieces of paper that ended up in a wad in his hand. The dog was right behind them, barking, jumping around at the excitement.

"We drew you some pictures," Crosby said happily. "Look – we drew you a whale!"

Beck smiled at the pictures, the crayon scribbles of little girls. "That's very good," he told her. "I love it."

"Can you take it to Mommy?"

He nodded. "Absolutely. She'll love them, too."

The girls squealed and ran out, followed by the dog, and Beck had to grin at the joyful bedlam they created. He set the drawings down on the kitchen counter.

"I think I'll go see how Cadee is," he said quietly.

He walked out of the kitchen and realized that Lizzie was following him by the time he reached the stairs. He turned around and she fell right into his arms, hugging him tightly. He hugged her back.

"What's the matter, baby girl?" he asked, his cheek against the top of her head. "Are you okay?"

Lizzie was in tears. "It was so scary, Dad," she whispered. "The cops came to tell us about Blakesley and we didn't know where you were. Marshall came and took care of everything. I heard him tell Grampa that Blakesley's car was cut in half and it was a miracle she survived. Is she really okay?"

Beck felt sick to his stomach to hear that, but he nodded. "She's going to be fine," he kissed her forehead. "Thank you for helping Gramma with the little girls. I'm proud of you for being so responsible."

Lizzie nodded, wiping at her nose. "They're my sisters," she said simply. "Dad, I know I told you that I liked Blakesley when I first met her, but I just want you to know... you know, that I love her, too. She's been really good to me and I feel like I can talk to her. I was so scared for her but I didn't want the little girls to see how scared I was. It's been really hard without you."

He sighed sadly, giving her a big hug. "I'm sorry, baby girl," he comforted, kissing the top of her head. "I'm going to see if I can change that, okay?"

"What do you mean?"

"I mean that I'm going to see if I can get a job that doesn't require me being gone months at a time."

Lizzie looked up at him, shocked. "You're going to stop being a S.E.A.L.?"

He nodded. "I'm getting too old to do that stuff. I'm going to see about getting a nice desk job at the base so I can come home every night to my girls. I think it's time."

Lizzie was torn between disbelief and excitement. "That would be great," she said. "We need you here. We don't want you out running around where something can happen to you. Blakesley didn't think I knew, but she cried almost every night after you left. She really missed you."

Beck patted her cheek. "I'll see what I can do," he said as he began to take the stairs. "Now, I want to see if Cadee is okay."

Lizzie let him go, mostly because Crosby and Charlotte started yelling in the playroom so she went to see what the ruckus was about. Beck went to the second floor of the old house, going to Cadee's bedroom and knocking softly on the half-open door. Not receiving an answer, he stuck his head inside.

Cadee was lying on her bed, hugging a big, blue teddy bear. The room was messy, clothes and shoes scattered on the floor. Cadee looked at Beck as he entered and he smiled at her.

"Hi," he said. "I came to see how you're doing."

Cadee seemed to find more interest in the bear. "I'm okay."

"Really?" he sat down on the edge of her bed, watching her pick at the toy. He could sense the fright, the frustration, simply by her manner. "Are you sure?"

"Yes."

"You're not, maybe, scared for your mom?"

Cadee didn't answer right away. She was poking the bear in the eye. "I just want her to come home, that's all."

"We all do, baby. She's getting much better, I promise."

Cadee just shrugged. Beck could see that she was having an increasingly difficult time pretending that she was okay. He felt a good deal of sympathy for her.

"You know," he said softly, "if you want to talk about it, I'll listen. I won't get mad and I won't laugh. I care about what you feel, Cadee. I know this has been hard for you."

Cadee's brow furrowed and she started poking the bear rather violently. "Everybody goes away," she complained.

"What do you mean?"

She poked the bear so hard that it fell out of her hands. She picked it up and threw it to the floor.

"My dad went away," she spoke angrily as she climbed off the bed. "Now my mom has gone away. You even go away. I live in a house with my sisters and people I didn't even know until a little while ago. I don't even know where my home is. This isn't my room!"

Beck could see how agitated she was. He wasn't quite sure what to say to her without setting her off. As he'd discovered, Cadee was quiet until she got on a roll. Then, it would all come out. He wanted to make sure she got it all out, even if it came flying out all over him.

"Your mom bought this house for you and your sisters," he said evenly. "This is your bedroom with all of your stuff."

Cadee was standing on the futon that Nikki slept on, looking out the window that faced to the south. The Coronado Bridge was in the distance and a faint haze hung over the bay. There wasn't anything she recognized in the view. It wasn't her city.

"I just want to go home," she murmured sadly.

Beck stood up from the bed. "You *are* home," he said gently. "Cadee, I know this has been hard on you. I know what happened to your dad and I know how hard it was on you. Your mom brought you to San Diego because she thought it would be better for you to be here, away from that life in Los Angeles. I was so lucky to meet you, your mom and your sisters, and I'm so lucky that you allowed me to come into your life. I love you and so does Lizzie and Gramma Elizabeth and Grampa Beck. We're so happy to be a family with you and we just want you to be happy, too. What would make you happy, honey? What can we do to help?"

Cadee broke down in sobs. "I want to see my mom."

Beck went to her, putting his arms around her and hugging her as much as she would allow. In fact, she rather caved in to him. He squeezed her tightly.

"I'll take you to the hospital tomorrow, okay?" he knelt down so he was at her level, his big hand wiping away the tears. "Don't cry, baby girl. I promise I'll take you to see your mom tomorrow. Would you like that?"

Cadee nodded, struggling to stop the water works. She wiped at her eyes furiously. "Is she really okay?"

He nodded. "She's getting better every day."

Cadee sniffled, wiping at her nose. "Can... can I bring her something?"

"Like what?"

"A present maybe. Like a gift?"

He smiled. "Of course," he said. "Let me change my clothes and I'll take you shopping, just you and me. Would you like that?"

Cadee nodded. "What about Crosby and Charlotte?"

"Do you want them to come?"

She thought on that, shaking her head after a moment. "No," she said. "They can stay here. Beck?"

"What, baby?"

"I... I'm glad you married my mom, but I don't like it when you go away for a long time."

He cocked an eyebrow. "Neither do I."

"Beck?"

"What?"

She wrinkled up her pert, little nose. "You're stinky."

He pretended to scowl at her, which made her giggle. He kissed her cheek and stood up, feeling relieved that Cadee was feeling better. He also realized that he was seriously feeling his exhaustion.

He made his way back downstairs, hearing Lizzie in the play-room with the little girls as he made his way back to the master bedroom. It was an odd experience for him when he entered the room that had so much of Blakesley in it, from her paintings on the walls to the comforter on the bed she loved so much. He could smell her everywhere. It was enough to bring a lump to his throat but he fought it as he made his way into the bathroom, which still had Blakesley's cosmetics and flat iron in it just where she had left them the morning she had been in the accident. It was like a time capsule, everything the way she left it.

He didn't touch a thing as he went about showering and cleaning up. It was easier to pretend everything was going to be all right if he could believe she was going to come through the door at any moment to clean things up.

———

Marshall and Beck Sr. were in on the covert op the next day.

Marshall ran interference with Gabrielle as soon as the hospital opened for visiting hours. He pretended to engage her in a serious conversation about his daughter's post-hospital care as Beck and Beck Sr. snuck into the ICU with Cadee between them. Beck Sr. was the lookout, waving Beck and Cadee into the ward when another nurse turned her back.

Beck was used to stealth and he moved faster when it was just him, so he scooped Cadee into his arms and made a break for Blakesley's room at his father's direction. Even though the rooms had glass walls, Beck made sure to position Cadee in front of him so no one looking in could see her. He took her right up to the bed where Blakesley was taking a nap.

She was without the big oxygen mask on her face and only a nasal cannula. Instead of multiple I.V.s, there was only one. Someone had washed her hair and braided it, because Beck could see that the braid draping over her shoulder was still damp. Her face was still bruised but it looked much better than it had the day before. She looked like she was quickly healing. Beck set Cadee down carefully next to the bed, leaning over to kiss Blakesley on the cheek.

"Baby," he whispered. "Wake up. I brought you a surprise."

Blakesley sighed heavily, coming out of a light nap. She opened her eyes, blinking the sleep from them, and the first thing she saw was Cadee's face looking back at her. Startled, she blinked her eyes again as if to regain her focus.

"Cadee?" she said hesitantly.

"Hi, Mommy," Cadee burst into tears.

Beck lifted the little girl onto the bed. Blakesley was bruised and extremely sore, but that didn't stop her from throwing her arms around her daughter. Cadee wept as Blakesley pulled her down against her, snuggling her close.

"Hi, baby," Blakesley rocked her. "I'm so glad to see you."

"Mommy, I miss you," Cadee sobbed. "Are you okay? Are you going to come home soon?"

They were making some noise. Beck Sr. slithered into the room and shut the door, but he wasn't fast enough. Gabrielle had heard the crying, too, and was making her way to Blakesley's room with Marshall on her tail. Beck Sr. hissed at his son that the nurse was coming so Beck flipped up the blanket on the side of the bed and covered Cadee up. Beck. Sr. tucked her feet into the cover just as Gabrielle came into the room.

Both Becks were lined up against the bed, blocking most of the view. Gabrielle looked at them suspiciously, cocking an eyebrow as she strained to get a look around them. Then, she crossed over to the other side of the bed as Marshall followed and tried to block her view. But Gabrielle was on to them. She began checking the oxygen flow and the various monitors that Blakesley was hooked up to. She pretended to be all businesslike.

"We're going to move Miss Blakesley into a regular room this afternoon," she said casually. "She'll be able to see more visitors there. I'm going to start unhooking her from the monitors so we should be able to move her by lunch."

Beck knew the woman wasn't stupid but, to her credit, she didn't call them out. "That's great," he said, obviously relieved. "When do you think we can take her home?"

Gabrielle shrugged. Then she leaned over Blakesley and flipped back the blanket that was covering Cadee's face. When she spoke, she spoke to the little girl.

"She should be able to go home the day after tomorrow if she eats well and continues to improve," she said. "Do you want to push your mama in a wheelchair and take her outside?"

Cadee's big, bluish-green eyes gazed back at the woman. "Yes."

"Then I'll go get one."

Gabrielle flipped back the blanket so it covered the girl up again and made her way out of the room. Marshall shrugged apologetically as she walked past.

"Sorry," he said feebly. "Cadee's had a hard time with her mom being gone and...."

Gabrielle wagged a finger at him. "Don't think you're so smart, Marshall Thorne," she snapped without force. "I fell for your charm, I admit it, but it's going to cost you dinner at a restaurant of my choice."

Marshall, a truly handsome and distinguished older man, grinned. "Any place you want, honey."

Gabrielle winked at him and left the room to go get the wheelchair. Marshall turned around to see both Becks and his daughter busting up with laughter. He pretended to scowl.

"See what I do for you?" he said to Blakesley. "I had to sell my soul to the devil."

Blakesley just laughed. "Stop pretending that you don't like it," she snorted, then she groaned and grabbed her belly. "Oh, God, it hurts to laugh. But it's worth it."

"Glad I could help."

As Marshall left the room, presumably to go find Gabrielle again, Beck leaned over Blakesley and Cadee, watching them cuddle, feeling a good deal of optimism and relief. Gabrielle came back in with the wheelchair and began carefully disengaging the monitors, keeping an eye on Blakesley to make sure she was handling the movement well. She even had Cadee help her take the blanket off of her mother and Cadee felt included, as if she were helping. It made the little girl feel much better.

Blakesley did so well with her move that the doctor cleared her to go home on the afternoon of the next day. She was under instructions to rest for the next month because of the major surgery and she couldn't drive a car for six weeks, but all in all, she was doing extremely well and was on her way to a complete recovery.

On a bright and sunny California afternoon, Beck took his wife home where she belonged.

———

"You're not going to believe this."

Beck was standing in the doorway of the master bedroom, looking at his wife with some amusement. Blakesley was in bed like a good girl, the television on and books spread out around her. The dog was even lying beside the bed, lonely, because the girls had started school the day before and he didn't have anyone to play with. Blakesley looked at Beck with curiosity.

"Believe what?"

Beck's grin broke through as he came to the bed and lay down next to her. "I was just at the base talking to Davis."

"I know."

He let out a noise that sounded like feigned laughter as he stretched out and put his big arms behind his head.

"It seems that Davis, my captain, has a date tonight."

Blakesley looked at him, smiling. "Really?" she said. "That's great. Anyone we know?"

"Sophia."

Blakesley's smile vanished. "What?" she hissed. "*My* Sophia?"

"Your Sophia."

Blakesley's eyes widened. "She called him!"

Beck nodded. "She did," he replied. "Davis gave her his business card at our wedding, remember? It seems that they're going out to dinner tonight."

Blakesley's smile returned. "Good," she said firmly. "Her boyfriend was such a jerk to her. Even though he was a big-wig doctor, he couldn't keep it in his pants. I'm so glad she finally broke it off with him."

Beck reached out to stroke her arm, somewhat tenderly. "Speaking of keeping it in his pants...."

Her grin broadened. "Are you hinting?"

"I'll spell it out if I have to."

She laughed softly. "So you've dropped the girls off at school and the house is empty, and now you want to have some fun?"

"I think I deserve it."

"Do tell."

"Well," he cocked his head. "I did what the doctors said. I left you alone for an entire month.

"Twenty-seven days."

"I took care of you, took care of the girls, made sure everything was handled."

"You're Superman. I don't know what we would have done without you."

"So I'm going to plead my case that I should get to have relations with my wife because I deserve it."

She just grinned, shaking her head at him reproachfully. Beck smiled back, hopeful, thinking of her soft, supple body and inevitably reliving the past few weeks when he thought he might lose her. Then he started thinking of the baby they had lost.

Blakesley didn't remember that part of it. In fact, the accident had wiped out her memory for three days prior to the accident. She didn't remember the baby or anything else from that time period, so the doctor advised Beck not to tell her. There was no point. Beck happened to be speaking with Sophia one day, who mentioned the baby, and Beck had to head her off from saying anything to Blakesley about it. He didn't want his wife weeping over something that had been out of her control.

For the past twenty-seven days, Beck had taken care of Blakesley with the attentiveness and compassion of a mother, making sure she was comfortable, cared for and tending the girls to make sure they were happy, and just generally being a house-husband, which he loved. He'd never had the opportunity before and he took to it quickly.

Blakesley was back to her usual gorgeous self and he was thrilled. She was a little thin from her time in the hospital and the spleen removal had left a couple of small scars on her belly, but he couldn't have cared less. She was still perfect as far as he was concerned, getting better every day to the point where she would get up and wander around the house, trying to do dishes or laundry until he chased her back to bed. She was still a little weak, and she slept a lot, but those were the only residual clues to the accident. He didn't see any reason why they couldn't start practicing for another baby.

As the dog snored beside the bed in the mid-morning sunshine, Blakesley pulled the books off the bed and neatly stacked them on the bedside stand. Slowly, as she still couldn't move her torso or left shoulder very well, she lay down beside Beck and wrapped her right arm around his neck.

"You're going to have to do all the work," she said, closing her eyes when he kissed her cheek. "I still can't move around much."

He wrapped her up in his big arms very carefully, very tenderly. "I'll do all the work," he whispered. "Tell me if I hurt you, okay?"

She simply nodded, giving in to his strength and passion. Between heated kisses and tender touches, Beck carefully undressed them both. He suckled her nipples, his fingers probing into intimate places as she parted her legs for him, inviting him in. He had never been so aroused or so emotional in his life, wanting to take his time with her but unable to restrain himself.

He kissed her tender belly and the little scars from the laparoscopic surgery to remove her spleen. He dragged his mouth over the left side of her torso, blotched with faded green bruises, and tears sprang to his eyes. He had come so close to losing her that a lump formed in his throat at the thought of never experiencing her again. He lifted himself up to kiss her deeply on the mouth and the tears in his eyes fell onto her face. Her eyes opened in a flash.

"Beck?" She had her hands on his face, concerned. "What's wrong, baby?"

"Nothing," he said huskily. He refused to look at her or even open his eyes. His mouth slanted over hers hungrily. "Everything is fine."

He made love to her slowly, with great feeling, careful not to lower his weight on her too much as he thrust. He was able to bring her to a climax twice before releasing himself. He lay with her, all cuddled up against him, before resuming again once he caught his breath. That went on three times that morning until he had to pick Charlotte up from preschool and even then, it had been difficult to tear himself away from her. He never wanted it to end.

When he returned with Charlotte and Spike Aguirre, who was in the same school as Charlotte because Gina had gotten a day job, he found Blakesley still asleep in the bedroom with the blinds pulled. He shut the door and tried to keep the kids and the dog quiet as Blakesley slept on into the afternoon.

As Captain Davis and Sophia had prime rib and lobster at an exclusive Coronado restaurant, Beck made macaroni and cheese for Cadee, Crosby, Charlotte, Spike and Lizzie, who was into her first week at high school at Coronado High School. Gina came by to pick up Spike and she ended up staying the evening, keeping Beck company in a house full of kids and a sick wife. Gina had never seen Beck so happy and they talked most of the evening about Butch and what he would say to all of it. They agreed that after making fun of Beck, Butch would have eaten all of the macaroni and cheese before letting the kids jump all over him. That was the kind of guy he was. Beck tried not to miss him too much.

Blakesley slept through all of it, awakening only when her husband finally roused her around ten o'clock at night when he came to bed. He kissed her and tried to get amorous with her again, but she ended up falling back asleep on him. With a grin, Beck just turned out the light.

It was good to have her home.

TWENTY-ONE

"YOUR FOUR MONTHS with the FMLA leave are up, Beck." Davis wasn't sure what more he could do. "First it was three weeks, then three months, then an extra month. I can't give you any more time off."

Beck was in his captain's office on an unseasonably warm, early-December day. He'd come in because, technically, he started back to work today, but he was clearly unhappy about being on base and not at home with his family. Dressed in his standard issue gray tee shirt, black combat pants and big black boots, he slouched angrily in the captain's guest chair.

"I told you I didn't want to actively participate with the teams anymore," he told Davis. "You were supposed to be working on that."

Davis nodded. "I am," he insisted. "Do you think this is going to be easy on me or the men to lose you? We've lost Butch and now you? That's like cutting both arms off of a healthy body. It's going to take time to re-learn how to function but until I can officially replace you, you're still on duty."

Beck's jaw ticked furiously. "You mentioned that you were going to try to get me transferred to Basic Underwater Demolition and S.E.A.L. training," he said. "Have you heard anything on that?"

Davis snorted. "Captain Bucklew can't wait to get his hands on you," he said. "He wants you badly, but they're fully staffed. They're trying to work some angles in order to make a slot for you, but until then, you're still a part of S.E.A.L. team 3 as one of my three commanders in charge."

Beck scratched his head irritably. "Any timeline on the transfer?"

"They're hoping by the first of the year," Davis replied, his gaze lingering on Beck. "They want to put you in charge of Advanced Phase 3 Training because of your record and your real-world experience. You'd get the boys who have almost graduated, right before they do their airborne phase. I told the commander I think you'd be great at training them in all of the hard-core elements of the job. There's no one better than you."

Beck nodded modestly. "I'd like that," he said. "The Naval Special Warfare Center S.E.A.L. training center is right here on Coronado, so I'd stay close to home."

Davis simply wriggled his eyebrows. "I know you want to stick close to Blakesley, Beck, but she's not an invalid, for God's sake," he said. "That accident was four months ago. You need to stop acting like she's going to disappear tomorrow. That's just not healthy for you."

Beck tried not to get defensive. "I know she's not going to disappear tomorrow," he said. "But she's almost three months pregnant and we've got four other kids at home. I've got a family now and a lot of responsibility. There's nothing wrong with me wanting to retire from active field duty that has me traipsing all over the world and finally have a job in the Navy where I can go home every night. What makes that so terrible?"

"Nothing," Davis snapped. "But I'll be honest with you; taking you out of the field is a waste of material. You're the best, Beck; you know that. You've done things that no one would ever believe if I was to tell them. You've got courage and skill that goes beyond a normal human being. I told your wife once that you were a real American hero and I meant it. I sincerely do not want to lose you."

"You won't lose me. I'll still be here on base."

Davis sighed, falling silent as he sat heavily at his desk. This wasn't an argument that he could win. After a long and pensive moment, he lifted his gaze to Beck.

"I'm going to tell you something that I shouldn't, but I think it's important." His voice was low. "I'm trying to get your transfer pushed through before the end of December because it looks like we'll be deploying for another six month rotation in January when the carrier George H.W. Bush sets off for her group rotation."

Beck's eyes widened. "Six months?" he repeated, horrified. "If I deploy, I'll miss the birth. I can't miss it."

Davis put up a soothing hand. "That's why I'm working on your transfer, Beck. Trust me that I'll do everything I can in spite of the fact that I don't want to lose you. I have a feeling that if you don't get what you want, you'll be a pretty miserable man to be around."

"That's a fair statement."

"So go get reacquainted with your troop," he said. "You've got fifteen new faces, so introduce yourself and let them know who's the boss. You've got training scheduled with your troop for tonight, touch and go boardings off the coast. Get yourself ready."

Beck stood up from the chair. "Aye, cap'n," he muttered.

"Hold on," Davis stopped him. "One more thing. The S.E.A.L.s have decided to put out a calendar again next year. Remember that? They did for a few years back in the '90's when that movie about S.E.A.L.s came out and was so popular."

Beck was standing by the door. "So?"

Davis lifted his eyebrows at him. "So you're going to be the cover boy."

Beck's face fell. "What in the hell...?"

"Your team decided it, so don't shoot the messenger. They voted you in. Solis is Mr. June and you are the cover and Mr. December. They wanted to wait until you came back to work

3639

4144

before doing the photographs, so someone from Navy P.R. is coming out tomorrow to take some shots of you. Look hot and sexy. The Navy wants to sell a bunch of these because the release is coinciding with the release of some big war movie in January. Proceeds go to the Navy Widow and Orphans Fund."

Beck's jaw was back to ticking unhappily. "I'm not doing it."

"Yes, you are."

"Absolutely not." Beck was furious. He pointed a finger at Davis. "And don't think you can boss me around just because you're dating my wife's best friend."

Davis lifted his eyebrows. "Actually, I can," he said. "I'm calling your wife. She'll have something to say about it."

"Don't you dare."

"Try me."

———

"You're doing it."

Beck faced off against Blakesley as she gave the little girls a bath in the upstairs bathtub. It was after dinner and she was settling them down for the night. He stood in the doorway, deeply unhappy.

"Baby, I'm *not* going to do it," he said flatly. "It's stupid. I'll be the laughing stock of the whole damn base."

"Are you the only team member doing it?"

"No, but I'm on the damn cover."

Dressed in yoga pants and a flowing top that concealed her growing waistline, Blakesley sat next to the tub as she washed Charlotte's hair. She was very calm and very firm with her stubborn husband.

"That's because you're the most handsome," she said frankly, scrubbing the little blond head. "You're going to do it. The money from it goes to the Navy Widow and Orphans Fund, so it's for a good cause."

He slumped against the doorjamb and rolled his eyes. "I can't believe Davis called you."

Blakesley had no sympathy for him. She began to pour water over Charlotte's head to rinse it clean.

"I'm glad he did," she said. "I'm going to buy five hundred of those calendars and send them to everyone I know. You're the best-looking man in the Navy and I'm very proud of you."

He lifted an eyebrow at her as he slouched against the door-jamb. "Would you be proud of me if I were a dog?"

She looked up at him but before she could answer, Crosby jumped up in the tub and splashed soap suds all over her mother.

"Beck, are you a dog?" Crosby crowed happily.

Blakesley pulled her daughter back down into the tub as Beck grinned. "I hope not," he said. "But your mother hasn't answered my question."

"Mommy's going to have a baby," Charlotte told him seriously, water running in her face. "He's in her tummy."

Beck laughed softly and went to sit on the toilet next to the bathtub. "I know, baby girl," he said. "I'm very excited about it."

"Why?" Charlotte wanted to know. "It's not your baby."

Blakesley started to laugh. "Sorry, Beck. That's a terrible way to find out it's not your baby."

Beck smirked. "That UPS man really gets around."

Blakesley continued to chuckle, calling for Nikki as she finished with Charlotte's hair. As Nikki appeared, Beck pulled Blakesley off the floor and they left the bathroom as Nikki got the girls out of the tub. Blakesley stretched her body, stiff from sitting on the cold tile, as they took the stairs down to the first floor. Lizzie and Cadee were in the living room watching television and doing homework as Beck and Blakesley moved into the kitchen.

A lovely meal was waiting for them, having been cooked by Blakesley earlier in the day. She waited until Beck got home so she could eat with him. But he had only come home to pick up some clothes because he had night training, so their meal was going to be very short before he bugged out. As she was dishing out the pasta, he put his big hand on her gently rounded belly and kissed her forehead.

"How are you feeling?" he asked as he sat on a nearby stool.

She shrugged. "Fine," she said. "I just eat all day but I feel fine. I have a craving for Tootsie Rolls, though. That, and orange smoothies."

He made a face. "Gross," he said, using Lizzie's favorite term. "You don't mix them together, do you?"

She grinned as she put the plate of pasta in front of him. "No, but today I crumbled chocolate cake on top of some lasagna. It was delicious."

He snorted, his mouth full of pasta. "Oh, God," he groaned. "That's really disgusting."

She laughed and sat next to him at the counter, eating pasta alfredo with vegetables. Beck seemed rather quiet and she eyed him as they ate.

"Other than the calendar issue, how was your first day back?" she asked.

He shrugged. "Uneventful for the most part," he said. "Davis is trying to get me transferred to the Special Naval Warfare Center at the base."

"What's that?"

"It's where they train S.E.A.L.s. I'd be in command of one of the training units. The best thing is that I'd get to come home every night for the most part. No more deploying."

She smiled at him, a gentle hand caressing the back of his head. "That's wonderful," she said, running her fingers through his soft, blond hair. "Does he seem confident you'll get the job?"

Beck nodded. "The center commander wants me badly," he said. "I'm pretty confident it will come through."

Blakesley congratulated him again but he still didn't seem too excited. In fact, he seemed fairly pensive, like his mind was somewhere else. She got up from her stool, went to the cabinet, and returned with a snack cake, which she promptly crumbled all over her pasta. That drew a reaction.

"Ugh," he groaned, trying to look away but was forced by morbid curiosity to watch her eat it. "How can you do that?"

She grinned. "Baby Beck tells me what to eat and I do. He likes it."

He just wriggled his eyebrows. "Then my son is insane," he said flatly. "Which reminds me; I was thinking of something today."

"What?"

"What would you think if I didn't want to name a boy after me?"

She looked surprised. "Are you kidding?" she said. "That was one of the first things you ever said to me. You told me your name in case I wanted to name a future child after you. Now I'm willing to do it but you don't want to?"

He remembered back to that day, grinning. "I do, sort of, but having three Becks in one family is a lot," he explained. "People were constantly confusing me with my dad, so now we want to add another Beck to the mix? What if he's in the Navy, too? That will make things crazy-confusing."

"So what do you want to name him?"

He shrugged, stuffing his face with pasta. "I'd kind of like to name him after my mother's father," he said. "His name was Colton. Everyone called him Colt."

She brightened. "I really like that," she said. "How about Marshall Colton Seavington the First? We can honor my dad and your grandfather. We'll just call him Colt."

He swallowed the bite in his mouth, grinning at her. "That sounds perfect."

"You like it?"

"Love it."

"But if it's a girl, can I name her Becky?"

"Absolutely not. Name her something else."

"How about Emma?"

"If you like it, I like it."

She giggled and he put his arm around her shoulder, pulling

her against him and kissing her temple. He looked in disapproval as she picked at her plate.

"Stop eating that stuff, will you?" he said softly, kissing her again before returning to his food. "That's not good for you."

She shrugged. "It's not too terrible," she said. "Besides, if it's what I want to eat, then I'm going to eat it. Being pregnant is no time to be picky or go on a health kick. Besides, I eat well enough. I had three orange juice smoothies today."

He chuckled and shook his head, finishing up with his meal. "Whatever makes you happy, baby," he said. Shoving the last bite in his mouth, he stood up and took his plate over to the sink. "I'll be back tomorrow morning, probably in time to take the girls to school."

"What are you guys doing tonight?"

He wiped his hands off and went back over to her, eying the mess on her plate. "Secret stuff. James Bond stuff," he repeated the standard phrase. "I'm not sure I can kiss you on the mouth now that you've eaten that concoction. It might make me sick."

She cocked an eyebrow at him, wrapping her arms around his neck as he enveloped her for a big hug. He held her tightly, rocking her gently. He buried his face in her neck.

"Hey," she said.

"What?"

"Why do you seem so depressed?"

He pulled his face out from the warm confines of her neck and looked at her. "Depressed? Are you kidding?"

"No," she said flatly. "I know you too well. What more is on your mind that you're not telling me?"

He sighed faintly, not surprised that she could read his mood as well as she had. She was very intuitive. "I don't want you to get upset but I don't want to blindside you, either."

"What about?"

He hesitated a moment, thinking on how to phrase it. "If this transfer to the Special Naval Warfare Unit doesn't take place before the end of the year, there's a possibility I may be deployed with my team on a carrier group in January."

Blakesley stared at him, her big, bluish-green eyes liquid with emotion. "Where?"

"We'd be at sea to deploy worldwide."

"How long?"

"Six months."

"Six months?" she repeated, horrified. "But... if you deploy in January, you won't be home until July and the baby is due in June."

He soothed her gently. "I know, baby," he kissed her forehead. "Davis is trying to get it pushed through as fast as he can but I don't want you blindsided in case the worst happens and I have to go."

She was tearing up already. "I don't want you to go," she sniffed. "You need to be here when the baby is born."

He pulled her into a snug embrace, kissing her repeatedly on the head. "I'm working on it, I promise," he murmured. "You know I don't want to be gone, either. Please don't cry about it, okay? You know I can't handle tears. I'm doing everything I can do."

She nodded, sniffling and unhappy. He kissed her salty lips. "I love you," he said. "I'll see you in the morning, okay? Get the girls into bed and get to sleep. I'll take the girls to school in the morning and bring you back some breakfast."

She nodded again, deeply unhappy, as he took her hand and led her out of the kitchen and into the dining room. Lizzie and Cadee were spread out all over the leather couches, with pens, paper and books scattered. Beck bent over and kissed his daughter on the head.

"I'm off to work," he said, pointing to the mess. "Make sure you and Cadee pick this all up, please? Don't leave it for Blakesley."

"We won't." Lizzie looked over her shoulder up at her father. "Dad, I've been invited to a party on Friday night. Can I please go?"

Beck knew she was trying hard to make new friends at school. Using Beck's old townhome address on Coronado, she'd started school at Coronado High School because the state test results were better than the high school in their current district and Beck already knew the campus. He'd attended it himself years ago. Lizzie had been very lonely over the summer with no one to hang out with, but Beck was naturally hesitant with her request.

"Maybe," he said. "We'll talk about it more tomorrow when I get back."

Lizzie wasn't happy with that answer. "Why not, Dad?" she begged. "These two girls have been really nice to me since I started school. I'd really like to go."

He gave her a pointed look. "I will talk to you about it tomorrow," he said clearly. "Finish up your homework and pick up the living room. Please."

He added the "please" as almost an afterthought, but Lizzie was pouting by that point. Blakesley caught her eye as she followed Beck into the kitchen, winking at Lizzie to let her know she was on her side. Leaving the girls picking up the living room, Beck collected his keys and gear sitting on the washer on the back porch.

"Got everything?" Blakesley handed him his sunglasses.

He nodded. "Yes." He looked around just to make sure. Then he bent over and kissed her on the lips. "Love you. I'll see you tomorrow."

"Okay," she said, following to the door. "Baby?"

He opened the door and looked at her. "Yes?"

"Do you want me to find out about the girls Lizzie is talking about?" she asked helpfully. "It really means a lot to her to participate with kids she's making friends with, you know that. She's been so lonely."

He sighed faintly, appearing torn. "I know," he muttered. "If you can find out something about them that would be good. I just don't want her going off to some wild party with no parents around. Back in my day, the rich kids on the island would have parties when their parents were gone. That haunts me."

"I suspect you went to one or more of them."

He nodded, ashamed. "I did; sex, drugs and rock and roll. I don't want Lizzie to fall into that."

Blakesley put her hands on his cheeks and kissed his lips. "I'll check it all out and report back," she assured him. "If I don't think it's a good idea, I'll tell you. You know I look after Lizzie as if she were one of my own."

He smiled. "I know you do," he said. Then he kissed her swiftly again. "I have to go. I'll see you tomorrow. I love you."

"I love you, too."

Blakesley watched him head off into the dark backyard with Alfie running up to him and begging for attention. He petted the dog as he reached his new truck, unlocking the door and throwing his gear into the back of the crew cab.

As Beck sped off into the night, Blakesley locked up the house, made sure the girls got to bed, and then got herself into bed with the television for company. She thought on Beck's transfer and the possibility that he might have to deploy in January.

It didn't sit well with her, no matter how much he reassured her.

———

"I got a call this morning from the State of California." Blakesley was following Beck around the bedroom the following morning as he threw off his clothes in the process of getting into bed. "Apparently, I told them I wanted to sell the old homestead but I don't remember. It was the day of my accident."

Beck was exhausted. He pulled off his briefs and slid into bed, sighing with satisfaction at the cool and soft sheets. It was comfortable and wonderful, smelling like his wife. He pushed his face into her pillow, smelling faint wisps of her perfume.

"What are you going to do?" he asked, eyes already closed as he snuggled down.

"I'm going to go over to the house this morning," she said, moving into the bathroom with his dirty clothes in her arms. "The guy that called me was from the real estate division. He wants to meet me at the house and talk about a possible sale."

Beck's eyes opened as he heard her banging around in the bathroom. "When are you going?"

She came out of the bathroom with her arms full of laundry from the hamper. "Eleven," she replied. "I'll go meet with them and still have time to pick up Charlotte and Spike from preschool."

He rolled over onto his back, looking up at her. "Will you do me a favor?"

"What?"

"Will you wait so I can go with you?"

She cocked her head. "Baby, if you go with me, you'll only get a few hours of sleep."

He lay there, bare-chested and gorgeous, gazing at her pensively. Then he held out a hand to her. Blakesley dumped the laundry on the end of the bed and took his hand, sitting down beside him. He tugged her over to him so she was laying on his chest, gazing down into his handsome face.

Beck studied her face a moment, tucking a stray piece of hair behind her ear. "The last time you went to the house," he reminded her, "you were in a terrible car accident. Please let me drive you over there. It just freaks me out thinking of you driving up on those roads again, knowing what happened the last time you were up there. Can you move your meeting to the afternoon?"

She smiled and kissed his dimpled chin. "Sure," she said. "I'll give them a call right now. We can pick up Charlotte and Spike first and then go over there."

"Sounds good."

"The kids are going to want chicken nuggets for lunch. We can feed them on the way over."

"Fine." Now that it was settled, he kissed her and she backed off the bed as he pulled the covers up. "Are you going anywhere this morning?"

"To the supermarket."

"I'm out of deodorant."

"I'll get you some."

She picked up the laundry and left the room, shutting the door quietly behind her. Alfie was inside, snoring on the couch, as she made her way back to the laundry room to start a load of wash. She spent the morning rearranging her meeting with the state, doing laundry, and tidying up the house, which exhausted her so she decided to wait to go to the market. With the chores finished and nothing to do until Beck woke up, she headed out to the big four-car garage in the backyard where Beck had set up one of the car bays as her painting studio.

Her accident had thrown a monkey wrench into a lot of plans she had, a big one being the Art Bar. The space in the Gaslamp Quarter was still hers but her health hadn't been terribly great since the accident and the subsequent pregnancy left her exhausted most of the time. She was okay to work around the house and paint in her studio, but more than that usually had her stressing out and crashing. Beck had taken such a huge load off of her that she sincerely didn't know what she would do without the man. In six months, she had become completely dependent upon him and he loved every minute of it.

The old Earp homestead had suffered, too. Marshall relocated to San Diego over the past couple of months to be near his daughter and grandchildren, and he had taken an active interest with the house in Blakesley's absence. With Blakesley recovering from her accident, Marshall had spent a lot of time dealing with the Earp homestead in her stead. When he wasn't at the homestead, he was dating Gabrielle, which thrilled Blakesley. Her father had been lonely since the death of her mother, and Gabrielle was a truly wonderful woman. The girls loved her.

So she painted in her studio until lunchtime, this piece of art a large abstract with gorgeous colors of teal, black and gold. Blakesley was more of an abstract artist than an impressionist or realist. She liked big, blocky colors that provoked the senses. At least, that's what she told people. Whatever it was, it was very modern and people really seemed to like it. The painting she was currently working on was going to be part of the Art Bar.

Finished for the morning in her studio, she locked it up and headed back across the yard to the house. Alfie was running around the yard, coming to her when he saw her walking up the back steps. He charged into the house before she did, his nails making clicking noises on the floor. As Blakesley shut the back door and moved into the kitchen, she heard her cell phone ring.

The phone was on the kitchen counter and she glanced at the caller I.D. before answering. She was curious and surprised to see that it was her lawyer from Los Angeles, the one who had handled her divorce and subsequent legal dealings with Ed. She hadn't heard from the guy in almost a year.

"Hello?" she answered.

Robert Karayan, Esquire, was an old and good friend. "Hey, Blakesley," he said pleasantly. "It's Robert."

She perched her butt at the breakfast bar. "Hi there," she said amiably. "Long time, no see."

"That's a good thing," Robert snickered. "No one wants to see their lawyer too much."

Blakesley giggled. "True," she said. "So how are you? What's new?"

On the other end of the line, Robert leaned back in his chair, settling down for the conversation. "I'm good," he said. "How are you? How's San Diego?"

"Well," Blakesley pondered the question, wondering where to start. "You and I haven't spoken in a while. A lot has happened. I got married, for one."

"Really?" Robert was genuinely surprised. "Anyone I know?"

She shook her head. "No," she replied. "In fact, it was one of those things that you read about in a romance novel. Cadee got sucked into the surf one day while we were visiting the beach and a group of Navy S.E.A.L.s were training in the area. I met my husband when he saved her from drowning. It was pretty much love at first sight."

"Wow," Robert exclaimed. "That's quite a story. How long have you been married?"

"A couple of months," she answered. "We're going to have a baby in May."

Robert was shocked. "Seriously?" he said. "That's really great news, Blakesley. You wanted to start a new life in San Diego. I guess you got your wish."

"I really did," she said sincerely. "My husband is the greatest guy ever and the girls love him. We're really lucky."

"That's great," Robert repeated. There was some hesitance in his manner. "Sweetheart, I really hate to mess any of that up, but unfortunately, I did call for a reason."

Blakesley grinned. "It wasn't just to shoot the breeze with someone who spent a half million dollars on you in legal fees?"

Robert laughed softly. "No."

"Trying to drum up more business? Sorry, but I'm not in the market for a divorce lawyer."

He snickered. "That's good to know," he said, sobering. "Actually, I'm calling about Ed. I've got some news."

Blakesley sobered as well. "About Ed?" she repeated. She hadn't thought of the man in almost six months. "What about him?"

"His lawyer had his case on appeal." Robert's manner softened considerably. "You remember that, right?"

Blakesley was starting to get a sick feeling in the pit of her stomach. She couldn't put her finger on why; it was more instinctive. She always felt sick when discussing Ed.

"I remember," she replied evenly. "Why?"

Robert sighed. "It seems that the key witness in the case, the sous chef from the Hollyhock who said he saw Ed trying to dispose of Maricelle's body, has recanted," he said quietly. "The man is swearing he lied on the stand and is saying he did it for you."

Blakesley nearly fell off the stool. "He what?" she nearly yelled. "I never... Robert, that's simply not true! I never told anyone to...!"

Robert calmed her down. "He didn't say that you told him to do it," he quickly clarified. "He said he did it because he felt sorry for you. Plus, he said something more about hating Ed and wanting to see the man burn in hell. All sorts of crazy things. Now, I'm not sure how much this guy was paid to recant his statement, but the gist of it is that Ed's case is being re-examined now and is scheduled to be brought before a grand jury next week. There's a very real possibility that he may be acquitted. I just want you to be prepared."

Blakesley couldn't help it; she sank to the kitchen floor, grief and horror such as she had never experienced filling her. She slumped against the dishwasher.

"Oh, my God," she breathed. "This can't be happening."

"I know."

"But they can't release him, can they? Even if a witness recants for the murder charge, he was still convicted of money laundering for the drug cartel."

"He may just be credited with time served for that conviction. We'll just have to see."

Blakesley exhaled heavily. "I... I just can't believe this."

Robert was deeply sympathetic. He had been with her every step of the way during the Hollyhock Murder trial, so he knew how she felt better than most. It had been hell.

"Believe me when I tell you that the Los Angeles district attorney's office is all over this," he said. "They'll put up a big fight."

Blakesley could feel the tears starting. "But...," she swallowed. "But he's a murderer. He killed that woman."

"I know," Robert said. "But the good news is that he doesn't know where you are, or where the girls are. I won't tell him and neither will anyone else. Blakesley, does your new husband know about Ed?"

The tears were streaming down Blakesley's face. "Yes," she whispered. "He knows."

"Well," Robert was feeling a good deal of her grief also, "that's good, at any rate. That way, if the worst happens and Ed is released, you two will be ready to deal with the fallout. I'm sorry about all of this, Blakesley. You can believe I'll be keeping a very close eye on it for you."

Blakesley was quickly reaching hysteria. She struggled to speak before she broke down completely.

"Thanks for calling," she whispered tightly. "Will... will you keep me posted on everything?"

"Of course," Robert assured her. "You'll know the second I do."

"I really appreciate it. Thank you."

"You take care, Blakesley."

"Thanks. You, too."

She hung up the phone and just sat there for a second, staring at it. Then she let it clatter to the floor as the sobs enveloped her. Huddling up in a ball, she sobbed her heart out.

Several minutes after the phone call, the door to the master bedroom opened. Beck had startled himself awake thinking that Blakesley had left to pick up the kids without him and, noting the time and the fact that her car was still in the backyard, he wandered out of the bedroom in search of his wife.

The dining room and living room were empty and as he was passing through the dining room en route to check the playroom off the entry, he happened to glance into the kitchen. At first, he didn't see anything and he was just turning away when he caught sight of something balled up on the floor.

Startled, he saw that it was Blakesley and he bolted into the kitchen, falling to his knees beside her.

"Baby, what's wrong?" he demanded, panicked. "Are you sick? What's wrong?"

Blakesley was weeping painfully. She threw her arms around his neck and he wrapped her up in big arms, hesitant to pick her up in case she had injured herself somehow. So far, she hadn't answered him and he was quickly growing frightened.

"Baby, what happened?" he asked again. "Are you hurt?"

Finally, she shook her head. "No," she wept. "I... I just got a call... my lawyer...."

Realizing she wasn't hurt filled him with relief. But the fact that she was hysterical had him almost hysterical, too. He sat down on the floor next to her and pulled her up onto his lap.

"Calm down," he hugged her, rubbing her back gently. "Baby, calm down and tell me what's going on."

Blakesley was quickly growing weak and emotionally incoherent. She felt sick and lightheaded.

"My... my lawyer from Los Angeles called," she struggled to explain. "He said that the witness who sent Ed to prison on the murder charge has recanted his statement and that Ed's case is going before a grand jury next week. It's possible that he'll be acquitted. I... I just don't...."

She faded off and suddenly went limp in his arms. Seized with panic, Beck checked her pulse, her breathing, realizing that she had passed out. The news she had sputtered out was just too much to take. In fact, it was almost too much for him to take. He was stunned. Sickened, he picked her up and carried her into their bedroom, laying her gently on the bed. Making sure she was still breathing easily and her pulse was steady, he went for his cell phone.

Marshall picked up on the third ring. "Hey, Beck," he said. "What's on your mind this fine day?"

Beck knew the man was with Gabrielle; he could hear her in the background. Besides, Marshall was way too jovial, which only happened when he was with the lovely nurse. Beck sighed heavily and with great regret.

"I need you to pick Charlotte up from preschool," he said, his tone tense and ominous. "Something's happened."

"Is Blakesley all right?"

"She's okay. But I need you to pick up the girls. It's important, Marshall."

Marshall swung by to pick up Charlotte and Spike, and had them back to the house in a half hour. Blakesley was sleeping at that point and as Gabrielle went in to check on her, Beck told Marshall what had happened and the man was nearly sick himself. He understood the implications better than most.

He knew what Ed was capable of.

TWENTY-TWO

BLAKESLEY WOKE up near dinner time but Gabrielle had her stay in bed and rest. Beck stayed in the bedroom with her while the girls, including Lizzie, cooked dinner with Marshall and Gabrielle. Grandpa took over while Blakesley pulled herself together and Beck remained with his wife. The girls knew that Blakesley wasn't feeling well but nothing more beyond that. Beck and Marshall decided it would be best not to tell them anything. It wouldn't have meant much to the little girls but it would have meant a lot to Cadee and neither man wanted to upset her.

Beck made his wife eat a few bites of dinner even though she was nauseous. She didn't feel like anything but lasagna, so he ordered some from a local Italian restaurant and went to pick it up himself. Blakesley had two very small bites of it, amounting to no more than licking the fork, as Beck phrased it, and then wanted cake with it. Beck groaned but dutifully went out to the kitchen for a snack cake, returning so she could mush it up and spread it all over the lasagna. It was the most disgusting thing Beck had ever seen, but she ate about half of her dinner that way so he couldn't complain too much.

It was a Friday evening in December and the day had been warm. Around seven p.m., Lizzie knocked softly at the door and

Beck let her in. She smiled timidly at Blakesley, who was lying down all surrounded by pillows, and Blakesley smiled back.

"Hi, honey," Blakesley said.

Lizzie moved towards the bed hesitantly. "Are you feeling better?"

Blakesley nodded. "Much," she said. "Thanks for asking."

Lizzie nodded in response, looking to her dad who was now stretching out on the bed next to Blakesley. He had the television remote in his hand and turned on the TV.

"Dad," she said. "Alex and Natalie want to know if I can spend the night at their house. Can you please take me?"

Beck was flipping through channels. "Who are Alex and Natalie?"

"My friends from school. The girls I hang out with. I went to their house a couple of weeks ago, remember?"

"Alex sounds like a boy."

Lizzie was swiftly losing her patience. She exhaled irritably, looking beseechingly at Blakesley, who took the hint.

"Alex is short for Alexandra," she said. "I've met her mother. Remember? I told you that a couple of weeks ago. You were out when Alex and Natalie's mother came to pick Lizzie up. She's a very nice lady and the girls seem very sweet. They seem like a nice family."

Beck was still looking at the television as he surfed the channels. "Yeah, sure; the Manson family."

Lizzie let out a grunt of frustration as Blakesley laughed. "No, they're not," she looked at Lizzie. "Ask Marshall to take you over. I'm sure he'd love to."

Beck was already climbing out of bed. "No," he grumbled. "I'll take her. Hey, wait a minute. I never agreed she could go. Why am I taking her?"

"Your keys are on the dresser," Blakesley said calmly. "Bring me back some ice cream. And why don't you take the little girls with you? My dad and Gabrielle have given up enough of their evening to babysit them."

Beck made a face at her to let her know he was displeased but he did as he was told. Thrilled, Lizzie squealed and thanked Blakesley before she ran out of the room and headed upstairs to get her things. Beck sat down to pull his shoes on but the door was still open thanks to Lizzie's exit, and Crosby and Charlotte ran into the bedroom and immediately jumped on the bed to see their mother. Blakesley snuggled with her little girls as Cadee wandered in and climbed on the bed as well. Gabrielle followed the little girls in, her focus on Blakesley.

"How are you feeling, honey?" she asked.

Blakesley had little girls cuddling up next to her and a blond head was in her face. "Better," she said, blowing blond curls out of her mouth. "Thank you for taking care of me and the girls."

Gabrielle smiled. "No problem," she said. "Have you tried to get up and move around?"

Blakesley nodded. "I'm okay," she said. "I just feel really tired."

"No dizziness?"

"Not at all."

Gabrielle nodded. "Good," she replied. "Call your OB/GYN on Monday, okay? Just tell him what happened and see what he says."

Blakesley nodded and thanked her again as Beck stood up from the chair, shoes on, and went to find Marshall. He was in the living room with Alfie lying next to him, an unlit cigar hanging out of his mouth as he watched the television.

"If Blakesley sees you on the couch with that cigar, she's going to have a fit," Beck pointed out. "I'd put that thing away if I were you."

Marshall snorted at his disobedience and petted the dog, sleeping next to him. "She hasn't seen me yet. She's in bed."

"I'm telling you, she'll smell that tobacco. She's got tobacco-radar."

Marshall continued to snort as Beck sat at the end of the leather couch to wait for Lizzie. "Your daughter says to tell you that you're officially relieved of kid duty," Beck said. "She doesn't want to wreck the rest of your date with Gabrielle."

Marshall waved him off. "There's no way we're going to Tijuana this late," he said. "I may as well just take her home and take advantage of her."

Beck chuckled. "You should probably get her liquored up first."

Marshall looked at him, stricken. "Why?" he demanded. "Just because I'm not a young buck like you doesn't mean I have to get my women smashed in order to get some action."

Beck was in full-blown laughter by then. He genuinely liked Marshall and the man's sense of humor. He started to reply but a knock on the front door interrupted him. He pushed himself off the couch.

"Hold that thought," he told Marshall. "I'll be right back."

Marshall grinned, stroking the sleeping dog and chewing on the cigar. Beck crossed into the entry and flipped on the porch light as he opened the door.

A familiar and unwelcome face greeted him. Beck found himself looking at Sharon.

"Hi," she said somewhat hesitantly.

Shocked, Beck nearly blew a fuse. "What in the hell are you doing here?"

Sharon backed away from her angry ex-husband. "Please, Beck," she said softly, sounding completely unlike the enraged woman who had threatened him a few months before. "I have to talk to you. Please. It's really important."

Beck stepped out onto the porch and closed the door behind him. He didn't want anyone, especially Lizzie, seeing her mother standing on the porch. With the day he'd had, this was the last thing he needed or wanted. The woman had been silent for the past four months and now, here she was on his doorstep. He resisted the urge to wrap his hands around Sharon's throat.

"You've got thirty seconds," he said. "I don't need you here or want you here, and if you don't leave...."

"Please," Sharon interrupted him, begging. "I just want three minutes of your time."

"Starting now."

Sharon looked uncomfortable and without confidence, unusual for the arrogant and proud woman. In fact, she looked rather drawn and pale, but Beck couldn't have cared less. He just wanted her the hell off his property before Lizzie or Blakesley saw her.

"I just wanted to tell you that I filed for divorce from Dan," she said. She was starting to look miserable. "You were right about him. I found pictures and texts on his phone from Lizzie's friend Meggyn that were sexual in nature. The stuff from her was bad enough but I saw that he was sending stuff to her as well. Terrible stuff. I was horrified. So I took it all to my lawyer and filed for divorce. Dan has already lost his teaching job. He'll be lucky if he doesn't go to jail."

Beck stood there with his big arms crossed, listening unemotionally. "Your daughter already told you all of this but you didn't believe her," he said flatly. "So what do you want? Congratulations that you finally came to your senses?"

Sharon shook her head. She looked around the porch, into the big picture window that faced from the porch into the entry hall, seeing the warmth of the house beyond. Her eyes found him again.

"Are you happy, Beck?"

He didn't have the patience for her conversation. "I'm not going to get into this with you," he said frankly. "You left me four years ago, leaving me when I was recovering from a life-threatening injury no less, so whether or not I'm happy is none of your business. We only share a daughter, Sharon, and nothing else. Wipe me from your mind."

She looked like she was going to cry but held herself in check. Suddenly, they could hear screaming as Crosby and Charlotte bolted in front of the entry window and into the little playroom beyond. Gabrielle followed them, saying something that was muffled by the walls. Cadee plodded along behind the nurse, all of them disappearing into the playroom. Sharon watched the little girls run around before looking at Beck.

"You always did want a big family," she said. "I see you finally got what you wanted. I'm happy for you."

"Your three minutes are up."

"Wait," Sharon was back to begging mode. "I wanted to ask... I wanted to ask if now that Dan and I are divorcing, would it be all right if I talked to Lizzie? I've missed her so much. I'd really like to fix whatever it was I broke between her and me. I want my daughter back."

Beck looked at her with disbelief. "You treated her like crap because of your husband and now you expect to re-establish a relationship with her?" He was growing livid. "Over my dead body, Sharon. Get out of here before I call the cops."

Sharon found her backbone. "Maybe you should let Lizzie make that decision. She's old enough to. You can't make that kind of decision for her."

"I just did," he snapped. "I'm done with this conversation."

He turned for the house but Sharon wouldn't let him go. "Beck, please!" she cried. "Please let me talk to Lizzie. It means so much to me."

Beck turned to her, preparing to snarl, when the front door suddenly opened and Blakesley came charging through with a baseball bat. Startled, Beck grabbed her before she could get away from him but she was able to get off a swing and caught Sharon on the shoulder. Sharon screamed and fell back, tripping off the porch and falling about five feet to the concrete below.

Marshall was already in the door, pulling the bat out of Blakesley's hands. Lizzie, having come down the stairs just about the time Blakesley charged through, saw her mother on the concrete walkway and began shrieking.

"Mom!" Lizzie screamed. "What are you doing here?"

Sharon wasn't injured but she was shaken. She sat up, her expensive designer jeans dirty from the fall, and began weeping.

"Lizzie," she sobbed. "I'm so sorry, baby girl. I should have believed you about Dan and I came to say I'm sorry."

Lizzie stood in the doorway, partially held back by Marshall. He had no idea what was going on and didn't want Lizzie involved. But he began to understand that the woman on the ground was Lizzie's mother.

"Beck," he reached out and grabbed his still-struggling daughter. "Let me take Blakesley. It looks like...."

"No," Blakesley roared. "I'm not going anywhere. I'm going to kill that bitch if she comes near my family again."

Beck had never seen Blakesley so furious. Truthfully, he was impressed, but he was also very concerned. Given what had happened to her today, he didn't want her working herself up so much. He was honestly surprised she was able to summon the strength, but on the other hand, she was extremely protective of her girls and, in this case, Lizzie as well. He knew how much she loved the girl. He grabbed Blakesley by both arms and forced her to look at him.

"Baby, listen," he shook her hard enough to make her focus on him. "I'll handle this, okay? Go back inside with your dad. Please."

Blakesley was enraged. She had gone out into the living room a few moments earlier, looking for Beck, and heard his voice on the porch. Seeing him talking to Sharon made something inside her snap and she ran back to the master bedroom to grab the baseball bat out of the closet. Probably not the best move, but she hadn't been thinking too clearly.

After the news about Ed, seeing Sharon threw her over the edge. She yanked herself from Beck's grip roughly, suddenly feeling very hot and very weak. She stumbled back, smacking Beck's hands away when he tried to steady her, and stumbled into the house. Casting Beck a long look, Marshall followed.

Beck was torn. He wanted to go with Blakesley but the greater issue was Sharon and Lizzie. His daughter was crying hysterically and as Marshall went after Blakesley, Beck put his arms around Lizzie.

"It's okay, baby girl," he held her tightly. "Your mom came to talk to you. If you don't want to talk to her, then just say so and I'll send her away."

Lizzie sobbed. "Talk about what?"

Sharon was climbing to her knees. "I'm so sorry, baby." She was struggling to compose herself. Tears made her vastly uncomfortable. "You were right about Dan all along. I'm so sorry I didn't believe you. I guess... I guess I didn't want to believe that someone I loved and trusted was capable of such things. I'm so sorry I didn't believe you."

Lizzie was calmer as her father held her. He gave her strength and she knew that nothing could hurt her so long as he was with her.

"You should be," she said, wiping at her nose. "I didn't lie."

"I know that now."

"So why couldn't you just take my word for it? Why did you have to treat me like I was trying to break you and Dan up?"

Sharon stood up and brushed off her pants. "I guess...," she said, "I guess I just didn't want to admit I had been suckered in. I left your dad for Dan, you know. Dan wasn't gone for months on end and didn't risk his life every time he went to work. I thought that was better for me and for you. I didn't want to admit that I'd been wrong."

Lizzie was done crying. The shock of the woman's appearance wore off and she stared at her mother, mulling over the conversation. She gently pulled free of her father's grip as she made her way to the edge of the porch.

"I get that," she said quietly. "But I can't get over the way you treated me when I told you about Dan. You're supposed to protect me and all you did was protect Dan. I don't feel safe with you. I don't trust you. I love my life here with Dad and Blakesley and the girls and I'm going to stay here. I don't want to go back to you, not ever. My life his here now and I'm happy with people who love and trust me."

She turned for the house before Sharon could say a word. Beck watched her disappear into the house before turning to his ex-wife.

"Now you've heard it from her," he said quietly. "She doesn't want to have a relationship with you so I would appreciate it if you would just stay away."

Sharon was coming to see that the damage she had done was irreversible. She had foolishly thought that an apology would make it all better and it was a bitter pill to swallow to know that it didn't. Unwilling, unwanting, to fight any longer, she simply lifted her shoulders.

"I'll respect her decision," she said quietly. "I guess I don't have a choice."

"No, you don't."

Sharon shook her head unsteadily, as if not sure what more to do or say. "So what do I do now?" she asked, rather despondently. "Can I... can I at least send her a birthday card?"

Beck didn't want to come off unreasonable. He knew Sharon was hurting but he didn't care. Still, he tried to stay as neutral as he could.

"Yes," he replied. "And Christmas cards. You're her mother and I don't want you to fade out of her life completely, for her sake. But... you just need to give her time. Maybe she'll change her mind in the years to come, but until then, do what she wants if there's any hope of having a future relationship with her. Don't push it."

Sharon nodded and, picking up her purse from where it fell on the ground, wearily made her way out to the curb and climbed into her rental car. Beck stood on the porch, watching the woman pull away. He should have felt bad for her but he just couldn't manage it. His concern was for Lizzie.

Going back into the house, he shut the door and locked it, feeling oddly relieved yet oddly hollow. It was a strange sensation. He turned off the porch light, trying to digest what had just happened. As he turned for the living room, he could hear the little girls upstairs, getting into their bath. He thought he heard Gabrielle's voice with them. The living room was vacant except for

Alfie still stretched out on the couch and as he headed back to the master bedroom, he saw Marshall in the kitchen with an open bottle of wine. The man had a glass in his hand.

"Hey," Beck pointed to the glass. "You didn't let Blakesley have any of that, did you?"

Marshall cocked an eyebrow, looking at the open bottle. "Actually, Lizzie has had a couple of belts," he teased. "I thought she needed it."

Beck appreciated the attempt to ease the tension. "I wouldn't blame her," he muttered. "Have you seen her?"

"She's in with Blakesley."

"How's my wife?"

"Upset. How's your ex-wife?"

"Upset."

Marshall grunted and waved him on. Beck went into the master bedroom to find Blakesley and Lizzie curled up together on the big bed. Blakesley had her arms around Lizzie, who was cuddled up against Blakesley. Beck couldn't help but be touched by the scene as he walked up on the bed.

"Hey," he said. "Can I be a part of that hug?"

Blakesley and Lizzie looked up at him and Lizzie nodded. Beck lay down on the bed beside his daughter, his big arms going around both women. He pulled them close, his hand stroking Blakesley's head. When she looked up at him, he smiled tenderly.

"Are you okay?" he murmured.

She nodded. "Fine."

"Sure?"

"I'm sure," she pulled one arm off of Lizzie and stroked his blond head. "Sorry I went a little crazy there. It's just been that kind of day."

He kissed her hand as it moved to his face. "I understand completely," he whispered. "You're pretty frightening with that bat. That's the second time I've seen you use it."

She was confused until she remembered she had nearly clobbered him the night he came to the house after she bought it. She grinned sheepishly.

"I don't know how to use a gun like you do."

"The bat is scarier."

"Is Sharon going to file assault charges against me? I don't care, you know. I would have cracked her on the head and been very happy about it. This is our world and she doesn't belong here."

Beck's smile faded and he kissed her hand again, to both agree and comfort her. Then he focused on his daughter.

"Baby girl," he gave her a squeeze. "Are you okay?"

Lizzie had her head against Blakesley's chest. She was pensive, deep in thought, wondering if she had made the right decision. She nodded.

"I'm fine," she muttered. "Can I still go to Alex and Natalie's?"

Beck looked at Blakesley, who merely wriggled her eyebrows. "Do you still want to go?" he asked Lizzie.

"Yes."

Beck stayed there a moment longer, his eyes on Blakesley, before giving the girls a final squeeze and climbing off the bed.

"Then let's get going," he told Lizzie.

Lizzie hugged Blakesley and slipped off the bed. Beck already had his keys, waiting for her to clear the bedroom. Before he followed, he looked at his wife.

"Are you sure you're okay?" he asked.

She nodded. "Fine."

"It's been a hell of a day for you."

"You, too."

He grinned. "I'm tougher than you are. I can take it."

She snorted. "In your dreams, buster. Trade places with me and let's see how well you handle things."

He put up a hand. "No, thank you," he said. "On second thought, you're tougher than I am."

"That's more like it. And don't forget to bring me ice cream."

"I won't." He winked at her. "Love you."

"Love you, too."

He quit the room and collected his daughter, realizing as he drove her over to Coronado Island that he felt better than he had in years. A weight of some kind had been lifted off his shoulders with Sharon's departure, although he really couldn't put his finger on it as to why. All he knew was that he felt free and Lizzie, too, was in control of her life now as much as a teenager could be.

TWENTY-THREE

THE STATE of California was apt to haggle on the price over the Earp homestead. Three people from the Office of Real Estate met with Blakesley, Marshall and Beck, and Blakesley's asking price was the subject of intense debate. Blakesley wouldn't budge.

She purchased the property for three million one hundred thousand dollars and that's what she wanted out of it. The real estate people came in with a seriously low offer and she almost got up and walked out. But they quickly changed their tune when they saw that she wasn't even willing to negotiate, so the offers kept coming back. Blakesley kept refusing. After the fourth such low-ball offer, Beck's displeasure became evident and the real estate people started getting intimidated by the big, blond husband. The offers became more serious.

Still, they weren't able to reach an agreement. The State of California was about a half million dollars under the asking price, so the meeting broke up with the real estate agents stating that they needed to return to their office and meet with their boss. Left alone at the old family homestead except for an archaeology crew in the public wing, Blakesley and Marshall took a look around.

The truth was that Blakesley hadn't been at the house since her accident and she was shocked to see how much it had been pulled apart by the people from the state. Every inch of the public wing had been combed over and examined, and the floor boards in every room had been lifted in sections to look for the pits and tunnels underneath. Beck held her hand tightly as they moved around the yellow caution tape, peering into holes and noticing that the archaeologists had methodically cut into the walls in their quest to study the structure.

The more Blakesley looked around, the more upset she became. "Look what they've done to my house," she pointed to the holes in the walls. "What in the hell are they doing?"

Marshall peered at the nearest hole. "They've used saws to cut into these walls," he observed. Then he looked around in general. "It had been years since I'd been here. It hasn't changed much."

Blakesley was still frowning at the walls, the floor. She put her hands on her hips in an irritated gesture. "Dad, have you heard of the Earp Curse?"

Marshall looked at her, surprised. "Who told you that?"

"Some old guy named Mike. He said he worked for Jimmy. He lived in one of these tunnels under the house until the state came in and chased him away. He seemed to know a lot about Ben Earp and the curse."

Marshall scratched his chin. "I heard of it," he looked up at the ceiling as if held some answers for him. "Mom's grandfather was Nicholas Walter Earp, and his grandfather was Robert Earp, son of Ben and Dulcinea. Old Nick spoke of the Earp Curse once or twice."

"What did he say?"

Marshall shrugged. "Just doom and gloom, mostly. He said the curse came from cursed money that Ben had stolen from the mission down here. Your mom thought it was a bunch of crap, of course."

"Did anyone ever look for the money?"

Marshall shook his head. "Not that I know of," he said. "Besides, Ben Earp was such a greedy bastard that if that money really existed, he probably spent it. He owned brothels and other crooked businesses in San Diego, and it's my guess that he spent most, if not all, of his money. His son and grandsons struggled to survive. This family really wasn't rich, you know. Whatever money Ben had, most of it was gone by the time he died."

Blakesley thought on that. She found herself looking up to the ceiling just like her dad had done. "What do you think, Dad?"

Marshall sighed faintly. "I think the whole damn Earp family is cursed," he said quietly, turning to look at his daughter. "And I think that if I were you, I would sell this place and never look back. This isn't a bright and shining family legacy you're preserving, Blakesley. This is a grave of failure, evil and sorrow. Even your mother knew that."

Blakesley looked at him with some surprise. "Wow, Dad. That's pretty dark."

Marshall nodded slowly. "Yes, it most certainly is."

He wandered into another room, leaving Blakesley and Beck alone in the great room of the public house. Blakesley just stood there, looking around the room pensively and gently rubbing her swollen belly. Beck walked up behind her, wrapping his arms around her.

"What are you thinking?" he asked, kissing the side of her head.

She sighed. "Maybe he's right," she muttered. "Maybe this whole places is really just a monument to failure and evil."

"What are you going to tell the state if they come back with another low offer?"

She turned in his arms, wrapping her arms around his neck. "What would you do?"

He looked surprised. "Me?"

"Yes, you."

He shrugged. "I don't know," he said. "You're the business genius in this family. The state was a half million dollars short of what you wanted. Thinking about losing that kind of money gives me the shakes."

She grinned. "Me, too, but I really want to stick to my guns on this one. If the state won't meet my offer, then I'll just put the property up for sale. I'm done thinking that we could live here. There's just no way I'd bring our family into this place."

"Not that I'm sorry to hear that, but what made you change your mind?"

"I guess I just love the Victorian too much. It's our home, Beck. Our family lives there and this baby was conceived there. This place... I guess I just don't get a good feel for it anymore. There are so many obstacles that have prevented us from moving in that I'm convinced someone is trying to tell us something. We need to stay where we're at."

He just hugged her and didn't say anything more. He was afraid if he did, it would sound as if he were celebrating. The truth was that he was, indeed, celebrating; Blakesley just didn't know it. Inside, he was doing the touchdown victory dance.

Dr. Welton picked that moment to enter the public wing on his way to the room where the original tunnel had opened up. He came through the doorway, surprised to see the owner and a big, blond man in a romantic embrace. He started to turn around and go back the way he came but Blakesley caught sight of him. She waved him over.

"Dr. Welton," she said. "This is my husband, Beck."

Dr. Welton stuck out his hand, shaking Beck's big mitt. "It's nice to meet you, Mr. Seavington," he said. Then he looked at Blakesley. "I heard you were going to be here today. I haven't seen you since before your accident. How are you feeling?"

Blakesley nodded. "Fine," she rubbed her pregnant belly. "We're all good these days."

Dr. Welton grinned at her obvious pregnancy. "Congratulations," he said. "So, how did your meeting with the real estate people go? They were here all morning looking the place over."

Blakesley's smile faded. "It didn't go all that well," she said. "They don't want to pay me nearly what I bought it for. They said they needed to talk to their boss and come back with another offer."

Dr. Welton crooked a finger at her. "Come with me," he said. "I'll show you something that may make them change their mind."

Curious, Blakesley and Beck followed. Dr. Welton took them into the room with the pit in it and Blakesley could see that they had tables and big lights set up, attached to portable generators. The tables were cluttered with all sorts of treasures taken out of the shaft, like a traveling antique show, and Blakesley approached the nearest table with great interest. There was a mish-mash of everything; old kitchen implements, a walking cane, broken pieces of bottles, forks, knives, a really nice jack knife, and other museum-quality relics.

Beck had his attention focused on the rifle that he had seen down there earlier. It really was a beautiful piece with a mother of pearl stock. As he admired the gun, his cell phone went off. Blakesley was over with Dr. Welton as he answered.

His conversation was brief. He was suddenly standing behind his wife, his hands on her arms.

"Sorry to interrupt," he said, looking at Blakesley when she turned around. "Baby, I need to go."

Blakesley didn't even hesitate. She was already following him from the room. "Sorry, Dr. Welton," she said. "We'll talk about this another time."

Dr. Welton lifted a hand. "No problem," he replied. "But I'm going to show the people from the state this booty and emphasize to them what a valuable place this is. Maybe that will help with the sale price."

"I'd appreciate it," Blakesley replied.

Dr. Welton waved one last time and turned back to his tables. Meanwhile, Beck had Blakesley by the hand and was leading her quickly from the house.

"Why are we leaving?" Blakesley asked as they crossed through the great room.

"I need to get to the base."

Blakesley suspected as much but it didn't prevent the nauseous feeling deep in her belly. The only time he moved that fast and with so few words was when it was work related. Beck took her out to the truck and helped her inside, driving her the few miles to the old Victorian in record time. He pulled into the alley next to the house and made sure she had her keys before he let her out of the truck.

Blakesley climbed out and collected her purse from the seat. Her bluish-green eyes fixed on him. "I'm going to pick up the girls from school in a little while," she tried to keep it casual, ignoring the usual anxiety that these swift departures provoked. "I don't plan on going anywhere else after that. Will you call me when you can and let me know what's going on?"

He nodded. "Absolutely," he said, his green eyes intense on her. "I love you, baby. Go inside now."

"I love you, too," she said, then her lip stuck out in a pout. "You didn't kiss me before I got out of the truck."

With her blossoming belly, it was hard for her to climb around agilely like she used to, making getting back in the truck to kiss him a rather tiring venture. He turned the truck off and bailed out, running around the front of the truck and taking her in his arms. He hugged her tightly, holding her fiercely against him. Then he kissed her repeatedly, deeply, soaking up the feel of her like a great, giant sponge.

"I love you," he murmured again, his lips against hers. "I'll call you in a bit."

She nodded, letting him go. He pointed to the front door and, grinning, she took the hint and went inside before he drove away. Blakesley stood at the window in the entry, watching his truck until it disappeared down the street. Struggling against the overwhelming depression his quick disappearance usually provoked, she went about her business and tried not to think about what Beck was doing, or what he was possibly facing.

He had promised her he wasn't going to serve with the teams any longer, but the fact of the matter was that until his transfer came through, he was an integral part of his team. She really was proud of him for his sense of duty and as he'd told her when they'd first met, he loved it. She knew he did regardless of his request for transfer.

She seriously wondered if he'd be happy doing anything else.

The rest of the afternoon at the Seavington home was something of a tribulation.

It all started when Cadee and Crosby came home from school sick. Crosby had been fighting a cold, which now had her full-bore, and Cadee was running a fever. While Blakesley was taking care of the older two, Charlotte fell on the back steps coming up from the backyard because Alfie inadvertently shoved her. Charlotte knocked out one of her front teeth and Blakesley left the older two girls with Nikki as she rushed Charlotte to the nearest pediatric dentist to have the tooth implanted.

Unfortunately, Charlotte's tooth had broken off at the gum line so the dentist had to remove the root. Charlotte was hysterical throughout the procedure, stressing Blakesley out as she held her weeping daughter. With all of that taken care of and Charlotte now displaying a gap-toothed smile, Blakesley had gotten a call from Lizzie, who had been waiting for her father to pick her up from school but he had never showed. With an exhausted and banged-up Charlotte in the car, Blakesley had made the trip over to Coronado Island to pick up Lizzie.

Lizzie was a Godsend, however, and took care of Charlotte while Blakesley tended to the older two, who were now both running a fever. Nikki had her hands full helping Blakesley, who was by now showing serious signs of stress and nausea. Nikki made a simple dinner for the girls, which turned out to be more of an ordeal. Cadee would only eat tomato soup while Crosby cried for ice cream. Charlotte, with the sore mouth and missing tooth, wouldn't chew anything so Lizzie fed her chocolate milk and soft, little pieces of mandarin orange slices.

Because there was so much going on, no one heard Beck drive up to the house around seven in the evening. He came in through the back door and into the kitchen, hearing Charlotte and Crosby's crying almost immediately. Frowning, he followed the sounds until he came to Charlotte and Lizzie, all huddled up in the playroom watching television. He stood in the doorway, his brow furrowed.

"What's all the noise?" he asked his daughter.

Lizzie was rocking sleepy and grumpy Charlotte. "Charlotte fell down today and knocked out her front tooth," she told her dad. "Blakesley's spent most of the afternoon taking her to the dentist."

Beck grunted sympathetically and went over to Charlotte, who gingerly opened her mouth at his gentle prodding to show him the damage. He clucked sadly at the missing tooth and kissed her on the forehead.

"Poor baby," he said. "How did she fall?"

"It was an accident," Lizzie said. "Nikki said that Alfie accidently pushed her over."

Beck pursed his lips irritably. "Damn dog," he grunted, hearing more crying coming from upstairs. "What's going on up there?"

Lizzie snuggled with Charlotte. "Crosby and Cadee are sick," she said. "Blakesley's been running all over the place for them. I'm glad you're home. She needs help."

Beck kissed Charlotte again and kissed Lizzie before standing up and heading upstairs. He mounted the top of the steps, hearing Crosby's crying. She was the loudest of the kids and it wasn't unexpected to hear her all over the place. The moment he showed his face in her bedroom, she yelled.

"Beck!" she cried. "You're home!"

Blakesley had been sitting beside Crosby's bed on a little, white plastic chair, trying to coax her daughter into drinking some juice. She turned to see her husband standing in the doorway.

"Hi, baby," she said wearily.

He could see how exhausted she was. "Why didn't you call me?" he very nearly demanded as he entered the room. "I could have come home earlier."

Blakesley let him pull her up from the chair. "That's never an option when you go to work." She cocked her head as if he had just said something outlandish. "Why on earth would I call you to come home because the girls are sick?"

Beck just gave her an intolerant expression, like he had expected her to call him, before bending down to put his big hand on Crosby's forehead. He looked at Blakesley. "She's running a fever."

"One hundred point three," Blakesley said. "Cadee has the same bug. They're both running a fever."

"Beck," Crosby said as she gave him the big, pouty face. "I want ice cream."

"What did your mom say about it?"

Crosby broke into tears and covered her face with the blanket. Beck looked at Blakesley, who shrugged her shoulders. "I told her she could have some if she had a few bites of sandwich but so far, she hasn't kept up her part of the bargain."

"A little ice cream isn't going to hurt her," he said softly.

Blakesley lifted an eyebrow. "No sandwich, no ice cream. It's the law."

Beck knew he didn't have any negotiating power at that point so he turned away from the bed and went into Cadee's room. Cadee was sitting up in bed, watching television with a cup of tomato soup in her hand. Beck went in to see how she was feeling, which seemed to please Cadee immensely. He kissed her forehead, just like he had with the other girls, and went back into the hall with Blakesley. He faced his wife.

"You look exhausted," he said. "Come downstairs with me for a few minutes."

Blakesley did as he asked and followed him into the kitchen. Alfie was lying on the floor, his tail wagging and thumping against the wood when he saw Beck and Blakesley. Beck frowned at the dog, silently scolding him for causing such chaos, before lifting his wife up by the waist and setting her on the stool against the counter.

"Have you eaten anything?" he asked.

She shook her head. "I've been busy with sick girls and a dentist visit."

"I saw Charlotte. Poor little kid."

Blakesley wriggled her eyebrows. "I told her that the Tooth Fairy would bring her a present," she said. "That was about the only way to calm her down. Last I saw, she was sitting with Lizzie."

"She still is."

"Lizzie is my lifesaver. Did you know you forgot to pick her up at school?"

Beck looked at her, stricken, before letting out a remorseful hiss. "It completely slipped my mind." He was deeply sorry. "I got so involved in... well, I just forgot. I'm so sorry, baby. Did you go get her?"

Blakesley nodded. "After I was finished with Charlotte."

He squeezed her arm gratefully. "Thank you," he said sincerely. Then he turned for the freezer and pulled out a frozen lasagna meal. "I'm going to make this for you so you eat something. With all of the running around you've been doing today, you need to keep up your strength."

Blakesley watched him pull the meal out of the box and read the directions. "I'm fine," she said, watching his focused movements. "But I have a question for you."

"What?"

"What's happening?"

He popped the meal in the microwave and turned it on. Then he looked at her. "What do you mean?"

"I mean that you're quiet, efficient, and subdued," she replied. "If you were home to stay, you would have your clothes off and a beer in hand by now. You're still in your casual uniform."

Beck looked at himself, the black combat pants and gray shirt that said "Seavington" in stencil. He leaned against the kitchen counter and hung his head wearily.

"I want you to eat before I tell you anything," he said quietly.

Blakesley couldn't help it; her breathing began to quicken and her palms began to sweat. "I'm not eating anything until you tell me what's going on."

He lifted his head and looked at her. "No food, no information. It's the law."

She just sat there and looked at him, not having the energy to grin at his twist on her No Ice Cream decree. The tears were instant because if he wasn't willing to tell her right away, it must be very bad indeed.

"Beck," she whispered, tears already popping out of her eyes. "Please don't tease me."

He was off the counter, moving towards her with his arms open. "No, no, no," he whispered, sing-song, pulling her into his powerful embrace. "No tears. I can't take that and you know it. Please don't cry."

She didn't listen to him. Her arms went around him and she sobbed as he rocked her gently. He kissed her head, her temple.

"Please, baby," he murmured. "Please don't cry. I haven't even told you anything yet."

That statement just made her cry harder. With a heavy sigh, he swept her into his arms and carried her to their bedroom, shutting the door softly. Laying her on the bed, he snuggled up beside her and hoped she didn't notice that his boots were on the bedspread. She would yell at him for that. He had her tucked up against his torso, her rounded belly against his stomach, when he suddenly felt a thump. It was a soft bump, as if someone had flicked his belly with a finger, faint reverberation against his skin. It took him a moment to realize that the thump came from Blakesley and his hand immediately went to her belly.

"Oh, my God," he breathed. "I just felt a kick."

She nodded, her face pressed into his shoulder. "He's been doing that for a couple of days now."

As he lay there, waiting, he was rewarded with a few more punches and what felt like a roll. He could feel the baby moving around and he grinned broadly.

"That's the most amazing thing I've ever felt," he declared, looking at Blakesley when she pulled her face from his shoulder. "Did you feel that? There he goes again."

There was such naked joy on his face that she couldn't help but smile. "He's been really busy today," she wiped at her cheeks, rolling onto back so he could put both hands on her belly. "Did you feel that?"

Beck was entranced. He pulled her shirt up so he could put his hands against her bare skin, feeling for the kicks with great anticipation. He wasn't disappointed; the baby kicked and fluttered. He laughed out loud.

"That's incredible," he said. "Does it hurt?"

She shook her head. "Of course not. Don't you remember feeling Lizzie kick?"

He shook his head. "No," he replied. "I was deployed when Sharon was about two months pregnant. I was gone for a year, so I missed Lizzie's birth. This is all new to me."

Blakesley put her hands over his. "I'm so glad you're here to share this," she said. "When I was pregnant with my girls, I was happy, of course, but I didn't feel the emotional thrill that I feel with this baby. To have a baby with someone I love so much... I can't think of anything more precious. I don't want you to miss a second of this."

His smile faded as he gazed down into her sweet face. "I don't want to, either, but I'm going to have to," he whispered. "We're deploying at midnight."

She stared up at him, her hands still on his as the baby kicked enthusiastically. "Where?"

"You know I won't tell you."

"How long?"

He drew in a long, deep breath, full of regret. "I don't know."

She began to get pouty again. "What do you mean you don't know?" she asked. "Will you please tell me where you're going? For my own sake. Please, Beck. I just want to know."

"I'm not going to tell you."

"Please?" she begged. "It helps me to know where you are. The not-knowing just kills me, Beck. How would you feel if I went away and you didn't know where I was? You wouldn't like it, either."

He hesitated and she could see that she had him. When he

finally spoke, she barely heard him. "All right," he murmured. "We're deploying to Afghanistan."

Blakesley exploded off the bed. "What?" she shrieked. "You're going to Afghanistan? They can't do that! They can't deploy you that fast!"

He was trying to keep her on the bed, keep her calm. "Yes, they can," he said softly, firmly. "That's the way we work sometimes. We go worldwide with a twelve-hour notice sometimes. That's just the way it works."

Her hands were at her throat, her breathing coming in sharp pants as she looked at him with utter horror. "But...," she gasped. "You can't go. Beck, you promised you weren't going to go away anymore. You promised!"

He remained calm, hoping it would soothe her. "Baby, do you really think I want to?" he asked gently. "My transfer to the Warfare Center is in the works but it hasn't come through yet. Until it does, I'm still part of the teams. I have to go."

"No, you don't!" her hysteria exploded. "You tell them that you can't go! You have to stay here, with us. You promised you wouldn't go away anymore!"

She was sobbing and he jumped off the bed, wrapping her up in his big arms. "Shush," he had her tightly, his face against the side of her head. "The girls are going to hear you. Keep your voice down."

"Please," she sobbed, holding on to him with a death grip. "Please don't go."

Her knees had collapsed and she was sinking to the floor. Beck tried to pick her up but it was like trying to hold spaghetti.

"Baby, please get a hold of yourself," he begged. "I have to go and no amount of crying is going to prevent it."

She collapsed on the floor, weeping painfully. He got down on the floor with her and just held her.

"Baby, listen to me," he was trying desperately to plead with her. "I don't want to go; believe me, I don't. I almost came to blows with Davis over it, but I literally don't have a choice. If I refuse to go, they'll throw me in the brig. I'll be dishonorably discharged, lose my pension, and God knows what else. Is that what you want? If you do, then tell me and I'll do it. But know the consequences."

She suddenly stopped crying and looked at him. Her face was wet with tears. "You... you'd do it?"

He wiped at her cheeks with his thumbs. "I'll do whatever you want me to do," he whispered. "I just want you to be happy. Tell me what you want me to do and I'll do it."

Upset and muddled, she could nonetheless see what he was saying. She understood. "I don't want you to get in trouble," she admitted. "But you promised, Beck. You promised you'd never go away again."

He just looked sad. "I know," he whispered. "I'm sorry I have to break that promise. It's not by choice. I wouldn't go unless I absolutely had to. I don't want to miss one minute of this baby, and I certainly don't want to be away from you, but I will make you this promise: come hell or high water, I will be at the birth. There is nothing on earth short of death that will keep me from it. Okay?"

She didn't have the heart to argue with him. "Okay."

"Do you believe me?"

"I always believe you."

She didn't sound convincing and he wrapped her up in his big arms again, hugging her fiercely.

"I love you," he whispered. "I love you so much. I swear this separation is really going to kill me."

Blakesley clung to him, feeling his warmth and power, drawing strength from it. She was much calmer now but still feeling weak and frail and vulnerable.

"Will you just hold me until you have to go?" she begged.

He picked her up and put her on the bed. "Stay there a minute. Okay?"

She lay there, sniffling, and nodded. Beck winked at her as he went out of the bedroom and soon, Lizzie and Charlotte appeared. They climbed on the bed with Blakesley, who put her arms around them both. It was an instinctive, motherly thing and she didn't hesitate. She even put Lizzie's hand on her belly when the baby kicked, drawing a great big grin from her step-daughter. Lizzie was thrilled. Eventually, Beck appeared again, but this time, he had his arms full. Crosby was in one arm and Cadee was in the other.

"I thought we could all lie on the bed together for a while," he said softly.

"Dad, why are we all here?" Lizzie wanted to know.

Beck had a hard time ever bringing forth the words. "Because I deploy tonight, hopefully for the last time, and I want to spend time with all of my girls."

Lizzie understood, more than most. Her entire life had involved her father shipping out. Blakesley thought his gesture to be genuinely sweet. She didn't even have the heart to tell him to keep the sick girls away from the others. He just wanted to lay with all of his girls and she wouldn't spoil that. Beck laid Cadee and Crosby down, moving to the other side of the bed so he could slide in behind Blakesley. He turned on cartoons and lay there with five girls, his eyes closed and his face planted in the back of Blakesley's head as Crosby and Charlotte tried to play patty-cake with his big hands. Lizzie ended up lying next to Cadee and braiding her hair.

They spent of the evening cuddled up on the bed, until the girls, one by one, fell asleep. Beck eventually turned off the television and the light so that it was dark and still in the room. He lay there listening to Crosby's baby snoring and to Charlotte's little grunts when she rolled over and over in her sleep. Blakesley had fallen into a deep sleep and he was thankful; she was exhausted and he didn't like seeing her so strung out. He just laid there, his hand on her now-still belly, absorbing the moment and tucking it away deep in his memory for the times that he would need it. It was such a precious moment that he couldn't even put it into words.

About an hour before midnight, he carefully climbed out of bed and pulled the covers up around everyone. They were all sleeping so peacefully and he stood there a moment, just gazing at the group. Once, he had described his career as his life. For twenty years, the Navy had been the most important thing to him. But looking at the huddle of girls on the bed, he knew that his career took a distant second to his family.

Cadee, Crosby and Charlotte weren't his biological children, but he loved them like they were. His life was richer for having known them. Lizzie was his flesh and blood, and he was deeply proud of the young lady she was becoming. And Blakesley... he couldn't put into words what he felt for her. Whatever it was ran deeper and stronger than anything he had ever experienced. He had that mad, passionate, deep and emotional love for her that most people never experience. He considered himself the luckiest man in the world.

Before he left, he took a notepad by the phone and wrote a note to Blakesley and put it in the bathroom where she would find it. Then he went back out to the bedroom and kissed her gently, one last time. It was enough to bring tears to his eyes. Lizzie was the only other person he could reach on the opposite side of the bed so he kissed her, too, before he quit the bedroom and quietly shut the door.

Pulling his truck out of the backyard in the darkness, he headed for the Coronado Bridge.

———

Blakesley had carried Beck's note around with her for almost four months. Beck had been gone that long with no word whatsoever. In the beginning, it had been extremely difficult. Every time the phone rang, she was running to it. These days, she didn't run to the phone and she didn't listen nightly for his truck pulling up the alley. She had settled into a rather calm routine and a calm life, taking the girls to school, painting daily, and focusing on the newly laid plans for the Art Bar. She had to put her focus on something other than Beck's absence; otherwise, she would have gone crazy.

She realized, sometime during the beginning of the third month, that she was starting to view Beck as kind of a dreamlike figure. He had taken on ethereal qualities in her mind and a larger-than-life persona. She thought of him daily and dreamt of him nightly. There were a few dirty clothes in the hamper he had left and she hadn't washed them. In fact, she had taken to sleeping with them because she could still smell him. She didn't want to lose that scent, that link between his body and her. She never told anyone that, not even Gina Aguirre, because she didn't want people to think she was crazy.

Spring was in full swing, as mild as it was in San Diego, and Easter was approaching. Lizzie had a huge social life at school and was at all of the parties and hung out with all of the cool kids. Blakesley kept a close watch on her, probably tighter than she should have, because she didn't want anything to happen to Lizzie while Beck was away. The old Victorian became filled with teenagers almost every weekend, girls as well as boys, as Lizzie's circle of friends grew.

Blakesley knew that Beck would have been wary of the boys hanging around, but she trusted Lizzie. She grinned when she thought of Beck returning home to a living room of teenagers hogging up his new flat-screen television. Both she and Lizzie were eager for the day. Lizzie missed her dad almost as much as Blakesley did.

On a particularly warm and dry Friday evening, Lizzie and some of her friends came home from a basketball game to hang out and eat. Gina had come over earlier in the evening, bringing Spike so the kids could play, and they were in the process of putting Spike and the little girls to bed but when they heard Lizzie and her friends, that became impossible. Blakesley let the children go downstairs to see the older kids, who fawned and cooed over Charlotte and Crosby, and allowed Cadee and Spike to hang out with them on the couch like one of the gang. Blakesley and Gina stood in the kitchen doorway, watching their children with the older kids, smiling at the general happiness going on.

Gina had a glass of red wine in her hand, watching Spike high-five it with one of the boys. "It's times like this when I miss Butch the most," she said softly. "I wish he could see Spike as he grows up."

Blakesley was leaning against the doorjamb, watching the little boy with the dark hair as he laughed and teased the high school kid. "He looks a lot like you." She looked at Gina. "Who does he act like?"

Gina grinned. "He's his dad all the way," she said. "He even has his goofy laugh."

Blakesley giggled, rubbing her belly. These days, she looked like she had a watermelon under her shirt, as the baby was growing very fast.

"I hope this baby looks like Beck," she said, eyeing her friend. "Did I tell you about the ultrasound last Friday? The doctor asked me if I wanted to know the sex."

Gina looked very interested. "And?"

Blakesley wrinkled up her nose. "I'm not sure I should tell you before Beck knows."

Gina was exasperated. "Then why did you say anything? Now it's going to drive me crazy."

Blakesley giggled. "Well, just don't tell him you knew before he did," she said, rubbing her belly affectionately. "It's official. We have a baby brother to balance out all of these girls."

Gina squealed with delight. "That's so exciting," she danced around. "Beck is going to be thrilled."

Blakesley grinned as she watched her friend's excitement. "I know," she said, inevitably sobering as she thought of her absent husband. "I just wish he'd hurry back. I don't know how you did it all of those years with Butch."

Gina's jovial expression faded. "It wasn't easy," she said honestly. "But he always came home, just like he said he would. At least, he did until the last time."

Blakesley reached out and touched Gina's arm comfortingly. "I refrain from asking you how you are all of the time because I don't want to keep bringing it up, but how are you doing? You seem okay these days."

Gina shrugged. "Nights are still tough," she said. "I still dream about him and then wake up expecting him to be there. I haven't had the guts to clean out his closet yet."

Blakesley went over and hugged her. "Don't do anything you're not ready to do," she told her. "When you feel strong enough, Beck will help you. You don't have to do it alone."

Gina nodded and sipped at her wine. She seemed more interested in watching her son, who was now being tickled by Lizzie. Blakesley let the subject go, her gaze lingering on Gina as she made her way back into the kitchen to clean up a little bit. She didn't hear the knock at the front door, which Lizzie went to answer, and she didn't see Gina as she caught sight of who was at the front door. Blakesley was scrubbing out the sink when Gina came back into the kitchen.

"Bee," she said hesitantly. "Uh... do you have a minute?"

Blakesley looked up from the sink. "Sure. What for?"

Gina went to the sink and took the scrub brush out of Blakesley's hand and set it on the edge of the sink.

"I need to talk to you," Gina said.

Blakesley shrugged, pulled off a paper towel, and wiped off her hands as she followed Gina into the master bedroom. Gina shut the door then went to the French doors that opened up into the backyard. She unlocked the panel and pulled it open.

Lizzie was the first person to step through from the darkness of the backyard. She was crying. Startled, Blakesley went to see what the matter was when another body stepped through the door. It took Blakesley a moment to realize that it was Captain Davis. He was followed by Anthony Solis and another Navy officer that Blakesley didn't recognize. She kept waiting for Beck to come in the door but he never did and she was momentarily confused. And then, it hit her.

Blindsided.

That's all Blakesley could think as she looked at the three men standing in her bedroom. She was stunned at the sight, but in the next breath, she knew why they were there. God help her, she knew. Beck wasn't here but they were. Gina came over to her, reaching out to put her arms around her.

"I thought it would be better if they came in through the back," she murmured. "All of those kids are out in the living room... and the little girls...."

Blakesley suddenly felt very hot. Her heart began to pound painfully in her chest and the room began to sway. She looked at Davis, and Solis, and the officer she didn't recognize... she could see crosses pinned to his collar. Chaplains wore that insignia.

Blakesley ripped herself from Gina's embrace and bolted into the bathroom and slammed the door, turning on all of the water faucets and letting the water blast. The shower was pounding, the tub, and both sinks. Steam began to rise. She turned them on full-bore, drowning out the people pounding at the door and calling her name.

No, she couldn't hear them. If she couldn't hear them, then they couldn't give her any bad news. She would stay right here with the water blasting out their voices so she couldn't hear anything. If she couldn't hear the news, then nothing had happened. Beck was still coming home. Her heart was pounding so hard that she was feeling faint, terror welling up inside her and there was no way to stop it. She couldn't control the rising tide. He promised he'd always come home to her, didn't he?

I'm sorry, baby, that I have to break that promise.

Screaming Beck's name, Blakesley passed out on the bathroom floor.

TWENTY-FOUR

"SHE'S NOT strong enough for you to tell her all of that. Can't it wait?"

"She has to know, Gina. Delaying it isn't going to make it go away."

Another female voice pitched in. "I agree with Gina," she said firmly. "Wait until she's capable of understanding."

Blakesley was vaguely aware of voices around her. She could hear Gina and Captain Davis, but she also heard a more familiar female voice. Muddled, half-conscious, she began to stir.

"Sophia?" she whispered.

She could feel the bed give next to her and arms going around her. "I'm here, sweetheart," Sophie said. "Don't worry about anything. I'm here."

Blakesley was very groggy. "My girls?" she breathed, trying to get up. "Where are my girls?"

"Honey, they're fine." Gabrielle was on the other side of the bed, helping Sophia keep Blakesley calm. A panicked call from Lizzie six hours ago had her and Marshall rushing to Blakesley's house where they had just broken down the bathroom door to get to Blakesley. "Marshall is with the girls. They're all fine."

Blakesley relaxed, collapsing back against the pillows. It took her a few moments to orient herself but the last memory she had washed over her and she burst into tears. Painful sobs filled the room and Captain Davis pulled away from Gina, planting himself next to Sophia. He was very close to Blakesley's head.

"Blakesley, I need for you to listen to me," he said in his firm, even tone. "It's important that you hear everything. For Beck's sake, I need you to be strong. He needs that strength."

Blakesley's eyes opened, great bluish-green orbs, red and watery. She struggled to calm herself. "I'm sorry," she whispered. "You're right. I'm so sorry. I... I just don't want to hear any of this."

Gina was suddenly beside the bed, her pretty face serious. "Bee, do you remember what you told me when Butch died?" she asked. "You told me to pull myself together because Butch deserved that respect. You were right. Beck deserves that respect, too, so you need to pull yourself together."

Blakesley's own words were coming back at her, wise words that were true. She knew they were right but her hormones and emotions were surging, and her control was weak. She swallowed hard, reaching out to hold the captain's hand. He squeezed it tightly.

"Okay," she took a deep breath, laboring for control. "I'll be calm. Tell me what happened."

The captain ended up sitting on the bed beside her. "I want to be very clear up front," he began. "As far as we know, Beck isn't dead."

"Then where is he? What happened?"

Davis took a deep breath. "Our callout five months ago was to aid a fellow S.E.A.L. team in the Paktia region of Afghanistan," he said quietly. "We received reports that a helicopter went down in a very mountainous area and that twenty-one U.S. Navy S.E.A.L.s were being held captive. Since Beck's team spent two tours in Afghanistan and knew the region, the customs and the warlords intimately, it was decided that Beck's team would deploy for the rescue mission. Are you with me so far?"

Blakesley nodded. "He wouldn't tell me why he went but I did know that he had gone to Afghanistan."

Davis wriggled his eyebrows, perhaps his way of saying that Beck shouldn't have told her and continued. "Beck spent almost six weeks negotiating with warlords for information and access to the downed team," he said. "To make a very long story short, he was able to discover that a warlord with loyalties to the Taliban held the men. Regional command decided that an armed rescue incursion was the best course of action, so we went in there with guns blazing."

He suddenly stopped and waved to someone standing at the foot of the bed. Blakesley looked over to see Anthony Solis approach, looking weary and sunburned, like he had spent a lot of time in the elements. He was dressed in a clean utility uniform but clean clothes couldn't erase the dark circles under his eyes or the exhausted demeanor. Davis indicated Anthony.

"Tony can tell you the rest," he said. "He was there when it all went down."

Blakesley stared at the young man, struggling to sit up in bed as Sophia and Gabrielle pulled her up.

"What happened?" she asked him.

Anthony seemed genuinely hesitant. He didn't like the fact that his captain had put him in a very touchy situation, especially with Seavington's wife. Still, he had been there. He had seen everything.

"It was a mess," he finally said. "We had ground forces and air forces, but the stronghold was up in the mountains near the Pakistan border and it was heavily fortified. Rockets, firearms, you name it. We were hit from all sides. We managed to get the chopper down and fought our way to within about a half mile of the compound where the S.E.A.L.s were being held. You know Beck; he was leading the charge all the way. He's not afraid of anything. When we got to the compound, he used a bullhorn to try and talk to the warlord. The guy came out and said Beck could come in and see the captives, but only Beck. So Beck threw down his weapons and walked in there even though we told him not to. About an hour later, the compound gates opened again and those S.E.A.L.s started coming out. Some walked out but some were carried. All twenty-one came out but no Beck. When we asked where he was, we were told that he exchanged himself for the release of the others."

Blakesley was listening intently. When Anthony finished, she just stared at him as his explanation sank deep. Then, her expression changed as realization dawned but surprisingly, she didn't become hysterical. She hung her head and thought on Beck's noble sacrifice, knowing how difficult it must have been for him to make it. But she respected his choice, strangely, seeing that the man was only doing what he felt right for the American hostages. He had done what he had set out to do. He had freed them. He had accomplished his mission and saved lives in the process. She just couldn't be angry about it.

"So he's not dead?" she finally asked, still staring at her lap.

Anthony shook his head. "We saw him after the release of the hostages and he was fine," he replied. "He was with the warlord on the walls of the compound. He was just watching us go."

Blakesley's head came up and she looked at the captain. It was evident that her mind was working. "How long ago was this?"

"Two weeks ago."

"So he's presumably still alive."

"I'm sure he is. The warlord that has him wouldn't kill him. Beck is more valuable alive."

She cocked her head. "Why would he still hold him?"

Davis shrugged. "More than likely to see if he can ransom him for money or weapons, or something like it. The man that has him isn't known for being particularly cruel but he is powerful. He controls a very large region near the Pakistani border."

"What's his name?"

"General Heckmytum."

She fell silent again, very controlled and thoughtful. After a particularly lengthy silence, she looked at Davis again.

"You said money," she said. "How much money?"

Davis shrugged. "It's hard to say," he replied. "You have to understand that even a few hundred American dollars is like a fortune over there. The warlords like money but they like weapons more. It's a power thing."

"What is the Navy doing about negotiating for my husband?"

Davis scratched his head, looking uncomfortable. "The United States doesn't negotiate with terrorists," he replied quietly. "That is, unfortunately, their stance at the moment, but you can bet that our contacts and patrols are keeping tabs on the situation. We won't give up and we won't let this drag out, I promise. I'm heading out again in a couple of days to see to the situation. Beck wouldn't leave me and I won't leave him."

Blakesley sighed and slowly, laboriously, climbed off the bed. So many hands were trying to help her but she shook them off, stretching and rubbing her back once she got on her feet. She seemed very calm, almost too calm. On the dresser was a big picture of her and Beck on their wedding day, his handsome face smiling back at her. She gazed into his face, feeling the longing, the pain and the pride. It was an odd situation.

"Richard," she turned to Captain Davis and addressed him by his name. "If I were to offer the warlord thirty million dollars, do you think he'd take it in exchange for Beck?"

Davis' eyebrows lifted. "Thirty million?" he repeated. "Where on earth would you get that kind of money?"

"It doesn't matter. Do you think he would take it for Beck's release?"

Davis was at a loss for words. He glanced at Anthony as he replied. "I don't know," he said. "Maybe. That's a hell of a lot of money. But I'm not sure the Navy would allow that kind of nego-tiation."

Blakesley's features hardened. "I don't give a flying fuck what the Navy would allow," she snarled. "Let me tell you what's going to happen. I'm going to fly to Afghanistan and I'm going to hire people to find that warlord and negotiate for Beck's release. I have thirty million dollars at my disposal and I will give it all up, and gladly, for the release of my husband. If you try and stop me, I'm going to the media with this and I'll make the Navy look like a bunch of assholes as they try to prevent a pregnant woman from gaining the release of her husband. Is this in any way unclear?"

Davis put his hands up to calm her. "Hold on," he stood up from the bed. "Don't get ahead of yourself."

"If she's going, I'm going," Sophia stood next to Blakesley, firing back at her boyfriend. "I'm not going to let a pregnant woman go halfway around the world alone."

Sophia, the beautiful, little, Italian woman, was all fired up and Davis continued to hold his hands up as if to protect himself from the furious pair.

"You two need to calm down," he said as he tried to get a handle on it. "First of all, Blakesley isn't flying to Afghanistan. She's going to..."

He was met with a chorus of interruptions, not only from Sophia and Blakesley, but from Gabrielle and Gina. Gabrielle was the tough mother hen as she inserted herself between Blakesley and Captain Davis.

"If she wants to negotiate for the release of her husband, then you can't stop her." Gabrielle was in his face. "In fact, I'm going with her, too, because she's my baby and I'm not going to let anything happen to her. If she wants to go, she'll go. It's that simple."

Davis was in over his head. He somehow managed to make his way to the bedroom door and open it.

"Marshall?" he called. "A little help, please."

Marshall was in the living room after having put his grand-daughters to bed. Lizzie was sitting with him as they both watched television. But Davis' plea had them both off the couch and heading for the bedroom. When Lizzie saw that Blakesley was up and moving, she went right for her and put her arms around her. Blakesley held Lizzie tightly.

"You're not going to stop me, Richard," Blakesley said frankly.

"Beck needs to come home and if I have to pay every dollar I have, I'm going to get him released. You can help me or you can stand aside. Either way, I'm going."

Lizzie looked at Blakesley, frightened. "Go where?"

Blakesley softened as she looked at Beck's daughter. "How much did they tell you about your dad?" she asked gently.

Lizzie blinked back tears. "They said he was in Afghanistan," she said. "They told me he was a hostage."

Blakesley looked at Davis, appreciative that he hadn't given Lizzie the full story. It would only have frightened her. Blakesley's focus returned to Lizzie.

"He is," she said softly. "I'm going to go to Afghanistan and see if I can ransom him. I've got the money."

"Wait a minute," Marshall was catching bits and pieces of the conversation. "What's this, Blakesley? What are you going to do?"

Marshall had been given the story by Davis when he had arrived earlier that evening, so he knew the details of Beck's captivity. Blakesley faced her father without reservation.

"I'm going to pay Beck's ransom." She took a defiant stance against the men in the room, which seemed to be very much against what she was suggestion. "Look, this isn't your decision to make, any of you. Beck would do the same for me or for any of you, so I'm not going to stand by while the Navy decides what they're going to do in order to secure my husband's release. I'm going to go to that damn country and buy my husband's freedom, and if any of you don't like it, you can kiss my ass. I mean it. You're not going to discourage me."

Marshall listened to her speech before looking to Davis in a sort of helpless gesture. He knew how stubborn his daughter could be and he knew she meant every word.

"She's not bluffing," he told the captain. "If she says she's going to do it, then she will. So now what?"

Davis just grunted. He turned away from the group, running his hand through his graying blond hair. He had a situation on his hands and he knew it; there was no way he was going to talk

Blakesley Seavington out of this. In truth, he really wasn't surprised. He tried to think of how Beck would handle his wife but he knew the man would have just caved in to her. Probably the only way to stop her would have been to tie her down and he wasn't ready to do that. Not yet. Finally, he turned to the group.

"Okay," he surrendered somewhat. "I'll tell you what; I'm going to Afghanistan in two days anyway. I'll take your offer to the general. You will stay here, nice and safe, and I will keep you updated daily. Is that acceptable?"

Blakesley frowned. "But I want to...."

Davis cut her off. "You can't always have everything you want," he interrupted. "More than that, Beck would kill both you and me if he knew you traveled halfway around the world, into a war-stricken region no less, in your condition. Do you really want to risk the baby like that? I don't think you do."

Blakesley looked uncertain for the first time. "Of course not," she said quietly. "But I want Beck back and I'll do whatever I have to in order to do that."

Davis sighed faintly. "It's my job to take care of my men," he said. "You let me do this, okay? Do you seriously want to offer thirty million dollars?"

Blakesley nodded without hesitation. "All of it."

Standing next to his daughter, Marshall blanched. "But that's everything you received from selling the janitorial business," he pointed out. "Blakesley, that's everything. You won't have anything left."

Blakesley looked at her father. "None of that matters if Beck isn't here with us. If I had more, I'd offer more. Don't you get it, Dad? The money means nothing. Beck means everything."

Marshall nodded reluctantly. He understood. Kissing his daughter on the cheek, he looked at Davis.

"You heard her," he said. "Thirty million dollars and not a penny more."

―――

Beck didn't think he'd ever be so glad to see the ass-end of a C130 Transport. At the Kandahar Airport, it waited in an extreme security area protected by the U.S. Military, and he boarded the barebones plane along with Davis, Anthony Solis, several more of his men, and Bill Hudson. In fact, there were about thirty men accompanying him from the general's compound all the way to the airport, about a three-hour drive.

Beck's only thought was getting home. He'd spent almost four months away from Blakesley and now that he was free, he was sick to his stomach with wanting to see his wife. He'd been holed up in the general's compound up until that morning, when Davis had come to the lair demanding to negotiate with the general. Davis had been surrounded by his own troops plus a platoon of Afghan forces that didn't look like regular army. Beck still hadn't been able to figure that one out. Davis had traveled like a king, spent two hours speaking with the general, and suddenly, Beck was free. He didn't know how or why, but he didn't care. When an American Humvee came for him in the fortified compound, he jumped in and off they went.

He hadn't spoken to Davis during the trip, as they were in different vehicles. They had just been trying to get the hell out of there before something really bad happened. Now that they were at the airport, he went straight for his captain as they boarded the aircraft.

"Beck," Davis seemed very glad to see him. "You're looking well, considering."

Beck was looking well, considering. He'd been treated very well, showered daily, had clean clothes, and ate regularly with the general. He'd been treated more like a guest than a prisoner. He had a reasonable amount of freedom but absolutely no communication with the outside world. That part had killed him; no phones, no computer, nothing. Beck looked around at all of the men, the aircraft, the vehicles.

"Is this all for me?" he asked, incredulous.

Davis grinned as he found his preferred seat on the aircraft. "Did you think we were going to leave you there?"

Beck shook his head. "No," he said honestly. "But what is all of this?"

"What do you mean?"

Beck pointed to the plane. "This," he said. "Air transport, a convoy, and it looks like a couple of platoons. Did you come to bust me out?"

Davis snorted as he put on his seatbelt. "Something like that," he said. "Are you sure you're okay?"

Beck was still a little giddy from his swift release but he nodded. "I'm fine," he noticed that Davis was digging into his gear bag and pulling out a cell phone. "How's Blakesley? Does she know about all of this? You didn't tell her, did you?"

Davis looked at Beck curiously, cell phone in hand. "Why wouldn't I?"

Beck had his answer and his jaw ticked furiously. He sat heavily next to his captain. "You shouldn't have told her," he growled. "For all she knew, I was still on the operation. She didn't have to know what had happened."

"Are you crazy? You're a hostage in Afghanistan and I'm not supposed to tell your wife?"

"No," Beck nearly barked. "It wasn't going to be forever. The general and I had an understanding and I'm pretty sure that I almost had him talked in to releasing me. Oh, God, I can't imagine she handled the news very well. You shouldn't have upset her like that. How did she take it?"

Davis put his hand on Beck's shoulder. "Beck, I had no way of knowing when, or if, we would ever get you back," he said. "Blakesley had a right to know. What did you want me to do? Wait a couple of years to see if we could negotiate your release and then tell your wife? I don't think you'd want it to go down that way. That's not fair to her."

Beck sighed sharply. He didn't want to argue about it but he didn't agree. "You didn't answer me. How did she take it?"

"Terribly. How did you think she would take it?"

Beck rolled his eyes. "Oh, my God," he breathed. "I didn't want her upset, not now. Is she okay? Is the baby okay?"

"The baby is fine. Your wife is fine. They need you home, not holed up in Afghanistan."

Beck felt better to know that Blakesley and the baby, in spite of everything, were all right. He began to relax somewhat. "I would have gotten out, eventually," he repeated. "I almost had the general talked into it. I feel very strongly that he was going to let me go at some point soon."

"But you couldn't be sure."

"Sure enough." Beck began to put his seat belt on. "So what did you do? Threaten him with a rocket assault if he didn't release me? Threaten to cut his satellite feed? That man thrives on his television. That probably would have done it right there."

Davis shrugged, regarding the cell phone still in his hand. "Like I said, we had no way of knowing that."

Beck's thoughts lingered on his beautiful wife and the hell she must have gone through. It made him sick to think about it. "The general and I had very long conversations every night," he explained. "I told him I had a family and a baby on the way. He said he didn't want to keep me from my family. He also said I was a man of honor and he respected that. I really think I could have talked him into letting me go."

Davis gazed at the man, wondering how much he should tell him about the lengths they went through for his release. He opted for all of it because he would find out eventually. He may as well know now.

"I wasn't going to wait for that possibility," he said quietly. "So I ransomed you."

Beck had no idea what he was talking about. "You ransomed me?" he repeated, shocked. "There was a ransom demand?"

Davis shook his head. "Not in the literal sense." He cleared his throat, increasingly uncomfortable that he would have to explain himself. "Afghan warlords are into money and power. The Navy wouldn't officially negotiate with the general for your release, you know that. They don't deal with criminals, especially not like that, not in this military theater. So I bought your freedom. I felt it was the only thing we could do; otherwise, you risked rotting away in that compound and we'd never see you again."

Beck still wasn't following him. "Bought my freedom? With what?"

"Thirty million dollars."

Beck's jaw dropped. "Thirty million...?" he sputtered. "Where in the hell did you get that kind of money?"

"Your wife."

Beck would have bolted out of his seat had he not been belted in. His roar was heard above the gunning of the jet engine as the plane began to taxi.

"What?" he bellowed. "What in the hell are you talking about?"

Davis put his hand on the man's arm to calm him down. "She gave me the money," he said as quietly as he could. "She liquidated every asset she had except for the house, the cars, and the girls' college funds. Marshall said she used all of the money she had from the sale of her janitorial business. Beck, if I hadn't come here to negotiate, she would have come herself and there would be nothing I could do to stop her. She was determined to come and buy your freedom. Nothing in the world was going to stop that woman. Would you rather have had her come to Afghanistan and not me? That's where we were heading, my friend."

Beck was pale with shock. He couldn't believe what he was hearing. "So you came," he muttered, suddenly feeling very weak and very ill. He sank back against the chair and closed his eyes. "Oh, my dear God. What in the hell did she do?"

"She bought her husband's freedom," Davis replied. "You can't get angry at her for it, Beck. She did what she felt she had to do. She did it for you."

Beck just sat there, dumbfounded. "But I'm sure the general

would have eventually released me," he said, despondent. "She didn't have to... oh, my God, I think I'm going to be sick."

"Hold it together, son," Davis said, handing him the cell phone still clutched in his hand. "Give her a call when we get in the air. Tell her you're on your way home."

Beck looked at the phone in the man's hand a moment before taking it. He held it in his hand as the plane took off, closing his eyes, seeing Blakesley and thinking about the huge sacrifice she had made for him. Assets she had protected through her ex-husband's trial were given up in a single day to buy his freedom. Thirty million dollars. He just couldn't believe it. It was the greatest act of sacrifice he had ever heard of, so deeply touched by her actions that he couldn't put it into words. That she would do such a thing for him had his senses reeling.

The plane hit altitude and Beck called his wife. It was three in the morning in San Diego but she picked up on the fourth ring. She sounded groggy and pissed, but at the first sound of her voice in four months, Beck couldn't hold back the emotion. Tears streamed down his face as he greeted his wife.

Davis could hear Blakesley weeping from where he sat.

———

Beck woke up in an empty bed. Blinking the sleep from his eyes, he lifted his head to look at the alarm clock, seeing that it was 1:32 pm. His mind was groggy, like he had been drugged, and he fought through the cobwebs to recollect when he went to bed the night before.

His flight from Afghanistan had been a twenty-four hour affair, finally landing at Miramar Air Station near San Diego around midnight. Blakesley and the girls had been there to greet him and it had been a sweet and joyful reunion, but by the time they got home and got to bed, it had been around two in the morning. Everyone had been exhausted. He'd been asleep almost twelve hours and he sat up in bed, shaking off the sleep, and got up.

Pulling on a pair of pajama bottoms, he opened the bedroom door to see three heads pop up from the sofa in the living room. Cadee, Crosby and Charlotte heard the door open, saw him standing there, and immediately screamed at the sight. Beck grinned as they came charging over to him and he picked up Crosby and Charlotte, kissing their little cheeks. He was able to set Charlotte down so he could hug Cadee, but Crosby clung to his neck and refused to let go. As he tried to make his way into the kitchen with his fan club hanging on him, Blakesley appeared in the kitchen door.

Beck's breath caught in his throat at the sight of her. He hadn't really gotten a good look at her last night because of the darkness, the fact that she was bundled in layers, and his fatigue, so he took a moment to drink her in. Her belly was quite large now and she wore a big, white collared shirt with leggings, looking about as adorable and pregnant as she possible could. Beck made his way over to her with Crosby still hanging on his neck, tears in his eyes as he drew close.

"Hi, baby," he whispered.

Blakesley could see the tears in his eyes. She put her arms around him, hugging him tightly and kissing him sweetly as Crosby still hung on to his neck, joyfully strangling him. Blakesley's impression of him last night had been brief, dark and exhausting, also, so to see him in the light of early afternoon looking healthy and whole did her in. She buried her face in his chest and sobbed. Beck managed to pry Crosby off his neck and put her down so he could put both arms around his wife.

"Everything is okay," he murmured, feeling her big belly against his torso. "I'm home. Everything is okay now."

Blakesley nodded, wiping at her face and trying to get a hold of herself so the girls wouldn't be frightened by her tears. As she struggled to collect herself, Beck looked at the little girls surrounding him.

"Hey!" He suddenly pointed to Cadee and Charlotte. "Why aren't you in school?"

"Mom said we didn't have to go today since we got to sleep so late last night," Cadee informed him. "She said we could stay home and see you."

Beck grinned. "She did, did she?" He looked at Blakesley, now wiping the last of the tears from her eyes. "You have a pretty cool mom. That was nice of her."

"Beck!" Crosby grabbed one of his big hands. "See the baby? He's gotten big!"

Beck put his free hand on Blakesley's big belly. "He sure has," he said with pleasure. Then he looked confused. "Wait a minute – do we know it's a 'he'?"

Blakesley had hoped to tell him under more private circumstances, but she couldn't hold back. Besides, the girls already knew and they wouldn't be able to keep the secret.

"Yes," she nodded, watching his expression. "It's a boy."

Beck stared at her a moment before wrapping her up in his big arms, unable to speak for a moment. He was overwhelmed with emotion. The tears returned and he shoved his face into the side of her head, smelling her hair, kissing her gently.

"Thank you," he whispered.

Blakesley put her hands on his cheeks, returning his sweet and gentle kisses. "I didn't have anything to do with it," she joked. "Maybe God just knew we needed some balance in this family."

He smiled, wiping at his eyes and putting his hand on her firm belly again. "I'm just speechless," he said softly, picking Charlotte up when she tried to jump up on him. "Does anyone else know?"

"My dad," Blakesley said, looking rather fearful to tell him the truth. "And... well, your parents know. Lizzie spilled the beans. Gina knows. So do Richard and Sophia."

Beck laughed softly. "So everyone knew but me."

"That's about the gist of it. Are you mad?"

He shook his head and kissed her cheek. "Of course not," he said, suddenly looking around. "Speaking of Lizzie, where is she?"

"School," Blakesley said. "She wanted to go today. I told her you'd pick her up from school."

Beck nodded. "Thank you, I will," he replied. "But for now, can a guy get something to eat around here?"

Blakesley grinned and had him sit down on one of the bar stools. Beck sat and ended up with Crosby and Charlotte in his lap, as usual. Cadee stood next to him, leaning against him, and he kept an arm around her. It seemed that all of his girls wanted to be with him and around him. He soaked it up, glad to be home, as he watched his wife go about making him something to eat.

Blakesley made him a chicken salad sandwich and pasta salad for lunch, pulling the little girls off of him so he could eat it. Crosby and Charlotte ran to the back door and let Alfie in, and the dog ran through the house with the girls chasing him, barking happily. Beck grinned at the joyful chaos as he wolfed down his lunch.

"God, I missed this," he breathed, kissing his wife with chicken-flavored lips. "I missed you so much. I still can't believe I'm home."

Blakesley was watching him with a rather dreamy-eyed expression until he said that. Then she got teary.

"Was it awful?" she asked softly. "Richard told me what you did to save those men. Beck, I swear, if I'd been anywhere near you, I would have slapped you silly for risking yourself like that. But on the other hand, it makes me so proud of you I can't even verbalize it. I can't believe you did that."

He shrugged modestly, taking another big bite. "About half of the S.E.A.L.s that were being held captive were wounded," he said quietly. "I had to do something to get them out of there or they would have died."

"But offering yourself up as a hostage in their place?" Blakesley still wasn't quite over his self-sacrifice. "You took a terrible risk."

He shrugged again, pulling her off the stool and hugging her against his body with one arm while he ate with the other. The way he felt right now, he didn't ever want to let her go. He just wanted to feel her, smell her, and touch her.

"Speaking of risks," he didn't want to talk about himself at the moment. "What's this I hear about thirty million dollars?"

Blakesley was cuddled up against him, her face very close to his. She watched him eat. "I did what had to be done," she said. "I wasn't going to let you stay there a moment longer than necessary. I had to do something."

He sighed faintly. "But it really wasn't your call." He was trying to be gentle. "The Navy had things in hand and I'm pretty sure I wouldn't have been a captive too much longer. Why didn't you just wait it out?"

She looked sad and horrified. "Wait it out?" she repeated. "Beck, I wasn't going to wait anything out. The Navy was just sitting on their ass so I had to do something. I couldn't let you rot away in that place."

She was getting upset and he kissed her to quiet her. "Let me tell you something," he whispered, kissing her angry face again. "I sincerely, deeply and wholly appreciate what you did. I understand where you're coming from. But please know that I wasn't being treated poorly and I wasn't in imminent danger. The general treated me kind of like a guest and I think he was close to letting me go. He knew I had a family to come home to."

She was still pouty but easing quickly. "I didn't know that," she complained. "No one knew that. I just wasn't going to sit around while nobody did anything to help you."

He just hugged her, not wanting to create a big scene. He'd said his peace and there wasn't much more he could add. "So you paid thirty million dollars?" He shook his head at her, baffled. "Baby, I didn't even know you had thirty million dollars."

She shrugged, putting her cheek against his. "You could have," she said. "But you never look at our bank records. You never look at anything that's financial relating to me or the house or anything else. You just leave that all up to me. Did you even know that half of that money was yours? I had it written in to the prenup."

He stopped chewing and looked at her. "No, I didn't know," he said, almost agitated. "I didn't want to know. I trust you and I didn't want to inspect every piece of paper you put in front of me like I didn't trust you to do the right thing for both of us."

"But you took it to a lawyer," she said.

"Yes, I did, but I didn't read it. That's why I paid him; to read it for me to make sure it was all in order."

She kissed his cheek because she could see he was getting upset. Money always made him upset. "It was the money I received for the sale of the janitorial company," she said quietly. "I told you that I had invested most of it. The thirty million wasn't all I had but it was close. I still kept the interest it had earned over the past couple of years, which amounts to a couple of hundred thousand dollars, plus I sold the homestead to the State of California."

He looked surprised. "You did? When?"

She toyed with the dimple in his chin. "The day after I began liquidating everything," she said. "I called the state and told them I'd take their offer of two point four million for the property. It's already in the works. So we're not completely destitute. I just don't have millions of dollars sitting in the bank anymore. It's not a big deal."

He was beginning to look sick again. "I can't believe...," he paused and took a breath. "Baby, I just can't believe you would do that."

"And why not?" she wanted to know. "Beck, I would have sold my soul to get you back. Don't you get it? The money doesn't mean a damn thing to me. You do. You're the most important thing in the world to me."

She was starting to tear up again so he kissed her cheek and hugged her to comfort her. He hadn't seen her in four months and he didn't want their first day together to be full of tears. He just didn't know what to say about the money anymore; it was done and over with. He wasn't sure he could say anything more.

"It doesn't matter," he said, finishing his sandwich. "We've got over three hundred thousand sitting in the bank from the sale of my condo, so we'll do just fine. Plus, I make a decent salary, around sixty-eight hundred dollars a month. Add hazard pay and it's another couple of thousand. We'll get along fine."

"I was thinking that I should maybe get a job."

"You don't need to get a job."

She sniffled, wiping at her nose. "But there's the Art Bar," she said. "I signed a lease on that. Before all of this happened, I was making plans for getting it up and running, but that's going to cost about thirty thousand dollars for everything I want to do. I'm thinking... thinking that maybe I should just let the Art Bar go for now. It's just not the right time."

He looked at her. "You will not let it go," he insisted. "That's your dream, baby. You're not going to give it up. You do what you want to do for that and we'll find a way to pay for it. I don't want you to worry about that, okay? Please?"

In lieu of an answer, she simply wrapped her arms around his neck and hugged him, just glad to feel him alive and well in her arms. It was difficult not to get emotional but she fought it, telling herself that there was no need. He was home and he was safe.

Beck finished his lunch and Blakesley put the dishes in the dishwasher as he made his way back to the bedroom to take a shower before picking Lizzie up from school. Crosby and Charlotte saw that he was up and moving so they ran after him, into the bedroom, and the dog followed. Alfie jumped up on the bed and Beck scolded the dog, who contritely climbed off, but Beck had a feeling that dog was used to getting up on the bed. He seemed very comfortable up there.

Beck coerced the little girls into leaving the bedroom so he could strip down and take a shower, and they eventually cooperated. He took his time cleaning up, soaking in the hot shower and taking the time to scrub himself down good. It was good to be in his own shower again. He eventually turned the water off and dried off, taking the time to shave off about a week's worth of growth. Clean shaven, he looked at himself in the mirror, thinking he needed a haircut. He could hear the little girls banging on the bathroom door so with a towel wrapped around his waist, he opened it.

The girls screamed with delight when he threw open the door and growled like a bear. They scattered like frightened rabbits as Beck went into the bedroom, grinning, noticing his wife was lying down on the bed. He eyed her as he went to the dresser to pull out his clothes.

"Why are you lying down?" he asked.

She motioned him to come over to her and he obeyed, tee shirt and briefs in hand. She patted the bed beside her.

"Sit down," she said.

He did, looking at her curiously. Blakesley took one of his big hands, unbuttoned her shirt, and put it on her bare belly. She watched his face, with its relaxed expression, until his eyebrows suddenly drew together. His eyes narrowed at her.

"What was that?" he demanded. "Your stomach got hard all of a sudden."

She smiled. "It's called a Braxton Hicks contraction."

He suddenly looked panicked. "A contraction?"

She patted his hand. "It's not like that," she said. "They're basically false contractions. It doesn't mean I'm in labor. It's just the body preparing itself for the birth. It's common."

He didn't look convinced. He set his underwear down and put both hands on her belly, feeling another weaker contraction a few moments later.

"Baby, that can't be normal," he looked rather frightened. "Do they hurt?"

She shook her head. "Not really," she said. "Sometimes they're uncomfortable, but they don't really hurt. Not like real labor, anyway."

He still wasn't convinced. "Does the doctor know?"

"Of course he does. This has been going on for the past month."

"I don't like it."

She laughed. "They're harmless," she said. "But I wanted you to know I've been having them just in case you see me take a pause some day because I'm having them. I'm at 36 weeks now, so we don't have much time left before Colt is born."

Beck bent over and kissed her belly, laying his cheek on it affectionately. "A boy," he muttered. "I can hardly believe it. I'm actually going to have a boy."

"Excited?"

He grinned brightly. "Do you seriously have to ask that? I feel like I'm on top of the world right now. Life just gets better and better with you."

She met his grin, stroking his hand sweetly and he kissed her fingers. She watched him as he went back to lavishing attention on her belly.

"So now what?" she asked.

"I'm going to get Lizzie. Do you want to come?"

"No," she replied. "I'm going to stay here and rest until these contractions go away. Besides, I'm sure she'd like to have some alone time with you. She hasn't really seen you yet."

He nodded, kissing her belly one last time before getting off the bed, closing the bedroom door, and getting dressed. Blakesley watched him, his magnificent body clad in casual jeans and a pullover shirt. He looked spectacular and her heart, as always, fluttered at the sight of him. He sat on the bed as he pulled on his shoes.

"I may get a haircut on my way back," he told her. "I feel shaggy."

She laughed. "Baby, your hair is barely a half inch long."

"It needs a trim."

"Okay," she wasn't going to argue with him. "Do what you have to do."

Shoes on, he lay across the bed and kissed her. "I will," he took a moment just to look at her, stroking her blond hair, reacquainting himself with her beautiful face. "I'll miss you while I'm gone. I won't be long."

"No worries. I'll be here when you get back."

He kissed her again and pushed himself off the bed. "Love you."

"Love you, too."

He winked at her as he slipped out the French doors to his

waiting truck. The little girls heard him leave and tried to run after him, but Blakesley stopped them. Unhappy, they pouted and jumped on her bed until she turned cartoons on. With the little ones drifting off to sleep in her arms in the mid-afternoon, Blakesley settled back on the bed and waited for the Braxton Hicks contractions to subside.

———

When Beck returned home a couple of hours later, he had no idea what he was walking in to.

He came in through the back door with Lizzie and the little girls were in the kitchen with Nikki, who had started dinner. Nikki had never said more than two words to Beck the entire time she had known him, so it was odd for her to go out of her way to speak to him. She literally blocked his path as he walked in the door.

"Mr. Seavington," she said hesitantly. "Blakesley... she wouldn't let me call you, but I think something is wrong."

His brow furrowed. "Wrong? What do you mean?"

Nikki pointed to the bedroom. "The baby, I think."

Beck bolted. The master bedroom door was closed and he tried not to charge in, but it was difficult. As it was, he startled Blakesley, who was lying all curled up on her side, facing away from him and watching television. Eyes wide with fright, Beck went around the side of the bed and fell to his knees beside her.

"Baby?" he grasped her hand. "What's wrong?"

Blakesley looked pale. She squeezed his hand. "Damn Nikki," she hissed. "Did she call you?"

He shook his head. "No, she didn't call me." He was bordering on panic. "What's the matter?"

She looked at him and sighed heavily. "I wanted to wait until you got back before making any decisions," she said, grunting as she rolled onto her back, "but the contractions have gotten worse."

He visibly paled. "Did you call the doctor?"

She nodded. "About an hour ago. He told me to drink some

water to make sure I'm hydrated, because dehydration can cause cramping, and then wait a little while to see if they go away."

"Have they gone away?"

"No," she shook her head. "I need to call him again but I didn't want to do anything until you got here."

Beck grabbed her cell phone next to the bed and went through her phone log, dialing the doctor's office. The exchange answered and Beck calmly but forcefully explained who he was and what he wanted. The exchange took his number and promised to have the doctor call him back shortly. Beck hung up the phone, put his hands on his hips, and studied his wife with concern.

"They're going to have the doctor call me," he said. "Is there anything else we can do?"

She shook her head and closed her eyes, tired. "Not right now," she said. "I had Braxton Hicks contractions a lot with the girls. They never amounted to anything which is why I wasn't worried. But they've been really strong over the past hour, like they're getting worse."

He watched her, brow furrowed, feeling helpless and sick to his stomach. "Were any of the girls born early?"

She nodded. "Cadee was three weeks early."

"But this baby would be almost four weeks early. Oh, my God, I can't even say that without feeling sick. I'm not ready for him to be born yet."

Blakesley opened her eyes, seeing his tense expression. She could tell he was starting to get worked up and she patted the bed beside her.

"Lay down with me," she begged. "Tell me about your trip to Afghanistan. I want to hear about this general who took thirty million dollars in exchange for my husband."

He didn't hesitate. Kicking off his shoes, he carefully lay down beside her with extreme care, cuddling up with her. Blakesley snuggled against him, feeling comfort with his strength. She'd missed it terribly.

He was worried and edgy, but he told her what he could of his mission to Afghanistan. Blakesley lay still and quiet in his arms, listening, and it took him a few minutes to realize that her hands, resting on his arm, were digging in to his flesh with regularity. He began to notice and it distracted him from his story. He told her about the harsh conditions, of eating local food that gave him the runs, and was in the process of telling her about a particularly hairy helicopter ride when she suddenly dug her nails into his arm and grunted softly. Stricken, Beck put his hand on her taut belly and began to rub it.

"Colt, you need to stay in there, buddy," he begged. "Stop scaring the crap out of your old man. Your mom and I love you but we're not ready to meet you yet."

Blakesley giggled softly as the cell phone rang. Beck moved so fast to pick it up that he nearly knocked it off the nightstand. He managed to keep it in his hand as he answered.

Within ten minutes, they were dressed and heading to the hospital.

TWENTY-FIVE

BECK WAS SITTING in the plastic hospital chair, his mouth and chin resting on his folded hands as he watched Blakesley. She was resting in a hospital bed, in a private labor and delivery room at Scripps Mercy, hooked up to fetal monitors and an I.V..

The ward was quiet, the hour late as he sat, waited and watched. The doctor on-call had hooked Blakesley up to the monitors and took a blood test. He had done an initial exam on her, noting her water hadn't broken and she wasn't dilating, but her cervix was thinning out, a sure sign that labor was approaching. He diagnosed the early stages of labor and wanted to run some tests on the baby before he took the next step.

So he put Blakesley in a room hooked up to some monitors and left, with Beck sitting beside his wife, terrified of what was going on but determined not to show it. He didn't want Blakesley to see just how worried he was. With everything he had faced in his lifetime, the death and battles, this was clearly the most frightening, mostly because he was helpless. It was out of his control and he didn't like that one bit.

Beck blamed himself, of course. All of the stress he had put on Blakesley with deploying to Afghanistan and his subsequent capture had taken its toll. Blakesley had so much to deal with in his wake and, as strong as she was, something had to give. He utterly blamed himself. Feeling sad and despondent, he simply hung his head.

Exhausted and in some pain, Blakesley eventually drifted off to sleep but Beck couldn't sleep. All he could do was watch his wife every single second as if fearful something would happen if he took his eyes off her. He had called Marshall on the way over to the hospital, who promised to drive over to the house in the morning and take the girls to school, and Marshall had in turn called Gabrielle. The woman was on duty this night and as Blakesley slept fitfully, she came down from ICU to Maternity.

Beck saw her in the hall as she got off the elevator. He stood up from his chair and went out into the hall to greet her. Gabrielle gave him a big hug.

"Thank the Lord you're back safe," she said, taking a good look at him. "How are you, baby?"

Beck smiled weakly. "I'm fine," he said. "No worse for the wear."

Gabrielle's smile faded as she studied him. "You sure gave us a scare. You gave your wife a scare."

Beck sighed sadly. "I'm sure that's why she's here," he said. "All that stress must have triggered this. This is all my fault."

Gabrielle peered around him, into the room, seeing Blakesley asleep. "Don't blame yourself," she told Beck. "These things happen. Has the doctor been back to see you?"

Beck shook his head. "He's still running some tests on the baby. He hasn't come back to talk to us yet."

Gabrielle nodded. "I read Blakesley's chart," she said. "Her vitals look good, so it doesn't look like she's in any danger. The baby's vitals look good, too. It's my guess they'll just let her go into labor and have the baby. He's not too early."

Beck sighed heavily, closing his eyes as if to ward off the horrifying thought of a premature birth. "Are you sure? She's not due for another month yet."

Gabrielle could see how upset he was and she patted him on

the arm. "Babies are born this early all of the time," she assured him. "Don't worry so much. I'm sure the doctor will be around soon to talk to you."

Beck just shrugged, not knowing what more to say, when he suddenly heard his name. Turning around, he could see Blakesley sitting up in the bed and he very quickly went into the room.

"Hi, baby," he said as he approached the bed. "What's...?"

Blakesley cut him off. "My water broke," she said, gripping the sides of the bed. "I just had a huge contraction."

Startled, Beck looked on the bed and he could see a big wet spot around her pelvis. Everything was soaked. Gabrielle was already buzzing the on-duty nurse as she went to Blakesley and put her arms around her.

"Looks like we're going to have a baby tonight," she said cheerfully. "I'd better call Marshall. He'll want to meet his grandson."

Beck was still rather dumbstruck. He just stood there and held Blakesley's hand, not even sure what to say as the on-duty nurse came in, saw what was going on, and swung into action. Between Gabrielle and the nurse, they put Blakesley into a supine position and the nurse checked to see if Blakesley was dilated. She was, about three centimeters, and suddenly everyone was all smiles because the baby was on his way. Everybody but Beck, that is; he stood there, struggling to process everything.

"Wait a minute," he finally said, concerned. "The baby is early. You have to stop this labor."

The on-duty nurse grinned; her name was Kelli and she had been a Labor and Delivery nurse for twenty years. She could see how rattled the man was, but she'd dealt with a lot of rattled fathers in her time.

"Commander Seavington," she said calmly. "The tests on the baby have come back fine. His lungs are developed, his heart rate is good, and there's no reason to stop the labor. Everything will be fine. We'll call your wife's doctor and let him know what's going on."

So that was it. Colt was coming whether or not Beck was ready for him. When Beck realized he was going to be a father that night, he looked at Blakesley with some shock. He kissed her hand and caressed it.

"How do you feel?" he asked her, worried. "Okay?"

Blakesley saw how apprehensive he was. "I'm fine," she assured him. "Please sit down and relax. This shouldn't take too long."

He looked terrified. "Why do you say that?"

She grinned at his expression. "Because my labor with Charlotte was only four hours," she said. "We should be holding Colt by midnight."

Beck's eyebrows lifted with astonishment. He started to grab around for the chair. "Oh, my God," he breathed. "I have to sit down. I don't know if I'm ready for this."

Blakesley laughed at him. "Baby, it's okay. It'll be fine."

"But... I've never seen a baby born before. Well, I mean I have never seen a child of mine born. I wasn't around when Lizzie was born. She was two months old when I first saw her, all pink and perfect and pretty."

Blakesley lifted a serious eyebrow. "You realize that the stork doesn't deliver them that way, right?"

He fought off a grin at her teasing. "No shit?"

"No shit."

"You're a smart ass, you know that?"

"Maybe so, but at least I'm not crying over the thought of a little bit of blood."

Beck broke down into soft laughter, holding Blakesley's hand and kissing it. Suddenly, he seemed a lot more relaxed than he had just moments earlier. Blakesley was laughing because he was. He seemed a little slap-happy.

"I swear," he said as he shook his head, "put me on the field of battle and I can take anything thrown at me. Battle wounds, guts hanging out, bullets flying over my head... you name it, I can take it. I'm still standing when others fall around me. But having a baby... I feel like an idiot. I feel like I'm going to vomit."

Blakesley kept laughing. "Buck up, Seavington. You can do this. Just breathe and push."

He stood up from the chair, leaned over, and kissed her. "You just tell me what you need me to do and I'll do it," he said, kissing her again. "But weren't we supposed to take childbirth classes for this?"

"Uh... you were in Afghanistan. You couldn't make the classes."

"That's an affirmative."

"No worries. I'll coach you through this. But if you don't do it right, I'll yell at you."

"Yes, ma'am."

"Are you in, then?"

"I'm in, baby. All the way in."

"Actually, I think that's what put us in this situation in the first place."

He laughed at her. She was in rare form, happy that Colt was on his way and thrilled that Beck would be at her side to experience it. He was fine, too, laughing and joking with her for about the first hour until the contractions became progressively stronger. The laughter faded after that but Blakesley was still rolling with the contractions, still in good spirits. As Beck fed her pieces of ice, her regular doctor finally showed up. The man did a quick ultrasound to make sure the baby was in the correct position and he was, already engaging in the birth canal.

By the beginning of the third hour of labor, the contractions were starting to come fast and heavy, and Blakesley had entered the realm of misery. Gabrielle came down from ICU and spent a few moments holding Blakesley's hand, comforting her when the strong contractions would hit, and braiding her long hair to keep it out of the way. Very quickly, the pains became very strong and very hard and Blakesley was having some difficulty breathing through them. But she managed, keeping her cool, focusing on what she needed to do to bring the baby into the world.

Although this was a new world for Beck, he was deeply

impressed with Blakesley's tolerance and demeanor. He could see on the monitor that her contractions were peaking at nearly 100% but she never let out more than a soft grunt. She breathed and remained focused, and Beck held her hand the entire time, telling her how well she was doing and how much he loved her. It was a bonding experience beyond anything he could have imagined, this woman whom he loved with all his heart and soul, giving birth to his child. He'd never known that kind of connection existed and it made him feel a part of her like he had never felt with anyone else.

At exactly three hours and twenty-three minutes since her water broke, the baby was beginning to crown. Blakesley was in a seated position, bent nearly in half as she pushed in response to the doctor's direction. The doctor was calm, working quickly to aspirate the baby's nose and mouth as his head came through the birth canal. Beck, holding on to Blakesley's right knee, could just see the red, little head. He was filled with excitement and fear.

Blakesley was controlled as she gripped her thighs and pushed. Beck gently teased her, telling her that she looked like someone who had done this kind of thing before, which drew a weak smile. She was exhausted and rightfully so. She'd done the entire labor and delivery without any medication even though they had offered it to her. She was too concerned that it might somehow affect the baby so she declined. She was coming to regret that decision but she wasn't going to let anyone know. Besides, it was too late for all of that.

A particularly strong pain gripped her and Blakesley grunted as she pushed hard. The baby abruptly slipped out into the doctor's hands and she fell back against Beck, exhausted, feeling the ultimate relief that the baby was finally out. The nurse clamped the umbilical cord as the doctor suctioned out the nose and mouth. A weak cry filled the air.

"Uh...," the doctor held the red, squirming baby up to the eager parents. "Does anyone see anything wrong with this picture?"

Blakesley was too wiped out to guess what he was talking

about. She counted ten fingers and toes, and a big screaming mouth. It was Beck who finally spoke up. He just started laughing.

"I'm firing you," he told the doctor. "Don't you know the difference between a boy and a girl?"

Blakesley blinked, focusing on what he was saying. It took her a moment to realize that there was a vagina where there was supposed to be a penis. She started laughing.

"A girl," she crowed. "It's a girl!"

Beck was giggling like a fool. He wrapped his arms around Blakesley, hugging her tightly, laughing with her. He realized that he wasn't disappointed. Now he had a little girl that would look just like his wife. No, he wasn't disappointed at all.

"Thank you, baby," he kissed her repeatedly. "She's beautiful. Thank you so much."

Blakesley kissed him, tears in her eyes, before taking the baby from the nurse and laying her on her chest. Blakesley and Beck inspected her, counting little fingers and toes, commenting on the fact that she had Blakesley's nose. The doctor asked Beck if he wanted to cut the cord, which he carefully did, returning his attention to his wife and new daughter, aware that he was feeling more love and contentment than he had ever known in his life. He never knew it was possible to love something as much as he loved Blakesley and the little girl squirming on his wife's chest.

The nurse eventually took the baby away and weighed and measured her, and the neonatologist declared her perfectly healthy. Little Emmalynn Rose Seavington weighed five and a half pounds and was eighteen inches long, not bad for a preemie. As her hair dried in the warm air, it was a shiny, brilliant blond and she had a lot of it. As the doctor threw a few stitches into Blakesley where she tore a little during the birth, Beck hovered over his new daughter in the incubator, marveling at her perfect beauty. He was a man in love.

Cleaned up and stitched up, Blakesley was moved into a private room with the baby, who she put on the breast right away. Baby Emma suckled ravenously while Beck watched with awe.

THE SUNSET HOUR   379

"Really?" he breathed. "Is this really happening?"

Blakesley looked up from her new daughter. "Really," she whispered. "I love you so much."

He looked up from the baby, tears in his eyes. "I love you, too," he murmured. "I feel like my life has come full circle somehow. I never truly thought I would have everything I ever wanted in life, but I do. I really do."

Blakesley smiled at him, touching his face as he kissed her fingers. When Emma was finished nursing, she handed her over to Beck, who showed surprising confidence with the newborn as he burped her for the first time. After that, he wrapped the baby up and just held her. Blakesley's last vision before she fell asleep was of Beck gazing adoringly at their newborn.

When she woke up some time later, it was to Beck's soft snores. In the darkness, she could see that he had fallen asleep on the chair, the baby curled up on his chest sleeping like an angel. His big arms were around the baby, holding her strongly and protectively. Daddy had his little girl, and he was bonding with her. It was the sweetest thing Blakesley had ever seen.

She watched both of them sleep long into the night.

TWENTY-SIX

IT WAS seven o'clock in the morning and Nikki heard her cell phone go off. That wasn't unusual since her mother, a lonely woman still living in Los Angeles, would often call Nikki early in the morning before the Masterson girls got up. On this foggy morning after the birth of Emma Seavington, Nikki rolled over and picked up the phone before she even looked at the caller I.D.

"Hello?" she said sleepily.

A familiar voice from the past was on the other end. "Hey, Nikki," the man said cheerfully. "It's Ed. Ed Masterson."

Nikki rolled over and nearly fell off the futon. She grabbed the edge of the night stand to keep from falling, so great her surprise.

"Mr. Masterson?" she repeated, startled and frightened. "Uh... hi...?"

On the other end of the phone, Ed laughed. "Sorry to call you so early," he said. "I called your mother last night and she gave me your cell phone number. I hope it's okay. She says you're with Blakesley and the girls."

Nikki was terrified. She sat up in bed, not sure what to say or do. "I... yes, sir, I am," she said, her voice trembling. "The girls are sleeping right now. I...."

Ed cut her off. "That's okay," he said. "I don't want to talk to them right now but I would like to know where they are. They're my girls, Nikki. I have a right to know."

Nikki was near tears. She didn't know what to do, very fearful of the man she had worked for. "I...," she stammered. "Mr. Masterson, I think you should talk to Blakesley. She should tell you."

"Well, I would talk to her if I knew where she was or knew her phone number. No one seems to know anything and I can't get a hold of Marshall."

Nikki was shaking as she sat at the end of the bed, trying to think fast but she wasn't very good at it. She wasn't very bright, either. "She moved, Mr. Masterson."

"I know, Nikki. Where did she move to?"

"Uh... you know, down to San Diego because of the family...."

"The old house?" Ed interrupted. "Did she really buy that old thing? She'd been talking about that for years. I can't believe she finally pulled the trigger."

"Yes, she bought the old house, but...."

"Thank you, Nikki. I really appreciate your help. But do me a favor and don't tell Blakesley I called, okay? She doesn't need to know. In fact, to show my appreciation, your mom is finally getting that new car she needs. It's a gift. So please don't tell Blakesley that I called. She doesn't need to know right now. I just wanted to know where my girls are."

Nikki was in tears. "What are you going to do?"

"Do? Nothing. Thanks again for your help, I appreciate it."

The line went dead. Nikki, knowing she had done something very bad, sat on the bed and sobbed.

———

"Mommy!" Crosby was jumping up and down. "Can I hold Emma, please? Please, please?"

Blakesley was in the kitchen, putting dinner in the crockpot, as Crosby and Charlotte clamored at her feet. Six days after Emma's birth, she was feeling great, although Beck often followed her around the house and scolded her if he thought she was doing too much. He was at the base now, which was why she had made lunch, cleaned up the kitchen and put dinner on. She felt active and alive. Throwing away the paper towel in her hand, she took Crosby's hand and went into the living room.

Betty and Beck Sr. were sitting on the leather couch, Betty cradling her new granddaughter. They had come down the day after the birth to see the baby and, so far, had been fixtures on the couch since their arrival. Baby Emma had hardly spent any time in her bassinet with a father and grandparents and siblings always wanting to hold her. Blakesley was afraid she was already raising a very spoiled child.

"How's she doing?" Blakesley asked, leaning over Betty to take a look at her sleeping daughter.

Betty was deeply in love with the little, blond bundle. "She's fine," she said rather dreamily. "She likes to snuggle."

Blakesley grinned at Beck Sr. when the man looked up and winked at her. "I wouldn't know," he said. "I haven't been allowed to hold her yet."

Betty shushed her husband as Blakesley laughed, quieting the jumping girls at her side. "Let Grandma Betty hold her for a while, okay?" she told Crosby. "You can hold her tonight, I promise. Right now, I want you to make sure the playroom is picked up, please? Help me out a little."

Crosby was unhappy and did as she was told, but not before stopping by Betty and kissing Emma on the head. As Charlotte and Crosby skipped off to the playroom, Blakesley stood in front of Betty with her hands on her hips.

"I'm sorry to break this up, but I need to feed her," she said.

Betty looked rather sad that she had to give up her prize, but she carefully handed the baby over to Blakesley. Blakesley turned for the bedroom.

"Do you want to come and watch?" she asked Betty.

Betty got up off the couch right away to follow. Beck Sr. passed on the offer before it was fully delivered, laughing as he turned on the big television. Blakesley and Betty went into the master bedroom and Blakesley climbed onto the bed, positioning pillows and getting comfortable as she settled in. Unbuttoning her shirt, she put Emma on the nipple and the baby began to feed eagerly.

Betty sat on the bed beside the pair, watching with a smile on her face. She reached out to hold a tiny little hand.

"She looks so much like Beck did as a baby," she said softly. "He was a good eater, too."

Blakesley stroked the blond head. "Was Beck a big baby?"

Betty nodded. "He was almost ten pounds," she replied. "After a child that size, I didn't want any more. He nearly tore me to shreds."

Blakesley understood. "I wondered why he didn't have any siblings," she said. "A ten pound baby might do me in, too. I've been lucky – all of my girls have been seven pounds or less."

Betty stroked the velvety skin, her gaze on the baby. "Beck had a sister born a year before he was," she said softly. "She was a stillbirth."

Blakesley looked at her, shocked, and tears filled her eyes. "I'm so sorry," she whispered. "I didn't know."

Betty smiled bravely. "He doesn't, either," she said. "There was no reason to tell him. We were just so grateful when Beck was born healthy that we really didn't think about having any more children."

Blakesley grinned, blinking away the tears. "And now you have five granddaughters," she giggled. "That's kind of an overload."

Betty laughed. "I love every one of them," she said. "Cadee, Crosby and Charlotte are such a blessing. I can't remember when I haven't loved them."

Blakesley clasped the woman's fingers with her free hand. "Thank you," she whispered sincerely. "My mother would have liked to have heard that. You're the only grandmother they have, you know."

"What about their father's mother?"

Blakesley shrugged, looking back at the baby. "She died before I met their father," she said. "I never knew her."

The conversation fell silent after that as Emma suckled furiously. As Blakesley was switching her to the other breast, Beck's truck pulled up in the backyard and they could hear the truck door slam. Betty stood up from the bed and pulled back the curtains from the French door, opening it for her son.

"We're in here, Beck," she called.

A few seconds later, Beck took the steps two at a time up the porch and appeared in the doorway. He was smiling the minute he came through, kissing his mother and heading straight for the bed where Blakesley was nursing. He sat down beside her and wrapped both her and the baby up in his arms, kissing Blakesley's cheek and nuzzling her sweetly.

"Hi, baby," he murmured, looking down at Emma and kissing her blond head. "How are my girls?"

Blakesley watched him as he kissed and stroked the infant. "We're fine," she said. "How are things at the base?"

"Busy."

"Saving the world?"

"Pretty much."

"Are you home for the night?"

He nodded and released them from his embrace. "As far as I know," he said. "Some of the guys want to come over and see Emma. I hope you don't mind that I invited them over tonight."

Blakesley shook her head. "I just started dinner," she said. "But it's only enough for us. I suppose we can order out with more coming."

Beck waved her off. "You let me worry about that," he said, bending down to unlace his big, black boots. "Where is everybody?"

Blakesley returned her focus to the baby. "Your dad is in the living room watching television, Crosby and Charlotte are supposed to be cleaning up the playroom, Lizzie and Cadee are

THE SUNSET HOUR 385

upstairs, and my dad and Gabrielle are coming over for dinner. Sounds like we're going to have a full house tonight."

Beck nodded, pulling his boots off. "I want you to take it easy, okay?" he said. "I'll take care of everyone. You just relax."

Blakesley shrugged in agreement, watching the baby as she alternately dozed and nursed. Beck went to go wash his hands and change his shirt, preparing for the opportunity to claim his child, which wasn't long in coming. When Emma was finished nursing, Blakesley handed her over to her father, who took her tenderly.

It was a little chaotic at the Seavington home that night. Along with the family of seven, there was Beck Sr., Betty, Marshall, Gabrielle, Gina and Spike, two of Lizzie's friends from school, and seven officers from Beck's team. Beck was rather regimented about who he let get near his daughter much less touch her; no one could be sick or recently ill. Everyone had to wash their hands. Beck's men just wanted to see her and no one really made an attempt to hold her; mostly, they just brought beer for Beck to celebrate him becoming a father again. It turned into a big celebration that went on into the night.

Gina had to take Spike home early because he had a belly ache. Marshall and Gabrielle bowed out early, leaving Betty and Beck Sr. to babysit with Emma as Blakesley and Beck put the little girls to bed. Crosby wanted a story, so Beck lay down with her on her twin bed and read her two stories. Even though he had a living room full of guests, his girls were most important and he took the time with them. With two stories read, he had to fight down additional requests for stories, kissing pouting faces as he shut off the light and closed the door. Blakesley was already in with Cadee and they put her to bed, too, with Nikki now sleeping in the very small fourth bedroom next to Cadee's room. Peeking in on Lizzie and her two friends, they completed their sweep of the upper floor and ended up back downstairs with Beck's men.

Blakesley sat with Beck and his men for about a half hour before pleading exhaustion and retiring to the bedroom. Betty and Beck Sr. were sitting on the bed, watching television, as Emma slept peacefully in her grandfather's arms. Blakesley grinned as she walked up to the pair and peered down at her child.

"Well," she said with satisfaction. "It looks like Grandpa finally got to hold his granddaughter."

Beck Sr. wriggled his eyebrows. "It was a battle, let me tell you," he exaggerated. "Betty is fierce. I almost lost an eye."

Blakesley laughed softly. "Well, I'm glad you got your turn," she said. "I think I'm going to go to bed now, so you two are relieved until tomorrow."

Beck Sr. and Betty climbed off the bed, and Beck Sr. carefully put his granddaughter in her lovely new bassinet. The baby fussed a little bit but Blakesley turned her on her side and put a pillow against her back, covering her with a fluffy blanket. The three of them stood there and watched the baby settle down, suckling her little pacifier furiously.

"The question now is how long she's going to stay there," Blakesley whispered. "Beck will come in here and bring her to bed with him."

Betty smiled. "He's attached to her."

Blakesley nodded her head. "Yes, he is, but I don't like him sleeping with her. It scares me. I'm afraid either one of us will roll over on her. Besides, she needs to learn to sleep in her own bed."

"You're mean, Mommy," Beck Sr. grunted.

Blakesley grinned at him as Betty silently shooed him out of the room. Whispering their goodnights, Blakesley shut the door behind them, went into the bathroom, and got ready for bed. She could hear the men laughing in the living room as she scrubbed her face and settled in to bed. Checking on the sleeping baby one last time and pulling the bassinet up next to her side of the bed, she turned off the light and began flipping through the channels.

Nothing much seemed to be on the tube on the late Thursday night. She watched the cooking channel for a while before flipping to the news. It was the top of the hour on the late news and after two relatively boring stories, she picked up the remote to turn the television off when a graphic of the Hollyhock Restaurant suddenly appeared on screen. Shocked, Blakesley turned up the volume. The female anchor with short, red hair was speaking in a monotone.

"... nearly two years ago convicted Ed Masterson of the murder for Maricelle Graciano at the Hollyhock Restaurant in Hollywood. Once the go-to restaurant for the stars, the murder caused sensational headlines with the trial that followed. However, our sources have received information that a key witness in the murder has recanted his statement, which put Masterson on appeal before a grand jury. With no physical evidence other than the eyewitness linking Ed Masterson to the murder, sources tell NBC news that Ed Masterson will soon be a free man. Now, moving on to the health report, Americans are...."

Blakesley shut the television off. She sat there, quivering uncontrollably, grabbing at her cell phone and going into the bathroom to call her lawyer so she wouldn't wake the baby. Robert's phone rang six times before going to voicemail and she left a rather rattling message.

Hanging up the call, she went back into the bedroom and tried to calm down. Climbing in to bed, she lay there for what seemed like hours, listening to Beck and his men out in the living room laughing and talking. It was comforting to listen to them, knowing that nothing bad could happen to her or the girls with Beck around. He wouldn't let it. He'd kill Ed if the man tried anything and that brought her a great deal of comfort.

Blakesley was finally drifting off to sleep when Beck came into the bedroom quietly. She could hear him moving around, going into the bathroom to brush his teeth, then coming back out to take his clothes off. She could hear the soft drift of his jeans as he tossed them aside. Then he came around the side of the bed and she peeped an eye open, watching him bend over the bassinet to look at the baby. The moment he stuck his hands in to lift her out, Blakesley stopped him.

"Hold it," she hissed. "Leave her alone, Daddy. She's sleeping soundly. You're just going to wake her up."

He retracted his hands like the kid who got caught with the cookie jar. She could see his teeth gleaming in the darkness.

"You're supposed to be asleep," he said.

She rolled onto her back and looked at him. "I knew you were going to come in here and try to steal her," she whispered, grinning. "Get into bed with me and leave her alone."

"Please?"

"Absolutely not," she pulled the covers back on the bed beside her. "Get into bed and snuggle with me."

He leapt into bed over her, jostling her, listening to her giggle as he swallowed her up in his big arms and nuzzled her neck. Nuzzling turned into heated kisses as he suckled her earlobe, and she could feel his stiff erection against her buttocks.

"You're going to make yourself miserable if you don't stop," she murmured.

He stopped kissing her and sighed heavily. "I know," he groaned. "I can't help it. Sorry. I'm a dirty dog, I know."

She laughed. "No, you're not, but you know what the doctor said. No sex for six weeks at least."

"Can I at least play with you?"

She turned to look at him. "Seriously?" she wanted to know. "I just had a baby six days ago and you want to know if you can *play* with me?"

He looked property contrite, but there was humor to it. "Bad question?"

She shrugged. "If you touch my boobs, they'll leak all over you, and if you try to touch something else, there are nine stitches down there that won't react too well. That's the price you pay for your new daughter. Sorry, I didn't make the rules."

He grinned and pulled her close, snuggling against her. "I don't care about the leaking part."

She gasped with soft outrage, slapping weakly at his arm. "No, Beck. Not now. Talk to me next week and see how I feel, but not now. I'm too sore and don't feel particularly sexy."

His humor faded and he kissed her, hugging her tightly. "I

know, I'm sorry," he said. "I'll leave you alone. But you're still the sexiest and most gorgeous woman I've ever seen, no matter what."

She grinned. "Nice save." She settled down with him behind her. As they lay there in the darkness, her eyes remained open and her smile faded. She couldn't help the heavy thoughts on her mind. "I saw something on the news tonight about Ed."

Beck had his face shoved into the back of her head, her hair all over his face and neck. He often slept like that because the scent of her brought him extreme comfort. Her statement had his eyes opening.

"What about him?" he mumbled.

"The news said that his case had been appealed and he'd be a free man soon."

"Did you call your lawyer?"

"I left him a voicemail. I can't understand why he wouldn't call me to tell me this personally. Why did I have to see it on the news?"

Beck rolled over and looked at her in the darkness. "You seem pretty calm about it."

She shrugged. "I don't know why. I should be freaking out, but I just can't seem to get worked up about it. I feel kind of numb, to be truthful."

Beck could see her lovely profile in the shadows, studying her expression for a moment. "Baby, I've never asked you what really happened with all of that," he said, "because I figured you'd tell me when you were ready. It's been almost a year and you haven't told me anything about it so now, as your husband, I'm asking. What really went on with you and Ed and all of that mess?"

She rolled onto her side so she was facing him. "It was pretty much just what I'd told you," she said quietly. "He murdered his whore and then the girls and I endured the trial that followed. What I didn't know was that through his mistress, he began laundering money for a branch of the Colombian drug cartel, a branch that called themselves the *la ira de Dios*."

"The wrath of God," he murmured in translation.

Blakesley nodded, snuggling up to him in the darkness. "Anyway, the whole trial was just sickening. The lawyers hammered away at witnesses, at Ed's character, and my character, all sorts of terrible things. The defense kept trying to pull me into it by saying I knew what was going on but the cops cleared me of that."

"Did you know what was going on?" he asked.

She shook her head. "Not a clue," she said. "I guess it was my fault that I didn't know. Ed and I had kind of drifted apart since Charlotte's birth, so I just didn't pay a whole lot of attention to him or what he was doing."

"Why did you drift apart?"

She shrugged. "I guess you had to know Ed and the kind of relationship we had," she whispered. "He was an extremely arrogant man. At first, I found that kind of attractive but as the years went by, it just got old. He was very hard on me, on my appearance, afraid I would let myself go and embarrass him."

Beck scowled. "Seriously?"

She nodded. "He was really adamant that I take care of myself, which I do anyway, but I was always afraid that if I got breast cancer or had a bad accident and was scarred, he would just up and leave. He was just that superficial. Anyway, I think I started distancing myself from him over the years just as an act of self-protection. He got mean and critical and aloof as time went on. By the time he was arrested, I was shocked and upset, of course, but part of me didn't really care. That sounds cruel, but it was true."

Beck digested the information. "Did he ever hit you or threaten you? I mean, the guy murdered his mistress. I'd be surprised if he didn't lift a hand to you or showed that side of himself to you during the course of your marriage."

She shook her head. "Never," she said firmly. "In all the years I knew him, he never even hinted at that, which is why a murder charge really shocked me. I had no idea he was capable of that kind of thing."

"So what did the Colombians do to you?"

"Do? Nothing. But they tried. Ed was preparing to spill the

names of the big gang leaders in Los Angeles so the Colombians thought that if they threatened or killed me, Ed would keep his mouth shut. They messed with my brakes, which ended up being nothing, thank God. Because my car crashed into a stop sign, the mechanic discovered what had happened. Then one day when I was picking Cadee up from school, someone took a shot at me but hit my car door instead."

He stroked her head. "That's awful. What happened after that?"

She shifted, settling down against him and feeling increasingly sleepy. "LAPD really stepped up my protection and the protection of the girls. Ed ended up not testifying about the cartel in a plea deal, so the Colombians left me alone. I haven't heard from them or about them since, thank God. That was really a scary time."

He kissed her forehead. "I'll bet," he murmured. "So if Ed is released, what then? Will he try to contact you? I'll bet the man will want to see his children and maybe have even some kind of custody arrangement."

Blakesley suddenly pulled away from him, sitting up and glaring at him. "I have full custody of my girls," she hissed. "He's never going to get anywhere near them. I came down to San Diego to start a new life, and that means a life without that bastard. I have you now and you're all the father my girls will ever need. I'll kill Ed if he tries anything, I swear it."

He pulled her back down on the bed next to him, soothing her gently. "No worries," he promised, kissing her angry cheek. "I'll kill him first. Those girls are mine."

She settled down quickly, snuggling into his embrace and closing her eyes. "Yes, they are," she whispered. "But... this was kind of what I was trying to warn you off of when we first met. Remember I told you the troubles that follow me around? I mean this, although I had no idea that Ed's release would come about."

"Like I said earlier, you seem much calmer than you did when you first found out."

She opened her eyes and looked up at him, seeing his handsome features outlined in the darkness. "It was a knee-jerk reaction," she admitted softly. "Don't get me wrong; I'm still upset about it. But I know that Ed can't hurt me or the girls with you around. We have such a happy life, Beck. Nothing can hurt us at all, not even Ed and the drama that surrounds him."

He smiled and kissed her, growing more amorous until she pulled away. He was growing engorged again and groaned miserably when she laughed at his agony.

"You belong to me, as do those three little, blond girls upstairs asleep," he whispered. "If Ed Masterson comes anywhere near my wife and family, he'll have to answer to me, pure and simple. And not even Ed and the entire Colombian drug cartel can survive a bout with the U.S. Navy, I promise you that."

"I know," she said as she kissed him. "I believe you."

"Do you think he knows you remarried?"

She shrugged. "No one from my side would have told him. I doubt it."

Beck sighed faintly and snuggled down with her, feeling pretty weary himself. "Maybe you'd better find a picture of him so if he shows up on our doorstep, I know who he is."

"I'll see what I can do," she agreed. Then she paused. "Beck?"

"What, baby?"

"Thank you. For everything, thank you."

He hugged her as they both began to drift off to sleep. Blakesley was just about there when fusses and cries came from the bassinet beside the bed. She sighed heavily and opened her eyes just about the time Beck was climbing out of bed. He went to the bassinet and picked the baby up as she began to cry for her midnight feeding, handing her off to Blakesley when she unbuttoned her pajama top.

Lying beside his wife and watching her feed the newborn, Beck couldn't help his thoughts from lingering on Ed Masterson and the man's potential release from prison. He'd never really given the man any thought the entire time he'd known Blakesley, but now, he was starting to think heavily on him, seriously wondering how he would react if Ed found out where Blakesley was and came to see her.

As Beck watched Emma tug hungrily at Blakesley's breast, he was starting to feel extremely protective and extremely territorial of his girls. Not that he wasn't always, but now there was more to it. He knew for a fact that if the man came around, he'd probably strike first and ask questions later. For the hell that man put Blakesley through, he deserved all that and more.

————

Blakesley had received a call that morning from the State of California Real Estate division about the Benjamin and Dulcinea Earp home regarding all of the artifacts and personal family possessions. As Beck got dressed to take the girls to school and head over to the base, Blakesley made breakfast and chatted with the real estate agent who had handled the transaction.

Lizzie wanted toast, eggs and sausage while Cadee wanted eggs and cheese. Crosby wanted everything everyone else did and Charlotte cried because she wasn't allowed to eat leftover cupcakes from the night before. Beck entered the kitchen to the chaos, kissing Blakesley as she cradled the phone between her shoulder and ear while manipulating the frying pan full of scrambled eggs. Beck just grinned at her multitasking, telling Lizzie to help Blakesley out and make the toast.

As Beck fussed with the collar of his khaki naval shirt, Charlotte climbed down from her chair and tried to talk him into letting her have the cupcakes. Somehow, Alfie got in and the dog wedged himself underneath the breakfast bar, waiting for any food to fall to the floor. Beck put Charlotte back on her stool and was trying to get the dog out from underneath the breakfast bar when the cry of a newborn filled the air to add to the bedlam.

Lizzie dropped what she was doing and ran into the master bedroom as the other three girls tried to follow. It was the most comical thing Beck had ever seen but something that was now commonplace in their home - Emma would cry and all four girls would go running to the source like a stampede. Beck kept the little girls on their stools while he followed Lizzie into the bedroom, but Lizzie was faster than her old man and carefully picked Emma up from her bassinet. The teenager was quite competent with the baby and Beck put his arm around her shoulders, grinning at his daughter as she cuddled her new sister.

"You kind of like her, don't you?" he asked.

Lizzie nodded. "She's so sweet," she cooed. "I love her so much. I never thought I'd have a baby sister, not ever."

Beck kissed her on the temple. "Now you've got four."

Lizzie grinned. "It's pretty cool."

He laughed. "Let's go get her fed, okay?"

Very carefully, Lizzie walked back to the kitchen with Emma in her arms. Blakesley, still on the phone with the real estate guy, saw the baby and went straight to the freezer. She pulled out one of the many bottles she had filled with breast milk and ran hot water into a cup, putting the bottle into it to defrost it. As the milk defrosted, Beck found himself begging his oldest daughter for the baby.

"Just let me hold her before I go," he pleaded. "I won't get to see her until tonight."

Lizzie carefully rocked the baby. "But you get to feed her at night, Dad. I don't."

Beck threw up his arms. "If you want to feed her during the night, be my guest. I have no problem with that."

"Can she sleep in my room?"

He shook his head, smiling. "No, baby girl," he said. "She needs to stay with her mother for now."

With a reluctant face, Lizzie handed over the baby to her father's waiting arms. Beck greedily soaked up the time with the infant, soothing her as she hungrily fussed until Blakesley abruptly hung up the phone. She went straight to Beck.

"Here," she said. "Give her to me. You finish with the eggs."

Beck made his displeasure known but he dutifully switched

places with her and handed over the baby. Blakesley sat on the stool vacated by Lizzie, uncovered a plump breast, and plopped Emma on the nipple. The infant quieted immediately.

Lizzie was still standing by the sink with the half-defrosted bottle of breast milk in her hand. She dramatically pouted.

"But I wanted to feed her," she whined.

Blakesley grinned at her step-daughter. "You still can," she assured her. "This will quiet her enough to give the bottle time to defrost. Pop it in the microwave for a few seconds. That will speed things up."

Happy again, Lizzie did as she was told. Soon enough, she was seated on the stool with the baby in her arms, carefully feeding her a couple of ounces of breast milk. Cadee, Crosby and Charlotte hung all over Lizzie, watching their sister eat and completely ignoring the eggs that Beck had laid out before them. As Blakesley buttoned up her shirt, Beck finished with his kitchen duty and put his arm around her.

"All of our girls," he grinned as he kissed her forehead. "All five of them."

Together, they watched for a few moments as the girls fed the baby. It was sweet and heartwarming. Beck finally gave his wife a squeeze.

"I hate to break this up, but we've got to get going," he told her, going to the stools and lifting Crosby and Charlotte down. "Go get your stuff. The bus for school is leaving in five minutes."

The little girls scattered and Cadee soon followed, but more slowly. She was jealous that Lizzie got to feed the baby and she didn't. As she stomped out of the kitchen, Beck went to gather his keys and wallet. Blakesley eventually took the baby back from Lizzie so she could go get her things. Alone in the kitchen feeding Emma the rest of the bottle, Blakesley glanced up as Beck came back into the room.

"I've got two meetings today and both should run long, so I'm not sure when I'll be home," he told her. "One of them is the final interview for the position at the Warfare Center, so keep your fingers crossed."

Blakesley smiled. "You'll do great," she assured him. "You know how much they want you."

He wriggled his eyebrows modestly, bending over to kiss Emma's head and then his wife's sweet lips.

"What are your plans for the day?" he asked.

She wiped her lip-gloss from his lips. "I'm going to head up to the old homestead to start looking through the old artifacts to see if there's anything we want to keep," she replied. "That's what the real estate agent and I were talking about when you came into the kitchen. I had it written into the sale contract that our family has first right of refusal for anything on the grounds."

Beck gave her a very unhappy expression. "Baby, I don't want Emma up there," he said. "I don't even want you up there. That whole place is...."

She put up a hand, cutting him off. "I know," she said softly, firmly, "but escrow is going to close at the end of the week and I need to get in there while I can. After that, it's out of my hands."

"Can you at least wait until I get off work?"

She pursed her lips irritably. "You just said you don't know when you'll be home," she pointed out. "I'm going to take Nikki with me so she can sit in the car and watch Emma while I check out the stuff they've found. Emma won't go in the house at all, I promise."

He still wasn't happy. "Can we go tomorrow?" he tried again.

She grunted, frustrated. "Beck, I promise I will be careful," she stressed. "I'll watch where I'm going, I won't go in the room with the pit unless someone else is with me, and I'll be very, very careful. Okay?"

"Do I have a choice?"

"No."

He rolled his eyes. "Fine," he was starting to get grumpy. "You just make sure Emma stays in the car with Nikki. I don't want the baby out and about. She's not even two weeks old yet, for Christ's sake."

Blakesley nodded with strained patience. "Yes, Daddy."

"I'm serious."

"So am I. Don't you trust me any more than that?"

He softened somewhat. "You know I do," his tone softened. "I just don't want to see you get hurt."

"I won't, I promise."

He scratched his head, knowing it was the best he could do with her. She was a stubborn and determined woman.

"Speaking of Nikki," he said, "does she seem a little strange to you since the baby was born?"

Blakesley shrugged, putting Emma on her shoulder to burp her now that the milk was gone. "No," she said. "She's always kind of quiet. Why? Does she seem strange to you?"

Beck thought on the question. "Nothing I can put my finger on." He lifted his big shoulders. "I don't really know her so I guess I can't make that judgment on whether she's been abnormally quiet lately."

"I think you scare her."

She was grinning so Beck leaned over and kissed her again. "I've got to go," he said, listening to the girls as they gathered in the entry. "I'll call you later. Love you."

"Love you, too. Good luck today."

He gave her one of his best sexy smiles, winked at her, and was gone.

————

Blakesley felt a good deal of sadness as she pulled into the driveway of the old homestead. So much of her family's history were here, a depth of history that a lot of American families didn't have, and she was sorry to have to let it go. Not that she regretted selling the place, but still, she felt somewhat guilty for having been the weak link in the Earp chain. She couldn't hold on to the house.

The day was mild and she parked her BMW SUV underneath a thick oak tree for shade. She had brought Gina along because the woman wasn't working that day and because she'd never seen the house before. Plus, Beck felt much better with Gina going along, convinced that Gina would keep Blakesley out of trouble and keep an eye on her.

Nikki sat in the back with Emma, who was sleeping peacefully. Rolling down the windows to provide some air in the mild temperatures, Blakesley told Nikki to stay in the car with Emma and under no circumstance should she leave or get out. Nikki had her cell phone and promised to call Blakesley if she needed her.

Satisfied, Blakesley and Gina climbed out of the car and headed for the public wing. She was still wearing her maternity jeans even though she'd lost almost all of the baby weight, and a pretty turquoise colored empire-waist blouse that made her look like she had enormous boobs. Beck thought it was the greatest shirt ever, but the truth was that it was comfortable. Blakesley couldn't resist wearing her platform sandals, shoes she had been banned from wearing during pregnancy, so feeling moderately fashionable, she strolled up to the public wing and stuck her head into the open door.

"Hello?" she called.

A faint response came from somewhere in the house. Wandering into the great room with its gigantic fireplace, Gina looked around with awe.

"Oh, my God," she gasped. "This place is amazing."

Blakesley looked around as well, the last look at something that belonged to her. "I know," she agreed. "It's been in my family for over one hundred and fifty years."

Gina was over by the great plugged fireplace. "Beck told me," she said. "He said that your cousin was Wyatt Earp."

Blakesley nodded. "My great-great-great-great grandfather and Wyatt's father were brothers."

"That's really cool."

Blakesley just smiled and shrugged. "It is, kind of," she said, pointing to the fireplace. "See that tile? It's all original to the house. Did you see it when we came in?"

Gina nodded. "Gorgeous," she peered at the fireplace. "This thing is massive, isn't it? If you get a good blaze going in there, you'd burn up the whole damn house."

Blakesley giggled. "It's plugged," she replied. "The contractor was in the process of trying to restore it but all of that was halted when I sold the house. I don't know what the state will do, if anything."

As Gina wandered over to look more closely at the hand-painted Mexican tiles on the mantel, Dr. Welton emerged from another doorway.

"Good morning," he said cheerily.

Blakesley turned to look at him. "Good morning," she replied. "I was talking to one of the real estate agents this morning and he told me to head over here to go through all of the stuff you found to see if any of it was near and dear to my family."

Dr. Welton nodded. "Absolutely. There's a ton of stuff."

Gina stepped forward and Blakesley introduced her to the archaeologist. Then she refocused on the gist of their conversation.

"Are you still cleaning out that tunnel?"

Dr. Welton motioned the women to follow. "Still," he said. "Watch your step when you come in the room; we've reinforced the pit but it's still dangerous. Just stay clear of it."

Gina took Blakesley's hand when they went into the big, dusty room, peering uncomfortably at the hole in the floor. Dr. Welton took the women around to the nearest table, an eight-foot long plank that was covered in artifacts. Everything was tagged and carefully set out, including the rifle that had Beck's interest. Blakesley pointed at the rifle.

"That's the first thing I'll take," she said. "My husband loved it."

Dr. Welton nodded. "It's a fine piece," he agreed. "Take a look over here. I think there's something you might like."

Blakesley and Gina followed him over to a second table that

had a bunch of smaller items on it. There was a conservator in a chair next to the table, using a giant, lighted magnifying glass to inspect a piece that Blakesley couldn't quite see. Dr. Welton gestured to the table.

"We found all of this stuff in old crates down there," he said. "I hate to say this, but it looks like robbers were using that cave that opens up into the canyon."

Blakesley looked at him curiously. "Why do you say that?"

Dr. Welton carefully picked up the nearest artifact; it was a bag of some kind, velvet, with delicate gold stitching upon the wine-colored fabric.

"This is a lady's purse from the 1880's," he explained. "There were dozens of them down there, some picked clean and some not. We found purses with money, watches, jewelry, you name it. Look at all of the jewelry we found."

Both Gina and Blakesley gasped as Dr. Welton indicated rows upon rows of very carefully organized jewelry. Ear bobs were kept together, a spectacular array with fine stones in them, brooches were kept together, rings and necklaces and other fine valuables. It was a magnificent cache of jewels and Blakesley reached into the midst, carefully plucking out a diamond ring that had to be three carats in size. It was gorgeous.

"You got all of this out of the purses?" she asked, awed.

Dr. Welton nodded. "Tons," he cleared his throat and motioned her to follow him. She did, with the diamond ring still in her hand and Gina on her heels, until Dr. Welton came to a halt near the big double doors that opened up onto the grounds. He faced Blakesley seriously.

"Look," he said softly, "I could lose my job for suggesting this, but I happen to know that the state didn't pay you nearly what the property was worth."

Blakesley kept a good poker face. "How would you know that?"

Welton wriggled his eyebrows. "People talk," he said frankly. "If you claim all of that jewelry, plus some other valuables we've found, it would more than make up for what the state screwed you out of. I know you have first right of refusal for all of these artifacts. You could just claim them all as a whole and then go through them at your leisure, donating what you wanted back to the Benjamin and Dulcinea Earp Museum so we can put them on display when this house becomes a public tour."

Blakesley's eyes were big on him. "I was thinking about doing that," she admitted. "I'll call my lawyer and have him put my claim in writing. There's nothing in the sales contract that says I can't take everything."

Dr. Welton shrugged. "If I were you, I'd do it," he said. "You can leave it here and let us work on it, but you would be the rightful owner."

Blakesley nodded eagerly. "I'll do it," she agreed. "Thank you so much for the suggestion. I'm surprised, actually."

"Why?"

"Because you're not only a state employee, but you're also an archaeologist," she said. "I would think you'd want to see this stuff in a museum."

He gave her half grin. "It will be, eventually, when you donate a good portion back to the Earp Museum. But the jewels and other valuables... call Christie's or Sotheby's. Auction them off and get your money out of it."

Blakesley grinned at him. "I will. Thank you."

He just nodded and headed back towards the table with all of the valuables on it. "Like I was saying," he said loudly for the benefit of the conservator who was in the room, like he hadn't been doing something covert moments earlier, "I think robbers must have used that canyon. We even found old mailbags."

Blakesley slid the big diamond ring on her finger; it fit perfectly and she grinned at Gina happily.

"That's really crazy," she said, peering at more jewelry on the table. "But I was also told that Ben Earp was an outlaw himself. Maybe he did the robbing and just hid the stuff down in the tunnels."

Dr. Welton nodded. "That's very possible," he replied. "There are stories about Ben hiring outlaws to rob stage coaches for him and then hiding the loot. I guess they aren't stories now so much as they're fact."

Blakesley found a big emerald ring with beautiful gold filigree work and she took Gina's hand, slipping it on her middle finger. It was huge and gorgeous, and Gina admired it happily.

"What a crook," Blakesley shook her head as she looked back to the table and focused in on a beautiful sapphire necklace. "But I guess I can't complain too much. His thievery is apparently my gain."

Dr. Welton fought off a grin as she very carefully lifted the sapphire necklace, setting it down and moving in on a luscious pearl necklace. Both Blakesley and Gina were in the process of admiring the pearl collection when someone cleared their throat behind them.

"Excuse me," came a voice. "I was looking for Blakesley Thorne."

Blakesley felt as if she'd been hit in the gut. She suddenly couldn't breathe. She knew the sound of that voice and even as she turned around, the room swayed and she nearly knocked some of the jewelry off the table as she grabbed for something to steady herself with.

As her gaze fell on Ed Masterson in the doorway, Blakesley truly thought she was going to become ill. Shock, horror, everything she could possibly feel was rolling through her head. It took her a moment before she could actually speak.

"Ed," she swallowed. "What... what in the hell are you doing here? How did you find me?"

Ed Masterson smiled at his ex-wife. He was a handsome man, tall, with big brown eyes and a winning smile. He wore an expensive suit with equally expensive shoes, something not out of the ordinary for him. Ed liked money and it showed.

"A little birdie told me you had purchased the old homestead." He looked around. "I've come here every day for three straight days hoping to catch you here and it looks like today is finally my lucky day. The last time I was here was before we were married, with your mother. It hasn't changed much other than the fact that it's apparently all torn up. What's going on?"

Blakesley's heart was pounding in her throat as she made her way to him on shaky legs. She wanted to get him the hell out of there before anything more was said. She was terrified of what he would say or do, knowing now what the man was capable of. She could hardly believe she was looking at him.

"What are you doing here?" she ignored his question and lowered her voice as she approached him. "When were you released?"

Ed shoved his hands in his pockets. "About two weeks ago."

"I didn't see it on the news."

"That's because my legal team fed the media a bunch of bull-shit. We didn't want to turn it into a circus."

"That's an understatement."

He regarded her carefully. "So your lawyer didn't tell you anything?"

She shook her head. "I haven't talked to Robert in a few weeks," she said, her voice trembling as she thought of the lawyer she hadn't been able to get a hold of. "Ed, you've really given me a start. Why are you here?"

Ed was calm. He didn't come across as threatening in the least as he gazed down at his beautiful ex-wife with really big boobs. In fact, she looked fuller and more luscious than he remembered.

"I wanted to see you," he said. "I wanted to see my girls. That's not a crime, Blakesley."

Blakesley was seriously verging on tears. She began to walk, motioning Ed with her. She was so scared she could hardly think straight.

"Ed, I moved down here to get away from you and all of the bad memories in Los Angeles," she said as they entered the big public room. "I didn't want you to know where I was for good reason. You had no right to hire a detective and hunt me down."

Ed's smile faded, thinking that he wouldn't rat Nikki out as the source of the information, at least not yet. "I know you're upset," he said patiently. "But I really want to talk to you. So much has changed, Blakesley. I've changed. I'm so sorry for... well, for everything that happened. I just never had a chance to tell you that."

Blakesley was starting to tear up, frightful tears. "You did tell me that," she said. "On the day of your sentencing when you stood up in front of the entire world and told them how sorry you were for what you did and apologized to me. It was the most humiliating day of my life."

Ed sighed faintly, playing the properly repentant husband. "I can't say I'm sorry enough," he said sincerely. "I was hoping we could talk."

"About what?"

"About the girls. About us."

She shook her head. "Ed, there is no 'us,'" she said flatly. "I've remarried. I just had a baby. I'm happier than I've ever been in my life and even if I weren't, I still wouldn't go back to you. You made my life hell and I can't forgive you for that."

The gentle expression vanished from Ed's face. Now it was his turn to be startled. "You remarried?" he blurted, his face turning red. "I never heard that."

"It wasn't any of your business. I divorced you, remember?"

"Who did you marry?"

"You don't know him," Blakesley replied steadily, feeling more comfortable now that she had the upper hand. "He's in the Navy. He's been wonderful to the girls and we're very lucky to have him. He's a great guy."

"Bullshit," Ed spat. "My girls have a father. They don't need another. I want to see my girls, Blakesley."

Her face hardened. "You're going to have to get a court order for that and I don't see them handing that out to a murderer."

Ed's face turned a deeper shade of red and he took a step back from her, his jaw ticking furiously. It was apparent there was quite a bit he wanted to say but he held his tongue, his jaw working, his veins pulsing in his temples. He had never once during the course of their marriage lifted a hand to her, but Blakesley didn't trust him anymore. She knew what he could do when cornered or infuriated, so she took a step back from him. But Ed suddenly reached out a long arm and grabbed her by the elbow.

"You and I are going to have a talk," he grumbled. "Let's go outside."

Blakesley dug her heels in. "I'm not going anywhere with you." She yanked her arm out of his grasp. "If you touch me again, I'll file assault charges against you. If you want to talk, we'll talk right here where there are witnesses in the next room. I'm not going anywhere with you alone."

That wasn't the answer Ed was looking for but he kept his cool. He just nodded his head, frustrated and angry, and began hunting around for a place to sit.

"Fine," he barked, planting himself on a step that led up to another room. "We can stay right here and have everyone hear our business."

Blakesley snorted ironically. "Like they didn't already hear it when you were on trial," she said. "Don't turn this around and make me out to be the bad guy. I did what I had to do to protect me and the girls."

"You took my girls away."

"You cheated on me and killed your lover!"

"You let those lawyers poison you. How could you not have faith in me?"

Blakesley backed away from him. "Gina?" she yelled in the direction of the next room. "Call Beck. Tell him to get over here now."

"Beck?" Ed repeated. "Who in the hell is... oh, I get it. The new husband."

Gina suddenly appeared in the doorway leading from the pit room. Her pretty face was dark as she looked between Blakesley and Ed.

"I already did," she said, her gaze lingering on Ed. "*Usted asno estúpido.* You're in big trouble, dickhead."

Ed threw up his hands like he had no idea why people didn't like him. "What in the hell is that all about?" he wanted to know. "Who is that bitch?"

Blakesley waved Gina away. "A good friend," she told him flatly. "Now tell me what you came here to tell me. I don't have all day."

He cocked his head. "Where are the girls?"

"School."

"I want to see them."

"No."

Ed lifted his eyebrows as if expecting more of an answer. "No?" he repeated. "If you don't let me see them, I'll track them down just like I tracked you down. You can't keep me from my children."

Blakesley stood firm. "Before this hour is out, I'm going to get a restraining order against you," she rumbled. "You're never going near the girls again. They don't want to see you. They're happy now and I'm not going to let you screw them up."

Ed laughed but it was without humor. "What in the hell are you going to base the restraining order on? I haven't done anything."

Blakesley crossed her arms and backed away from him even further. She moved just about as far away from him as she could get without actually leaving the room, crossing her arms stubbornly as she leaned against the wall near the fireplace.

"I really have nothing more to say to you," she said. "I'm sorry your trip here was wasted. You should have just gone through the lawyers."

He lifted an eyebrow at her. "Don't worry, I will," he said. "I'm going to get my girls back."

Blakesley fought down her anger and fear. "Ed, they're happy and well-adjusted now in spite of your attempt to ruin them," she said quietly. "If you really loved them, you'd just leave them alone for now. They're just little kids, for Heaven's sake. Why do you have to screw with them?"

"Who says I'm screwing with them?" He threw up his hands. "All I want to do is see my children."

"You never wanted to see them before," Blakesley fired back. "In fact, you went out of your way during our marriage to make sure you came home after they were in bed for the night and left in the morning before they got up. It was rare if you had breakfast with the girls or even played with them. You weren't really father material."

His jaw ticked faintly. "I was trying to make money for my family," he said quietly. "That meant time away from the girls. It wasn't by choice."

Blakesley gave him a disbelieving look and turned away, her arms crossed protectively over her chest. She was coming to think about Emma out in the car with Nikki, not wanting to draw Ed's attention to her newborn as a target for his venom. She was also increasingly concerned about Beck and where he was in all of this.

Gina said she had called him and undoubtedly, Beck was already in the car making his way to the homestead at double the speed limit. She just had to hold Ed off until Beck arrived. The best way to do that was to keep him calm and talking. She was no longer terrified at his appearance, but she was still very uneasy. She kept her distance.

"Fine," she said. "Have it your way. So it wasn't your choice. Even if I let you see the girls, what then? Why do you want to see them? Charlotte doesn't even remember you."

A look of pain crossed his face, but Blakesley was sure it was fake. "I know," he admitted. "She was so young when all of this went down. I'd really like the chance to establish a relationship with her."

There was no way Blakesley was going to allow that but for the sake of keeping the conversation going and keeping Ed calm, she entertained it in theory. She had to keep the man talking until the cavalry arrived.

———

It seemed like forever. Blakesley had been discussing Ed's intentions towards their children, not promising the man anything but listening to him present his case. He talked about the past, the present, the future. He talked about working hard to win back his family. He even talked about his hellish stint in prison and glad he was to have been given a second chance. More than once, he apologized for his bad judgment when it came to his affair. Blakesley just stood there and listened. She couldn't manage to feel anything for him, good or bad.

Gina, who had been standing in the doorway between the pit room and the great room during most of the conversation, had abruptly vanished. Blakesley could see the doorway but Ed could not. In fact, the entire house seemed eerily still, as if everyone had disappeared. Increasingly curious, Blakesley was sure that Gina hadn't gone far. She knew the woman wouldn't desert her, and that was her last thought before chaos exploded.

Men dressed from head to toe in black suddenly burst in through every entry point. The window next to Blakesley exploded as someone leapt in through the glass, weapon held steady. In fact, all of the men had weapons and gear, yelling something she couldn't quite understand because she was so startled. As she yelped and dropped to her knees, covering her head, a shard of glass from the exploded window cut her on the arm. Blood streamed.

Someone pulled her to her feet. She began to realize that the men were yelling "U.S. Navy, U.S. Navy" very loudly, identifying themselves as they filled the big room. She turned to the man who had her by the arm, startled, to see that it was Anthony Solis. He was dressed for battle.

"Mrs. Seavington?" his young face was full of concern. "Are you okay?"

Blakesley nodded, still a little stunned. "I'm fine," she said. "Where's Beck?"

Anthony was looking at her bloodied arm but he pointed over to where Ed was now being surrounded by several armed men.

"He's right there," he said. "What happened to your arm?"

Blakesley hadn't even realized she had been cut. Before she could open her mouth, Anthony yelled over to Beck.

"Commander," he boomed, holding Blakesley's bloodied arm up as evidence. "We've got an injury."

Beck had been in the process of hauling a very startled Ed to his feet. His only objective when entering the room had been Ed Masterson. He was blinded by it. Having arrived minutes earlier, he had been met by Gina out in the yard, who had assured him that both Blakesley and the baby were fine. Knowing that, he could focus on the ex-husband who had unfortunately decided to show up. Beck didn't know how or why, but that didn't matter. All that mattered was that he was here and Beck was going to deal with the man.

Hearing Anthony's declaration, Beck looked over to see blood streaming down Blakesley's arm. She looked very frightened. It was all Beck needed to unload on Ed.

The first blow from Beck's huge fist caught Ed in the jaw. The man went reeling, falling off the steps and ending up on his knees. Beck handed his weapon off to the nearest man and went after his prey with a vengeance. Two more blows caught Ed in the head and in the belly, sending the man to the ground. Beck pounced and began pounding him.

Blakesley should have stopped it. God knows, she should have. She watched Beck beat the crap out of Ed and felt absolutely no remorse for it at all. For everything the man did to her, to her girls, for every humiliation and hurt, she just couldn't pull Beck off of him. It was wrong and she knew it. Still, she was afraid that Beck might kill him and she couldn't stomach the thought of Beck being prosecuted for the crime. She pulled away from Anthony.

"Beck, stop," she cried. "Don't kill him."

Ed was a battered mess as Beck came to a grinding halt. He turned to look at his wife, standing there fearful and bleeding. He could feel his rage all over again.

"I'm not going to kill him," he rumbled. "But I'm going to make him understand what will happen to him again if he touches you."

"He didn't touch me," Blakesley said. "I was cut from the glass when you guys busted in through the window."

Beck's gaze lingered on her bloodied arm before he fixed her in the eye. "Do you swear?"

A painfully disappointed expression crossed her face. "Do you really think I would lie to you, ever? For Ed, no less?"

Beck could see that he had offended her but he had been so blinded by hatred and fury that it was difficult for him to calm down. Still, Blakesley was his priority so his focus shifted to her. He pushed himself off of Ed and moved in her direction.

"What happened?" he asked quietly. "What did he do? Did he try to hurt you?"

She shook her head as he came close and his big arms reached out for her. But he was strapped down with a Kevlar vest, among other things, so he couldn't pull her close without bringing her into contact with cold, dangerous things. So he cupped her head with his big hands and bloodied knuckles, kissing her cheeks and lips. Blakesley allowed herself to feel her fear for the first time, her eyes filling with tears. His comfort was her undoing.

"He didn't hurt me," she whispered tightly. "He didn't try. I don't know how he found me, but he just showed up here and wanted to talk about the girls. He wants to see them."

"Bullshit," Beck spat. "The only thing he's going to see is my fist to his face if he shows up again."

Blakesley, frightened, just nodded, noticing the Ed was becoming more lucid now and struggling to sit up. One of Beck's men pulled the man into a sitting position. Beck glanced at Ed over his shoulder before returning his focus to Blakesley. He kissed her frightened face again.

"I want you to go home," he said. "I'll deal with Mr. Masterson."

Blakesley nodded. "Okay," she eyed him warily. "Don't kill him, okay? I don't want you up on a murder charge."

"If I kill him, they'll never find the body and they'll never pin it on me. I can make him disappear like he never existed."

She looked at him with some unease. He meant every word and she believed him implicitly. It began to occur to her that he was in battle mode and his entire personality had changed. He was hard and calculating and deadly. Concern filled her.

"Listen to me," she whispered. "I hate Ed and I don't want him around the girls, ever, but killing him... Beck, you can't do it. What if the girls ever found out the truth? If he came at you with a knife, it would be different, but to outright murder him isn't acceptable."

Beck's brow furrowed. "Don't you think I know the difference?"

"Do you? Look at you; you're ready to do it now because you thought he hurt me. If you kill the man, you're no better than he was when he killed his whore. I can't condone anything like that, for your sake."

Beck stared at her. "What do you mean?"

"I mean I can't let you kill, not like this. I love you too much to let something like that happen. If I go home, I want you to come with me. I won't leave you here with him."

Beck was coming to see what she was saying, having difficulty separating the furious husband from the trained killer.

"Baby, I love you, too," he murmured. "I'm not going to kill him. I just want to talk to him."

"Then let's do it together."

Beck grunted and gave her a long look, unhappy. Then he turned to one of his men and snapped his fingers, indicating Blakesley's arm. The man was already digging in to one of the many pockets on his body, pulling forth a roll of gauze. The young, silent man took Blakesley's arm gently and professionally wrapped the cut, sealing it off. Beck stood and watched silently.

"What in the hell is going on?" Ed had become lucid enough to speak even though he had three loose teeth and his mouth was swollen and bloodied. "Blakesley, who in the hell are these guys?"

Blakesley could see, just from Beck's expression that Ed was in for another beating if he didn't shut his mouth.

"Ed...," she warned.

Beck cut her off. "I'm Blakesley's husband," he snarled, moving in Ed's direction. "And you're on borrowed time if you ever try to see or talk to her, or the girls, again. Do I make myself clear?"

Ed looked up at the big, blond bear of a man, blinking his muddled eyes. He was quite surprised and, truthfully, quite intimidated by the man. "You're Beck?"

Beck nodded once. "For everything you've done to her, I should gut you here and now. How in the hell did you find her?"

Ed didn't want to give up his source but he had a feeling if he didn't, it might end badly for him. He was arrogant but he wasn't stupid. He could see very bad things for him reflecting in Beck's green eyes. He surrendered the information without a fight.

"Nikki," he said. "I called her. Don't get mad at her; she's not smart enough to deal with me. I got the information out of her."

Beck looked stricken, turning to look at Blakesley, whose eyes were wide with surprise. But in the next second, Blakesley was bolting for the front door with Beck right behind her. Racing from the front door to the driveway, Blakesley began searching frantically for her car.

It was missing. She screamed in terror.

"The car's gone!" she cried. "Nikki took the baby!"

Beck was perhaps more panic-stricken than she was only he held his control a little better. Blakesley was starting to cry hysterically and he put his arms around her, snapping orders to his men over the two-way. Inside, the S.E.A.L.s began to move.

"Where's Gina?" Beck looked around anxiously. "Where did she go?"

As if on cue, Gina suddenly emerged from the front door. She had been hiding up in the gallery above the big room, watching the action. "Where did you guys go?" she demanded. "What happened?"

Blakesley was weeping with panic. She whirled to Gina. "Where's my car?" she demanded. "Where's the baby?"

Gina looked confused. She went to Blakesley, putting her hands on the woman's arms. "I had Nikki move it down the driveway to the street when Beck and his men got here," she explained patiently. "I didn't want the car caught in any crossfire. Why? What's wrong?"

Blakesley was weeping too hard to explain, now seized with relief. Beck took off at a dead run down the driveway with Blakesley behind him, the two of them running down the driveway of the property until they reached the street beyond. Beck moved much faster than Blakesley did and he reached the street first, finding the car parked down the block. He tore down the street to the car, finding a terrified Nikki huddled with the baby inside.

Nikki was sobbing as Beck tried the door. "I'm sorry," she cried. "I'm sorry, I didn't mean to do it!"

The door was locked and Beck's panic began to rise again. He struggled to stay calm. "It's okay," he said steadily. "I'm not mad. Please open the door."

Weeping, Nikki moved slowly for the door and flipped the lock. Beck yanked the door open, hit the unlock for the entire car, and then threw open the back door. Emma was sleeping peacefully in her car carrier and Beck was driven to tears by the sight. The baby was safe. As he reached down to pull her out of the seat, Blakesley came running up behind him.

"Is she okay?" she sobbed.

Beck lifted the baby out and handed her over to Blakesley. "She's fine," he assured her, wiping at his eyes. "She was sleeping."

Blakesley burst into fresh tears as she cradled her daughter, who was starting to stir. Gina and several of the S.E.A.L.s came running up on the car.

"Bee, I'm sorry," Gina said urgently. "I didn't mean to scare you. I thought it was safer to move the car."

Blakesley just nodded, hugging Gina to let the woman know she wasn't mad. Still inside the car, Nikki continued to weep. Beck was watching Blakesley reconcile herself to Emma's safety but the nanny's tears distracted him. As Blakesley and Gina held each other and cuddled Emma, he turned his attention to the chunky young woman.

"Nikki," he knelt down beside the open door so he could look at her more on her level. "I promise I won't get angry, but why didn't you tell me that Ed Masterson had called you?"

Nikki was a mess. She was terrified of Beck as it was, more so now. She huddled back against the opposite car door as if cowering.

"He... he called my mother and got my cell number," she sobbed. "He wanted to know where Blakesley had taken the girls and I tried not to tell him, but it just slipped out. He thanked me and told me he was going to buy my mother a new car. She really needs one, you know. So... so I got scared and didn't want to tell you. I'm so sorry. I didn't mean to do anything wrong."

It was the most Beck had ever heard her say. He was still angry but he let it go for the moment. There wasn't any point. The baby was safe, Blakesley was safe and that's all that mattered. So he simply nodded and stood up, moving away from the car.

Blakesley had calmed sufficiently by this point, rocking the baby gently. Emma had fallen back asleep. Beck put his big hand on the baby's head, kissing her little forehead before kissing his wife.

"Put her back in the car and then you and Gina go home," he murmured. "When I get off of work, we're going to have a serious talk with Nikki. I can't say that I trust her anymore and that's a problem. I won't have her jeopardizing my family."

Blakesley knew he spoke the truth, nodding with some reluctance. "It will be hard on the girls," she said. "They've known Nikki all their lives."

"She betrayed us."

"I know. We'll do what needs to be done."

"Then you and Gina go back to the house. I'll see you there later." He kissed her. "Love you."

"Love you, too."

"You sure you're okay to drive?"

"I'm fine." Her gaze lingered on him. "What are you going to do with Ed?"

Beck's expression was stony. "Make sure he gets the hell out of San Diego."

Blakesley didn't say anything more. She went back to the car, strapping Emma back into her car seat as Gina went to the front passenger side and climbed in. Blakesley shut the car door on Emma's side and turned to Beck to kiss him goodbye when a shot suddenly rang from the house, followed by two more in close succession. The S.E.A.L.s that had followed Beck out onto the street were already jabbering into their radios as all of them, including Beck, took off at a dead run back up the driveway towards the house.

Startled, Blakesley watched her husband and half his team tear back towards the house. She was torn with curiosity and apprehension. Something, a little spark of intuition, told her to go with them.

"Stay here," she told Gina. "I'll be back."

Before Gina could stop her, Blakesley was running back up the driveway after the S.E.A.L.s. She could hear Gina yelling behind her but she ignored the woman as she ran up the driveway, sheltered by the great oak and eucalyptus trees. Beck and his men had already disappeared inside the public wing and she followed on their heels, running into the great room in time to see Ed lying on the floor in a growing pool of blood. She gasped in horror.

"Ed!" her hands flew to her mouth in shock. "What happened? Has someone called an ambulance?"

Beck hadn't realized she had followed them. He had been gazing down at Ed Masterson with some curiosity but now moved towards his wife as she stood in the doorway. He put his arms out, collecting her against him.

"We don't need an ambulance," he told her grimly, his gaze returning to the man lying prone on the floor. "He's dead."

Blakesley gasped again and turned away. She didn't want to see the carnage anymore.

"Oh, my God," she breathed. "What in the hell happened?"

Beck was looking at Ed. "I don't know," he said honestly, looking to the men he had left behind to watch over Masterson. "Miller, what happened?"

He was addressing one of his men, a young half-Asian man who had been with him for four years. The kid tried not to look too contrite or emotional.

"It happened pretty fast, Commander," he said. "I was standing next to him and suddenly, he kicked out my knee and grabbed my sidearm. I stumbled sideways and the guy fired off a round. I think it went into the fireplace or something. Before he could cap off another round, Guerrero and I capped him."

Beck was listening intently. "So the first shot we heard was Masterson's," he clarified.

"Yes sir."

"Then the second two were you and Guerrero, shooting the man because he took a shot at you."

"Yes sir. He was aiming to kill us, sir."

Beck just stood there, a little dumbfounded, looking at Ed's body on the old, adobe tile floor. He thought that it probably wasn't the first time that floor saw bloodshed considering the history of Ben Earp and the house in general. But the severity of the situation began to weigh on him and he turned to Anthony, standing a few feet away.

"Call Davis," he said quietly. "Tell him what happened. Tell him he'd better get up here."

Anthony nodded sharply and pulled out his cell phone, moving outside to make the call as Blakesley uncovered her face and dared to turn back around again. Ed was very dead, dark red blood ruining his expensive new suit.

"Oh, God," she breathed. "He's really dead."

Beck nodded faintly. "Yes."

Blakesley sighed, feeling braver about looking at the dead man. "I can't believe it."

Beck just shrugged. He wasn't going to apologize for what happened. He was glad and that was the truth.

"I wonder why he made a swipe for the gun?" he wondered aloud. "Did he really think he could get away with shooting one of us?"

Miller thought the question was meant for him. "He didn't say anything, sir," he replied. "He just kicked out my knee and grabbed the sidearm. He must have been aiming for Guerrero based on the shot he got off. He just missed his head."

Blakesley and Beck looked over to the massive fireplace, plugged up and useless for so many years. They could see a hole right above the bricked hearth.

"But that's so stupid," Blakesley shook her head. "He's in a room with armed men and he tries to grab a gun? It doesn't make any sense."

Beck thought so, too. "Maybe he was trying to make an escape. He knew I was coming back for him... maybe he was just trying to be a tough guy and get away."

Blakesley shrugged. "He was pretty arrogant," she agreed. "He didn't like anyone to tell him what to do and he really didn't like cops. I'm sure the fact that you beat him up pissed him off a lot. But to grab a gun... that goes beyond anything I thought he was capable of."

"Prison changes people."

"I would believe that."

Blakesley pulled away from her husband and wandered over to the fireplace, giving Ed's body a wide berth. She really didn't want to look at him but she wanted to see the damage that the bullet caused. Not that it was her house anymore but still, she cared.

The hollow point armor piercing round had made a big hole. It was about at eye-level, taking a chunk of the old tiled mantel with it. In fact, as Blakesley peered closely at the hole that was, more or less, a couple of inches in diameter. She could see pieces of the yellow painted tile pushed back into the bulk of the big, stone hearth. At least, she thought it was tile until it oddly seemed to glimmer back at her. Curious, she cocked her head and gingerly stuck her fingers into the hole.

Something cold, hard and loose met with her fingertips. She could feel some kind of texture. It took her a few tries to get a grip on it but she finally managed to, pulling the cold, hard object back out of the hole.

Blakesley stared at the object in her hand. It took her a couple of seconds to realize that it wasn't a piece of broken tile at all. It was dark gold, heavy and round. Looking more closely, she could see some kind of lopsided cross stamped on it and intricate designs around the edges. It was a gold piece. Startled, she held it in Beck's direction.

"Beck!" she called to her husband. "Oh, my God! Look at this!"

Beck had been speaking with Miller but he looked up when Blakesley called his name. He could see she had something in her hand and he went to her, curious, as she began to grow more excited.

"Look!" she was practically jumping up and down by the time he reached her. "It's a gold piece! Beck, it's gold!"

Startled, Beck took the piece from her and took a hard look at it. It was, indeed, a gold piece, with Spanish writing on the edges and a cross emblazoned across the center. He blinked as if he didn't believe what he was seeing.

"Where'd you get this?" he demanded.

Blakesley was already sticking her fingers back inside the bullet hole, pulling forth two more round golden pieces.

"In here," she said excitedly. "It's in the mantel. Gold coins!"

He wriggled his eyebrows, peering inside the hole and seeing more gold pieces glittering back at them. His men began to crowd around, watching curiously, as he pulled out several more gold coins, all of them emblazoned with the same Spanish marks.

"Holy crap," he exclaimed. "Who in the hell would have put this in there?"

Blakesley was looking at some of the pieces in his flat palm. "Have you ever seen anything like this before?"

Beck shook his head in awe. "Never," he replied. "It looks like there's Spanish writing on them, which I guess would make sense since this entire area was under Spanish rule about the time this place was built. But why hide gold coins in the fireplace? It seems like a strange place to hide money."

Blakesley was still staring at the coins in his hand. "Not...," she paused and looked up at him. "Not if you're Ben Earp and you just stole this stuff from the padres at the San Diego Mission."

Beck's eyes widened. "The cursed gold?"

Blakesley couldn't help but grin. She was genuinely excited and amazed by what they were seeing. "It makes sense," she insisted. "No one has been able to find it before now. So Ben steals the gold and hides it until the search for it dies down. I don't know why he left it here, but he must have had a reason. Maybe... maybe that's why the fireplace has been blocked all of these years. Maybe it's because Ben stashed the gold in it."

Beck could only shake his head in wonder. "So that's where old Ben put it."

"Maybe. I'm sure Dr. Welton's going to spend a lot of time trying to figure it out."

Dr. Welton spent the next two years excavating the cursed Bouchard gold from the fireplace. In fact, the entire exterior of the mantel and fireplace had been built around the stash, including a big section of it that blocked off the chimney so that smoke couldn't escape. It was only one in a series of mysteries that the Benjamin and Dulcinea Earp House revealed, like layers peeling off of an onion. Some mysteries had no answers, but most did. Dr. Welton would spend the rest of his professional career trying to figure them out.

The cursed Bouchard gold ended up with an estimated worth of over one hundred million dollars. Beck and Blakesley donated some of it back to the San Diego Mission, some of it to the Benjamin and Dulcinea Earp Museum, while the rest of it, along with many valuable pieces from the jewelry collection, were auctioned off through Christie's of London, netting them more than enough money to replace the thirty million Blakesley had paid for Beck's release and then some.

Blakesley and Beck, and their family, were set up for life with an astonishing amount of wealth. For whatever bad deeds Ben Earp had accomplished in his lifetime, he finally did some good with it in seeing that his descendants were financially well taken care of. The curse was gone.

Naval Criminal Investigative Services and the San Diego Police Department eventually determined that the death of Ed Masterson had been in self-defense, clearing anyone associated with his death of any charges. He was quietly buried in Encino next to his father and mother, with Marshall Thorne and Cadee Masterson in attendance.

Cadee, the only one of the three sisters that truly remembered or had any connection to her father, decided that she wanted to be there when he was buried because she felt bad that he was going to be buried alone. So Marshall escorted his granddaughter to the burial because her mother didn't want to go, and the two of them said their farewells to a man who had done little good for them in life. Cadee never asked how her father died and those who knew never offered up any information. He was dead and that's all she ever knew.

Nikki ended up going back to live with her mother after Blakesley fired her. In Nikki's place, Blakesley hired an older woman who had already raised her own three children, and the three Masterson girls loved Ms. Sarah. Ms. Sarah, in turn, grew very attached to the Masterson girls, Lizzie, and little Emma as the baby grew into an adorably angelic toddler. It was a good thing that Beck and Blakesley had hired the woman because their child-bearing days were apparently not over.

When Emma was fifteen months old, Blakesley went into labor and, in roughly an hour and forty-two minutes, delivered a nine-pound baby boy who came into the world screaming his lungs out.

Beck had wept when the nurse handed him Marshall Colton Seavington, a healthy boy who howled and screamed his displeasure as he was held by his father for the first time. Between the baby's crying and Beck's weeping, Blakesley had her hands full trying to calm both of them down. Putting the newborn on the nipple shut him up quickly, and soft kisses and gentle comfort pretty much did the same for her husband. Finally, they had the tow-headed healthy boy they had been waiting for. Mother, father, sisters and grandparents were thrilled.

The first time Charlotte and Emma put a princess crown on little Colt, they didn't have to call an ambulance for Beck. But Blakesley did have to ply him with drink, enough so that he calmed down and fell asleep on the couch as the children played around him. It was his mistake.

When he woke up, the crown was on *his* head.

EPILOGUE
FOUR YEARS LATER

BECK HAD NEVER SEEN anything like it.

He had expected the opening of the Art Bar to be an event, but he had no idea just how much of an event. Blakesley had hired a publicist to arrange for a grand opening and the man had used the Hollyhock notoriety to its full advantage. When the sleek and modern Art Bar opened for business at 5 p.m. on a balmy Friday night, there was a line out the door to get in.

Everyone who was anyone in San Diego had shown up for the event, plus a lot of people that Blakesley knew from Los Angeles had come as well. It was an invasion from the north of people driving expensive cars and wearing expensive clothes, including some actors that Beck had seen on television. He could hardly believe it.

Dressed in clothes that his wife had picked out for him, he looked like he had just walked off the pages of a Tom Ford ad. With his stunning good looks, he had the attention of every woman, and some men, that walked into the place as he and Blakesley greeted the throng.

"This is crazy," Beck hissed to his wife as they finished greeting a group of high-powered restaurant publicists. "I've never seen anything like this in my life."

Blakesley grinned at him; clad in a designer gown that flattered her delicious figure to a fault, she looked amazing. "Impressed with my contacts?"

He rolled his eyes. "I had no idea you were so popular."

She laughed softly. "Stick with me, sonny. I'll take you places."

"I kind of like where we are."

She put her arm around his waist, hugging him as he squeezed her shoulders and kissed the top of her blond head.

"So do I."

"Are the kids coming around later?"

"Yes." Blakesley waved at a group of well-dressed men who had waved at her. "Ms. Sarah is bringing them over later."

Beck caught sight of the men waving at his wife. "Great," he said, rather sarcastically, as his eyes narrowed. "Who are they?"

Blakesley stopped waving, smiling at him. "My attorney from Los Angeles who handled my divorced with Ed."

"He's good looking. You're forbidden to talk to him without me."

She laughed again. "Baby, your jealousy is flattering but unnecessary. He'd date you before he'd date me. He's gay."

"Oh," Beck felt much better. "Then feel free to talk to him all you want."

She shook her head reproachfully at the man as another group of well-wishers came through the door. One of the happy visitors was a very old woman who had been a big "B" picture starlet back in the 1950's and she entered the Art Bar on the arm of a man who was young enough to be her grandson.

Wearing a fur and a bullet bra, the overly made-up woman was quite solicitous of Beck until Blakesley politely pulled him away. Even then, the old woman slipped him a note with her phone number on it. Beck and Blakesley laughed about that one, and laughed harder still when Beck slipped the note into Anthony Solis' pocket. He told him it was from a pretty woman across the room who was admiring him and Anthony fell for it.

Blakesley had to tell Gina, who was working the bar. They

had a huge laugh over it. Having worked in restaurants most of her life, Gina was in charge of the bar and was doing a smashing job. She was lovely, charming, and ruled with an iron fist, which worked well in the position. She was swift with service and always had a few words and a smile for the patrons, who quickly came to like her. Her boyfriend of two years, another Navy officer, had been a distant acquaintance of Butch. He showed up early and sat at the end of the bar, keeping her company while she worked. Beck kept glancing over the bar, seeing how happy the woman was and knowing how thrilled Butch would have been.

Aside from his wife and Gina, Beck's attention was on a third woman in the bar. At the front of the house, Lizzie was the official hostess as people entered, showing them to their tables with her tall, blond, and beautiful elegance. She had no shortage of male admirers, much to Beck's concern. Two hours into the opening, she already had three date offers and, to her father's horror, she was considering all of them. As a junior at San Diego State University, Elizabeth Seavington was a very beautiful and very popular Communications major.

Marshall Thorne and his new wife, Gabrielle, came later in the evening, thrilled to see how successful the opening was. Marshall had helped Blakesley pick out the selection of wines she would carry. He and Gabrielle shared oysters on the half-shell and a fine bottle of pinot grigio, and he reflected on how his daughter had come to such a happy place in her life. From the hell of nearly seven years ago until now, it was like day and night. He'd never seen her happier or more beautiful.

As Blakesley had said, Ms. Sarah brought the Seavington brood over to the bar somewhere around seven at night because Blakesley had wanted her children to see and be seen by her friends and patrons. Cadee, now a teenager, hung at the front of the house and helped Lizzie as Crosby and Charlotte, the social creatures, made the rounds with their mother. Beck had charge of Emma and Colt, five years and four years old respectively, and he proudly showed them off to his friends and fellow officers who had showed up for the opening.

"Baby," Blakesley came rushing up to him, no easy feat with the high heels she was wearing. Crosby and Charlotte tagged along behind her. "Guess what? I've already sold four of my paintings!"

She was so excited that she was nearly jumping up and down. Beck, his arms full of blond toddlers who, now that their mother was near, began to whine for her, grinned.

"That's great," he said happily. "Who bought them?"

Blakesley reached for Colt when the little boy practically threw himself at her from his father's arms. With her son on her hip, she turned and pointed to a group near the bar.

"See that guy over there, kind of round, with the dark hair?" she asked.

Beck was following her finger. "The balding guy"

She nodded. "He owns a very prestigious art gallery in Beverly Hills." She turned to her husband again. "The guy carries all kinds of art for sale. He bought four of my paintings. We just made about $18,000."

Beck's eyebrows lifted in surprise, in pleasure. "Wow," he exclaimed. "That's really great. Congratulations."

Blakesley was thrilled. With the somewhat sleepy and crabby Colt in her arms, she made her way back over to the group of art gallery owners, charming the socks off of them. Beck watched her, so proud he could nearly burst. He just watched his wife, her beauty and charisma, feeling like he felt every day since he had known her. He was absolutely the luckiest man in the world.

"Beck?" Crosby, now ten years of age and already an exquisite beauty, tugged on her stepfather's arm. "Can Charlotte and I go help Lizzie?"

Beck looked to the front of the house, crowded to the rafters. It was standing room only, spilling out onto the sidewalk beyond.

"Okay," he said. "But listen to what she tells you. If she doesn't want your help, come back and find me, and we'll figure something else out for you to do."

With a grin, Crosby skittered away with Charlotte close behind. Beck smiled as he watched them go, turning to look at his youngest daughter when she yawned and laid her head on his big shoulder. Emma was the spitting image of Blakesley with her doll-like face and slightly tilted eyes. Instead of Blakesley's bluish-green, however, she had her father's intense green eyes. She had his temperament, too, rather laid-back and accommodating.

"Daddy, I'm tired," Emma yawned again. "Can we go home now?"

He kissed her little head, his eyes searching for his wife, who seemed to have disappeared. "Let's find Mommy," he said. "Are you hungry, baby girl?"

Emma nodded her head, still cuddled up on her father's shoulder. "Uh huh," she said, suddenly spying Marshall and Gabrielle over at the bar. Her head came up and she pointed. "Grampy Marsh is eating something. Can I have some?"

Beck made a beeline over to the bar and handed Emma off to Gabrielle, who hugged and kissed the child. Emma declared she was starving and Marshall ordered her a Shirley Temple and homemade potato chips. Beck stood behind them, searching for a glimpse of his wife, when he caught sight of her above him in the loft. She was directing two male employees down the stairs from her studio with a giant canvas between them.

Beck went around the bar to the staircase just as Blakesley reached the bottom step. She directed the employees with the canvas to take it over to the bar.

"Hi, baby," she said brightly. "Where's Emma?"

"With your dad and Gabrielle," he replied. "Where's Colt?"

"With Sophia and Richard."

Beck looked at her as if she were crazy. "You left him with Davis to babysit?"

She laughed. "Relax," she said, taking his arm and pulling him back over to the big, modern bar where they were hanging up the canvas she had just brought down from the studio. "Richard's his godfather, so I don't know what you're upset about. He wanted to hang out with him for a few minutes."

Beck just shrugged, not entirely sure he wanted to burden his former captain with watching his son, but he went along with his wife as she pulled him towards the bar. The two employees were working on hanging the canvas as Blakesley, in her lovely evening gown, held out her arms to her husband.

"Set me up on the bar, please," she asked.

Beck did as he was asked, lifting her up by the waist and setting her on the long, wood bar with the beautiful, pounded-metal siding. With a wink, Blakesley stood up and all Beck could see were her gorgeous, tanned, smooth legs in those sexy, silver shoes. He found himself grinning up at her, leaning against the bar, his eyes all over her legs. He didn't even care what she was doing up there; he just wanted to sex her up. Not entirely oblivious to her husband mentally undressing her, Blakesley held up her hands to the crowd and let out a loud whistle.

"Everyone," she held up her hands, getting the attention of the packed bar. "Welcome to the Art Bar. I'm Blakesley Seavington and I just want to thank you all for coming out tonight. I really hope you like everything you see and taste, and we hope to see you all back frequently."

Everyone clapped and roared, and Blakesley grinned broadly, the big dimple in her left cheek flashing.

"Thank you so much," she said, waving off into corner by the door when someone whistled loudly at her. "And thank you. My husband thanks you."

The crowd laughed as Beck was acknowledged. He grinned at the crowd and then looked back to his lovely wife, who had his attention, and everyone else's. Blakesley continued.

"As you know, the concept of this place is a little different," she said, pointing around the room. "Every painting on the wall is my work. I've always loved art and I hope you like what I've done. It's all for sale, so don't be shy if you see something you like."

Again, the crowd clapped loudly and whistled, and Blakesley

took a couple of bows before continuing. "Now, as a kick-off for the Art Bar tonight, I have a little surprise for you." She glanced at Beck, who was gazing up at her adoringly. "My husband doesn't know this yet so I hope he doesn't get too angry, but we have a representative from the Navy Widow and Orphans Foundation here tonight and I'm donating a percentage of the evening's proceeds to the foundation, including a percentage of the sale of the art."

Everyone clapped heartily, including Beck. He had no idea she had arranged for that and was deeply touched. The NWO Foundation was something near and dear to their hearts, especially since it was something Gina benefitted from. They had generously donated to it over the years. Blakesley smiled down at Beck.

"If you haven't met him yet, this is my amazing husband, Beck," she pointed to her husband at her feet. "He works at Coronado Amphibious Base training new S.E.A.L.s. Before that, he was a S.E.A.L. himself for many years and, as someone told me once, a real American hero. He's the love of my life and I'm very proud of him."

The crowd was on their feet, clapping loudly for Beck, who was a little embarrassed by all of the attention. He acknowledged the applause modestly before turning to his wife, giving her an "I'm going to kill you" expression, to which she simply smiled. She held up a hand to quiet the crowd down.

"Here comes the good part," she said. "A few years ago, my husband did a Navy calendar where the proceeds all went to the Naval Widow and Orphans Fund. In fact, he was the cover boy, so I had that picture blown up and I'm going to auction it off tonight to benefit the NWO Foundation."

Stunned, Beck watched as the two employees pulled the soft cover off the giant canvas that had been brought down from the loft. It was a picture of him emerging from the surf, bare-chested, clad only in his black combat pants and boots. It had been taken at sunset and the colors were reflected off his tanned, muscular body as he gave the camera a deliciously smoldering look. It was the sexiest pose to ever grace the cover of a calendar and the crowd went mad.

People began screaming monetary amounts at Blakesley, who stood on the bar and laughed at her husband's mortification. Beck, seized with embarrassment, suddenly leapt onto the bar next to his wife and grabbed her as the crowd screamed with delight.

Blakesley was laughing as Beck tried to spank her, much to the thrill of the crowd, but he just ended up hugging her tightly as everyone yelled and clapped. It was evident how much affection there was between the pair. The old woman who had slipped Beck her phone number pushed her way to the front of the bar and lifted a piece of paper up to Beck which, on closer inspection, was a check. He hesitantly reached down and took it, his eyes bugging when he saw the amount. As the crowd demanded to know what he held in his hand, at Blakesley's prompting, he held it up for the crowd to see.

"It's a check for the photo," he said in his smooth, deep voice. "Seventy-five thousand dollars made out to the Navy Widow and Orphans Foundation."

The crowd roared in approval but there was more drama to come. From the table where Robert Karayan sat with his gay friends, one of the men ran up to the bar and handed Beck another check. This time, Blakesley took it and she began laughing loudly.

"Oh, my God," she held up the check. "I have a check for double that amount. One hundred and fifty thousand dollars. My lawyer wants to hang it in his office."

Once again, the crowd went crazy. They were cheering and clapping loudly. Everyone but the old woman, that is. In her fur and bullet bra, she marched over the table of gay men and slapped one of them across the face. A couple of Beck's men, who happened to be close enough, jumped in before a brawl could start but the entire restaurant was roaring with laughter over the old woman and the gay lawyer. It was just too funny to believe. Up on the bar, Beck watched the scene, holding Blakesley, his cheek against hers.

"You are so dead," he murmured. "When I'm done with you, you're not going to be able to sit down for a week."

Blakesley laughed softly, her arms around his neck. "You sexy beast," she nuzzled his cheek with her nose, kissing his lips. "You just bring out the animal in everyone."

He grinned, looking at her. "You're the only one I want to bring it out in."

"Do you even have to ask that? Ever?"

He shook his head, kissing her again, catching a glimpse of his picture over her shoulder. "Oh, God," he groaned. "I can't even look at that. I'm so embarrassed."

She glanced over her shoulder at the sizzling shot. "If that was me in a bikini, would you be so embarrassed?"

He scowled. "God, no," he said. "But I wouldn't have auctioned it off, either. You in a bikini is my dirty pleasure and no one else's."

"You get to take the bikini off."

He cocked a sexy eyebrow. "And I have done just that, many times."

Blakesley giggled and moved in for another kiss but she felt someone tugging on the bottom of her gown. She and Beck looked down to see Cadee pulling at her.

"Mom," she said, "Colt's crying. He needs to go home."

Beck dropped off the bar, holding his arms up for his wife, who slid down into his embrace. The realities of family needed her attention and Blakesley would give her children her full focus, but not before she went to the table with the still-angry old woman and furious gay men and arranged to get them both a big canvas of Beck to soothe everyone's ruffled feathers. She also made that promise to seven other people that night and before all was said and done, the Navy Widow and Orphans Foundation had eight hundred thousand dollars in donations. It was the biggest fundraiser they had ever had.

The opening of the Art Bar was an overwhelming success.

THE END

HISTORY OF THE BENJAMIN AND DULCINEA EARP FAMILY TREE

Benjamin Outsen Earp was the brother of Nicholas Porter Earp, father of Wyatt Earp. Ben was born in 1817, came to California (San Diego) in 1837, worked as a lawman and by 1847, was town marshal of San Diego. Ben married a Spanish woman, Dulcinea, and had one son. Benjamin fought in the Mexican-American War at the battle of San Pasqual and was rewarded for valor.

He was also a crook, thief, murderer and outlaw.

Son Robert Manuel Earp b. 1849

Robert married a Mexican woman in 1875, had one son and one daughter
   Nicholas Walter b. 1877
   Margarita Earp b. 1880

Nicholas Walter married an Irish woman in 1901, Mollie Kathleen Kelly. They had two boys
   James Robert b. 1904
   Walter Kelly b. 1906

James married Amelia Blakesley and had two daughters
    Kelly Kathleen Earp b. 1936
    Mollie Virginia Earp b. 1942

Mollie married Marshall Thorne (b. 1942) and had one daughter
    Blakesley Amelia Thorne b. 1986

ABOUT THE AUTHOR

ABOUT KAT LE VEQUE

KATHRYN LE VEQUE is a critically acclaimed, USA TODAY Bestselling author (having hit the list over 30 times), an Indie Reader bestseller, a charter Amazon All-Star author, and a #1 best-selling, award-winning, multi-published author in Medieval Historical Romance with over 150 published novels. Kathryn also writes Romantic Suspense as Kat Le Veque.

Kathryn has received praise for her writing and has won several awards for her work, including two nominations for the Holt Medallion. Her books have topped bestseller lists, and she has gained a loyal fan base that eagerly anticipates each new release.

Kathryn is a talented author who has made a significant impact on the world of historical romance fiction. Through her captivating storytelling and meticulous research, she has enchanted readers with her tales of love, adventure, and the enduring power of the human spirit.

Kathryn loves to hear from her readers. Please find Kathryn on Facebook at Kathryn Le Veque, Author, or join her on Twitter @kathrynleveque, and don't forget to visit her website at www.kathrynleveque.com.

ALSO BY KAT LE VEQUE

The Unholy Angels

Hour of Surrender

Trent Chronicles

Valley of Shadow

The Eden Factor

Canyon of the Sphinx

The Eagle Brotherhood

The Sunset Hour

The Killing Hour

The Secret Hour

The Unholy Hour

The Burning Hour

The Ancient Hour

The Devils Hour